Novels by Rick Stiller

Fiction

Dealer

The Redemption Series
Nellis Gray – Volume I
SunnyBreeze – Volume II

Young Adult

The Morgan's Knot Serial Fantasy

Morgan's Knot
Island of the Children
Ice Island
Islands of Concrete and Steel
Islands of the Mind
Islands in the Sky
Islands of Dark Miracles
Islands of Wisdom

Visit: www.rickstiller.com for more of his books,
photographs, and music and www.morgansknot.com for
the latest on the Morgan's Knot series.

MAC MURPHY

The Redemption Series
Volume III
By
Rick Stiller

For Bonnie Leighty
Mark Leavitt
& Matt Presby

MAC MURPHY

By

Rick Stiller

Milly Clark knocked on the window of the engineer's booth at radio station, WBFK, 'World Broadcasting from the Konfederacy', ten-forty on the dial, just outside Cincinnati. "Congressman's here, where's Murphy?"

Station manager Jack Hannah pulled off his headphones, "Damned if I know. He'll show, he always does."

"I'll bring the talent into the studio, so at least he's ready."

"Great! Time's a'tickin'."

The secretary guided young Congressman Morgan Nance along narrow hallways, snaking through the little cinderblock structure that anchored a gigantic tower flashing W-B-F-K in vivid magenta twenty-four hours of every day. "Let me get you settled into the studio before Mac arrives. Can I get you coffee or ice water or anything?"

"You got a cold beer?"

"I'm sure I can rustle one up," laughed the little woman pushing through the soundproof doors into a cramped and crowded studio built around a broad desk covered with piles of files, trinkets and memorabilia from the last three or four Republican conventions. One of several white WBFK coffee cups containing brown puddles of yesterday's beverages overturned, dribbling into an overflowing orange ashtray and seeping under a well pawed-through stack of radical right-wing newspapers and magazines filled with salacious photos which had no connection to scandalous stories based on hearsay and rumors. Raw material for alcohol and amphetamine fueled hours of hateful rambling rants to rile up the ignorant and the gullible. Legions of dedicated small town listeners coughed up tens-of-thousands of dollars to bolster a phantom defense against legions of brown-skinned, pagan-worshipping immigrants waiting just beyond the horizon for an opportunity to pour into the country to steal our jobs, seduce our women, and contaminate 'White America'.

The Congressman sat on a stiff, unpadded straight metal chair, a vantage point that offered tunnel-vision through the clutter into the host's lair. A large gray microphone erupted from the litter on the desk within easy reach of a well-worn executive chair framed by a tattered American flag and a smaller Confederate battle banner opposite a window into the engineer's booth beneath photos of Woodrow Wilson, who segregated the federal government during his stay in the White House, a portrait of an intense bespectacled Barry Goldwater pasted over a nuclear explosion, Ronald Reagan speaking at the Berlin Wall, and Alabama governor George Wallace blocking the entry of black students to the University of Alabama with the comment, 'Segregation now, segregation tomorrow, segregation forever!' in shiny silver text.

She set a sweating can of Schlitz on the desk, offered a worn pair of headphones, and adjusted the microphone to hang just above his nose, where he would be forced to lift his chin to speak into it. "Murphy should be here any moment because we're getting close to airtime. He's always late but he almost always makes it before Jack Hannah's finished the intro. If there's anything else you need, just pick up that white telephone and dial 117, I've got to go check the phones."

"Thank you."

The green metal door at the back of the building flew open with a crash and Mac Murphy stumbled inside, bouncing from one side of the hall to the other to avoid piles of renegade equipment, stands, chairs, and junk that piled up over the years. Hannah opened the door from the control room and reached to grab him as he staggered towards the studio, scanning his bloodshot eyes, drool dribbling from the corner of his mouth onto the lapel of a rumpled blue blazer. "You're in fine shape!"

Murphy straightened up, brushing his soiled old-school tie to cover brown coffee stains spilling down the front of a once-white shirt, "Never better."

"Are you sure you can handle this?"

"Who's the talent?" barked the opinionated barker.

"Representative Morgan Nance – 7th District – Missouri."

"That piece of shit's got his eyes on the big prize but he's no more qualified to run for the presidency than I am," rumbled Murphy, ramming through the door into the studio, bellowing, "Congressman, it's so good to have a true-believer on the show tonight!"

Nance started to rise from the chair to shake his hand but the short cord yanked the headphones off his head and he fumbled to catch them. Murphy patted him on the shoulder, "Sit down sonny, the world is waiting breathlessly to hear your bullshit."

"But…"

The host pulled off his jacket, loosened the tie, plopped into the big comfy chair, popped a couple of black pills with a swig from a bottle of Jim Beam that appeared from a drawer, pulled on headphones, adjusted the mike, propped his feet on the desk, and lit a cigar. Thin lips curled into a sadistic grin, his blue eyes dancing in amusement, as he glanced at the clock on the wall and pointed at Hannah in the booth, "Count us down."

"Live in four, three, two, and…"

"Good evening folks, this is Mac Murphy broadcasting unfiltered truth to the world from WBFK in the heartland of America. Please welcome second-term Congressional Representative Morgan Nance from the seventh-district in Missouri, as our guest this evening. Nice to have you on the show."

The young Congressman took a sip of his lukewarm Schlitz, wiping the froth from his lip with the back of his hand, "Thank you, it's an honor to be here."

"Rumor has it that some influential people have a surprisingly high opinion of you and there's talk that you might have a very promising future."

Nance blushed, "I don't know about that, I'm just trying to do my best to represent the people of Missouri and protect our state from the over-reach of the federal government. I will say that I think when we have a competent conservative Republican president to partner with our Republican Congress, this country can begin moving forward again."

"But for now, you've just started your second term as another incompetent cog in the broken machinery of the federal government."

"I ran on a platform of dismantling the status quo, eliminating unreasonable restrictive regulations, reducing the highest taxes in the world, rescinding the laws that allow doctors to butcher unborn children, heathens to threaten our religious freedom, and traitors to oppose our right to carry a firearm for self-protection anytime, anywhere."

Murphy laughed and took a big swig, "So, tell me about your solution to the Middle East crisis and how many troops do we really need in Central Africa and why they're there in the first place and why can't we stop Russian intrusions into the Ukraine? What do you think about the president's appointment of a new Chairman of the Federal Reserve? Do you even have a clue about monetary policy or what the Fed does?"

"Well, I..."

"How many times have you spouted that same list of platitudes since you started your first campaign three years ago?"

"It's the whole point of my candidacy - to take power from the deep-state conspirators and give it back to the working people of this great nation."

"Sonny, the folks who run the deep-state conspiracy bought you some fancy suits and pumped your meager little brain with simplified triggers, designed to piss off ignorant voters, until you could work through their script without missing a beat."

"I'm sorry, I don't know what you're talking about."

"Of course you know exactly who I mean! You spent three weeks in all-expense paid intensive training at a very exclusive private resort in Utah, over the summer, along with two-dozen other promising candidates and a small army of future campaign officials, being drilled on the latest research on turning voter preferences, the most effective propaganda, carefully crafted to rile up the fanatics and sully the reputation of any and every opponent. Then they gave you an experienced campaign director to guide you through the most effective use of the millions of dollars that are flowing into your campaign from deep-pocket sponsors around the country. We both know they'll expect your absolute loyalty to their best interests in return for their generosity and when they're done with you, they'll toss you out like one of their purebred dog's messes."

"That's completely insane," snapped the Congressman, taking a hit from the beer can.

"You're not even a good liar," replied Murphy, slugging his whiskey. "I might support everything you claim to stand for but we both know you don't really believe any of the crap you're spewing. Your scripted talking points use the exact same words and phrases as all the other numbskulls that graduated from 'Gee, I'm gonna be the next president U.' and none of you have the brains to be much more than an incompetent dog-catcher in a very small town."

"I don't have to put up with this," shouted Nance, "I'm a Congressional Representative!"

Murphy started laughing and leaned close to the mike, "Folks, he doesn't seem to understand that there are a million patriots out there listening to his hokum and all of you understand that the power brokers pay idiots like this moron to recite their lines in exchange for reliable votes. The big guys bolster his campaign with millions of dollars, soggy with the musty mildew of corruption and manipulation. My friends, I'm willing to bet that all that cash doesn't buy your vote! They can't empower these fools to actually think, to comprehend that the world is a complicated and unforgiving place, or to value anything beyond blind ambition because every second of their miserable perverted lives will be exposed for all the world to see. I guarantee that every one of these carbon copy candidates lack any qualifications for the offices they occupy for the moment, let alone the ones they might lust for in the future."

"You're finished as a spokesman for the conservatives," said Nance, tossing the headphones on the desk and dumping the metal chair to the floor with a clatter as he stood to leave.

"No, sonny, I don't think you understand how this works. I'm gonna be here talking to my people tomorrow night and every night and I'll predict that we'll see your resignation within the next couple of weeks, because it's become painfully obvious that you're a terrible actor and don't have a clue about what it takes to represent the American people. After this fiasco, I'm fairly certain that your handlers will be anxious to move on to your replacement."

"I guess we'll see about that," yelled the Congressman, slamming the door as he rushed into the narrow hallway. Murphy's raucous laughter echoed through every speaker in the station, as Nance stumbled through the clutter searching for an exit.

"If those powerbrokers plan to control the world, why would they put that punk kid up as a candidate? Everyone knows he's a frightened fraud!" yelled Murphy. "Hell, I ought to run for president. At least y'all know that everything I say comes straight from the heart!"

The light on the intercom in the booth blinked and Hannah picked it up, "What?"

"Put your board on auto-pilot and come help me answer the phones! As soon as Murphy said he ought to run for president, the lines lit up! This is crazy, they think he's serious!"

"Yeah, he's just spouting off, I'll be right there," said the engineer. He motioned for Murphy to cut to a taped promo and said, "You hit a note with that last bit, keep going, the phones are ringing off the hook!"

As the jingle ended, Murphy took another swig and a long slow drag on the cigar. "Seems some of you think my candidacy isn't such a crazy idea, that the Republican Party hacks represent the elite and arrogant one-percent, who are dedicated to maintaining the Wall Street barons and the status quo, while our voice speaks to the soul of America - the factory workers, miners, farmers, and truckers - the folks who built this country with their bare calloused hands, the folks who raise their kids with rock solid traditional values, and believe in the teachings in the Good Book.

We're the people in all those Rockwell paintings, who defend our flag, rights, and freedoms with our blood, sweat, and tears, and we demand protection for our most cherished beliefs against liberal domination of the laws and the courts! The weak progressive agenda is destroying everything that America stood for in the world before we became the laughingstock of the entire planet!"

He put a gray Confederate infantryman's hat on his head and swiveled the chair to salute the flags hanging on the wall, "If you're sick and tired of insane bureaucratic incompetence, followed by the same old fumbling excuses, when big government screws things up...if you want the administration to keep its nose out of your business and its hand out of your wallet...if you want to put an end to a perpetual migration of undocumented immigrants pouring across our borders to sully our pride and purity...if you want real change for real people, then send your contributions to the 'Elect Mac Murphy' Exploratory Fund at WBFK, P.O. Box 1040, Cincinnati, Ohio. I promise every penny will go to shutting down the noise, so the voice of the people can finally be heard!"

∼

Murphy tumbled off the couch onto a pile of empty bottles, pizza boxes, and greasy white bags that smelled as if they once contained something that might have been edible, scattered on a precious antique Oriental rug, now stained and tattered, as he took a wild swing at the ringing telephone buried in the clutter on the coffee table, launching the handset into flight along with the overflowing contents of a giant ashtray that erupted into a gray cloud shrouding leaded glass tinkling to the floor from the ensuing impact with a window in the intricately carved door of a fine old French cabinet.

His thoroughly scrambled brain sputtered electrical impulses that fired spastically between completely disconnected synapses, disrupting any potential for cognitive function. Bloodshot eyes drooped like an aging hound in the August heat, his tongue thick with fibrous tufts of something dead and furry, and the bile in his stomach threatened ignition at the scent of noxious poisons oozing from his rotund body.

A muffled voice, emanating from someplace in glittering shards of glass impaled in a heap of crumpled newspapers and trash, kept yelling, "Murphy, pick up the damned phone! Murphy, are you there?"

The table tipped over with a painful crash of broken crockery, moldy food, and mysterious liquids splattering in all directions when he tried to crawl over it to retrieve the handset so he could bash it repeatedly on the stone hearth, until that voice stopped screaming at him!

Finally, he held the receiver in front of his face, trying to figure out why Jack Hannah would interrupt his ruminations at this early hour on a weekend. "What the fuck could you possibly want at this hour of the day?"

"Well, it's three-thirty in the afternoon and I've been trying to reach you since this morning."

"The question remains, what could you possibly want?"

"I take it you haven't seen the paper?"

"What paper?"

"The newspaper, you old drunk. Someone's taking your candidacy seriously. They wrote an op-ed suggesting that you aren't any worse than all the boring traditional candidates, who are vying for president by repeating the same old tired crap that didn't work the last time and won't work the next time either. It even offers a compliment about how you could probably offer a refreshing perspective on the political turmoil we're going through."

"If they could see me now they'd have second thoughts," mumbled the prospective contender, rubbing his eyes, trying to focus on the hands of the clock on the mantle that had not been wound in months.

"Well, lots of people seem to be reacting. The post office box was overflowing this morning and Milly Clark's desk is covered in stacks of cash and checks."

"How much?"

"I have no idea but I'm pretty sure it's just the beginning. You need to sober up, so we can have a chat about what the hell's going on, before it gets completely out of hand."

"Buy me a whiskey and a steak and we'll talk."

~

Jack Hannah pulled into the unpaved parking lot of Katie's Chicken House, just down the highway from WBFK, noting Murphy's aging gold Cadillac convertible angled across three spaces in the flickering yellow radiance of the colossal neon chicken on the roof of the building. Gusty breezes swirled trash off the floorboards through the open driver's door and the canvas top was suspended part way out of the trunk. With dark clouds rolling in and the probability of rain, he walked over to slam the door and tug at the accordioned roof, until it settled on top of the windshield.

Katie's giddy daughter, Sara, was tending the register and guiding guests to tables in the tiny restaurant to the right. She nodded toward the 'Tropical' lounge, where Murphy was slumped against the faux teak bar with two empty shot glasses and a third halfway to his mouth. He raised his glass to the station manager, "Glad you finally showed up, I was just getting ready to order another round!"

Hannah slid onto a stool and Katie's husband and barkeep, Bernie, grinned while he poured a Rhinegeist draft into a tall tapered glass, "You guys got folks riled up with that show last week. I had a table-full of drunks screaming and yelling over there in the corner and had to threaten to turn your show off, if they didn't simmer down." He pointed to Murphy, "This guy keeps telling me he doesn't know nothin' about running for president."

Jack lifted his glass, "We're going to have a big coming out party. Maybe we should have it here."

"I'll go for that," laughed the bar tender. "You say when and I'll only charge you double."

"Hell, we haven't even started negotiating yet," said Murphy, offering an empty shot glass. "Fill 'er up."

Bernie filled the glass and wandered away. Hannah surveyed the future candidate who had managed to shower, rake a razor over parts of his ruddy face and dress in a fairly clean white shirt and a blue blazer that was only terminally rumpled. The flabby muscles in his jaw clenched and released, an amphetamine rush grinding his molars, and tremors in his hand sloshed the whiskey in the tiny glass while he attempted to lift it to his lips. He coughed, wiped his mouth with the back of his hand, and turned to Hannah, "What the fuck is happening?"

"Some very stupid people think you're serious about running for president after your shtick on the show the other night. Folks are sending in envelopes full of cash and we're getting calls from networks and wire services wanting interviews. Hell, someone claiming to work for the RNC, called wanting a biography for their donors."

"Anyone who knows me, could give you twenty good reasons why I'm completely unqualified and ill-suited to be president," said Murphy, hoisting his empty glass, "and this is just one of them."

Hannah tipped the tapered schooner and leaned on the bar, "We've had a hell of a run and we've produced some great shows but you know and I know it's all bullshit. You don't believe any of the crap that goes out over the air, so how are you going to rectify the dichotomy?"

The candidate straightened up, "Shit, you know more about this than I do, I'm just the talent, an actor playing a part in a nightly comedy. It's kept us out of the poorhouse for the past four years and given a voice to a whole bunch of folks who've been ignored and ridiculed, since before they started keepin' time. They might be dumber than mud but that's the price of democracy and they deserve the chance to scream and shout about the stuff that's important to them, even if I, personally, don't agree."

He took another swig, "If we do this, it's just a bigger tent, wind me up and lemme go. We'll cash in until someone figures it out and the whole charade falls apart. Then we can retire to earn millions of dollars writing books that justify our bad behavior and unbridled bullshit. I'm not proud, hell, I'm not even greedy, and we both know there's no chance in hell of winning the Republican nomination, let alone the election. That's not even worthy of consideration."

Jack's tension relaxed into a schemer's grin, "So, you'd do it for the money?"

"Yeah, make that lots of money, good booze, and some fine pussy and I'm in!"

"I'll make some calls."

Chapter Two
The conspiracy's fortieth anniversary

Nellis Gray fed the dogs, cats, chickens, goats, and horses, stroking and greeting each in turn, as their waking chatter rose to echo around the rafters of the barn. He collected the newspaper and sauntered across the drive, his breath blooming into clouds of ice crystals glittering in the first golden rays of sunshine stippling through the grove of bare pecan trees lining the lane out to the main road. He skipped up the steps following the rich aroma of coffee on the stove in the kitchen and silently pulled the bedroom door closed, poured a cup and headed out to the screened porch to read his paper.

He tossed another log in the wood stove, eased into the rocker and covered his legs with an old blanket, inhaled the earthy scent rising from his cup, took a sip and reached for a smoke. Having Katherine's calm presence in the house provided incentive and he was down to a few a day but, combined with a jarring jolt of thick Columbian caffeine, that first puff in the morning still kicked his juices into high gear.

The red-tail hawk cawed, as it swooped over the house, diving after a rabbit scurrying through the barren vegetable garden in search of shelter. One-by-one the dogs wandered up to the porch and perched according to pecking order - with Mamasan - the matriarch, closest to the fire, Cha-Cha - the aristocrat, at her side, Brandy snuggled next to the rocker for a gentle rub under his ear, Cody sprawled on the other side, and Gracie snuggled in with her butt near the stove and her head resting on the worn toe of Nellis' boot. Betsy, the momma cat, arrived with five downy kittens to curl up in the blanket on the lounge. None of the animals would lie on his pet pig Chester's roost in the corner, perhaps honoring his memory after he was slaughtered by a pickup full of rednecks trying to intimidate Nellis into abandoning his clandestine campaign to expose a conspiracy to buy the Cameron, Oklahoma election for a well-funded but totally unqualified candidate for Congressional Representative.

Certainly, there were adjustments to be made to accommodate his new roommate but she slipped right into the rhythm of caring for the sixty-acre farm and a herd of assorted animals, filling his life with kindness, intelligence and a passion that had been absent from his heart for longer than he cared to admit.

All of which made him confess to his no-bullshit inner-self, that his disposition these past few years had been something less than joyous - something more akin to dour and angry and miserly. Now, for the first time since he finally gave up life on the road playing music in honkytonks and reluctantly settled into the old homestead, the farmhouse was actually beginning to feel like a home again.

He sipped and puffed, pondering his deceased wife's ghost's initial reception of Katherine - slamming doors, popping lights on in the middle of the night, and splattering water whenever she passed near a sink. Her things in the frigid guestroom were rearranged every morning, sometimes neatly, sometimes in a pile on the floor. Nanny's tantrums went on for contentious days before something mysteriously changed and as the new woman of the house approached, doors began to open, lamps would light, the temperature would warm, and the second bedroom remained neat and orderly.

"Nanny, I feel like you've realized that Katherine is a decent, caring, and fairly feisty woman," He chuckled, *"sort of, way too much like you and I'm pretty sure we both agree she's good for me. Between her and the Spratlin girls, I feel like I've finally got something to live for, besides just keeping this ol' homestead running in case our wayward kids might want it someday. But I need you to remain a part of it, if you can, 'cause I don't think we're anywhere near done yet."*

He didn't wait for a response, there was never a direct response, but her presence permeated the old house and she was quick to remind him of his failings with an unmistakable prank.

His eyes traced the headline: 'Hurricane Dot Devastates West Coast of Florida', with a large photo of the appalling damage and a three-column story, accompanied by a smaller image of a huge crowd of drenched people, under a smaller headline that read:

Workers Rally through Storm for Rights

In the hours before the eye of hurricane Dot dragged devastation along the west coast of Florida, demolishing thousands of homes and displacing hundreds-of-thousands of residents, a brave confederation of protestors gathered in the town square of Dolphin Bay to bring faces and voices to the desperate struggle of the swelling segment of our society known as the working poor.

Dolphin Bay Times owner, Tabitha Hall, said, "These people braved brutal thunderstorms with gale force winds and a series of attacks by a small group of counter-protestors, who set off explosives and shattered storefront windows in an attempt to panic the crowd. In spite of the obstacles, the protesters showed the world that they are upstanding citizens, people who work two or three part-time jobs just to feed their families and keep a roof over their heads. They don't get raises or vacations and they don't receive benefits, like health insurance or profit sharing or 401K's, because they've been marginalized by a callous system owned and controlled by corporations.

Many of the companies that employ these people are making record profits for their investors at the expense of the workers, who make their products and provide their services. This might be the very first mass protest by an oppressed working class against the disproportional incomes between the have's and the have-not's in more than half-a-century and it certainly won't be the last."

It seems obvious that this rain-soaked rally of brave and determined souls will provide a template for expanding this movement to every corner of the nation and beyond. This soggy but determined first step is likely to expand into a political and economic crusade.

The door creaked and the toe of Katherine's fuzzy pink slipper appeared, testing the temperature, before the rest of her long leg emerged. She was swaddled in a heavy housecoat, cradling a steaming mug of coffee with both hands, and carefully stepped over Brandy to kiss Nellis, "You can't claim that it's toasty warm out here."

He stood up, "Here take the chaise with the kittens in the blanket. I'll throw another log on the fire and get a couple of these hounds to cuddle up to keep you warm."

"How can you be so chipper this early in the day? The sun's just barely crawling over the trees."

"It's a fine morning and it's going to warm up fast."

As she stretched out on the lounge, gathering a churning pile of meowing kittens and pulling the blanket up to her chin to sip her coffee, "Sounds like you've got an agenda."

"Stuff to do," he laughed, "there's always stuff that needs doin' to keep up with this place."

"You're incorrigible."

He picked up the paper and tapped the article, "Looks like there's a whole bunch of working folks in this country who aren't too happy with the way things are going."

She unfolded her reading glasses and scanned the article, "The more I see of the world from the base of the gilded tower, the more aware I've become of the disparity between the people who live in the manor houses along the ridge overlooking town and the rest of the serfs down in the valley, which makes me wonder how long it will take before the people at the bottom of the economic ladder become so desperate, they explode into revolution and anarchy."

"Darlin', for a brainy broad who spent her entire life in corporate witlessness, you've come a long way," laughed Nellis. "Hell, even some of your guys at Spratlin's plant give off that vibe of not being sure they'll be employed next week or next month, that anxiety of being dependent on an employer who has the power to decide when his bottom line makes them expendable. They're well paid and I'm sure they get great benefits but, like it or not, their fate and the welfare of their families lies in someone else's hands."

"I think our little town of Cameron kept that unspoken apprehension pretty well buttoned up until the strike but, once that snake slithered out of the bottle, there was no putting it back."

Nellis grinned, "Speaking of snake pits, I hear the governor's sending your old boss and our future Representative Spratlin to Washington to fill in until they can run a real election."

"I've got to meet him at the plant at nine o'clock to organize his schedule and get everyone else lined out to fill in while he's gone."

"He depends on you."

She stared into her empty mug, "Yeah, I know."

"I'll fetch us another round." He reached to take her cup, "Is all of this awkward for you?"

Katherine brushed back thick auburn hair and wrapped her arms around his neck, "I wouldn't trade sharing this wonderland with you for anything and, no, I wouldn't go back to my sheltered life before that ended and this started."

"That doesn't answer my question."

She pursed her lips, "I think Stanton has some doubts about the commitments he's made but he's the last of the true aristocrats, subject to the Victorian covenant that honor and obligation are far more profound than matters of the heart."

"Miss Kennedy, I do believe he's still in love with you."

Her dark eyes focused on his, "We shared our intimate secret for years and I doubt that either of us will ever stop caring for each other but we both knew it would end badly, when it first started. He has to put his family back together and become a responsible member of Congress and I have to build a life of my own."

Nellis kissed her forehead, picked up the cups, and started for the door but turned when she said, "I'd very much like to figure out whether I might build that life with you."

~

Just before eight o'clock, Spratlin's shiny black Fleetwood Cadillac pulled up to the steel gate in a cloud of grit from the dry gravel on the lane and disgorging a half-dozen children, who scampered over the fence to unlatch the gate. Mr. Charles tipped his driver's cap, as he eased out of the car and brushed dust from his black suit, before ambling up the path after his stampeding flock of hope. The dogs whined and yowled with tails wagging, as Sissy and Sammy Spratlin trotted up the steps with Maybelle Brown's children; Daniel, Hubby, Muriel, and Martin, to hug and pet them all.

Katherine stepped out from the parlor, adjusting an earring, as Nellis asked, 'What brings all of you here at this hour of the morning?"

Sissy grinned, "We got everyone together for a family meeting last night and we decided that we want to spend Thanksgiving this year with the family we choose."

"And we all wanted both of you to be there," added Samantha.

Nellis glanced up at Katherine, who smiled and said, "We'd be honored to join you."

"Great," said little Martin, "we've never been to a feast before."

Daniel added, "We've never had turkey before."

"It's just a giant chicken," laughed Sissy, "with stuffing, mashed potatoes and gravy, and green-bean casserole, and big fluffy rolls."

"My tummy hurts, just thinking about it," tittered tiny Muriel.

"Just leave room for the sweet potato pie," said Mr. Charles. "Louise's pies are so light and airy, they're food worthy of the gods."

"I don't see how anyone could be foolish enough to turn down a Thanksgiving dinner prepared by Mama Louise and your mother," said Nellis, squinting at Hubie with a sly grin, "even if we do have to put up with all you noisy children."

The whole group feigned hurt feelings, until little giggles and grins erupted into laughter and hugs, and the herd of children and dogs trooped out the door.

Mr. Charles said, "Six-thirty, Thursday a week."

"Can we bring anything," inquired Katherine.

"Just yourselves. I can guarantee that there'll be more delicious food than all of us could possibly eat in two sittings."

"We'll be there," said Nellis, watching his jaunty retreat across the drive, the shepherd wrangling his rambunctious flock before pulling the gate closed and turning the long car around to deliver them to school. Having saved the Brown children from a murderous gang of Klan thugs and Sissy and Sammy from a tornado and all of them from kidnappers, he'd developed a protective affection for each, even if he never quite displayed it to them. He looked up at Katherine, "Are you okay with this?"

She bit her lower lip, "It's strange, in spite of the affair, I don't feel much tension when I'm alone with either Stanton or Marjorie but it's a completely different tone when the three of us are together."

"I hate to say 'that's to be expected', when each of you and all of you are rearranging your lives and your commitments around each other. I spent too many years going through the 'what-ifs', until you made me see that the only thing we can control is what's right in front of us. Yesterday's gone and tomorrow might never get here."

"We'll get through it and, in a weird way, I'm kind of honored that they all wanted us to be there." She glanced at her watch, "I've got to go or I'll be late."

"Especially the kids." He stood to kiss her cheek, "You sure smell nice, I'm thinkin' I should be jealous."

The ravishing brunette grinned, "In case you've forgotten, you <u>are</u> the other man."

Nellis cackled, "You be careful. You know where to find me when you get finished with that other guy."

"You take it easy, I know how hard you work," said Katherine, with a kiss and a hug.

He marveled at her rhythm, as she hustled across the yard to the barn to retrieve the company station wagon - on loan until she selected something to replace her demolished Grand Prix. He reached for the pack of Winston's then pulled his hand away, muttering, "Beautiful women should not be allowed to wear spiky heels in public, especially first thing in the morning."

Big snowflakes drifted down through the thin forest of bare oaks, sycamores, and maples, majestic sculptures silhouetted against the last golden wisps of sunset tickling tumbling gray clouds racing north ahead of an arctic blast. The old pickup trundled beneath the arch bearing twin lions supporting the burgundy crest surrounding an ornate 'S', along the winding drive to Spratlin House, under the portico and through the courtyard to park near the kitchen door.

Nellis leaned over to kiss Katherine, "You sure look beautiful tonight."

She grinned, "And I never would have believed that you owned a tie, let alone would wear one out in public."

"Well, this is family…sort of." He fingered the deep blue silk, embellished with tiny golden guitars, and hopped out to walk around to help her. The pavers were slippery and he lifted her over an icy puddle, "Are we breaking some damned nicety by arriving at the back door?"

"I don't think anyone is going to care," laughed Katherine. "Although it does say something about the status of our relationship with these people."

"Aw, we've all been to hell and back together, plus, we beat the bad guys in the process. Hopefully we'll have fair and honest elections when the State Board finally gets through cleaning out the conspirators."

The kitchen door opened before they reached the bottom step and a mob of children poured out to greet them. Little Muriel grabbed Katherine's hand, "Come inside, where it's warm."

They trooped into the cozy kitchen, drawn by rich aromas beckoning everyone to a giant golden turkey, resting on the stove amid pots bubbling with goodness. Louise and Maybelle turned from their preparations to greet the guests with hugs.

Mama Louise put her whisk on a saucer and reached to pull on Nellis' tie, "You almost look domesticated but I wouldn't put money on it lasting."

"Let's just pretend it's Halloween and call it good."

"Well, I think you look downright handsome," said Maybelle.

"Thank you," replied Nellis. "It doesn't happen often."

Stanton followed Marjorie from the dining room to shake hands and exchanged cheek kisses with Katherine. Embarrassed, she reached for Marjorie's hand but the older woman pulled her close, "I need to thank you for the support that you've provided for Stanton, for me, and for our family. These are difficult times, suffered under awkward circumstances, but I think we all see that. Like it or not, we're participating in a drama that affects the entire country and we're all dependent on each other to see it through."

Before she could respond, Spratlin said, "Why don't we head into the living room and let these ladies finish this wonderful meal."

A noisy parade tramped along the gleaming parquet floor of the hallway into a very formal drawing room warmed by a large fireplace, dancing orange flames reflecting in a square glass coffee table with a large bouquet of yellow roses in a cut-glass vase, between twin sofas, end tables with upholstered side chairs, and other groupings to accommodate a large gathering in comfort and classic style.

Mr. Charles appeared with a silver tray, "May I offer you something to drink?"

Katherine replied, "Chardonnay, please."

He turned to Nellis, who shook his gloved hand and inquired, "Got any brews in the fridge?"

Bruce walked in with his older brother, Brad, who said, "One thing you can always count on is at least a case of something tasty in the cooler."

"With you two hanging around, it's a wonder there's any left." They shook hands and Mr. Charles continued collecting orders, before disappearing to a bar in the hallway opposite the pantry.

"Actually," said Bruce, "Dad's the only one who's still drinking alcohol and if you watch he'll only have one. We both decided to try to figure out who we really are by getting straight and going to therapy and Mom's off everything except her blood pressure medicine."

"Do your relationships feel…different," asked Katherine.

Brad leaned close, "For the first time, since…I don't know, maybe never, they feel genuine."

"In spite of years of weirdness in our family, these kids getting kidnapped by those stupid Klan guys taught us what it feels like when we're all looking out for each other," added Bruce. "Might not be perfect…but better."

"That's about as good as it gets," said Nellis.

Miss Sibble, aging nanny for generations of Spratlins, gathered the children around a table for a rousing game of Clue, while the adults settled in on the matching couches and Stanton said, "I had an interesting call from the publisher of the newspaper in Dolphin Bay, Florida, earlier this evening, asking about how we kept the Brantley's from stealing the election. Seems she's involved with the leaders of that protest they had over oppressive wages and phantom benefits, just before the hurricane wiped out most of the towns along the Gulf coast."

"I read about that in the paper," said Nellis.

"Well, it turns out that the lady I spoke with, Tabitha Hall, rose from cub reporter to own the newspaper so she's seen both ends of the social spectrum and we have a surprising number friends and associates in common."

Marjorie added, "American aristocracy is intertwined between old money and the nouveau riche, who have acquired their fortunes more recently, without the benefit of tradition or principled restraint. It's a very small club and everyone knows at least some scandalous tidbit about everyone else, so we're all aware of political affiliations and targeted contributions."

"And that's why it's not surprising to identify some of the mysterious donors on your list and dozens more, who used Billy Joe Hardman's ministry to funnel untraceable campaign funds to their chosen candidates."

"I wondered about that," said Bruce. "They can't be true-believers."

"He and his surrogate preachers around the country are paid handsomely to deliver coordinated messages to their flocks of the faithful, straight paranoid racist propaganda to rile the ignorant and bolster Republican candidates, who seem to be sponsored by an extremist federation of the wealthiest families in this nation and beyond."

"So, in spite of bringing down the local conspiracy, we zeroed in on their greed and failed to recognize the size of their role in a larger conspiracy?" asked Nellis.

Spratlin stood in front of the fireplace, "There is sufficient evidence to believe that our skirmish was merely a minor episode in an exceedingly coordinated campaign to stack this election and I wouldn't be surprised to find that it's affected every ballot at every level through every cycle for decades."

"Decades?" inquired Katherine.

"It's odd how getting appointed to become a temporary representative reveals a treasure trove of connections, information, and intriguing back stories that no one in power would dream of sharing with the common folk."

"And…?"

"Theory follows the roots back to 1958, in Indianapolis, when Robert Welch, a right-wing businessman founded an organization dedicated to exposing or inventing a Communist plot behind every piece of legislation proposed by the Federal Government. They called it the John Birch Society, after a missionary and military intelligence officer who was killed in China just after the end of the Second World War and, incidentally, had nothing to do with them or their cause. They held him up as a martyr, claiming he was the first American to die in the Cold War."

"I read about that in a political science class," said Bruce. "I'm pretty sure they morphed into a well-financed political arm of the fanatical right, just like our Klansmen, white supremacists, and ultra-nationalists. But they provide big bucks dedicated to financing gerrymandering and getting fanatics elected to state legislatures, boards of education, and city councils. The powerbrokers were never out front but lined up their people to make the deciding vote on whatever issue was beneficial to them."

"That's absolutely right," said Stanton. "An alliance of extraordinarily wealthy families and thoroughly corrupt evangelical ministries seem to have toiled to put a civilized face on sabotaging our democratic process. They're manipulating a large invisible segment of white society that feels threatened by anyone of color! Anyone from another country! Anyone who speaks another language or worships another religion! The brain trust was smart and started small on the local and state level but after decades of effort they've built up their base to elect enough radical nutcases to take control of the House and, once things finally get settled from our most recent mid-term, they have a good shot at seizing a majority in the Senate. The next election, they'll seize the presidency."

"With the recession, jobs disappearing overseas, and unemployment climbing, they've got plenty of supporters who are so desperate, they'd vote for a toad if he promised them a paycheck," said Katherine.

"What's the gold ring they're trying to grab?" asked Nellis. 'What's the ultimate goal?"

Spratlin tipped back the last few drops of his favorite Cragganmore single-malt Scotch, letting the fiery essence sear across his tongue, "I know some of these people. I've listened to their logic, their…strategy at cocktail parties and over dinners, so I'm sure that the power brokers are committed to eliminating intrusive government regulations and taxation, withdrawal from participation in multilateral trade and military treaties, deportation of immigrants, rescission of all the Amendments to the Constitution after the tenth…"

"Undelegated powers remain with the States and the People," interrupted Brad. "Although, I'm pretty sure the Founding Fathers were referring to wealthy white landowners not dirt farmers or factory workers."

"And eleven through twenty-seven address the rights of our modern society…" added Marjorie.

"Including the right for African-Americans and women to vote," said Mr. Charles, refilling the children's glasses of lemonade.

Stanton said, "They're fixated on the sixteenth, which gives the federal government the right of taxation. They see no reason why their profits should be confiscated to help or protect the indigent classes."

"I don't mean to interrupt your conversation but Mama Louise asked me to tell you that dinner is served," said Mr. Charles, with a broad grin.

The children cheered and applauded, before darting through the double doors into a formal dining room and around a very long table dressed with an intricately patterned damask tablecloth, Waterford crystal, fine Wedgewood China with the gold Spratlin 'S' centered up between twin lions on each plate, gleaming silverware and three fragrant flower arrangements glowing under twin chandeliers scattering sparkles across fine carved mahogany paneling and scenic French wallpaper.

Nellis walked in with Stanton, "You didn't answer the question."

"They want to own everything and everyone, simple as that. They consider 1850 the pinnacle of western civilization, when white landowners could own women and people of color and abuse, rape, or even kill them on a whim without threat of interference, let alone justice." He paused, "I'm considered a wealthy man but I can only imagine a level of affluence where money has no meaning, no finite value because no matter how much they spend or invest they're always making more. It's merely a tool to buy influence and power to feed the inflated narcissistic egos of people who honestly believe that they were born to privilege, so they should rule the world and a subservient population should be organized to serve them."

"Bullies always amaze and disappoint me," said Nellis, "and I've never seen one yet who could survive for two-seconds in a fair fight."

Everyone took a seat, with Katherine on Stanton's right and Nellis next to Marjorie, the children along each side with three empty chairs. Mr. Charles, Mama Louise and Maybelle placed delectable plates before the ladies, then the gents, and finally the children, who started to pick up forks and spoons. Marjorie said, quietly but firmly, "We'll wait until everyone is seated, if you don't mind?"

Forks and spoons returned to the table and little hands to laps as the three servers took their seats. Stanton stood and raised his water glass, "I'm so very proud that all of us are here together to celebrate this occasion as one big family because that's who we are! That's who we've always been…in spite of the fact that some of us were too preoccupied to notice the wonder and goodness of it all. When threatened by violent thugs, we pulled together to save these precious youngsters and expose a national conspiracy and we have Mr. Gray and Miss Kennedy to thank for guiding us through our nightmare."

The children clapped and cheered.

Sibble stood. The tiny waif barely taller than the back of her chair but her voice carried that perfect pitch guaranteed to freeze her many young charges in mid-flight. She looked up at Stanton, "I remember the day, the joyous day, when we brought you into this world, into this home. Your father was so proud and your mother elated and I think they would be pleased to find us, all of us celebrating together as one growing family." She paused to look from one face to the next, "And I'm proud to be one of you."

Stanton held up his glass and continued, "So, let us be thankful for our blessings, for each other, for caring neighbors and for this magnificent feast! Let's eat!"

The calm was overwhelmed by the tinkling of silverware on China and it was several savory bites before Nellis said, "My compliments to you ladies, this is wonderful."

Mama Louise laughed, "I'm sure we have plenty for seconds."

"Just be smart enough to save room for dessert," added Maybelle. "We have my pumpkin and Mama's sweet potato pies that'll knock your taste-buds into culinary rapture."

Katherine asked, "What did your publisher lady want?"

"They're trying to organize a conference of like-minded people to coordinate a national campaign to support the effort they've started in Florida. Tabitha pointed out that their rally in the storm was populated by people of every color and faith, every ethnicity and culture, so they're calling it 'All People Matter' for the moment and they're bringing in activists from all over the country. Several senators and representatives as well as a public relations firm, lawyers and finance guys are supposed to be there too."

"Sounds like they're trying to be professional."

"Do you remember that glamorous couple, Mavis and Tate Sloan, who were all over the tabloids for years?"

"Yeah, he was a star quarterback for OU back in the day. Didn't he disappear in that hurricane?"

"Yes, tragically, and their luxury development on the coast got wiped away by the storm but his wife is one of the leaders of this movement and in fact she and her people have put together a number of self-contained miniature cities within cities to house and employ thousands of destitute people."

"From all the tacky stories, that's not what I expected."

"Actually, she's financing this summit and she's even sending a plane to pick us up next week."

Katherine's lips curled into an inquisitive smile, "Us?"

"Well, of course. I'm invited, so I need you with me and Mr. Charles and of course we need Nellis' insight."

"They need Nellis, they just don't know it yet," laughed the beautiful brunette.

Stanton touched her hand, "I know things have changed but we make a great team and I think we have an opportunity to make a difference in the world. I hope you'll help make it happen."

"This is an awkward situation."

"I don't know, nor do I care to know, about your involvement with Mr. Gray…until you decide to make it my business. Until then, I intend to keep our relationship as professional as it's always been."

Katherine laughed, "As it appeared to be."

"You know what I mean."

"I do and I agree. After dinner, we'll ask Nellis if he'd care to join us."

The fire crackled, warming the study against a blizzard of fluffy snowflakes crafting a glittering wonderland outside leaded windows, overlooking the distant golden glow of sodium lights at the Stanton Oil plant on the opposite bank of the meandering river flowing through the city of Cameron. Sibble and Maybelle ushered the children towards bed and Mr. Charles served decaf coffee in delicate cups decorated with cardinals perched in green holly, before easing into an upholstered wing chair.

Stanton toasted the room with his coffee cup, "During dinner, I told Katherine that Mrs. Hall, the publisher of the Dolphin Times, requested our presence at a conference of volunteers from all over the country next week in Houston. It's being hosted by Mavis Sloan, who developed the infamous SunnyBreeze resort with her late husband, Tate. She's lined up a sympathetic group of moneyed families who have chosen patriotism over greed by investing in the construction of a rapidly expanding number of little self-sufficient cities within cities, where they house, train and employ thousands of indigent people."

"What's the point of this get-together?" asked Nellis.

"To create a coordinated national campaign to defend and assist the millions of middle-class workers and their families, who are being shoved off the edge of an economic cliff into desperation, while a fanatical faction of the super-wealthy have joined in a feeding frenzy, gobbling up ever larger chunks of commerce and industry to consolidate a world economy. Our allies and the growing protest movement are obviously, completely opposed to the conspirators who are bent on turning this country into their private piggy bank. So, enlisting vast armies of eager volunteers and dedicated voters to reclaim our democracy is fundamental to meeting the challenge."

"From our perspective," said Mr. Charles, slowly, quietly, "it seems like the chatter is getting louder from the white honkies, blaming immigrants and people of color for stealing their jobs and threatening their dominance over their white nation. Black kids, all over the country, are getting gunned down by white cops who get off with an acquittal and back pay. Hispanics are eight times more likely to get pulled over and ticketed or arrested than a white person.

You hear it on the radio, on television news programs. Hell, I heard one Senate candidate, from the deep South, saying that the country was at its best back in the days before the Civil War, when white families stuck together, even if there was slavery. I'm pretty sure my ancestors didn't feel the love."

"I saw a pickup racing down Maple Ridge, the other day, with a pair of battle flags flappin' in the breeze," added Louise. "It's like folks don't need to bother hidin' their prejudices and hate anymore. We seem to have lost the ability to pretend that we know how to behave and interact with each other in a civil manner."

"I think we've all realized how prevalent and acceptable this closet bigotry has become in our town, the next town and the one after that," said Katherine. "Except, now, it's out in the open."

"I hate to say this but I could see this turning into a race war," said Mr. Charles, "when folks finally realize that the Republicans have always bowed to bigots, because they're terrified of losing money from big donors and the votes of the racists."

"I think you're right on it," said Nellis. "That 'good ol' boy' mentality runs through the South and up through the Midwest into the rustbelt, where jobs have been disappearing for decades. I spent years traveling those roads, playing honky-tonks from Chicago to Atlanta, so I know that most of those ignorant bastards possess one talent, one thing they know how to do really well, like mining or manufacturing or whatever.

When that inherited birthright disappears, they'll hang on, desperately hoping their industry will magically come back to life, in spite of logic or common sense. But you know and I know and they know it won't. They're too proud to get retrained to do something else so, they've got no income and no future and they've gotta have someone to blame, which makes them easy pickings for right-wing propaganda."

"And they're desperate to find someone, anyone who can offer them hope," said Marjorie.

Stanton looked from one to the next, "The plane leaves the airport at 8:30, Monday morning. I think everyone needs to be involved in this because it's much bigger than a few greedy tycoons trying to get their puppets elected to vote for their tax cuts."

Chapter Three

Mavis Sloan padded through the kitchen to plant a kiss on Chen Chen's cheek, as he prepared the ingredients for his scrumptious Southwestern omelet, packed with enough spicy goodness to clear out the cobwebs. She settled into a banquette in the breakfast room with a hot cup of coffee and a copy of the New York Times. Her eyes strayed from the text, following flickers of warm sunlight bursting through scraggly gray clouds spilling northeast and illuminating snowy canopies dusting the forest surrounding the steely-blue Lake Travis. A mockingbird, pecking fermenting berries from a holly bush outside the window, worked through a repertoire of songs that almost soothed the jarring headlines in the newspaper:

'Rate of Foreclosures Surging', 'Republican Congress Refuses Budget Compromise, Threatens Government Shutdown', 'Supreme Court Rejects President Gonzalez' Executive Orders', 'Markets Rally Despite Uncertainty'.

She laid the paper on the table and sipped her coffee, tracking fleeting streaks of sparkles rippling across black waves to vanish into the gray haze reflected from the gloomy sky, thinking about her late husband Tate...dear Tate. Her public persona was marching forward with meetings and schedules, lawyers and lawsuits, but there were moments during each day when his voice would appear in her mind or his scent would tease her nostrils or his soulful eyes would peer from the empty space he would always occupy in the core of her being.

They both knew that their idyllic public image and private marriage could not and would not last forever...but she was not ready for it all to end so abruptly with his death and the complete annihilation of SunnyBreeze, their extravagant and exclusive housing development, in the frenzy of hurricane Dot. It felt as if the gods had completely ransacked the structure of her life, jumbled a tender tangle of emotions in her heart and exposed her soul to the harsh realities of a cruel world in preparation for whatever this next chapter demanded.

Selby Simonson removed a battered Stetson, as he strolled through the kitchen in his socks, nodding to Chen, his houseman and general counsel, who commanded that the boss's mucky riding boots remain in the mudroom to avoid contaminating his spotless kitchen. Mavis offered a cheek for a kiss, "How was your ride?"

"We rode up to check on a herd that's been grazing up in the high meadows. It looks like it's about time to bring them back down for the winter."

"It was really warm until the storm blew through the other night," replied Mavis.

Her father grinned, "We both know a blissful autumn can't last forever and this snow will be gone as soon as the sun breaks through those clouds."

Chen brought two gorgeous plates with stuffed omelets, thick slices of bacon, fruit salad, fresh squeezed orange juice and a basket of scratch-baked blueberry muffins as Simon sat down and topped off their coffee cups. "Enjoy."

"Thank you," replied Mavis. "This looks great!"

"Well, try eating some of it today. Your plate's been coming back untouched and you don't need to lose any more weight, my Precious Lotus Flower."

Selby cocked an eyebrow, "Why aren't you eating?"

Mavis picked at her eggs with a fork, "Too much to think about…"

"Like?"

"Like a big conference of activists from all over the country coming in on Monday."

"Knowing you, you've already got that covered because you're the most organized person on the planet. What's really bothering you?"

She fidgeted for a moment before looking up at her father with tears in her eyes, "I guess I'm not really over Tate's death yet."

He put down his fork and reached for her hand, "Honey, you might be strong and tough and think you're invincible but you're still just a lovely human being with a big heart who's suffered a staggering loss and it's going to take some time to grieve through everything that's happened. I admire your instinct to throw yourself into your work as a distraction but that's all it is, a distraction that will not heal the wounds that you've suffered."

She broke down and he wrapped his arms around her, soothing her sobs, until she finally slumped against his shoulder.

"It's all about regrets, isn't it?"

"Uh-huh."

"What?"

"In spite of everything we built and experienced together, I feel like I didn't do enough to make sure that he knew that I actually loved him for who he was, not the character we projected on TV and in the magazines."

"He adored you," replied her father.

"I know, but I was so busy promoting our brand that I neglected the husband and wife part a lot."

He pulled back a little to look into her eyes, "You're not pregnant, are you?"

She burst into tears, "No, I wish I was but we hadn't been together in months…because I pushed him into a relationship with Ned Flint. I made him prostitute himself for the good of the project!"

"I'm in no position to judge your relationship with your husband, after being married or involved as many times as I have," he pulled her close, "but I can attest that a man, with his sights set on a major goal, would not consider using his manhood to leverage success as prostitution."

She looked up, tears streaming down her cheeks, and he wiped them away with a gentle finger, then kissed her forehead. "So, first, it's not like you sent him to the gallows, after all. Pleasure is pleasure, but more important, however you worked this out, each of you entered into this agreement without duress, understanding that it was for your mutual benefit."

Mavis pressed against his shoulder, "It's more than that."

"What?"

"I never welcomed him back."

~

Nellis pulled the pickup up to the entrance of the private hangar and an attendant in a black windbreaker with starched white shirt and a sky blue bow-tie, appeared next to his door before he turned off the ignition. He reached for Katherine's hand and rolled down the window.

"Hi, I'm Kevin. Will you be joining the flight to Houston?"

"Yes. I'm Nellis Gray and this is Katherine Kennedy."

The young man checked his list and grinned, "If you have any luggage, I'll be happy to load it onboard and park the car for you."

Nellis nodded, said, "Thank you," and rolled up the window.

"Are you nervous about this?"

"Why do you ask?"

"Because, I'd expect you to hop right out, ready to rock, but you're not. You're hesitating." She pursed her lips, "You've never flown before, have you?"

"Never had the opportunity."

The attendant was still waiting patiently outside the closed window with a confused half-grin.

She kissed his cheek, "C'mon, it's fun. Besides, I'll hold your hand until we reach cruising altitude."

"How high's that?"

"Oh, probably twenty-five or thirty-thousand feet."

"Why do they have to fly so high?"

"To get above the weather and stay out of the way of other aircraft."

"How come planes don't run into each other, anyway?"

"Think of it as a layer cake with planes going east at one altitude in well-defined lanes, those going north at another, west at yet another, and southerly flights at their own height. They really do have this thing worked out, they've been working on it since the Wright Brothers' first flight at Kitty Hawk more than a hundred years ago."

"If you say so."

She kissed his cheek, "Promise."

The tension around his eyes melted into a smirk, "How 'bout parachutes?"

"Now I know you're just messing with me!"

The Lear landed on a damp slippery runway and turned onto an auxiliary taxiway to line up with seven sleek silver jets in front of a massive white hanger bearing the 'Simonson Air' logo, where dozens of people were loading into a parade of limousines.

The pilot's calm professional voice filled the cabin, "Welcome to the Simonson Air facility at the George Bush Intercontinental Airport in

Houston. The temperature is an unusually cool forty-two degrees and it's misting, with a forty percent chance of heavier precipitation this afternoon. Our crew will be on standby, when you're ready to return to Cameron. We hope you've enjoyed your flight and look forward to serving you this evening."

Temporary Representative Spratlin, as he preferred to be called, emerged from the plane and turned to help Katherine down the few steps to the tarmac, followed by Nellis, and Mr. Charles. Mavis Sloan, dressed in a reserved gray suit with a creamy chiffon scarf, flashed her magazine-cover smile and reached to shake hands, "In case anyone doesn't know, I'm Mavis Sloan and, if truth be known, only half the stories in the magazines were true but I'm not tellin' which! This is Marvin Standler and the Reverend Jimbo Combs."

Spratlin turned, "This is Katherine Kennedy, Nellis Gray, and Mr. Charles - all of whom played critical roles in bringing down a political conspiracy, as well as a fraudulent ministry."

Reverend Combs reached for his hand with a hardy smile, "I might be the king of evangelical entertainment but I preach against those who promote hatred and bigotry and my ministry has nothing but contempt for Billy Joe Hardman's 'Praise the Lord' alliance."

He shook hands with Nellis and Katherine, then took Mr. Charles' hand but Spratlin's houseman returned the grip, demanding, "Explain the difference."

"Billy Joe is a racist pig, who used the sacred word of God to fleece his ignorant flock out of money they can't afford to contribute, to finance his opulent lifestyle and his support for the white-nationalist's twisted quest. He worked in conjunction and coordination with Joshua Godwin and a network of lily-white evangelical ministries bent on destroying democracy and cleansing our society of brown-skinned vermin."

He paused to gaze deeply into Mr. Charles eyes, a technique he used to hypnotize thousands of his followers, but he found only quiet resolve. "I joined up with Mrs. Sloan after she made me face the inevitability of the coming catastrophe and we started organizing another group of wealthy families and corporations who are dedicated to preserving our national heritage. I took on the role of re-educating the population, not only to accept the risk of fighting back but to embrace the revolutionary responsibility of building a better future for everyone...together. An educated populous is our only defense against extremism."

Mr. Charles smiled and patted the former basketball player's enormous hand, "I believe you're sincere in your intentions."

"Welcome aboard, brother."

Katherine asked Standler, "How many are attending?"

"We've already sent about seventy-five on to the club, plus more than a dozen from Dolphin Bay, your crew, and another group from Chicago. So let's call it a hundred plus."

"The plane from Florida should be landing momentarily," said Mavis, "and then we'll get the last caravan heading out."

"Any reason we're traveling in a pack?" asked Nellis.

Mavis scanned his weathered face and the gleam of terminal irreverence in his eyes, "Representative Spratlin told me a little about your part in taking down the conspiracy."

"Are you avoiding the question?"

"Are you always this direct?"

"Pretty much."

She pursed her lips, "Alright, we tried to keep this gathering as quiet as possible but we've received some warnings that a local branch of extreme nationalists who call themselves 'White America', might attempt to disrupt our conference with protests or even violence."

"Have you informed the authorities?" asked Spratlin.

"Yes, all entrances have been sealed and we'll have an honor guard to escort us, when we leave here," replied Mavis, as a pair of bigger 'Simonson Air' jets pulled up to park at the far end of the row.

Several long white Cadillacs pulled up and drivers hopped out to load the guests from Florida and the Midwest. Mavis climbed into the car and took the back seat between Standler and Reverend Combs. Nellis sat on a side bench with Katherine, opposite Spratlin and Mr. Charles.

Two police officers on white motorcycles pulled up to lead the caravan of long white vehicles the few miles to the conference center.

"It seems that everyone we've contacted is seeing different pieces of a much broader conspiracy. We've had major protests and strikes in Florida to promote fair wages and benefits and to solicit help for the millions of middle-class people who are being driven into poverty," said Mavis. "Your situation seems completely different and yet, it's part of the same conspiracy."

"Economically, Cameron is probably a unique situation because we're a small town that depends on one primary industry and we've learned that when demand turns south or that single employer hits hard times, the troubles get shared through the whole community."

"Spread that uncertainty across the entire country, from the coal mines in Appalachia to empty factories in Detroit, Illinois, and Indiana. From farmers throughout the Plains who are fighting giant international corporations driving commodity prices down and land values up, to truck drivers transporting goods, or stockers in the giant wholesale distribution centers who will lose their jobs to robots and automation in a few years. There can be little doubt that the demise of the middle-class isn't an accident caused by economic circumstance. It is, in almost every case, the result of a long-term strategy by the very wealthiest of our neighbors who want to own and control everything." said Standler. "I should know, I'm one of them."

Mr. Charles' brow crinkled, "I don't understand."

Standler leaned forward, "I'm the CEO of Brinksman Investments, whose sole purpose is to leverage companies that are in deep financial trouble, by utilizing financial schemes that are barely legal but extraordinarily rewarding. Once our people take control using other people's money, we dismiss all but the most critical assets, sell off the lucrative bits and pieces, extract enormous profits, and abandon the rotting carcass of the debt-ridden corporation for the vultures to fight over.

I spent most of my professional life destroying iconic brands, until Mavis convinced me that the world needed expertise to turn this imminent disaster around before it consumes us all. So, I've reverse-engineered my skill to build seventeen rather impressive enclaves that house, educate, and employ thousands of unfortunate people, who had been cast out by society…and we're just getting started."

"I'm getting a mental picture of a cancer consuming our republic. A disease that started as a gleam in some greedy bastard's eye, growing and metastasizing into a self-perpetuating deconstruction of our democracy and a conquest of our economy at the expense of the working men and women who built this country," said Nellis.

"That was about as succinct as it can be put!" laughed Reverend Combs.

"Representative Spratlin warned me about you, when we spoke on the phone the other day," said Mavis, glancing at Stanton. "I can't wait to see what happens when you and Jessie Cotton get together."

"Who's Jessie Cotton?" asked Katherine.

"Oh, you'll love Jessie, he's an incredible landscape artist as well as the free-thinker who started the movement."

~

Lincoln Todd, hardened biker, ex-con, and stanch white-supremacist pulled the first of three battered school buses out of Autumn Creek Hollow to block both lanes of Talbot Road, just around the bend from a tangle of State Police cars guarding the private conference at the Houston Links. He opened the doors for two video crews and dozens of nationalists, neo-Nazi's, and radical-fundamentalists to pile out, oblivious to a persistent rain, igniting torches and raising placards tacked to heavy clubs, reading 'Save White America' and 'Stop Deep State Conspiracies', "Deport the Mongrels' and 'Death to Liberals'. They spread across four lanes of traffic to threaten drivers from both directions, as five limousines, accompanied by an escort of four motorcycle cops, slowed to a stop.

Torches and signs waved, as the crazed crowd chanted, "White America First!" and surged to surround the two officers leading the procession, toppled their bikes to block the lane, and pinning them against the hood of the first car. Two shots rang out but the mob disarmed them, beating the men to the ground and attacking the limos with clubs, while the front tires of the leading pair of vehicles in the motorcade were punctured and deflated.

Thunderous blows hammered the car and window glass crinkled before Mr. Charles shouted, "Push the pedal to the metal and don't stop!"

The chauffer gunned the engine, slammed the transmission into drive, and pushed the fallen motorcycles through the swarm of attackers. Their angry faces twisted with rage as they brushed past shattered windows screaming obscenities and death threats. Two rioters clamored over the hood to jump up and down on the roof before the car swerved left, pitching flailing bodies tumbling onto sopping asphalt and sped through a parking lot to escape along a service road that curved around to the police blockade.

Sirens wailed and most of the security vehicles charged up Talbot Road towards a barricade of abandoned burning buses but the remaining two squad cars backed out to allow the battered limousines to slip through the gate to refuge under a magnificent canopy of branches reaching from ancient southern oaks to shroud the plaza.

The officers hesitated as the last car raced through the gates before easing their cruisers forward to block the entrance, gauging the intent of a rusty gray panel truck racing around the bend, aiming to breach the gap between police cars. Their front bumpers closed just a moment late, pinching the rear wheels of the gatecrasher which flipped the truck up onto the trunk of the fifth limo, where it erupted in a blistering orb spewing orange flames and detonating an explosion that shattered windows across the complex and launched lethal shards of molten debris in all directions.

The blast battered the lead car, shattering windows and pitching the passengers to the floor. Nellis covered Katherine and yelled, "Don't stop! Keep going!"

Deflated tires shredded, steel wheels ground through tarmac as the car plowed to a side entrance of the clubhouse at the far end of the parking lot. Reverend Combs heaved the door open and carried a barely conscious Mavis, whose blond hair was matted with blood, to shelter under the eve of the building.

Nellis kissed Katherine's cheek, "Are you okay?"

"Do you think, just once, we could go on a regular date?"

"What, and miss this?" He helped her crawl out the back door to find three other cars jammed in tight, discharging rattled travelers who ducked for cover from fragments of the bomb raining down through the charred and shredded foliage of the oak trees above the blazing carcass of the truck, inverted and impaled in the back window of the twisted shell of the last limousine just beyond two incinerated police cruisers.

Katherine lifted her fist to her lips, "Oh, my…"

Nellis pulled her close, "We're alive. Let's see what we can do to help."

They scrambled to Standler and Combs kneeling over Mavis, applying pressure to a wound on her scalp. Katherine offered an embroidered handkerchief, "Here, use this."

Marvin pressed the cloth against the gash and Mavis winced, "Leave it to me to get hit by the wayward lash of sadistic fascists."

The minister inspected the lesion, "Yeah, a half-inch lower and you'd be dead, girlfriend. Sit tight, we've got medical help coming, I can hear the sirens."

Bobbie Warmington climbed out of the third car and raced to Mavis, "Are you alright? Here, let me look at that wound, I've got three kids and some medical training."

Mavis struggled to sit up, straining to see the wreckage, "I'll be fine but everyone should be more concerned about helping anyone who might have survived that blast."

Spratlin wrapped an arm around her shoulders, "I'm not sure anyone could survive that."

Police cars and ambulances eased past the inferno and wedged into the driveway. Two State Patrol troopers ran up to begin escorting the milling crowd out of harm's way, as Kate, Benny, and Sammy assisted a shaken Tabitha Hall from a crumpled limo.

A woman with a medical bag appeared, "I'm April Willow and I'm a doctor. Can I help?"

Bobbie Warmington looked up, "Yes, this young lady has a laceration to the scalp. I think we've got the bleeding stopped but she needs your expertise."

The young doctor knelt to inspect the laceration and opened her bag, "You're a lucky lady, this could have been much worse. I'll have you fixed up in no time but you're going to need a few stitches and we should probably keep an eye on you for a possible concussion."

"Fine, get me stabilized so I can help all these other people." She looked through the crowd to Tabitha's pale face, "Are you alright?"

The Florida contingent eased the publisher down next to Mavis and the doctor on the curb, "Every time I rally with you people we're attacked by subhuman troglodytes, crowds of the innocent and defenseless are forced to flee in panicked pandemonium. Things keep exploding, and it's raining again. How could I possibly resist?"

A black Ford sedan pulled up and two dark suits with wraparound sunglasses jumped out, walking directly to Mavis. The taller flashed a badge and inquired, "Are you Mrs. Sloan? I'm Detective Miller and this is Detective Roberts."

"Yes, I am. Can you tell me what happened?"

They glanced at the remaining people exiting the cars to gather around, "We believe the protestors were members of White America, a shadowy cult with political connections to right-wing militants. As soon as your limos pulled away, they torched the buses as a diversion and escaped in waiting vehicles. The attack was well-planned and executed and we haven't apprehended any of them yet."

"What about casualties?" asked Spratlin.

Detective Roberts hesitated, "The off-duty officers who were escorting you were pummeled by the crowd and have been taken to the hospital."

"What about the explosion?" asked, Nellis, pointing to the smoldering ruins.

"An initial assessment leads us to believe that two officers, the driver of the panel truck, and three people inside the car were killed and five others are being transported. I've noticed several other injured people being helped out of these other cars, as well," said Miller.

Bobbie Warmington opened a leather satchel to withdraw a sheaf of papers, "I've got the attendants' directory, so we can figure out who's missing."

Benny said, "You might also want to make sure that we don't have any extra folks, who slipped in during the chaos."

"Good thinking," said Roberts, taking the list. "We'll check this out and get it back to you."

"Should we expect a third wave?" asked Spratlin.

"We've sealed off the area, so I'm confident that we can contain our perimeter." He looked back to Mavis, "I understand that you have a fairly large gathering here for a political meeting and I want to assure you that we'll maintain your security, until you've finished your business."

"You might want to add more precautions at Simonson Air, we've got an expensive fleet of aircraft waiting to take these folks back where they came from," said Standler.

"We'll make sure the airport's covered."

"So, you don't care what we're talking about in there?" asked Nellis.

"No, Sir, I don't believe that my personal political opinions should affect my service to any citizen," replied Roberts, who offered a slight grin. "Although, I'll admit that we've been briefed on your meeting and we'd be hard-pressed to have anything but respect for your movement. Everyone who knows anything about what's going on in this country, has heard about the 'All People Matter' demonstration during the hurricane."

Miller saluted Tabitha and pointed to Kate, Benny and Sammy, "Mrs. Sloan might be famous but these faces have been all over the news for all the right reasons."

~

Standler helped a woozy Mavis shuffle down a hallway to an impromptu clinic in a small luxurious lounge where Dr. Willow and Jonathon Capehardt, a medical student from the Texas Medical Center, who was earning extra cash working in the kitchen, were scrambling to tend to several injured people, as medics wheeled the most critical to waiting ambulances.

Mavis turned as Jessie Cotton rushed down the hall, "Before they cart me off, I want you to meet Nellis Gray, your counterpart from Cameron, Oklahoma. Jessie was the driving force behind our rally and, from what I hear, Nellis tends to employ rather unconventional strategies to take down bad guys."

They shook hands and Mavis added, "I'm fairly sure that you two will deliver this conference to a successful conclusion in a most unusual manner or have a ballroom brawl going in the first ten minutes and I'm honestly not sure which."

Nellis looked at Jessie, "I'm guessin' you're preceded by a reputation?"

"Not by choice."

"I know what you mean, brother, but I can guarantee I've been accused of worse." He glanced at Spratlin and grinned, "How 'bout we let Reverend Combs get things cranked up, then your team can start this shindig and we'll jump in?"

"Works for me," replied Jessie, turning to Kate, "This is Kate Crocket - director and documentarian, Benny Young - our spokesman and soul of the organization, Sammy Ball - the guy who started all the trouble in the first place and Bobbie Warmington, who's taken over keeping track of us and everything else. Tabitha Hall is the wise strategic facilitator and publisher of our local newspaper, who transformed a rowdy protest into a movement. She's being attended to by the doctors and I'm hoping she'll be able to join us soon."

Nellis shook hands, "This is newly appointed Representative Stanton Spratlin, our secretary and coordinator, Katherine Kennedy and

Mr. Charles, who inspires us all with authentic pride and dignity. His impeccable sense of all that is right and proper and his belief that standing up for the downtrodden is the obligation of every decent human being."

The roar of a raucous crowd rattled down the hallway, drawing them into a large ballroom, where a churning congregation of anxious volunteers were chattering and vying to be heard. Reverend Combs strolled up to the tiny stage and picked up the microphone, "Ladies and gentlemen, may I have your attention?"

The furor died to a moderate frenzy, as the audience slowly recognized the six-ten former MVP basketball star turned tele-evangelical phenomenon. "I know that the violent attack, which culminated in a massive explosion out here in the parking lot with multiple casualties and the deaths of several of our volunteers was not anticipated in the agenda for our meeting. That terror was not part of the enthusiastic commitment any of us made, when we agreed to come together to talk about how to change the future to protect millions of tyrannized citizens and revive the essential core of our society." He paused, looking from one brave and frightened advocate to the next, their eyes filled with confusion, horror, and shock, "But I have to believe in God's wisdom. By permitting this catastrophe, He provides a miraculous tremor that jolts us into accepting the responsibility of our place in reality with crystalline focus and inspires us to act with deliberate determination. That's what's happening right now!"

He hooked a thumb over his shoulder, "Our comrades were murdered for their beliefs and their dedication. Now it's up to the rest of us, the survivors, to create a coordinated organization that allows us to speak with one voice, to rise up against those who would go to suicidal extremes to see us fail, and to demand the return of our rights and our dignity."

A voice called out above the murmurs, "How do we know they're not coming back to finish off the rest of us?"

"We don't," whispered the enormous minister. "We know that the state and local police have this facility sealed off from the outside world, emergency personnel are dealing with the tragedy outside and the FBI is opening an investigation. Everything that can be done is being done to ensure your safety, so I would suggest that we get on with what we came here to do."

He looked over at the co-mingled Florida and Cameron contingents, standing just inside the door, "I know that Mavis Sloan and Tabitha Hall were planning to open this session and guide our initial discussion and I hope they'll be joining us shortly but considering all that's happened today, I think it only appropriate to begin our program with two men who have been in the thick of it and know how to make things happen, Jessie Cotton from Dolphin Bay and Nellis Gray from Cameron, Oklahoma."

Applause.

He held up a gigantic hand and his infectious smile and boundless energy collapsed beneath the weight of the moment, "Before I hand it over to these two leaders, I want to share one more thought. What happened here today was just the first skirmish in a war for the hearts and minds of these hopeless people we're trying to help and while we're about it, the future of our democracy.

I can promise you that this won't be the last act of violence against common sense and human decency. I see it as a call to arms that demands that we stand together to fight for what is right and true, no matter what they throw at us. If we are to succeed, we cannot and will not condone violence of any sort for any reason. Like Gandhi and Reverend King, our strength and our conviction depend on the honor and integrity of our intentions and our actions." He paused, "If any of you want to bail out, we'll provide you with immediate transportation to a safe location, no questions asked, no judgement offered. Just raise your hands and you'll be on your way."

Jessie and Nellis dawdled for a moment, scanning the crowd, but there were no takers. They applauded the audience, before taking two stools and two microphones, while the crowd settled into scattered chairs.

"I'd like to thank all of you brave patriots for coming here to share your thoughts, ideas, and experiences with everyone else, in spite of the intimidation. As Nellis and I can attest, we've all seen how regimented economic repression is crushing our friends and families, destroying our neighborhoods and towns and gutting our state's and our nation's ability or inclination to provide even the most basic services and benefits to those who need them most. The middle-class is under attack to satisfy the greed of the richest of the rich, who value profits over community and sanction a return to feudal oppression over democracy."

Nellis added, "Most of you probably already know about our adventures in Cameron, Oklahoma. We exposed a very coordinated and well-financed effort to elect, not just our totally unqualified numbskull candidate for a seat in the House of Representatives, but almost a dozen more imposters and some of their sponsors.

What we didn't realize was that they were all supported by a radical national fraternity, dedicated to expanding their considerable holdings at the expense of whole classes of our society. They're like threatening storm clouds on the horizon but they've been building for a thousand miles before they found us. The swirling turmoil isn't just happening by chance, there's a whole industry working to perpetuate our fear and anxiety with a constant barrage of lies and misleading propaganda.

You'd be foolish to believe that these calamities are occurring because of a downturn in the economy or slow times in certain industries. The markets are soaring but hard-working men and women are losing their jobs. It's happening all across the country because the families that comprise the real power in this nation have been working on this campaign of political and economic deconstruction for decades and they won't stop until they take it all."

He pointed to a black woman with a large red ribbon in her hair, who raised her hand. "What's your name and where are you from?"

"I'm Ashley Wood from Raleigh. Jobs are disappearing and families are being forced out of their homes and into bankruptcy and foreclosure. Even with a master's degree, I'm working three part-time jobs, with no benefits or paid overtime just to put food on the table."

"What about you?" asked Jessie of a tall slender man.

"I'm Henry Deater from Detroit and everyone knows that the car companies ditched their workers and abandoned our city. Hell, they shipped heavy industry overseas, piece by piece, until the industrial Midwest and everything we used to stand for withered up into a sad memory. We had almost twenty-thousand protesters march on City Hall and the mayor and some of his City Councilors came out to make proud promises about retraining programs and dealing with city blight, but they only showed up because it gave them a 'concerned and involved civic leader' advertising clip for the next election. They have no interest in resurrecting the past or protecting those who survived it."

"It's the same all over!" shouted a young black man in the back of the room. "My wife got the cancer and my boss fired me because he didn't want to take a hit on the company's health insurance."

Jessie pointed, "And you?"

A stocky man with a goatee shook his head, "I'm Marvin Tur, fisherman from Maine. My family has been fishing the North Atlantic for seven generations and we're being driven out of business by giant international companies that have raped and devastated the richest fisheries on the planet and destroyed our industry."

A craggy man's dark eyes peered out from beneath a scruffy cowboy hat, "Hell, it's the same out in the plains states. There ain't no such thing as a family farm anymore, handed down from one generation to the next, like my daddy and his daddy before him. Big agriculture is taking over, destroying the land and the environment and putting the little guys out of business."

Nellis shook his head, "All of this is the result of decades of coordinated efforts to terrorize the population into supporting unqualified political candidates who wave Bibles and hoist the flag. They blame the other party or minorities or immigrants or anyone else who isn't a fat, white, ignorant evangelical racist for all the problems in our country without actually offering any plausible solutions other than lowering taxes for the rich and eliminating regulations. Chaos and anger are the fuel that compel our desperate neighbors to support these charlatans and hijacking those people into our world will be a high priority in the coming months.

Their agents take control of school boards, local councils, and state governments to pass laws that have destroyed services, infrastructure, education and trashed regulations that protect the public from big companies poisoning the water or polluting the air we breathe, while they twist voting laws and boundaries to disenfranchise minorities and guarantee Republican majorities."

"We've all seen the lies and complete nonsense that's being broadcast as 'News', the appropriation and poisoning of our children's minds by religious fanatics who believe that scientific facts are inconveniently incompatible with their ignorant but literal interpretation of disjointed Bible verses and the result of a worldwide conspiracy to make illiteracy a badge of honor. They demand that all textbooks include 'alternative' explanations for subjects like evolution or that state's rights, not slavery, was the real reason that our nation fought the Civil War. They eliminate any mention of past mistakes or transgressions that might sully their glorified patriotic technicolor version of history, like eliminating references to the internment of tens-of-thousands of Americans of Japanese descent during World War II or the wholesale slaughter of American Indians, as the federal government gobbled up their land and appropriated their resources," added Jessie.

"The people who tried to bust up our meeting and their backers believe that they can force a despairing population to accept their complete domination of independent thought, freedom of speech and the press and our economic future. They've built a propaganda machine that's spewing outrageous lies to rile up the masses, to capture their votes through a campaign that gives the frantic working stiff someone to blame for their troubles, someone to hate together…and that's anyone who isn't just like them, which is us."

A tiny Hispanic woman raised her fist and shouted, "We, all of us are the face of real America!"

"They want a revolution, we'll give 'em one!" added a burly factory worker, as the crowd reacted.

With dignity and grace, Tabitha Hall appeared in the entry, leaning on the ivory head of a carved cane. A black eye and bruised cheek testified to a fall in the car during the explosion but she carried herself with strength and determination.

Jessie lifted the microphone, "Ladies and gentlemen, may I introduce the true guiding spirit of 'All People Matter', Mrs. Tabitha Hall!"

The audience fell into a hush and applauded her slow progress, as the two men helped her onto the little stage and Nellis handed her a microphone.

She looked out at the curious faces of volunteers from all over the country, people who gathered, hoping to find a solution to the complete disassembly of society without fear or hesitation. "Thank you all for being brave enough to attend and for staying after such a horrific assault on not only us but our right of free speech and unimpeded congregation. This is the first convention of 'New Americans' and I promise you, it won't be the last!"

The crowd cheered.

"I must report that Mavis Sloan, one of the driving forces behind our organization, has suffered a laceration and a concussion from flying shrapnel. She is awake and alert and she's been taken to a local hospital for care and observation but she wanted me to tell you that she has no intention of becoming a martyr at the hands of 'those bastards', to use her terminology and neither should any of you!"

Warm applause.

"I don't know whether you heard about the little ruckus we had down in Dolphin Bay?"

The room erupted.

"Well, what started as a small group of city workers trying to organize for fair pay and benefits turned into an enormous crowd of desperate people who braved a hurricane looking for truth, looking for action." She paused, "I made them a promise that we would shut down one large employer every week and if they didn't resolve the dispute with their employees, we'd shut down the next one and the next until now, we've turned off the lights in city government and seven large businesses with a walkout planned for an eighth next Monday."

Applause.

"Just before we left Florida, I got a call from some of our people saying that management at two of the companies had requested the resumption of negotiations." She smiled, "If one falls, they all fall."

Everyone stood to clap.

"I overheard and agree with most of what Nellis, Jessie, and Reverend Combs told you but I would like to offer several thoughts." She paused, "First, we are all here to find a way to coordinate our efforts across these United States to expose shady politicians and the wealthy owners of international criminal corporations, who are dedicated to supporting their stock price at the expense of the workers who make the products or deliver the services."

"Here, here!"

"Right on!"

"To that end, we must all understand that every individual in this group and in our national organization, holds the responsibility for our success in their hands...and that through one inaccurate statement or thoughtless action, they can destroy everything that we're trying to achieve." She pointed from one to the next, "Each of you is accountable and responsible to everyone around you for how we, as a group, present ourselves, our integrity and our message to the world. Those terrified former workers will be watching, listening, wondering whether we are worthy of their support, their contributions, or their commitment to fight for all that we champion. We cannot give our enemies or their counterfeit press any reason or excuse to sully our image or cast doubt on our purpose or reputation in any way."

Murmurs.

"Each of you will go back to your communities to build and lead local organizations that will expand into regional movements, that will merge into a national campaign to retake our government, our democracy and our dignity. They have money and power. We have truth, honor, and a firm belief in the Declaration of Independence, the Constitution, and the Bill of Rights."

Applause.

"I'd also suggest, no, I will demand that every one of you go out and not only read but understand every word, idea and concept enshrined in those documents. It's obvious that the players behind the Republican Party have every intention of rendering those guiding principles irrelevant and unenforceable. We must not allow that to happen!"

Cheers.

"We all know that the Republican Congress has vowed to block or stymie any act or initiative offered by President Gonzalez and to pass legislation to block his executive orders, simply because he is a Democrat of Hispanic descent. Perhaps more so because he was elected by a sizable majority of the population in spite of their Congressional domination.

It doesn't take any stretch of the imagination to foresee the turmoil and destruction that will result from the Republicans gaining control of all three branches of government. So, while we're trying to force commerce to value the workers who make this country run, we also have to begin building a machine to reclaim our government.

But even that is not enough because we can't convince people to join our righteous cause, to work and fight for their rights and our future just because we claim we're the good guys. We have to offer real concrete plans and ideas to stop the demolition of the very foundations of our society. We have to repair the damage, mend the wounds and resurrect the rights guaranteed to all of us in the Constitution and all its Amendments."

Enthusiastic applause.

"We need feedback from every corner of the country. We need to know what people are thinking, their fears and their dreams, their challenges and frustrations and we need to assimilate all of that information to tailor our program to fit the needs of different communities across the nation. Our enemies didn't put together their coalition of incongruent groups who consistently support everything in the Republican Party platform. They found a way to play to the rawest nerve and tender resentment, to pluck the strings of a dissonant chord that resonates with the personal anger and hatred of each voter in each region."

She paused, gazing around at the staunch devotion in the eyes of a sea of attentive delegates, "To compete with a political machine that's been painstakingly assembled over decades, infiltrated the media, subjugated the minds and spirits of a huge portion of our society, and seized control of every political lever in the country from the school boards to the Congress…we'll have to coax millions of scared and desperate neighbors back across an invisible divide to sanity and responsibility.

Unless we can paint a believable and all-encompassing mural of the path back to the American dream. Unless we can persuade them to join our crusade to reclaim truth, hope, and honor. Unless we can join together to restore the profound moral principles that are the very bedrock of our nation, we will surely fail."

Murmurs and whispers rippled through the audience but no one moved or applauded, until Tabitha's crystal blue eyes glistened in a ravishing smile, "Failure is not an option. Giving up on all that our nation stands for is not an option and allowing wealthy criminals and thugs to control the government is not an option either. I know what we must accomplish and so do you! We have a deadline of election day. Let's get started!"

Chapter Four

A doting Standler rolled Mavis' wheelchair into the hanger at Simonson Air to join the last of the delegates awaiting flights home. She sat very erect, her head encased in a white bandage with blood splatter flecking the chiffon scarf and her beautiful suit, but her eyes were focused and intent. Tabitha, Bobbie Warmington, Kate, and Katherine gathered around, "What'd the doctors say?"

"Nice gash, fourteen stitches and a mild concussion but he cleared me to fly, as long as I stay inside the airplane."

"You're lucky the Lord has other plans for you, darlin'," said Reverend Combs, with a gentle kiss to her cheek. "I've been praying for you."

She looked up at him, "And I've been praying for all those souls we lost in that damned explosion! Last I heard, we had six dead and eight in intensive care. How could we let that happen?"

"Having a massive movement takes more than good intentions," said Nellis. "It takes organization, informed intelligence, serious security, and professional public relations, and it can't be a democracy!"

"Yeah, the PR folks you invited to the conference were prepared to show us slick logos, sample websites, and reams of demographics but they were clueless about how to react to the attack," added Benny, "and I'm a landscaper, I know more about manure than I'll ever know about advertising."

"It doesn't matter," said Kate, "you're both right. I've been handling the editorial narrative with Tabitha since this whole thing started but this is on a different level altogether."

"We need some pros on staff," said the publisher, "and I think I know just the people to call."

"What we need is an executive committee to set up a master plan and address all of these issues," said Stanton, "and it needs to happen immediately."

"I'll send a plane for you next week," said Mavis.

"I have to be in Washington on Monday and Tuesday," said Spratlin, "so, we could start on Wednesday, if that works for all of you?"

Nellis stood up, "Let's do this the other way 'round."

"What do you mean?" asked Jessie.

"I mean it'd be a whole lot easier to provide security in a little berg like Cameron, than in a sprawling resort town that's crawling with anonymous tourists. We can put everyone up at the one and only hotel and destroy your cholesterol levels in just a couple of days of eating good country cooking."

"I think you're right," said Sammy Ball. "Besides, I've always wanted to visit Oklahoma. Do the Indians still ride into town on horseback on Saturday night?"

"You've been watching too many old westerns," laughed Katherine. "Our 'good ol' boys' ride around in fancy pickup trucks."

"I do have one more question," said Nellis.

"What's that?" replied Tabitha.

"How did they know that we were meeting here today? Who else knew?"

Everyone glanced around at everyone else, until Sammy Ball said, "Hell, we were talking to people from all over the country. It's not like it was a big secret, we were trying to get people to attend."

"You're right," said Jessie, "but this was so carefully planned and executed, these guys weren't just Harry and Drew out with forty or fifty of their best buds to protest liberal support for a woman's right to choose, they had a plan."

Bobbie Warmington raised her hand, "I think I might be the one who gave it away."

"What do you mean?" asked Kate gently.

"During days of endless phone calls, while I was getting everyone set up, I got a call from a guy in California, I think his name was Ethan, wanting more information. He was very polite and apologetic for not knowing what was going on but I never did get the name of his organization. I told him all about who was going to participate and gave him the time and place and didn't think any more about it, until now. I might have made a note in my notebook but I gave that to the police with the list of the attendees. I'm so sorry, it never occurred to me that someone would try to sabotage the meeting or actually hurt anyone." She started to cry, "All those people died because of me."

Kate and Jessie wrapped her in a hug and Jessie said, "No, you had no way of knowing and don't doubt their responsibility for the dead and the injured."

Benny looked at Mavis, "You might want to order up a bigger plane, we'll be bringing some of our security people."

"And a few more," said Tabitha.

"Fine. We'll provide the transportation a week from Wednesday," said Mavis to Spratlin. "You provide the hospitality."

Katherine said, "I'll have everything set up on our end but let's keep communications inside our little group. I'll communicate through Bobbie and everyone else needs to maintain radio silence, agreed?"

"Absolutely," said Jessie.

~

Johnny and Bobbie waited impatiently, as Jessie edged the runabout into the slip on the battered dock below their little gray rental house. The artist tossed a line and Johnny pulled her in to tie the rope off on a cleat, admiring the shiny aluminum hull and the Johnson 25 hanging off the transom, "Where'd she come from?"

Jessie climbed onto weathered planking and hugged them in turn, "Well, I made a deal with ol' Joel Myers, up at the Pelican Bay Marina. He said if there's any trouble just bring it by and he'll take care of maintaining her."

"I can do most everything myself," said Johnny, hopping in to finger the throttle.

"Yeah, but it's nice to have someone who knows their stuff to count on when you don't know how to fix something," said Bobbie.

The boy looked up at Jessie, with big tears in his eyes, "I felt so proud that you let me help save all those people, that I almost didn't mind Miss U getting chewed up in the storm."

"Almost?"

"Well, yeah, she let me get around and we got to go fishing…and she reminded me of my dad."

Jessie climbed into the boat to give him a hug, "I think your dad would be really proud of the young man that you've become. I know I am."

Johnny squeezed him back, "That means a lot to me."

"We need to establish ownership."

"What do you mean?"

"Well, this is when I wish I could hand you the keys, because she's yours but you're going to have to ferry me around until we find another one, okay? Whatcha gonna name her?"

"Thank you," the boy hugged him. "'Miss U Too', of course."

"I should have known. I think I've got some paint that'll work, when you're ready."

Johnny rubbed his fingers across the rounded edge of the smooth gunwale, "Thanks for her...and for being you."

"Shall we try her out?"

"Sure!" said the youngster, checking the gas and tugging the rope on the little engine, which sputtered to life.

Bobbie handed down his rods and a tackle box, "You boys have fun, but...please, try to stay out of trouble."

"Fat chance!", laughed Jessie as he pushed the little boat out of the slip and they tacked into moderate westerly winds with a mild chop, to head down the Little Bay. It would take months to remove submerged boats, rebuild shattered docks, and clear away crumpled cottages that collapsed into the bay during hurricane Dot and certainly, years for flora and fauna to recover from ravaging winds, thrashing tides, and flooding rains.

Johnny piloted the little boat close to the narrow beach on the lee side of the key, reading flocks of gulls diving on schools of shiners, swirling and scattering in glittering clouds just beneath the surface as squawking birds plunged into the blue-green water vying for a meal against a half-dozen tarpon darting through the chaos.

He turned into the wind and Jessie handed him a rod, "You even have the right lure!"

"Saw the gulls when I got off the bus from school and I knew they'd be down here," replied the boy, flipping his line across the rippling water, to whip it through the minnows. On the third pull, his reel whined as a feisty fish wheeled to starboard and Jessie brought the stern around to allow Johnny to play his line.

"Work him, he'll get tired."

"Yeah, maybe it's the same guy as last time, only it feels like he might have put on some weight."

Jessie laughed, "I wouldn't be surprised if some of the fish that lived in our favorite fishing hole before the storm, are swimming around off the coast of Texas or Mexico."

The line glided north and Jessie eased the bow downwind, while Johnny reeled slowly, as the fish swam closer, paused, and sensing the restraint flashed into open water. Line screamed through the arching tip of his rod, trailing the quarry as it zipped through the shimmering school of shiners to flip around, aiming straight at the bow of the silver skiff. Water spit from the reel as the boy cranked fast, struggling to keep the line taut. Jessie ducked as the fishing rod whirled around to follow a three-foot silver torpedo erupting from the water just behind the stern, arching its back and flipping a gleaming tail before plunging back into the dark water with a mighty splash.

The line went limp and Johnny reeled slowly, until the fish bolted under the boat and the tension on his rod released with a snap. Slack line floated to the surface. "Rats! I had him!"

"Reload, there are more out there," said Jessie tossing a lure into the churning frenzy and gazing around at the landscape and two new inlets farther down the key. "Sure looks different out here."

Johnny sat on the bench seat to tie on a shiny new temptation with a Palomar knot that Jessie taught him to use when he was in a hurry. He paused, eyes scanning the shoreline, "It's almost like Mother Nature took a comb and raked it across the land, tearing everything away except a tree here or a shrub over there."

Jessie pointed, "Did you notice that mother fox with her kit? What, five of them, over there near the little channel into George's pool?"

"It's good they still have cover," he said, absently staring at the entry. "That seems so long ago."

"Our favorite gators might be gone but neither of us will ever forget how it felt to spend time feeding them marshmallows."

"I can't believe anyone is mean enough to shoot them for no good reason."

"I'll never understand that mentality." The artist reeled in his line, "I think we should motor down to the marina and see what's left, sort of revisiting the scene of our crimes."

"There was one kind of life, before SunnyBreeze, but it's different now that it's gone."

Johnny tucked his rod under the seat and started the little engine. Patches of battered palmetto and seagrape on Breezy Key opened into a vast moonscape of barren land, gouged by rivulets that grew into raging rivers that hauled the shredded remnants of hundreds of homes into enormous tangled mounds rising out of the shallows. Cranes and bulldozers worked relentlessly, each swipe clearing away another fragment of the splintered carcass of an audacious gambit that defied the ultimate supremacy of Mother Nature and failed to stand up to the fury of a category four storm.

Westerly winds and an incoming tide carried the dingy across the bay to motor along the shoreline to a pair of barges, balancing giant hoists to unravel the last snarled remnants of the boat bridge that provided escape for more than a thousand terrified SunnyBreeze guests through the worst of the savage storm. Ragged sections of the undulating aqua seawall and a few of the dock's hundreds of pilings remained upright - the last survivors of a proud brigade and all that remained of the marina. Waves washed in from the Gulf through another new inlet, cleaved through the mountain built to support The Commons.

"It's kind of hard to believe that this was jam-packed with hundreds of homes," said Jessie.

Johnny grinned, "It's hard to believe how little is left of all those boats we tied together."

"Let's be glad no one's pointing the finger at us."

"Well, we did save their lives."

"Yeah, but that junk they're pulling out of the water used to be worth millions and there are a lot of somebodies, who can't be too happy about it. Actually, the insurance companies are the ones who are going to want to find someone to cover the bill."

"Why do people have to blame someone else for when bad stuff happens?"

Jessie poured two cups of lemonade and pulled peanut butter sandwiches from his tackle box. "That's something I want to talk to you about."

The boy took a big bite of his sandwich and wiped a slurp of jelly from his lip with the back of his hand, "Every time you want to talk about something serious, I usually don't like it much."

"Well, I don't know how the next few months are going to go, but I'm pretty sure your mom told you what happened in Houston, so you know what we're up against."

"Yeah, it sounds like it's not safe to hang out with you anywhere," laughed Johnny.

"Smart Alec!" replied Jessie. "No, that tragedy just reinforces my belief that there are some very bad people manipulating our government and our economy to make huge profits for themselves at the expense of everyone else. It's not just here or even in just a few places, working folks are getting pushed out of jobs and into poverty all across the country and we've gotta get organized to fight back."

"And you're going to be in the middle of it, right?"

"Yeah, I feel like we started something that's growing way out of proportion to anything we could have imagined, and I have an obligation to see it through."

"That's why I love you."

"Why?"

"Because, I know that you'll do the right thing and you'll step up to defend the person who needs your help, that's who you are."

"Yeah, I guess you're right but it took me a while to learn it."

"Everyone figured that out when you started teaching kids about art in the park every summer. My mom says you're a hero in this town."

"I'm not a hero."

"You are to me."

"Well, after everything you did, you're a hero to me, too."

"So, we're going fishing as soon as you get back from wherever you have to go."

"Oklahoma," laughed Jessie, toasting with his cup of lemonade. "Deal."

~

The offices of ImageSculptor Public Relations were housed in a sprawling contemporary architecture of interlocking geometric forms nestled behind meandering gray walls overlooking Dune Point, in Malibu.

Ethan Tomlinson, ultraconservative public relations guru, leaned back in a plush leather chair behind a thick slab of burnished redwood burl that served as an imposing desk. A wispy fog crept over the point, rising from a slow sedate surf to devour the view. The intercom buzzed, "Will Terry on line three. Shall I take a message?"

"No, I'll take it, thank you." He pressed the button and stood to pace back and forth across the width of a curved wall of glass, gazing at the misty monochromatic charcoal landscape, ghostly vignettes vanishing behind swirling gray veils, ethereal portals into his vaporous netherworld of tyrannical trolls and greedy goblins. "Will! How are things going?"

"Oh, you won't believe the footage we got from that confrontation down in Houston. It's dynamite, more than we could have hoped for."

"Usable?"

"Yeah, we can edit this twenty-seven different ways to appeal to every market - from right-to-life evangelicals to raging white-supremacists and hook, line and sinker for the angry unemployed factory worker. Whoever organized this was stupid enough to transport their people in white limousines, which plays right into 'Common folks don't have a job but these arrogant bastards are riding around in limousines!'."

"That's beautiful."

"Then the fun begins. Our protestors looked like ordinary working people, who arrived on local school buses to picket what we'll be calling a 'secret' meeting of the elite core of the ultra-left deep-state conspiracy, trading money for power behind very exclusive closed doors. Our guys beat the crap out of a couple of cops and trashed the first three limos before the motorcade escaped and the buses erupted in flames, making it appear that our peaceful protesters were under attack. Then we got a sweeping shot of our suicide van crashing through a police barricade to explode in the back of one of the cars just inside the entry to the Houston Links, which is elite and ritzy. They made this too easy."

"Sounds like they could use a good PR firm," laughed Tomlinson. "Did our people get out clean?"

"Yeah, no problem. We created a little traffic jam of waiting cars and vans and they all went in different directions before the cops got anywhere close."

"Okay, mock up some ads and we'll get together at the end of the week. We can use the new material to fire up the base and motivate our sponsors to replenish the coffers, so we can roll out the first batch of prospective candidates."

"Can do," replied Terry. "Hey, I gotta ask, how'd we know when and where they were going to hold their conference?"

The ad man smiled, "It's amazing what you can find out by just being polite."

"You're a real charmer! Gotta go. See ya'."

He had been guiding the real titans behind The Forge, a secret and exclusive fraternity of mega-wealthy families, to develop and implement their campaign for political and economic dominance for decades, with an ultimate goal of total deconstruction of the government. They invested billions of dollars into cultivating candidates, buying down-ballot elections, gerrymandering district boundaries and cultivating a broad base of bigots and racists, the Klan, white-nationalists, and evangelicals, who would vote for anyone claiming to be against abortion.

Many of the companies and corporations owned by the richest fraction of the population, shipped jobs overseas or replaced humans with robots, adding millions of desperate souls to the ranks of the unemployed. Their surrogates in state and federal legislatures were tasked with destroying unions, public education, voting rights, and dismantling the safety net of benefits and programs for the poor. The disinformation machine hammered away, pinning all the problems to minorities and immigrants stealing American jobs, providing a common enemy for the desperate and unemployed.

ImageSculptor created an endless flow of propaganda that was pumped through their own network of broadcast and print news media, vilified legitimate journalists and traditional news organizations for relaying factual information that did not support the party line, manipulated the content of every textbook published in the country, and endowed many of the most prestigious law schools with millions of dollars and carefully selected conservative deans to shade the basic tenets of our system of justice to support the rights and enterprises of a few-hundred families, as interest on their status and their philanthropy.

Their philosophy was simple enough - society is, was, and always will be naturally divided into two castes - those who have and those who serve. The fortunate few, who accumulate massive wealth, have every right to feel empowered to dictate to the world around them and should bear no guilt, responsibility, or pity for those left to suffer the consequences of being deprived of privilege by birth or fate.

Having competition for the hearts and minds of the enormous congregation of the downtrodden was an impediment that needed to be crushed before it had a chance to bloom into a competing national movement, just when success was cresting the horizon.

Hoping the attack in Houston would scare them away was wishful thinking at best, so the cult of the radical right was primed for any hint of another assembly. They are your neighbors, the guy who works on your car, the factory worker and the cabbie who sees everything - invisible because they are everyman, everywhere. All that raw human data gets processed through the system to become weaponized intelligence for the firm's strategic team.

~

Brad rubbed the ragged scar on his cheek, subconsciously stoking memories of his own indefensible depravities in a quest to redeem his spirit and wipe away the nightmares of savagery and slaughter. He leaned back on the seat of his cycle, outside Cameron Municipal Airport's private facilities, watching a gleaming silver Boeing 727 transport with a gray Simonson Air logo on the tail, roll to a stop on the tarmac.

The fading wail of whining engines resurrected the chaos of a front-line landing strip carved into desert sandstone, under the thump-thump of Super Stallions ferrying troops, supplies, and equipment for a rolling assault. A swarm of Vipers defended the perimeter and ventured out to dissuade enemy advances, while scouting squads laid out trails for advancing packs of Abrams M1's to cut off and confront enemy defenses in open territory but taking small towns and villages was left to the Special Forces.

Brad's unit was known for removing threats of resistance with brutal efficiency, until they advanced into an ambush in an apparently demolished and abandoned town that held no strategic value to either side. Trapped in a blind alley and blinded by grenades and IED's, snipers rained bullets from three directions until the soldiers charged through a fierce gauntlet to clear an escape, losing seven of their own men.

His recollections were jolted by a wide flap opening in the body of the airplane, just in front of the left wing, discharging a long ramp that spewed a dozen chopped Harley-Davidsons to line up, rumbling thunder, waiting for the chain link gate to roll back.

Spratlin walked over to shake Eddie Glover's hand, "I'm Brad Spratlin, glad you're here."

"Yeah, man, us too. That was the shortest long ride in history!"

"Saves on gas and your ass."

"Amen, brother, amen. Hey, this is Nomad and Jimmy James, my best guys and I'll introduce everyone else when we land."

They shook hands and Nomad said, "So, you ride alone man, 'cause no one wants to hang with you?"

"Hell, if you knew the truth you wouldn't want to hang with me either!" Brad cracked up. "Hey, we've got digs set up at the hotel downtown where our folks are meeting and we've staked out a whole floor of the parking garage as our base. My guys are already on it. I'll show you the layout of the city on the way in and then we're going to have lunch with our Police Chief, Joe Billings. He's a straight up guy and you'll dig him. We need him and he needs us."

"Cool," said Jimmy James. "Does he smoke dope?"

"Probably not. This is redneck Republican Bible country," said Nomad, "and remember why we're here, we get to be the good guys."

"Amen, again."

"Nice ride brother, I like the way she's stretched out," added Eddie, eyeing the extended chrome forks on Brad's bike. "Does that thing ride as cush as she looks?"

"Twice as nice," laughed Brad, kicking the knucklehead engine into a low growl. "Follow me, we're going to do a loop, so you can see the four main roads leading in and out of town, then we'll spiral into the city. We'll start towards town on Osage Boulevard, which is pretty much a straight shot into the square, but I'm going to take you across Apache Drive on the northern edge of our thriving little metropolis, then down along the river. We'll cross Prescott Avenue that turns into Highway Four to the southwest, then Tribal Way to the south and I'll bring you back in on Prather Post."

"Osage Boulevard and Tribal Way I get, but who were Prescott and Prather?"

"Prescott hit the first big oil strike in the region and Prather was an Osage chief who designated the Council Oak Tree as the peaceful meeting place for all the tribes, a large open site overlooking the river with a generous fresh water spring."

"Cool. Lead on!"

The pack of motorcycles turned west off Osage and rumbled along a winding two-lane through a forest of bare trees, save a few pines and thickets of cedar, standing resolute against the gray glare of a cold winter afternoon's gloom. They turned south and dropped down to follow the meandering River Road, tailed by two pickup trucks full of rowdy partiers honking and hollering, until Brad pulled off on an overlook and killed the engine, watching the rednecks racing south.

Nomad stared after the trucks, "You have some weird drunken welcome tradition or were those fools looking for trouble?"

"Let's hope they're just drunk fools," said Brad, eyeing a dozen Florida license plates.

"You don't think they're scouts, do you?" asked Eddie.

"If they are, we'll know soon enough."

"That ain't what I want to hear," said Jimmy James.

"You and me either."

"I kinda had my heart set on buying me a nice cowboy hat, maybe some of them fancy boots, and chasing down an Indian maiden to share a couple of brews and some kick-up-your-heels dancin' on Saturday night," laughed Jimmy.

Brad pointed to the little city, nestled into a hollow in the hills, "Indian legend claimed that tribes who built their camps in the crook of a river would never suffer a tornado strike. The city fathers took their advice and tiny Cameron has been spared by horrific twisters that leveled towns all around us."

Nomad nodded towards the industrial plant across the river with a huge 'Stanton Oil' sign, "What's that?"

Spratlin laughed, "That's my old man's oil refinery."

"So, why isn't your bike gold-plated, rich boy?" laughed Jimmy James.

"Well, first, 'cause I'm happy with old-school and, second, he's been appointed temporary Representative to replace the guy we ousted. Plus, he's the front man for our organization."

"Sure is nice, when families get their shit together."

Brad grinned, "Believe me, we proved how hard that can be. Let's head out, I'll take you around south and then we can get you settled in at the hotel and our little command center."

The next afternoon, Nellis met Jessie and Kate at the airport gate, gathered their bags, and headed out to his truck, "You have a good flight?"

"Yeah, other than making two stops," said Jessie, stretching his back against the bed of the old pickup.

"Sorry, we don't have limousines in Cameron, except Spratlin's Fleetwood, 'cause nobody'd use 'em if we did. I think Mr. Charles is going to pick up the Misses Hall and Sloan and a couple of others in it tomorrow but everyone else is going to have to ride in whatever we can send."

Kate laughed, "I used to write for "American Style' magazine, covering resort openings and doing stories on fabulous houses and once in a while, they'd send a limo to pick me up at the airport, but I drive an old beat-up BMW 320 and Jessie putters around in a vintage Volkswagen bus."

"Just drop your bags in the back there," said Nellis, cranking the engine. "I'm glad you kids could come in a day early, gives us a chance to get to know each other before the troops start demanding plans and answers."

"I agree," said Jessie. "Besides, I've always wanted to check out this part of the underbelly of our nation. I know Big 10 country but not Big 12."

"Well, it's fairly laid back, folks are friendly and helpful even if too many of them qualify as evangelical morons who vote for anyone waving a Bible and claimin' to be against abortion. This part of the state is called 'Green Country' because we're right on the western edge of the Great Eastern Forest, thirty miles west and it melts into the prairie and grasslands. Go southwest and it's red dirt and scrub, southeast there's ancient mountains then marshes, down near Louisiana and high desert mesas out towards the panhandle. This area is mostly farming and ranching, with patches of oil and gas production, but Cameron's blessed with the Stanton Oil plant which processes crude into all sorts of derivatives. Stanton Spratlin, our 'temporary' Congressman, who you met at the Houston meeting, runs the company. It was started by his grand-daddy. Might even be his great grand-daddy, just after World War One and they employ or support the whole damned town."

"What's the population?" asked Kate.

Nellis stroked the stubble on his chin, "You know, I don't honestly know. I'd guess maybe twenty-five to thirty thousand, another ten or fifteen if you count all the little burgs scattered around nearby."

The old truck rolled down Osage Boulevard into the town square where broad walkways intersected a brown lawn surrounding a gurgling fountain of golden angels. The tidy plaza was graced with gnarly old oaks overhanging quaint shops, stores and the Great Plains hotel around the perimeter, all dwarfed by the hulking temple of the Praise the Lord Ministries at the top of an endless staircase that was wide enough for a line of twenty true-believers to huff their way to heaven without touching each other. The gilt citadel was looking rather neglected and certainly vacant of parishioners now that Billy Joe was under house arrest on Federal charges of corruption, money laundering, conspiracy to commit fraud and on and on.

Nellis pointed, "I don't know whether you're familiar with Billy Joe Hardman and his Praise the Lord ministries?"

"He was one of the facilitators that you took down, wasn't he?"

"Yeah, sad little weasel under all that blubber and bluster."

"Haven't seen much of him on TV," added Jessie. "He used to be on Wednesday nights and all day Sunday, screaming and hollering about how God had touched him or moved him or demanded some penance that was going to require an extra tithe or twenty, each and every month, from every one watching or the good Lord would strike him dead."

"He's spending time awaiting trial, under house arrest at his mansion out east and doesn't get out much, besides court appearances."

"Amazing how fast he fell from grace," said Kate.

"Ya' think, maybe the parishioners figured out that God was pissed off at their lying sack-of-shit preacher?" laughed Jessie. "Hell, God decided that instead of frying his dumb ass in a stupendous bolt of lightning, he'd make him spend the rest of his miserable life in a tiny cell someplace cold, dark, and lonely with someone large and angry."

"Actually, we did some research on him during our campaign and he started out doing tent revivals all across the south with his old man, until his father got shot dead by a jealous husband. The kid didn't miss a beat and took over as a teenager, building his whole empire from nothing. Even if he is an unabashed scumbag, gotta give him credit for having the vision and the guts to see it through."

"I guess, but I'm having a hard time finding much respect for bizarre religions that try to force their extreme and distorted beliefs on everyone else," said Kate.

"Well, first, he's a world-class celebrity in the business of religious entertainment, with millions of followers around the world who devoured his every word and contributed an amazing stream of money into his own private zip code." He pointed, "See that brick building tucked in next to the grand staircase? That housed the accountant's offices and his private bank."

"We picked the wrong business," laughed Jessie.

"I'm bettin' they'd rather be riding around with us in an old pickup than facing serious jail time," snickered Nellis, heading south and up Maple Ridge Boulevard, past the estates and mansions, then south on the main road to the lane into the farm.

"Reverend Combs has a huge persona but he isn't like that," said Kate. "I'm spiritual not religious but I never feel like he's putting his beliefs on me…it's more like he supports your right to believe whatever you believe."

"Yeah, I enjoyed the few minutes we spent together in Houston and look forward to getting to know him. I'm aware that he's famous for hypnotizing audiences of thousands of people, planting seeds in their brains that allow them to do outrageous things, like walking on fire or breaking boards with their bare hands," laughed Nellis. "How do you know he's not doing the same to you and all of us?"

"I don't know it. I just believe in the rightness of his influence on the rest of us. Even after all the weird stuff we've been through, he keeps us focused on what's right and what's possible."

Jessie grinned, "Plus, he's a hell of a showman, pitchman and he knows how to grab an audience and focus their attention on his shiny object."

Kate slugged him in the shoulder, "You know he's a good guy."

"Yeah, he is and I'm glad he's on our team."

Nellis eased up to the gate and hopped out to swing it back, Kate slid over and drove up the drive to park near the house. Jessie got out, gazing around, "I know it's winter, but this place is amazing. How much land do you have?"

"'Bout sixty acres give or take. Most of it's in pecans, plus a few cows grazing in a nice pasture down at the south end," said Nellis as a herd of hounds bounded across the yard to sniff and nuzzle. "All y'all simmer down, now. That's Mamasan, ChaCha, Cody, Brandy and Gracie."

Jessie knelt down to pet the Shepherd mix, who cocked her head inquisitively, "That's amazing."

"What's that?" asked Nellis.

He stood up to fetch a photo from his wallet, "Meet my Gracie."

Nellis peered at the image and held it up in front of Gracie. "It's like the same dog, only with reverse coloring. Where she's black, yours is blond and vice versa. I agree, that's pretty strange. I bet she's as smart as this one."

Jessie grinned, "Her latest trick was helping us evacuate a thousand people from SunnyBreeze during the worst of the hurricane."

Nellis leaned to pet Gracie, "That sounds like something you'd do."

"I don't mean to intrude on your life, but is Katherine your lady?"

"It's complicated, but yeah."

"So, I've got a Kate and you've got a Katherine, we have almost identical dogs named Gracie, we both value the serenity of being surrounded by nature, and we're tasked with saving our country from being snuffed out by a merry band of rich maggots who are committing terminal treason. I'd say the gods might be trying to tell us something."

"There's just one more thing I've gotta know."

"What's that?"

"Country smoked ribs?"

"Does a wild dog bay at the full moon? What kind of question is that?"

"The one that says that I'd best go check the Hasty Bake to make sure everything's on schedule. Take your stuff through the porch and the kitchen to the bedroom at the end of the hall. I'll be with you in a jiffy."

The red-tail hawk cawed as it swooped across the yard chasing a bouncing squirrel, zig-zagging across the gravel in search of a tree trunk, setting a flock of doves to flight in a frantic flutter of squawks and feathers. Jessie hugged Kate, before the pack of hospitable pooches ushered them up the path to the porch. "I want to paint that little explosion of nature, we just witnessed."

"That's great but if his ribs are half as good as they smell, I'm gonna propose marriage," snickered Kate.

"Hey, what about me?"

"I love your paintings but my tummy thinks you need to take a lesson on smoking meat!"

"Oooo, that sounds carnal and sexy."

"Yummy too," replied Kate, stepping into the comfortable little parlor with sunrise yellow walls, antique cabinet pieces and furniture upholstered in rich florals, beneath vivid artwork. "Wow, isn't this lovely?"

"Not what you'd expect from the outside," said Jessie, turning into the kitchen with the Chinese-red textured walls, silver appliances, and a skinny island, to the dusty-gray dining room with walls of books illuminated in pools of warm amber and into a tiny bedroom with pale blue-green walls and a large spool bed. "This place is incredible."

Nellis appeared in the doorway, "That was my daddy's bed and it's mighty comfortable, even if it is kinda stuffed into this little room. The bathroom's next door, fresh towels all laid out for you, if you want to freshen up."

"That'd be great," said Kate.

"Katherine should be home in a little bit," said their host. "I've got beer, wine, and I can brew up some tea, if you like?"

"I could go for a brew," said Jessie.

"I'll take a nice warm cup of tea," said Kate, disappearing into the aqua bathroom.

Nellis popped the tops off of two bottles of cold Olympia and handed one to Jessie.

"We don't see Olympia in Florida."

"Hell, it's clear on the other side of the country."

"Yeah, but we get great French wine at almost reasonable prices."

"See, that's the problem with America today, the 'can-do' attitude that built this country only applies until someone with money says you can't. That's usually a Republican with their head up their ass, because competition interferes with their monopolies."

"Used to be you could get yourself educated, go to the polls and vote for someone who was actually qualified for the job and win, lose, or draw feel good about participating."

Nellis grinned, as Kate wandered into the kitchen, "Now we're supposed to accept the puppets the paymasters choose."

"I love your house, it's so warm and homey," said Kate.

"Thank you, it's finally starting to feel like a home again, after much too long." He handed her a steaming cup of tea and grinned, "I should warn you that we have a real live ghost in our midst. It's my former wife, Nanny, who died a while back but never quite left the property. She's friendly enough but don't be surprised if she pulls some prank to let you know she's near."

"Really?"

"Really. She didn't like Katherine moving in and was really mean for the first few weeks."

"How?" asked Kate.

"Oh, slamming doors in her face or turning off the lights and the heat when she walked into a room. Or turning the faucets on full blast when Katherine walked past a sink, or dumping all her clothes on the floor in the middle of the night."

"Sounds jealous to me."

"Absolutely, but it stopped suddenly. I don't know or want to know why, but now everything is just the way Katherine likes it and I'm not about to mess with any of it."

"I don't blame you," said Jessie. "You've got too many women."

"Well, you haven't met the Spratlin girls, Sissy and Sam, yet. Between the four of them, I've got no chance of reverting to my miserly old self."

Jessie clinked bottles, "Amen, brother."

The dogs on the porch pranced and whined, announcing Katherine's entry, "I'm glad to see you guys made it okay."

Kate walked over to offer a hug, "Nice to be here and love the house."

She hugged Jessie and took off her coat, "Think a girl could get a glass of Chardonnay?"

Nellis kissed her cheek, as he pulled a bottle from the fridge, "Coming right up."

Katherine leaned close to Kate and whispered, "Do you guys get high?"

Kate giggled, "He's an artist, what do you think?"

"Cool, I didn't really get into it until I got hooked up with this guy. Now, it's become ritual especially after a day sitting in a windowless office on the phone coordinating everything." She reached under the counter and pulled out a shallow wooden bowl, bearing papers and a pinch of pot.

Nellis pulled out a rolling paper, sprinkled shredded bud into the crease, rolled from the center and, with a lick and a flip, handed a perfectly cylindrical joint to Katherine.

Jessie whistled, "That technique takes some practice."

"How 'bout more than twenty years on the road, playing honky-tonks from Chicago to Atlanta."

"What's your instrument?"

"Guitar, singing. I play a little bit of everything, mostly blues and easy-going country story songs," mused Nellis, taking a deep drag.

"He's way too humble. You should watch him take over a crowd." Katherine coughed and handed the joint to Jessie, "I hear you do a little painting."

Kate laughed, "Well, he had a stunning collection of natural fantasies...you know raging oceans, billowing storms and beautiful scenery with birds and animals...that make the viewer feel like they've just witnessed the very best nature has to offer. They were selling like hotcakes, until a gang of bogus cops broke into the house one night, destroyed everything in the place, and kidnapped us to try to stop the protest rally from happening."

Nellis grinned, "Before you say another word, I'm bettin' big money was behind it."

"Give the man a gold star," laughed Kate. "It seems like these guys have staked a claim on the future of our country and they're not going to take 'no' for an answer."

"And they don't take kindly to anyone standing in their way," said Jessie.

"I don't know about you but the road block and explosion really blew my mind in several different ways...sure, I was scared shitless, stunned that there really are people who carry around enough hate to murder anyone who disagrees, but now, I'm angry, determined, and ready to build an organization to take back our democracy," said Katherine, sipping her wine.

Jessie shook his head, "Six dead, eleven injured, two still in the hospital...no one claimed responsibility and the cops never caught any of the 'protesters'."

"They never would have caught the crew that snatched us and tried to blow up the rally, if the hurricane hadn't flushed them out," added Kate. "They could have merged into the crowds of tourists and vanished, because they are every man - your neighbor or your postman or your kid's teacher."

"The only tell-tail is that they're all white men."

"True, but now, it seems fairly obvious that the herd is being directed by a very well-organized and funded elite, who have found a formula to transform racism and bigotry, frustration and anger into votes for their hand-chosen surrogates," said Katherine.

"They'll retake the House for sure," added Jessie, "and, probably the Senate. All they need is the White House to claim a commanding trifecta."

Nellis refreshed the drinks, "Not to change the subject but ribs in twenty."

"They smell divine," said Kate.

"Aw, they'll be better than that," laughed Nellis, leaning against the sink. "We can get off on organizing rallies and marches, strikes and voter drives...and we need to do all those things, but the underlying problem that we need to solve, this week, is what's the ultimate goal, what are we willing to risk to get there, how are we going to protect our people, and then, what are we going to do if we figure out how to win this war?"

"That kind of sums it up in a tidy little package," said Jessie, "but, if you want to take it a step further, it's going to come down to a question of mass...who has the most folks willing to get out there and make it happen and most of the people we're appealing to need a damned good reason to choose our side verses theirs. The powers behind this conspiracy have been organizing their campaign of hate and destruction for decades, we've got less than a year to turn it around."

"If you want to take the White House, you'll need something close to 50 million votes," said Katherine. "Everything between now and then is just one more step towards that goal."

"I think we're done here," said Jessie. "Can we eat now?"

Brad and Eddie rotated squads of bikes to escort cars and trucks ferrying guests from the airport into town, the only vehicles breeching a secure perimeter of police cars blocking streets along the west side of the square. Officers from the surrounding towns and counties, guarding every entrance to the Great Plains Hotel, checked and accounted for every vehicle, person, or package entering or leaving the building.

Nellis pulled up to the road block and rolled down the window to greet Chief Billings, who was wearing an official dark blue poncho, a plastic cover over his gray Stetson, and a scowl to suit the weather. "Sorry to drag you out in this cold nasty weather, Chief."

A little rivulet of water dripped from the rim of his hat, as he glared, "I'd blame you, if I could, but I can't, so I won't."

Nellis jerked his thumb towards his passenger, "This is Jessie Cotton, one of the leaders at the rally down in Dolphin Bay during the hurricane."

Billings leaned into the window, "I admire everything you stand for but I'm still going to blame you for bringing this lousy weather in."

Jessie laughed, "This is nothing compared to Dot, she was every bit a lady - vicious, relentless, and terrifying."

"You can hide from a tornado but you can't outrun a hurricane."

"Any signs of our favorite bad guys?" asked Nellis.

"Yeah, actually there's a fair-sized crowd of evangelicals, over on the steps of Praise the Lord, waving signs and singing hymns, but Klan guys, nothing yet."

"Brad thinks they got spotted, when he was bringing the bikers into town from the airport, so anything's possible."

The Chief grinned, "Can't you do anything without causing a ruckus?"

"We both know I never start these things but I usually have to finish them off," replied Nellis.

"So, you keep saying." Billings glanced at Jessie, "I'm betting the two of you are way more trouble than I need right now, so behave yourselves."

"Yes, sir!"

Katherine and Kate followed the pickup into the parking garage and up to the second floor, in the well-loved company station wagon, which she learned to value for its bland inconspicuousness, the comfort of a plush interior, and enormous capacity to haul her things, one batch at a time, from storage to the farm.

Brad and Eddie wandered over to greet them and Nellis asked, "How're things?"

"We've got all the cars cleared out of the lot, caravans running back and forth to the airport, a communications base set up, eyes on the roof and the street, and our people logging everyone in or out."

"Anyone scouted the protestors across the square?"

"Yeah, we're watching. We're also keeping an eye on the perimeter, in case the noise might be a diversion from a real attack," replied Brad.

"We've got faith in you," said Jessie.

"So, the cops haven't arrested any of your guys...yet?" snickered Nellis.

Eddie laughed, "Yeah, well, we all...and I mean us and them...think it's kind of ironic that we're working together for something we all support but it seems to be a smooth ride so far."

"If we're going to succeed, it's going to take all different sorts of people, setting aside their differences and joining together, to make this all work," said Katherine. "There can't be a hierarchy, it's one for all and all for one or we all go down in flames."

"You do your best in there and we'll do our damnedest to keep you safe."

The ladies hugged them, with a kiss to each cheek, and headed for the conference in the library, on the second floor behind the balcony of the turn-of-the-century lobby. The din of passionate voices echoed from a hand-hammered tin ceiling arching over walls of bookcases, broken by soft puddles of cold blue light spilling across a magnificent Persian rug, through heavy curtains veiling leaded windows.

Tabitha's eye was still bruised and swollen and Mavis wore a stylish aqua head-wrap to conceal her bandages, as they greeted the new arrivals. Katherine hugged Mavis and kissed Tabitha's cheeks, "You ladies look as if you're barely recovering."

"Well, neither of us would miss this chance to get things rolling," said Mavis. "I'm pretty sure everyone's arrived, so, I think we can start in a few minutes."

The publisher leaned on her carved cane, with a pert grin, "Stanton and I will get the party started and then you troublemakers can have your say."

"Ah, we're not that bad, are we?" asked Sammy Ball, with a pout.

"Speak for yourself," said Benny. "The crowds seem to love an angry black kid, especially a good-looking angry black kid, with a big smile and a sense of humor."

Stanton tapped a spoon on a water glass and waiters wandered through the conferees offering water, tea, and coffee, as everyone took a seat and the noise dissipated into murmurs.

Spratlin raised the glass, "I applaud every one of you for being brave enough, dedicated enough to journey to this distant uncharted and undomesticated corner of the planet, to learn how you can relinquish the next couple of years of your lives to saving our nation from the traitors for little or no pay or recognition. The very idea of taking on a wealthy, formidable, well-established political machine that controls all the levers, is totally ridiculous. They have the overwhelming advantage and we are ill-prepared and late to the game."

"What we do have is the righteous and revolutionary tradition that all of us are created equal, that we all have value, and that we deserve the same rights as our rich neighbors," said Tabitha. "There is an enormous segment of society being pushed into poverty by our greedy foes, who believe that profits take precedence over humanity and common decency, that an ignorant and destitute populous will bow down to worship them as gods, gratefully accepting meager crumbs that trickle down from on high as sustenance. Their arrogance sanctions the assumption that their immense and boundless wealth gives them the right to mold the future of our nation and our world to suit their whims…I think not! We will march and rally and strike for the oppressed workers of America until we win!"

The audience applauded.

"I have to believe that the attack on our gathering in Houston was the work of well-coordinated radical extremists but the ranks of the opposition also include some indigent souls we need to rally to our cause. Winning over the allegiance of a whole caste of wounded and abandoned people, who have lost their relevance and status in this bleak new world of dashed hopes and broken promises, is not going to be easy," added Stanton.

Nellis raised his hand, "With the endless flow of absurd propaganda they're spewing all over newspapers, magazines, the internet, and television, blaming everyone who isn't fat, white, and stupid for the collapse of our social structure, they have an advantage. They're marketing hate and it's easy to get all different kinds of folks to unite to fight against a common enemy. That's how wars get won."

"We've already suffered our own casualties," said Mavis, "and I want to make damned sure they perished for something worth dying for!"

"There will be a short service for our lost or injured colleagues before lunch," said Spratlin, "as well as an update from the hospital."

"Mourning those we lost is all well and good," added Nellis, "and we can yammer all day about what we intend to do, but nothing will get accomplished until we've worked out security for all of our people. The defense that Chief Billings, along with Brad and Eddie's volunteers have devised is robust and visible, which should give protesters or troublemakers something to think about. Defending our own turf is one thing, taking this show on the road with twenty or thirty-thousand people in the crowd is a whole different ballgame."

"I have nothing but admiration and appreciation for those guys out there in the street making sure we're safe inside our little fortress," said Katherine, "but, if we're going to carry our own security around the country, we're going to have to disguise them to be more palatable to the folks we're trying to lure into our campaign. The Klan and the Nazi's are belligerent and violent bullies, you can spot them a block away, but our security force can't make people afraid to join us."

"You've made a valid point. That can be worked out, once we have a clue about who's going to run the security detail," said Stanton, "and before we get to that, we need to decide who's going to run the national organization. Who's going to have final authority to run the front office?"

Nellis raised his hand, "There are a dozen people in this room, who could do a bang-up job of putting and keeping our stuff together. Unfortunately, Tabitha has a newspaper empire to run, Mavis has countless corporations that would certainly prove a conflict of interest, when the right-wing press starts chewing on us. Stanton's going to be spending time in Washington, as well as running a thriving business..." He squeezed Katherine's hand, "We could put out a search for the best people in the country but we don't have time for that, so I propose that Katherine Kennedy take charge. She knows how to run a corporate structure, she knows how to communicate with people, to delegate duties and responsibilities, and she looks great on camera."

"I'll second that," said Stanton. "I can attest to her professional prowess, her intelligence, drive, character...and her commitment to defending her moral compass. Given options, she will always choose the correct path."

The willowy brunette blushed, "I'm not qualified..."

Tabitha placed with pale delicate hand on her shoulder, "M'dear, we both know that you've been working your entire life, preparing for this duty. You are eminently qualified and I have every faith that you'll become the anchor, the conscience, and the soul that keeps us pointed towards all that is right and true...for the salvation of our country."

Mavis looked around the faces in the small crowd, "I agree, how about all of you?"

A rousing 'Aye' rose to echo off the hammered-tin ceiling.

Katherine looked around, "Fine, I want an executive secretary, starting now, and an executive committee, to coordinate our campaign, by the end of the day."

Nellis groaned, "Give a woman access to power and she goes bonkers right from the git-go."

She pursed her lips, "You better watch yourself, Buster, now that you've crowned me Empress, I'll demand that you become my personal secretary, which will mean planning, attending, and recording every meeting and conference, filtering every phone call, message, or letter, and keeping me attentive with lots of fresh-brewed hot coffee."

"Lady, you can have your way with me but I ain't your personal secretary." Nellis hung his head, as the room exploded with laughter, and Katherine kissed his cheek, whispering, "You claimed to be a feminist."

He grinned, "And I think you're gonna do a bang-up job, so let's get started."

Katherine glanced over to Bobbie Warmington, who was scribbling in her notebook, "Bobbie, I know you've got kids and other responsibilities, but would you consider keeping me organized?"

"I've never done anything like this before," said Bobbie.

Jessie walked over to hug her, "You're perfect for this job and your kids are going to be really proud of you…and you'll make a decent salary for a change."

She hesitated for a long moment, "I'll give it my best shot."

"That's all we can ask," said Stanton.

"And I want Tabitha, Mavis, Sammy, and Benny to be out front on all of this. Each of you represents the best of who we want to be."

A young woman's hand shot up, "We're here from Atlanta and…"

"What's your name?" asked Katherine.

"I'm Althea Dodson and this is Amy Martin, we represent the Worker's Union of the Unemployed. We have nearly twenty-thousand people signed up for a protest rally in two weeks at Piedmont Park in Atlanta and, in spite of the fact that you people seem to attract horrendous weather, I was wondering whether we might coordinate our efforts?"

"Even though we haven't even agreed on an executive committee," said Katherine, "I will guarantee that we'll be there in some capacity and we'll spread the word to everyone in our network."

"That would be wonderful," said Althea.

"Think you can handle two or three times that many people?"

"We've got the room but I'm not sure we've got enough security to guarantee their safety."

"We'll give you everything we can muster," said Stanton.

It was past midnight, when the headlights of the old truck swept into thick black smoke rolling down the lane, spawned by hungry orange flames licking low clouds streaming over the charred remnants of his beautiful new barn.

The dogs yelped and barked, as Nellis piled out of the truck and pushed through the gate to grab a hose. He started towards the faucet but Jessie held him back, as a wave of flaming shingles fluttered off the roof, "C'mon, man, you can't save it!"

Kate and Katherine pulled him away from the roaring inferno to huddle with the dogs, cats, chickens, and goats, as blazing timbers collapsed through billowing showers of orange sparks into a crackling pyre.

Katherine knelt to hug him, as Gracie and Mamasan licked his face, "I'm so sorry."

"Nothing to be sorry for, the horses are out to pasture and no one got hurt, but those bastards will pay, I promise you that."

"We should call Chief Billings," said Kate.

"And Brad and Eddie," added Nellis, turning to trudge towards the house, escorted by a howling chorus from his menagerie.

Chapter Five

Brad and Eddie stood on a broad stage, constructed on a flotilla of flatbed trucks beneath brilliant spot lights blazing through a sedentary fog to illuminate a dazzling banner that read *Workers Union of the Unemployed – All People Matter*, scanning across the misty field at the south end of The Meadow at Piedmont Park in Atlanta, to glimmers from Lake Clara Meer in the background. Brad pointed, "There's no way to secure any part of this place, except this patch right around the stage, and all these trees provide perfect cover for snipers and shielding for escape. We'd need lots more guys than we're gonna have and a couple of miles of fencing to secure a perimeter around the whole park."

"I can see twenty or thirty-thousand filling this space with some room left over, but what happens if fifty or seventy-five-thousand show up?"

"Lots of folks waiting for the head?"

"Too many bodies crammed into a confined space is asking for a riot," said Eddie. "That's what happened at our rally in Dolphin Bay, tons of people jammed into the town square with all the exits blocked by police cars, when the trouble started. Best we can do here is station our people in all the choke points to maintain the flow, if people start running."

"Maybe we should be looking at this the other way around," he paused, flashing back to moonless night patrols through desert landscapes full of traps and rabbit holes, where a silent invisible enemy could pick off his men and vanish into the darkness. "If we were trying to rain on this parade, where would we start, what's the easiest primary target, and how do we get out?"

Eddie sauntered across the stage, surveying the elevated sound and light booth, a hundred yards out, and pairs of light and speaker towers staggered on either side of the field, where video cameras would be mounted to record the stage and the reaction of the crowds. A broad road provided access and parking on the right and curving paths surrounding the meadow, leading off around the lake to other areas of the park behind clusters and rows of trees. He waved his hand, "It's too open and, with tons of panicky people stampeding, there's no way out."

He turned to look across Tenth Street, to the Grady High School football field, flanked by soaring stadium seating and a sheltered press box. "I'd set up over there."

"I agree absolutely, it's close but clear of the crowds, easy egress, and places to hide out. Hell, they could drive a tank into that parking lot and it'd be a straight shot at the stage. Boom! One and done!" Brad grinned, "What if we set up our staging area over there? It'd be easier to maintain and coordinate and get our guys where they're needed. Two birds and all that…"

"Yeah, man. The cops can handle the audience and we'll look after the event."

"We'll run it by the new security guys, if and when they get here."

They turned as a prattling parade climbed the stairs at the back of the stage, led by a tall athletic black woman and her partner, whose pale complexion suggested extended captivity in a dank dungeon or working on top-secret potions, while locked in a sealed laboratory for months at a time. Brad extended his hand, "Hi, I'm Brad Spratlin and this is Eddie Glover."

"I'm Althea Dodson and this is Amy Martin and we're certainly glad you're here. We've brought Abe Sheldon and Brandon Beal from Eagle Security to help keep everyone safe."

Beal, slender, tailored, with a tidy moustache and blond hair curling over the collar of a worn leather flight jacket, reached to shake Eddie's hand, "Brandon Beal, pleased to meet you, this is Abe Sheldon."

Eddie held on to his hand, as he looked him over and then his older stocky partner, "Military intelligence, Navy, I'd guess, top of your class, served overseas, the Middle East is an obvious stop but I'm betting on the political capitals of Europe, but they didn't kick you out, there was something more that you wanted."

Beal grinned, "You're close."

He turned to Sheldon, "Career New York City cop."

"How'd you know?"

"The spit-polished black tie shoes with silent rubber soles and the way you carry yourself, as if you're a lineman used to pushing through a crowd, with a holster under your left arm and another on your ankle."

"You're very good," said the cop, stuffing a blunt unlit cigar into his craw. "Where'd you learn that?"

Eddie laughed, "There aren't too many people who are actually native to Dolphin Bay. It's a town where everyone's running or hiding from someplace else and no one's hurrying to go back. I'm betting we'll all know way more than we ever wanted to know about each other, before we're done here."

"You're right about that," said Beal.

"So, we've been going over the maps with the guys on the local force and they're used to handling parking and big crowds for concerts and festivals out here, and they'll have the area around the stage sealed off. They know how to deal with stoned kids and folks being stupid but I don't think they understand that this is could be ground zero for a violent clash of opposing political forces. Both of you have been through attacks, so we'd sure like to get your slant on a worst-case scenario."

Brad waved his hand across the field, "There's no way to secure this space, too many trees and obstructions, and any saboteurs are going to have a hard time making an escape through the crowds. If someone's going to attack, they'll either do it right in front of the stage or they'll launch lethal fireworks from the parking lot of the football field across the street."

Sheldon and Beal appraised the stadium, "Direct access."

"Well, we've got a solution for that threat," laughed Eddie.

"What's that?"

"We'll set up our security base in the press box, where we can see everything and run the bikes out of the parking lot."

"Brilliant!" said Beal.

"So, what's your contribution?" asked Brad.

"Oh, we'll coordinate between our people, your people, and the cops. We've got forty guards, all with military backgrounds, plenty of secure radios to share, and two experts in weapons and explosives."

"Okay," said Eddie, "we've got more than fifty volunteers and we want to station them on Harley's as rotating emergency teams on either side of every choke point, as well as internal security around the stage. People will move out of the way, when a mean looking son-of-a-bitch on a hog growls at 'em."

"Cool," said Beal, "let's add spotters on those towers and a couple on the sound booth."

"And the stage," added Sheldon.

"Speaking of which, has anyone inspected the stage and all this rigging? What about the crews that set it up? Anyone know what their political affiliations are?" asked Eddie.

"Yeah, actually, all of this was volunteered by the people we're trying to organize, the unemployed folks who do this for a living," said Amy. "They're on our team."

"That's great," said Brad, "but I still want the demolition guys to go over this whole area."

"I'll get 'em on it," said Sheldon.

"So, we're thinking lethal explosives or some other catastrophic strike but the guys, who attacked our rally in Dolphin Bay, used big firecrackers, set off in a coordinated sequence, to panic the crowd and drive them into a stampede for the networks to broadcast. They weren't out for a body count, it was all staged PR panic for the cameras." Eddie shook his head, "We got that under control with the help of a badass hurricane and the calming words of a towering woman, but the same thing could happen here and any chance of containing a really big frightened mob is dicey at best."

"The episode in Houston was on a totally different level," added Brad. "Their mission was intimidation and their goal was to decapitate the competition before we could get rolling. Their intel was perfect, they had all the founding members in one place, but even though their timing was off by just a smidge, we lost eight very special people, plus lots of injuries."

Eddie added, "Lethal fireworks and dead bodies strewn about the grounds leave a lasting impression on civilian volunteers."

"Either they turn rabbit and run or they stand and fight," said Beal. "As desperate as these folks are, I'm bettin' on them standing their ground."

"Let's pair up some of your best and ours and let them wander around as scouts, maybe save some bad guys from the vengeance of the crowds, if they're stupid enough to try something out there," added Sheldon.

"Done."

Althea leaned in, "There's just one more thing, that you might want to consider."

"What's that?" asked Brad.

"Well, there's been some talk about ending the rally with a spontaneous march on the Capitol. We've got the mayor on our side but he's already a sympathetic Democrat. What we really want is to push Jasper Kline, the hard-right Republican governor, to get behind jobs and retraining, restoring welfare and medical benefits for all his citizens who are getting laid off every day, paying teachers a competitive salary to actually educate our kids, the list goes on and on but bottom line is that folks are desperate for hope, for a champion to defend their withering American dream, for someone who has a plan and the guts to make it happen."

"Either, he publicly endorses our crusade and promotes legislation that solves problems or we'll make sure he sweats every day, until he loses the next election," added Amy. "I'm voting for both."

"Keeping the lid on things here is one thing but a march through the city is a whole different animal," said Eddie. "How far is it?"

"A little over three miles," said Althea. "I drove it this morning."

"What do the police think of your idea?"

"Well, we haven't really mentioned it to them, because we had to jump through hoops just to get the permit for the rally, getting one for a parade and a gathering around the Capitol was way beyond our means," said Amy.

"So, you're just going to suggest it to the crowd and then kind of let it happen?" inquired Sheldon, in a fatherly tone.

"Yeah, I guess," said Amy, shuffling her feet on the blue painted plywood covering the flatbeds. "Sometimes it's easier to ask forgiveness than permission."

"That's bullshit and you know it," snapped Sheldon. "People's lives are at stake."

"Yeah, well, so are thousands and thousands of good, hard-working people, who are losing everything...their jobs, their homes, every dime they ever made. They can't feed their kids without handouts and the fucking government is defunding every program that helps provide food or shelter or medical care. They have nothing! What could be worse than that?"

"You're passionate about this, aren't you?" asked Brad.

"It's personal," replied Amy, "but that doesn't change anything. If the crowd wants to march, we march. This is our chance to make those arrogant bastards listen."

"Then at least give us a heads up, so we can send out advance patrols to clear traffic and secure potential sniper nests. If the bad guys knew about our semi-discreet meeting in Houston, you can bet your booty they know about this."

"Deal."

Jessie, Nellis, and Stanton stepped onto the stage, followed by a pack of children, who danced across the platform.

Brad walked over to shake hands and ask his father, "How'd the kids get here?"

"Well, Jessie brought his friend Johnny, who's Bobbie's son, for a lesson in community action and I thought our herd could stand a little education too."

The eldest son made no attempt to hide his annoyance. "I'm worrying about security and the bad guys dreaming up some horrendous stunt and now I've got to worry about my sisters' safety too?"

"Once things get started, we'll confine them to the secure areas," replied Jessie.

"Great! You guys are in charge of keeping them safe, because I still haven't figured out whether it's even possible to control a mob this big."

~

Georgia's all-star band, Peachtree, launched into a warmup set of romanticized story songs about the courage and gallantry of most unlikely heroes, struggling against overwhelming forces of a heartless bureaucracy and the condescension of big money to defend the vanishing rights of common people.

Waves of the desperate and despondent streamed into The Meadow, brooding human eddies swirling into rivulets amassing bodies into islands, partisan amoebas swelling to fill the field and all the open spaces beyond, under a sullen mantle bristling with whispers of insurgency.

These were not stoned-out youngsters gathering to hear their favorite act, or athletes who attend the annual road race, or socialites sampling delicacies at the food and wine festival. These people were displaced from their jobs, their neighborhoods, and their former reality, to exist at the mercy of a heartless and shrinking bureaucracy that was being systematically deconstructed at the behest of the powers who paid for their demise. These were the victims of all those tragic songs, the workers who built this country, being scrapped like so much obsolete machinery.

At high noon, Althea and Amy stepped up to the microphones, peering out over a dense crush that oozed around clusters of trees and spilled into every breech or break within the sound, if not sight, of the stage. Flashes of colorful coats popped up here and there, beneath a flutter of signs and placards waving over a sea of blue denim, with as many hardhats as children, and almost everyone shared an expression of despair, of shock and disbelief that their worlds had vanished, their dreams had dimmed and, considering the tens of thousands gathered together under gloomy gray skies, any hope of salvation seemed just beyond their grasp.

Althea shouted, "How y'all doing?"

A loud murmur wafted through the crowd, a soggy blanket masking desperation and anger.

"I asked, HOW Y'ALL DOING?"

Cheers and applause.

"I'm Althea Dodson and this is Amy Martin and we run the Worker's Union of the Unemployed, which represents all of you." She pointed to the banner with a giant 'WUU' in electric pink waving in the breeze and shouted, "Can a get a Woo-Woo?"

The audience responded with the roar of an approaching train whistle.

Amy chipped in, "We want to thank everyone for coming out today. We hope to talk about some of your more serious challenges, with people who can actually make stuff happen, provide you with nutrition for body and soul, and options you might not know about, as well as entertain you with some dynamite music from Peachtree and Jazz Taggart!"

Althea pointed, "There are food tents along each side of The Meadow, offering as much great southern cooking as you can eat for as much as you can afford. If you're hungry, we've got ya' covered, with special thanks to The Atlanta Food Bank and volunteers from Community Kitchens. Can we have some appreciation?"

The crowd cheered and applauded, as little streams of people, especially those with children, meandered through the throng in search of sustenance.

"There's a cluster of tents at the north end of the field, where you can find advice and assistance with a whole slew of folks who want to help. We've got housing and shelter, medical care with a pharmacy, legal aid, getting signed up for unemployment or state benefits, and a whole tent full of phones, so you can call whoever you need to contact."

"Check it out!" bellowed Amy. "There are all sorts of people ready to help in any way they can. So, take advantage, make contact, and connect!"

"Same goes for the folks you're hanging out with. Everyone here shares the same fears and worries but every one of you has knowledge or a skill that someone else could use. Hug your neighbor, they're hurting too! Help each other out!"

"We've got some heavyweight speakers lined up for you, including our very own Mayor Tyrone Turner, Representative Stanton Spratlin from Cameron, Oklahoma, as well as publisher, mentor, and soul of the All People Matter movement, our Grande Dame - Tabitha Hall, and most of the leaders from the rally in Dolphin Bay! But we're going to start things off with some music from Nellis Gray, who helped take down the shady election in Oklahoma, along with Jazz Taggart and his Band of Merry Men for a little funky blues, while you get to know each other, eat, and take advantage of all those helpful volunteers around the flanks of this incredible gathering."

"We'll be back in a little bit but let's hear it for Nellis Gray and Jazz Taggart!"

The crowd roared and Jose started a tickety-tak, tickety-tak on the snare, as Harvey built deep heavy Hammond B3 chords chasing screaming guitars into a crescendo that dropped into a pulsing beat and Nellis stepped up to the mike, "Here's a little tune to remind everyone that the good times will roll again and we'll get back to complaining about all that trivial stuff that never mattered in the first place. Maybe we should recognize this moment, because this is where we all realize that we can change the world, if we stick together. Everyone put your hands together for 'Too Much of a Good Thing'."

> *Living in a house*
> *Full of gorgeous girls*
> *Blowin' through my life*
> *Like a storm.*
> *A cold wind blowin' south*
> *You know what I'm talking about!*

Too much of a good thing
Lord, save me from myself

The crowd's malaise melted into musical communion, shared terror shrouded under a funky rhythm, inducing thousands to dance and sway and join on a brief sojourn through an altered reality fashioned from their memories of the carefree time before…

Fell for a vixen with velvet eyes
Said I was her reason to live
Loved me, left me
Took all I had
Now I got nothing left to give, nothing left to give
Too much of a good thing
Lord, save me from myself

Rolled the dice
And hit it twice
Now Uncle Sam
Wants a slice of my life
It ain't right
Too much of a good thing
Lord, save me from myself!

The audience clapped and cheered and Nellis said, "You know, we're all here for the same reason."

"What's that?" yelled a fat lady with a sparkly pink bow clinging to an explosion of mangy brown curls.

"We were feeling pretty proud of busting up our little conspiracy, when we shut down the bogus election in Oklahoma and sent a bunch of political crooks up on Federal charges…but then, what's happening to all of you made us realize that our skirmish was just a little piece of something way bigger and scarier than we could have imagined. We didn't understand, we couldn't even begin to conceive of the idea that this hell, that millions of our brothers and sisters are suffering through, was the goal.

I know this sounds audacious but there's plenty of evidence that a small group of very wealthy people sat down, years ago, and planned all of this out. They've been throwing elections to eliminate taxes that pay for benefits and services for all of you, for public education, roads and bridges, medical care, food stamps, unemployment, and, hell, even police and fire departments. They're succeeding in my home state of Oklahoma, which went from being a secret treasure to being at the top of the worst list and the bottom of the best in every category you can name. I'll bet it's happening in every state in the union. It's just that no one seemed to notice that it was happening everywhere and it was all coordinated by the greedy few, who masquerade as staunch patriots defending the Constitution and the 'intentions' of the Founding Fathers...and I can guarantee they don't give a damn about what those first patriots thought or intended.

Your jobs didn't just disappear, these guys shipped 'em to Asia and South America to increase profits for their international corporations, which pay little or no taxes to anyone. The middle class is disappearing because these folks want to deconstruct our government and our society, to seize complete domination of a two-class system, arranged exclusively for those few hundred families, at the expense of everyone else."

The crowd booed.

"I look out over this crowd and I see real patriots, every size and shape, color and ethnic background all mixed up together, ready to take a stand against tyranny and greed, to fight for our rights and our country and our dignity!"

The Meadow roared.

"We're going to ask you to sign up to help out with all sorts of things, before this day is over, but every one of you can begin by going by the four blue tents we've got set up in the corners of the field, where you can register to vote. I ask this because we can march all day, every day, but we'll make things happen faster, if we can vote these bums out of office and replace them with candidates dedicated to resurrecting our democracy and the future of our nation. If you have any qualifications, please talk to our voulnteers in one of the blue tents. We need people to run for every available office in the state and then the nation!"

The band jumped into 'For All That's Right and True', a revolutionary anthem disguised as a rousing bar song, that had tens-of-thousands singing the chorus by the second verse. They dragged out an extended jam with a chorus of thousands and kept the positive spirits flowing through a half-dozen songs, before Althea and Amy strolled up to the microphones again.

Sissy, Sammy, Daniel, Hubie, Muriel, Martin, and Johnny Warmington huddled in their secret hideout under the stage of flatbed trucks and Sissy said, "I want to go see what's happening out in the crowd."

"Yeah, I'd like to see what they're doing in the service tents," said Daniel.

"But Jessie and your dad said we have to stay inside the secure area around the stage," said Johnny.

"Aw, we've got these passes, we can go anywhere we want," said Sammy, holding up a bright green stage pass. "C'mon, we'll sneak out and make a sweep around the crowd and be back inside before anyone knows we're gone."

"Let's stick together, so Muriel and Martin don't get lost," said Sissy, taking Muriel's hand.

"Cool, let's do this," smirked Daniel, who had never had the confidence or freedom to embark on a lark to spite adult restrictions but Sammy was smart and Jessie said that Johnny helped save lots of people in a hurricane, so he was pretty sure they would get everyone back safe.

He took Martin's hand and followed the pack through the security gate, where a policeman saluted with a jovial smile, and into a rush of people moving in every direction. Sammy and Johnny trotted along but Hubie, Muriel, and Martin were running hard and darting between grownups to keep up.

The children stopped to regroup at a blue tent, where hundreds of people were lining up to register to vote. Sissy grabbed Sam, "The little guys can't keep up and I'm afraid we'll get separated in all these people, it's like the land of the giants!"

"Aw, we can do this," said Johnny. "We're just getting started."

"No!" said Sissy. "We've at least got to take Muriel and Martin back where they'll be safe."

"Okay, compromise," said Sam. "Let's walk through the edge of the crowd on the way back, so we can at least get a feel for the energy."

"Fine but slow down, so we keep everyone together."

"C'mon, follow me," said Sam, zig-zagging through a forest of adults who shifted in waves of feet and knees, barely noticing the convoy of youngsters snaking through the madness.

"Let's hear it for Nellis Gray, Jazz Taggart, and the Band of Merry Men!" shouted Althea. "These guys are cookin'!"

"We want to thank all of you for believing that we can change the world because we can!" yelled Jazz.

Amy applauded as the band disappeared off the back of the stage, "You know, Nellis is right, we're up against some powerful people, who have no respect for humanity or the people who built this country. They don't care what happens to the vast majority of our society and they're working every day to make sure that they win and we lose."

Booo's.

"But the only way they win, is if we give up the fight and bow down to beg for scraps, until we hand over the last of our dreams, our values, and our dignity," said Althea. "This isn't going to be easy and it isn't going to be fast but we'll be relentless in our quest to take back our democracy!"

"Someone just told me that we already have more than a hundred-thousand people here, with more folks pouring in to add their voices, and I can tell that all of you aren't about to give up or give in. They might have a head start but we have each other and we're going to keep growing and growing until we take back our country!" Amy scanned the signs waving above a churning crush of hopeful faces, peering up with the expectation of possibilities and the terror of disappointment. 'Feed my children!' – 'Save Democracy!' – 'Give Me Hope!' - and 'Fighting for Freedom is Not a Choice'.

New thickets of signs appeared almost simultaneously, in several areas just inside the exits, bearing menacing messages, 'Save Our Jobs – Deport Immigrants' – two signs bobbing together 'White' 'America' - 'Protect the Second Amendment' – 'Crush Liberal Elitism' – 'Global Warming is a Hoax'.

She glanced at Althea, who was raving about using our communal power to force change, and pointed to a scuffle, where those hateful signs became spears and clubs against the people who objected with raised voices and flying fists…then another, and another, and more back near the trees. The chaos rippled out through the packed crowd, ringlets rolling away from the violence, only to intersect another human wave surging from a distant confrontation, squashing confused and fearful protestors in panicky gridlock.

Althea yelled, "Today is all about coming together and the folks trying to start a ruckus over here and over there, need to join in or ship out!"

"We have no tolerance for hate or violence!" added Amy. "So, I'd ask security and those folks around the trouble, to escort these people to the exits."

Samantha and Johnny led the children around picnic blankets, coolers, lawn chairs, and the occasional drunk or amorous couple sprawled on the grass. Lots of people were waving signs and yelling their support for the speakers, until the kids broke through a wall of adults who were shouting 'White Power' and 'Deport the Immigrants', wielding signs with 'White America First!' which were transformed into poles and lances against angry protestors screaming obscenities, throwing fists and employing any improvised weapon they could find.

Sissy clung to Muriel and Martin, while Daniel and Hubie tumbled away as a burly fighter stumbled and fell, a writhing blockade isolating them from Samantha and Johnny, who were carried along by the roiling crowd and vanished. Amy's voice sounded sharp and distinct, through the giant speakers staged around the field, over the roar of the crowd, as the fight rolled closer and agitators tossed onlookers catawampus in their struggle to clear a path to freedom, brandishing spears and swinging ax handles to crush any challenger.

Daniel and Hubie scurried away, while Sissy grabbed Muriel and Martin to roll down a little hill on the grass to escape being mauled by lethal truncheons or falling bodies as the floundering rogue wave plowed through the angry mob.

Brad and Beal followed Nomad and Jimmy James on a pair of chopped bikes, slowly herding folks to clear a path toward flailing bodies to quell the fray but the boiling brawl doubled back, as the thugs bulled their way to the exits and waiting cars, that blasted into the streets to scatter into Atlanta's traffic, chased by rumbling Harley Davidsons.

Brad spotted Sissy, Daniel, and Hubie hugging Muriel and Martin in a cluster of overturned coolers and ran through the chaos, "Are you alright? How'd you get out here anyway?"

The children started crying and Sissy's brother wrapped them in a hug, "Where's Sammy and Johnny?"

Sissy looked up, with tears streaming down her cheeks, "They disappeared into the crowd, when the fighting started and the people were pushing and shoving in every direction, and we couldn't catch up."

"Why are you out here?"

"We just wanted to see what it was like to be in the middle of all these people," said Daniel.

"That turned out to be a dangerous adventure, didn't it?"

"Yes," replied the boy, patting his little brother's back and wiping tears from his eyes.

Brandon appeared out of the wall of people with Sammy and Johnny in tow. They ran to Sissy, Daniel, Hubie, Muriel and Martin, "I'm so glad you're okay. We got carried along in the crowd and couldn't find you. I was so worried," said Samantha, hugging each in turn.

"You should have been worried," said Brad, "and you might get ready for Dad being really pissed off at the danger you put all these other kids in. I know I am!"

"I'm so sorry, I never thought we'd get in trouble, we just wanted to go out and see what it was like."

"And what was it like?" asked Beal.

"At first it was exciting and inspiring, then it turned scary and I was worried that something bad had happened to these guys," sobbed Sam. "I'm so sorry."

Brad hugged her, "I won't tell Dad, if you promise to do as we ask. This is serious stuff because there are some dangerous people out here, the same kind of folk who kidnapped all of you back in Cameron, and we don't have any idea of who's a good guy and who's not."

Sam buried her face in his jacket, "I promise."

Johnny stepped up, "She doesn't deserve all the blame, it was partly my idea too."

Brad pulled him close, "I've a mind to tan your hide son but, considering you're a certified hero, I'll give you some advice instead. Your job is to protect other people not put them in danger. Are we clear?"

"Yes, sir."

"Fine, then let's get all of you kids back where you belong, so the rest of us can get back to doing the job we came here to do."

The two bikers cleared a route to the stage gate followed by a slinking herd of children eager to slip inside unnoticed, while Brad and Beal headed to the closest exit.

They found Eddie and Sheldon near the Beltline trail, "Catch any?"

"Naw, that was flawlessly coordinated," said Eddie. "I doubt any of our guys will catch up with them."

"That was just a warm up, to remind us that they're here, they're watching, and they can strike when they want to," said Brad.

"Words of wisdom from experience in the bush?"

"Been pinned down more than my share."

"Then we should treat this as a diversion and guard the perimeter,"

"That whole thing was for PR. Images of the melee are already out on the airwaves and we won't have a chance to refute them until this is over."

"Score one for the bad guys," said Eddie. "We need to win the next one."

Twenty minutes after the first signs appeared, Althea took the mike, "Ladies and gentlemen, I must apologize for a few of our guests who refused to follow decorum. Fortunately, they've chosen to leave. I hope the rest of you can settle back, knowing that we're all going to stand up for each other!"

The crowd cheered.

"I'd like to introduce Tabitha Hall, owner of the Dolphin Times Newspaper, wise and steady inspiration for everyone who knows her, and, as I said, the soul of this movement. Let's hear it for Tabitha Hall!"

She wore a fluffy floral scarf beneath a long burgundy coat that fluttered in the breeze, as Benny escorted her to the microphone, with a kiss to her cheek. The crowd applauded and she gazed over thousands of hopeful faces that demanded hope and feared retribution.

"Ladies and gentlemen, I am honored to be here, flattered by the introduction and humbled by the weight of my expectation for your future."

Cheers and applause.

"We, all of us and our millions of brothers and sisters across the country, have every right to reclaim our democracy, our rights, and our future from a fistful of greedy families, traitors in every sense of the word but powerful, dangerous, and ruthless too. We face terrifying enemies too arrogant to realize that they are not invincible. The only way to get their attention is to march and rally and strike!"

The audience responded with a gigantic roar of enthusiastic approval.

"The real question is – do we have the will? Do we have the guts to see it through? And do we have the wisdom and determination to ensure that we don't make things worse?"

Laughter.

"I'm serious, history proves that revolutionaries make lousy administrators, Chairman Mao managed to kill off almost half the population of China, before the few surviving bureaucrats took over and saved his revolution." She paused, "Desperation makes for convenient allies but victory tests the character and integrity of the victors, when the purpose of the struggle transforms into mending the wounds and rebuilding the country for everyone."

Silence.

"That's what we must do, tear down the gilded bastions of tyranny and restore common sense and decency. Look around at your neighbors, you need them and they need you and, when this is over, we want a country that values and includes everyone. We want a country that defends our rights and our freedoms, our dreams and the promise of our children's future. We can't accept the disgusting mess the Republicans have made of this nation over the past five or six decades. We're going to rebuild the America our Founding Fathers intended and we're going to begin today!"

The crowd cheered and thinned, as people wandered through the sponsor and service tents around the perimeter, as a succession of speakers shared life-changing stories and pleas for unity, until Stanton was presented to introduce Atlanta's Democratic Mayor.

"I've got to say that I'm excited to see so many true patriots here today. In case you don't know who I am, you might be familiar with the story about the candidate running for Congress in Cameron, Oklahoma, who got arrested instead of elected. My name is Stanton Spratlin and I'm the replacement Republican candidate and temporary Representative."

Booo's.

Spratlin laughed, "I know anyone who isn't a diehard Democrat is the enemy but, if you want to judge my dedication to eradicating the current version of the Republican party, which has been hijacked by their extremist sponsors, you might consider the fact that the half-dozen children who were kidnapped by racist thugs and rescued by some of the people here today, those were my children."

The audience was silent.

"Today, we're rallying to demand replacing our fraudulent economy to renew the middle class with jobs and opportunities. Behind the very real nightmares that too many of you have suffered, we exposed a conspiracy that has been rigging elections from Maine to California, from Florida to Alaska. The people running this campaign of 'deconstruction', as they call it, want to 'privatize' every function of our government, meaning they want their companies to provide all of those services at a fat profit."

Jeers.

"They want you to be poor, your children to be raised without a real education, so they'll be more inclined to believe hateful and totally false propaganda and accept subservience to evangelical hypocrisy. They want to take everything you have and put you so far in debt that there's no way out, except capitulation of your hopes and dreams, your rights and your dignity in exchange for subsistence living, if you cooperate."

Booooo!

"I know this sounds like a bad dystopian novel set in some third-world country but that's why I'm going to Washington, to add one more vote to end this madness before it destroys our country! Are you with me!"

"YES!"

"Thank you! I'm honored to be a part of your movement! Now, help me welcome Atlanta's own, Mayor Tyrone Turner!"

The flatbed trucks beneath the blue plywood floor shifted in rhythm as the six-six former Rhodes Scholar, with a doctorate in economics from Yale, and all-star linebacker for the Atlanta Falcons, strode across the stage to shake his hand. He leaned close and laughed, "These folks believe you but the right-wing Republicans don't want to listen to experts like us! Truth can't coexist with the farcical party line."

"I'm an ugly duckling, an old-time moderate Republican, and I used to get the same reaction before I started calling out their lies. Now they don't want to talk or listen to me either."

"We need more patriots like you." The former linebacker patted Stanton on the shoulder with an enormous hand and turned to the microphone, with a baritone that birthed every word from deep in his gut, massaged and refined into elegance as they passed his heart, where each syllable ripened into melodious thunder growling through the ether to touch every person in the audience with inspired clarity.

"Ladies and gentlemen, my fellow citizens, and eminent guests, thank you, every one of you, for coming out today to stand together against the tyranny and oppression being foisted on America's workers by a gang of gilded traitors. An economic revulsion designed to suck the lifeblood from the souls of the middle class to feed the profits of the greedy few. Those same people filled the ranks in our legislature with corrupt Republicans and put Jasper Kline in the governor's office!"

The crowd roared!

"They've made the basis for their agenda clear, in spite of the public rhetoric, and it includes the elimination of all taxes for the highest earners and their corporations, abolishing the EPA and any and all restrictions that might interfere with industrial scale pollution that is killing the planet, the reduction or elimination of funding for all state sponsored health clinics, homeless shelters, welfare, unemployment benefits, and training programs…ensuring the destruction of the middle class.

They're well on their way to shifting the budget for public education to a voucher system that will benefit newly opened private evangelical schools across our state, which are owned and managed by CCP Education, a private company founded by the State Superintendent's sister, who makes no secret of her extremist beliefs. I've heard that CCP stands for Christ's Chosen People, so you can imagine the criteria they'll use to admit or reject prospective students and the choice of subjects for a rather incoherent evangelical curriculum."

Boooo.

"It's time for the people of the great state of Georgia to inform our government that we've had enough of their con game. We want change and we want it now!"

The Meadow reverberated as he raised his fist, reminded of the stories he heard from former mayor Andrew Young, who marched with the Reverend Martin Luther King as a young activist, "Boot 'em out, make 'em pay! Boot 'em out, make 'em pay!"

The crowd joined in a rousing chant as all the other speakers and players trouped onto the stage to join the mayor, who shouted into the mic, "Let's go visit Governor Jasper Kline, down at the Capitol with all his cronies, and deliver our message in person!"

The protestors erupted and thousands streamed out into the streets, shuffling impatiently in a chilling drizzle, waiting for the dignitaries to lead them south on Monroe Drive. Brad, Eddie, Beal, and a posse of Eagle Security and police officers, along with a cavalcade of chopped Harley's, escorted some of the elder luminaries and the children to waiting cars, while most of the dignitaries lined up at the front of the parade.

Brad clicked his radio, "Listen, we need to spread our resources from the front of this conga line to the last straggler. We don't want muggers nipping at our tail or trying to punch a hole through the middle of the march by popping out of some side street, we all understand the potential threat."

"Roger that," replied Beal, "Sheldon's got advance teams setting up along the route, so we'll place uniforms and security at intervals in the crowd and let the Harley's cover the gaps."

"I'm on it," added Eddie.

Atlanta's stout take-no-prisoners Chief of Police, Monica Hayes, stepped out of a cruiser and marched over to walk with the mayor, who was striding along between Althea and Amy and made no attempt to slow or stop. "You do realize that no one filed for a permit for this carnival and none has been issued?"

"I'm issuing it now," replied the mayor.

"I'm in complete sympathy with everything these people need and deserve but we both know you can't do that."

"I just did," snapped Turner, turning to take in miles of humanity, jamming up and pushing forward, determined to deliver their message. "Do you really think you're going to stop this? This is a spontaneous demonstration, which wasn't planned or instigated by anyone. It just happened."

"I heard your speech, it was recorded and transmitted live to the world."

"Good, then I'll have lots of witnesses when you bring charges! I'll demand that you depose every single witness."

"I'm not going to arrest the mayor."

"Then get the hell out of the way or saddle up, your choice," snapped Mayor Turner. "We've got a very important appointment at the Statehouse."

"Fine, I'll coordinate closing off your route."

"These hundred-thousand citizens appreciate your help."

Sheldon led ten groups of four-man squads to scout and secure potential points of danger along the first largely residential mile of the route, trusting the uniforms to block or divert traffic. They dropped a crew at Greenwood Avenue, more on either side of the intersection at Ponce De Leon, and another in front of the Pizza Hut on Monroe. Then every few blocks along the remainder of the route, which exposed the marchers to open areas with tall buildings and expansive parking lots, where snipers might set an ambush or a crazed zealot in a truck full of explosives might crash into the crowd.

Within minutes, police vehicles began shutting down cross-streets a mile ahead of the marchers, as the leaders advanced towards the turn onto North Avenue, while thousands were still pouring out of The Meadow to populate an endless pulsating human ribbon. Harley Davidsons rumbled back and forth between security points, on either side of the chanting human chain.

"Jasper Kline's crossed the line,
so, we'll keep marchin'
'til he resigns!"

"Sack the Assembly
they've destroyed the state,
respect and honesty
will replace their hate."

Several camera trucks from local television stations waited at Ponce De Leon and pulled out, jockeying for position ahead of the mayor, Amy, Althea, Spratlin, Nellis, Katherine, Mavis, Kate, Jessie, Sammy, Benny, Mavis, and Standler interspersed with a host of activists from across the country, bearing a broad banner that read, 'You're Fired!'

The trucks had been cleared through a police road block but Brad and Eddie's bikes growled ahead for a rolling inspection of the vehicles and their crews, who seemed to be genuine reporters trying to capture and report the story. The chants of thousands echoed and reverberated through the neighborhood as demonstrators marched past tidy homes, until the aromas from Popeye's Chicken and Dunkin' Donuts tempted more than a few to peel off for a quick snack and a momentary reprieve from the damp chill.

Katherine leaned to Nellis, "Can you believe how fast this whole thing blossomed into a movement and I have no doubt national TV coverage will spread it everywhere."

He pouted, "You're going to be a busy lady, I hope you remember me in your spare time."

Katherine punched his arm, "You're gonna be right in the middle of this, just like always, and, with all the hubbub, Nanny's not going to be lonely."

"And you're gonna become the international face and voice for millions."

Katherine blushed and kissed him on the cheek, "I know I'm not ready for any of this but I don't think there's any turning back now."

As the leaders pivoted west on North Avenue, Nellis turned to take in the rowdy column snaking back along the roadway to distant overhanging trees gushing a steady stream of protestors strolling along together. The power of being a member of this unrelenting train of a hundred-thousand guardians helped transform terror and anger into a giddy comradery of resolve and purpose. Although they might not claim victory today, lonely individuals and forlorn families merged into an army marching on a common enemy to land the first blow in a rebellion to reclaim even a tiny morsel of their lost pride.

The Cameron Scandal, as it came to be called, exposed a greedy fraternity manipulating the political framework to entice naïve voters to elect completely unqualified candidates, who would propose carefully crafted legislation to benefit the few at the expense of the many, by appealing to their desperation and their ignorance.

The overwhelming noise and explosive energy of this relentless procession proved that the whole scheme was just a microcosm of an international conspiracy to turn the clock back to a time before women's or minority rights desecrated white male dominance, before the overindulgence of workers, who were thankful for a job for whatever wage they could get, before unions had the gall to demand better working conditions, limited hours, and benefits for workers and their families, before the government taxed the rich to help provide pensions and health care to the commoners. They want to go back to a fictional time when a tiny group of extraordinarily wealthy families controlled key industries, the economy, the government, and the courts.

A resounding chant, rolling forward and back along the line, roused him from his exasperation with the realization, "What astounds me is that we've made it this far without some kind of confrontation or attack."

"Don't jinx it!"

Brad pulled up to idle along next to the leaders and his radio squawked, "This is Eagle dispatch, we've got a mob pouring out of Central Park and forming up around the intersection at Piedmont. Are you expecting more protestors?"

"Anybody got eyes on them?"

"Roger that."

"What do their signs say?"

There was a pause, "They're definitely not promoting peace, love, and equality."

"Can you deal with them before we get there?"

"We assumed they were friendly's but we'll try to keep them from blocking your path."

Brad clicked off and back on, "We've got a counter-demonstration waiting for us at Central Park, let's tighten up security front to back and send some squads to help the advance team."

Eight bikes and two black Suburbans eased along the shoulder to the front of the march and raced past Grady Medical Center and the Cosby-Spear Highrise at full throttle.

Professional right-wing agitator, Roger Stanislawski led nearly a thousand paid true-believers, who, after long bus rides from Mississippi, Alabama, Tennessee, Kentucky, and South Carolina spiked with an ample supply of amphetamines and perpetual mind-numbing sermons, were eager to kick some ass to save White America from a liberal-financed invasion of brown people bent on destroying racial purity.

The disciples were coached to believe that the Worker's Union of the Unemployed and the All People Matter movement were promoted by deep-state socialists bent on repealing the Second Amendment, expanding abortion rights, and abolishing religious freedoms. If the mongrel marchers needed someone to fight for their rights, this brigade would demonstrate why they picked the wrong side.

Police road blocks paid little attention to hundreds of people flooding through the neighborhoods to gather in Central Park and the open areas west of the medical center, assuming they were late to join the march, rather than congregating for a violent confrontation.

A dozen men produced bolt cutters and knocked down chain-link fencing to provide access to the street and the ringleader yelled, "Pick it up!" The counter-protestors jumped into formation with heavy boots stomping a menacing cadence, signs and banners waving, and a thunderous chant of "Make America White Again!".

The police moved more cars to block the side streets and armed officers joined Eagle security personnel and rumbling packs of bikers to cordon off the insurgents. Monica Hayes, Sheldon, and Beal moved forward, as the tramping supremacists marched in place at very edge of the sidewalk with the precision and flair of a shoddy wannabe quasi-Aryan paramilitary unit.

Stanislawski stepped to the front, "What gives you the right to block a peaceful demonstration by real Americans?"

Chief Hayes surveyed the column of white thugs waving battle-flags and hateful racist placards tacked to ax handles and thick clubs, "I'm the Chief of Police and I'm fairly sure you don't have a permit for this assembly or permission to block traffic. Considering the possibilities, I'd suggest that you turn your people around and take them back where you came from, before we have to start arresting people."

"You and who else, girly?" laughed a tall gangly man with straggly hair sprouting from beneath a ballcap. "We have every right to march on this road, our tax dollars paid for it!"

"It seems quite obvious that you couldn't possibly have the intelligence to earn enough to pay taxes to cover the cost of the asphalt that goes into a pothole and, from the Crimson Tide decal on your hat, I'd guess that you aren't from Atlanta or maybe even Georgia. This is Bulldog country, you moron, so shut your mouth, before I take you in for being an obnoxious bigot."

"Fuck you, bitch!" shouted the man, waving his fist.

Hayes walked calmly up to the man, who was almost a foot taller than the Chief, pulled a black nightstick from her belt, and knocked him flat with one unmerciful blow to his left cheek. She took two steps back and the crowd erupted in laughter, a frenzy surging forward in an attempt to push through the blockade, but she pulled and pointed her pistol at a patch of grass next to the road and fired one shot. The insurgents froze, silent, unsure and unmoving, until the leaders of the Workers' protest with the giant 'You're Fired!' banner approached the intersection, singing, "We shall overcome!" to drown out the racist screams of the angry crowds lining the sidewalks.

Brad, Eddie, and a dozen Harleys set up barriers on either side of the street to shield the marchers and to keep them from precipitating a riot. A grizzly roar erupted from the rowdy intruders, who shoved Stanislawski forward to crowd the Police Chief, who dropped him to the pavement under hundreds of feet stumbling over his cowering body. Beal, Sheldon, and a phalanx of defenders repelled repeated surges attempting to break through security, on both sides of the road, to breech and halt the animated and vocal procession marching past with taunts and laughter.

Nellis leaned to Katherine, "Well, now we know how the television stations knew about the march."

"At least they're recording the right message. Our people are orderly and theirs are rioting!"

Two columns of police cruisers, followed by armored personnel carriers with squads in full riot gear eased along the curbs against the flow of bodies to reinforce the resistance and extend the blockade down Central Park to corral the counter-demonstrators.

The mayor and the protest leaders turned south on Piedmont and the rioters charged through the park and down Pine Street, to swarm through Renaissance Park, in an attempt to breach the blockade and fill the street just as the march arrived, but barricades and baton-wielding riot police held them at the sidewalks. Amped up rebels stormed the officers' line of shields again and again, shouting profanities in their faces, while their comrades chanted, "White Power!" "Lynch the Liberals!" and "Deport the Migrants!"

Nellis grabbed Katherine and Mavis to shield them from a torrent of deadly debris raining down on the security forces and the march leaders. Officers replied with volleys of teargas and flailing nightsticks in unyielding ranks to push the rioters back. Jessie and Benny shifted to either side of a determined mayor, who marched ahead without fear or hesitation. Someplace in the mayhem, a sports whistle trilled and, on cue, the counter-demonstrators scattered through the park to dissipate into the neighborhoods.

Mavis hugged Nellis, "It's getting dangerous to hang out with me, those bastards keep trying to take me out."

"Are you alright?" asked Katherine, brushing cement dust from her hair.

"Yeah, I'm fine," replied Mavis, pointing, "but…"

Katherine turned to Stanton, who was holding a handkerchief to a bleeding gash above his ear, Kate was tending to Jessie, who had a trickle of blood running down his forehead, and Sammy was sitting on the pavement rubbing his temple. "Oh my, here let me help."

They guided the injured to sit on silver metal furniture pieces on a pedestal in the Art Park on the far side of the street, just as a medical team appeared. Kate said, "These two guys have lacerations but our friend Sammy might have a concussion."

The medic leaned to inspect the wounds, while his female partner knelt down to check Sammy's eyes and press a gauze pad against a contusion on the back of his head. "I'm Phillip and this is Rachelle. These two gentlemen could use a couple of stitches and they'll probably have whopping headaches starting in the next few minutes."

Sammy pulled away and glanced at Jessie, "We survived getting the shit kicked out of us by that bastard down in Naples. We won't let this stop us."

Rachelle turned to her partner, "He got his bell rung but I don't see signs of a concussion."

"Patch me up, we've gotta get back to lead the march!"

"I noticed that you have some cars ferrying folks who couldn't make the hike, how 'bout we compromise and you agree to ride to the Statehouse, rather than me putting you in an ambulance?"

"Deal, get cracking, these folks are anxious to have their say."

Within minutes, the three were bandaged and a car circled around the block to pick up Stanton and Sammy, while Katherine, Kate, Jessie, and Nellis trotted along the sidewalk to catch up with the leaders.

The mayor asked, "What happened to our little friend, Sammy?"

"He got bonked in the head during that storm of stones and concrete. A medic confined him to one of the cars, Stanton too," replied Mavis.

Nellis moved to walk next to Mayor Turner, "Anyone got a plan about what's going to happen when we get there?"

Amy said, "Rumor has it that they've got a microphone and speakers on the steps to the governor's office."

"The street on that side of the building is fairly narrow, with the Legislative Office Building on the opposite side," commented the mayor. "If the cameras are set up for a speech, he knows the crowd will look small, even if we cram folks in."

Althea leaned in with a big smile, "The crowd for his speech will look small but we've got a mike set up on the steps of the main entrance on the west side of the building, where there's more room and I'm told that the television stations are sending choppers to cover the sheer size of the event!"

"I see no reason to share a stage with that racist bastard and I certainly don't give a damn about his excuses for the damage he's done to our state and our people," said the mayor quietly. "We'll march around the building, past his office, and finish on the front steps. He can come listen to us."

"There's a decision," said Jessie, rubbing his bandaged head. "I'd vote for you."

"I think you live in the wrong district, son," laughed Turner, "but I appreciate your approval and you taking that shot that was aimed at me."

"I lived here for several years and voted for you, because you're a leader with intelligence and compassion," said Kate. "I'm proud to walk with you."

"So, you gave up Hotlanta for Dolphin Bay?"

Kate laughed and hugged Jessie's arm, "No contest! It's got a gorgeous beach and way less traffic!"

"I think Atlanta's loss is Dolphin Bay's gain," said the major, over rowdy chants rippling along the endless procession.

Police secured every cross street with squad cars and uniforms, as the boisterous pageant marched through the edge of the Georgia State University campus and picked up hundreds of sympathetic students who melded into the throng.

The leaders emerged into Capitol Square on Piedmont and turned west on Mitchell, blocked by a thousand counter-demonstrators blocking the street to defend the governor's entrance, which was guarded by a squad of State Troopers in riot gear, who were accused in the local press of acting as Jasper Kline's private army.

"Damn!" swore Jessie, pushing Kate behind him. "These bastards show up everywhere!"

"Good thing there are more us than there are of them!" yelled Mavis, looking up to catch a glimpse of Jasper Kline's pudgy face peering down from a second story window, the confrontation erupted into a scuffle. "Bastard!"

Brad, Eddie, and the bikers, as well as Eagle Security and the city police were pinched off by the narrow street as the marchers' momentum propelled the leaders into the ambush. The State Troopers guarding the entrance made no attempt to restrain the rioters, who brandished ax handles and clubs to attack defenseless demonstrators.

A dozen men in black hoodies pushed through the front lines aiming for Mayor Turner, Althea, and Amy but Nellis, Jessie, Benny and Standler closed around the them, grabbing the pole bearing the 'You're Fired!' banner as a battering ram to charge ahead, knocking most of the attackers to the ground and heaving the rest tumbling back into their flailing troops.

Angry, profane, and terrified screams reverberated off the buildings, blurring into a pulsing piercing din washing over thousands of demonstrators pouring into Mitchell Street, their momentum driving the riot past the governor's entrance. Under the tension of hundreds of bodies pushing and shoving, the banner dowel snapped near the center eliciting a momentary panic as the attackers advanced and the demonstrators retreated a step.

The leaders at the front of the march grabbed the shards to form a flying wedge around the human cocoon protecting the mayor and trampled over the fallen rioters to battle through a vicious mob wailing away at everyone who happened into range, including women and children being carried along in the flood of humanity.

Television cameras captured the battle as a squadron of Harleys rumbled into the melee to separate the leaders from the attackers, just ahead of the city police and security who waded into the brawl from the west end of the street, gradually clearing a path through the gauntlet to open space on the far side of the plaza.

Benny released his grip on the mayor's jacket, "Are you okay?"

"I'm fairly sure I have all of you to thank for making it through that ambush alive." He shook Benny's, Nellis', Jessie's, and Standler's hands in turn. "I owe you guys."

"No, you owe these citizens, they need your help," said Nellis, hugging Amy and Althea.

"Then, let's tell the world the truth about who and what we're up against."

"And how we got here," added Benny.

Nellis grabbed Katherine's hand, "C'mon, we need to get to that mike before the governor's goons try to shut it down."

Swept along by a cresting wave of diversity, they raced across the crowded lawn to the broad staircase beneath a half-dozen towering columns, where they found a microphone and a narrow lectern on the first landing and a trio of uniformed guards backing into the entry. Nellis spied the escorted convertibles pulling up to the curb on Washington Street to discharge Sammy, Stanton, Tabitha, a dozen elders, and a well-guarded posse of children, who scrambled through the crowd to join their parents.

Kate took Mayor Turner's arm, "I think it only appropriate for you to open this protest with a frank and honest assessment of what we just endured. As you said, it's time for the world to accept who and what we're up against, so they can decide just whose side they want to be on. The networks are already showing clips of the riot, so I'm fairly sure you'll have a national audience."

The mayor smiled and waved his hand across the crowd, packed shoulder to shoulder in every direction, "By speaking truth to these patriots, I'll be including every beleaguered citizen in every state in the nation."

"Then, you choose the moment to begin."

He crooked a finger to Amy and Althea, "I know this is your show but…"

"You have to speak first, don't even ask," said Althea.

"This enormous demonstration just went international," added Amy. "This is your time and these are your people."

He glanced at the leaders gathering on the landing, then at the thousands and thousands of despairing souls who had been forged into an army of desperate determination by the violent confrontations with the militia of the oligarchs…and this was just the first skirmish in a battle to resurrect democracy from tyranny.

Mayor Turner stepped up to the microphone and stood there, silent and unmoving for several minutes, until the raucous din dissolved into silence. "Ladies and gentlemen, I must say that I am proud to have had the opportunity to march with each and every one of you. In spite of being intimidated and attacked, you joined into this incredible invincible army marching for all the oppressed and persecuted citizens of this country, who have been ostracized and discarded by this conspiracy. You are true patriots and you are the future of this nation! Give yourselves a hand!"

The commons exploded in applause and cheers.

"Something extraordinary happened today. A hundred-thousand patriots came together in cold dreary weather to speak with one voice, to expose the Republican con-game that has destroyed the very fabric of our society, dismantled our government, our rights, and our future, and wiped out an economy built by the middle-class, the backbone of our country."

Boooo's.

"As the world just witnessed, our peaceful gathering in the Meadow at Piedmont Park was disrupted by well-coordinated packs of counter-demonstrators attacking innocent people and, in order to assemble here, we had to fight through a raging gauntlet of paid thugs to demand our rights and benefits.

After the organized ambush over on Mitchell Street, we also demand the resignation of our corrupt governor, Jasper Kline, and his ignorant and deceitful legislature! Not at the next election, we want them impeached and carted away right now!"

Cheers.

"We demand an investigation and indictments of the money-men behind this madness, the people who crafted this campaign to destroy our democracy to satiate their greed and arrogance!"

"Yeah!"

"This is not simply a problem for Atlanta or the great state of Georgia. No, this conspiracy was years in the making, crafted to eliminate government in favor of feudal fiefdoms administered by a tiny group of rich white tycoons.

Look around at your neighbors, your compatriots, every one of them is suffering the same oppression, the same degradation and disparagement, but we all share a common determination to end our national nightmare!"

The crowd erupted.

"You have the power to demand change by marching and by voting in every election that comes up. It's not just about who's president or governor, it's about who's on the city council, who's on the school board, what are their goals and beliefs, are they righteous in their intentions or just pumping more swamp gas to cover their lies and malice?"

He paused, "We're not going to win this war today but we're sure going to shine a light on the cowards who accept money from the rich to deconstruct our democracy. The world is watching and we won't stop marching, we won't stop fighting for justice, and we sure as hell won't stop exposing the traitors, until our government is once again of, by, and for all the people of this great nation!"

The demonstrators screamed their approval.

Nellis leaned down to Sissy and whispered in her ear. She nodded and walked over to take Tabitha's hand and lead her to the podium. The old woman leaned to hug her, as the little sprite said, "Those bad people scared me so, that's why these people need to hear from you."

Tabitha straightened up to scan the thousands of gleeful faces, faces full of hope and resolve, faces willing to fight to reclaim their futures. She adjusted the microphone, "Ladies and gentlemen, my name is Tabitha Hall. I am the owner and publisher of The Dolphin Times, published in Dolphin Bay, Florida. My newspaper takes pride in accurately reporting the facts and the whole truth, as we learn it, every day. Many of you are here because of the articles that our marvelous writer, Kate Crocket, wrote about how this whole movement began with a handful of municipal workers trying to find a way to be valued, to be paid fairly, and to be treated as human beings.

Journalism has been called the fourth estate, because we're the citizens' watchdogs, tasked with keeping our elected officials honest by exposing the unvarnished truth behind the punditry and blather, and reporting those findings to you, the people. In every edition, we have an Opinions Page, where we and our readers can express thoughts, reflections, and objections openly, but real news in the rest of our newspaper is not based on opinions, it's based on irrefutable facts.

I'm sure we all expect our elected officials to exaggerate or bend the truth to justify their political positions but the nonsensical gibberish being spewed by Republicans on every level of government is not only laughably false but just another layer in a propaganda campaign to lull the ignorant into believing that everything they hear is bogus. It was Adolph Hitler's second commandment, 'Tell the big lie often enough and the masses will believe it.' By extension, our 'conservative' leaders have added, 'Admit nothing, blame your enemies, and distract the populous from every accusation with some outrageous gambit, a shiny object to draw our attention away from the real embarrassment'.

The only way to expose the lies is for you, every one of you, to take the time to learn your own truth from reliable sources, instead of falling victim to the hateful propaganda that's coming at us from every direction. Demand truth and nothing less than the truth…and then act on it!

I'm surrounded by people who have fought for your rights and your future. I believe in all of these splendid patriots and I believe in you, so I know that if we stick together we might just win our country back. To that end, we're organizing a one-day strike to draw attention to your plight and we'll get the word out as soon as a date is set. All People Matter!"

The plaza echoed with cheers.

She waited for the crowd to settle, "We'll hear short messages from most of these exemplary people in due time but, first, I want to introduce the lady who has gracefully accepted the role of spokesperson for 'All People Matter'. Please welcome Katherine Kennedy!"

Katherine kissed Nellis on the cheek and then Stanton, before she was surrounded by a herd of children who escorted her to the microphone, under the watchful eyes of their temporary biker nannies. Sam and Sissy took Tabitha's hand and guided her to Jessie and Kate amid cheers and applause.

"So, this is what democracy looks like!" She beamed with that radiant smile and paused to take in the sheer size of the crowd, the contagious roiling energy shared in the union of every kind of person – young, old, thin, fat, black, white, purple, green – and in these momentous hours, every one of them made the transition from terrified victim to engaged activist.

"How's everyone feeling now?"

The crowd exploded in raucous approval. A black girl in a vibrant blue jacket standing on the steps yelled, "We're doing just fine, lady!"

"That's what I want to hear! My name is Katherine Kennedy. Along with Stanton Spratlin, Nellis Gray, and a host of dedicated and fearless friends, we uncovered and exposed an attempt to buy an election in Cameron, Oklahoma, actually a bunch of elections, by a well-organized conspiracy of wealthy benefactors.

What we didn't realize was that those directors were working in coordination with a nationwide confederacy that infiltrated and stole elections in every state in the country, from your local school board to the Congress. And they've been working on this since the 1960's."

An angry murmur rippled through the crowd.

"It seems kind of obvious that they've got an incredible head start on us. They control the political machinery to elect their candidates to local, state, and national offices. They own the House and the Senate, with majorities in both, but they don't own the White House, yet."

The audience chanted, "Gonzalez, Gonzalez!"

"I have every admiration for our president, he's waging a righteous battle to preserve our nation against overwhelming odds. Think he needs some help?"

Cheers!

"How about if all of us get together to give him a hand?"

The plaza echoed with their approval.

"Nothing is going to change for any of us, until we take the responsibility to fight for what we know is right and true. We're going to march and rally and protest until we expose every lie, every false news story, every crafty insider deal or bogus piece of legislation, and every traitor who's participating in the destruction of our democracy and our society!"

Cheers.

"Our greatest weapon is our right to vote for candidates who represent our beliefs and who believe in our future. The leaders of the opposition have installed hand-picked candidates to pretend to be patriotic defenders of the Constitution when, in reality, they're dismantling the entire system piece by piece. The only solution is to find, nominate, and elect people who believe in the America our Founding Fathers intended."

Near silence.

"We're working very hard to put together a national committee to coordinate our efforts from coast to coast and we need every one of you to become an active representative in your community, to educate your friends and neighbors, and all the workers who are terrified about the prospect of losing their jobs, if they haven't lost them already.

The Republicans are selling fear and hate, blaming immigrants and minorities and liberals for their failures, and filling the airwaves with persistent propaganda lacking any trace of truth. They offer desperate workers someone to blame, someone to hate together, but they don't offer solutions, they don't propose legislation to ease the burden of the poor or the unemployed. In fact, they eliminate rights and benefits and cut taxes for rich people with the savings…instead of providing for the destitute, educating our children, fixing our roads, or cleaning up the environment and banning the pollution their sponsors' companies are producing.

We have to counter their most powerful incentive – HATE – with an even more powerful alternative – HOPE! We have to show their supporters, who find it easier to believe the lies, how to face their responsibility to demand truth. We have to convince those people that we can and we will take back our country, our place in society, and our dignity and we won't stop until we have attained complete victory for every American!"

Songs and chants rolled across the plaza, protestors danced with complete strangers, and the feeling of unity and purpose surrounded the golden dome of the Capitol building.

"We've got people in purple shirts going out to collect your information. Please fill out the short form. Give us a brief description of your situation and any talents or abilities that you might contribute to the cause. If you're part of an organized movement in your area, let us know. We want to include everyone everywhere and we need lots of worker bees to coordinate everything we're going to do, so sign up!"

Chapter Six

Mac Murphy slumped against the bar of the Tropical Paradise in Katie's Chicken House, with five empty jiggers lined up, chugging shots with practiced proficiency. His drooping bloodshot eyes keyed in on the fuzzy news reports of the worker's rally in Atlanta on an ancient television surrounded by garish bouquets of dusty blossoms dangling from shelves supporting hundreds of partially consumed bottles of booze, most dulled by a coat of grime accumulated over years and unmarred by human finger prints. "Tyrone Turner's running for president and that woman's going to become the mouthpiece for truth, justice, and the American fucking way, you watch!"

"How d'you know?" asked a barely sober Jack Hannah.

"He's got the right stuff - intellectual, principled, superior, even if he is a black guy. And that dame's gorgeous, sophisticated, and intelligent. Look at those faces, every guy in the crowd wants to jump her bones and they'd follow her anywhere just for a whiff of her scent."

"What stuff? Turner's an uppity black mayor struggling to govern a predominantly black southern city in a state ruled by Republican rednecks. And, a few minutes of media exposure doesn't translate into national elections."

"He's got the moxie to make the cabal's racist governor look scared and timid, while he looks classy and dignified rallying a homogenized crowd of more than a hundred-thousand, who are pissed off at what the rich white folks did to them. That carries a lot of weight in liberal circles."

"Yeah, but the entire system's rigged to elect Republicans. That's why you're going to make out like a bandit. The old-time straight-up conservative politicians don't stand a fucking chance," said Hannah, slugging a fourth Rhinegeist brew.

Murphy pointed at the energized crowds on the screen, "Those folks are mobilized and they're going to elect the next president. We need to be talking to them!"

"That's your audience already."

"Naw, my audience has the collective intelligence of a gnat. Most of them couldn't read a Dr. Seuss book, let alone a real newspaper, so they're easy prey for loony conspiracies, preposterous propaganda, and rabid religious bullshit." He pointed again, "Those folks had real jobs and real lives and now they don't. That's a lot of collective anger spread across every district in the country, except maybe Aspen or Palm Springs."

"So, how do you bring those people into the fold? Those folks might be pissed off but they're every color under the rainbow. Most of our listeners only see white."

"We give them someone to hate together and make endless outrageous promises that sound plausible enough to maybe, someday, rescue them from damnation. Somehow, we've got to convince them that all the boring pussies currently running for president are losers and I'm their guy. Which means we need a whole bunch of free publicity and the easiest way to get national coverage is to come up with something so outrageous, the press won't be able to resist putting it at the top of the broadcast or above the fold on the front page of the morning paper."

The studio manager stared at him, "What have you got in mind?"

"I don't know yet, it's brewing. Something really offensive - like Gonzalez isn't really American or he's got fourteen illegitimate children with ten different white women or he's gay!" He grinned, "One of those prove-you-didn't-do-it gambits."

Hannah took another sip and grinned, "Guilty until proven otherwise?"

"Something like that. Folks remember the scandal but they don't pay much attention when later reports say it was all a bunch of hokum."

"Then I suggest you get your shit together and dedicate tomorrow night's show to the patriots who demonstrated in Atlanta."

"I'll provide the fireworks, you make sure it's on the front page!"

~

Murphy staggered into the studio a half hour late, flopped a folder of cuttings from the latest conspiracy and propaganda rags on the desk, peeled off his jacket, loosened his tie, and eased down into the leather executive chair, spinning to pop a handful of amphetamines with a belt of bourbon from the bottom drawer. He leaned back, lit a cigar, and looked up at Hannah in the booth, with a big grin.

The intercom squawked, "You look like you're primed."

"I'm just hittin' my stride, brother. Count us down for liftoff into the stratosphere!"

"Live in four, three, two, and…"

"Good evening folks, this is Mac Murphy broadcasting unfiltered truth to the world from WBFK in the heartland of America on this beautiful Monday evening.

I'm sure most of you saw the rally and the staged 'impromptu' march on the Capitol in Atlanta on the television and I think far too many in our world are feeling that same desperate determination, because poverty and unemployment affect more than half the population of this country." He paused for a long toke on his cigar, "But it seems obvious to me that no one in the press bothered to mention that most of those folks were illegal immigrants, the endless unimpeded flood of freeloaders who have been invading our country to take away the jobs of real Americans.

The people who organized the protest are the same bunch of elite blowhards who survived that horrible attack on their secret rendezvous in Houston a couple of months ago. We know who they are and who's supplying the money to finance this charade and we'll call them out in due time. I'm guessing the whole production was staged to launch Mayor Tyrone Turner's entry into the presidential race and I guarantee that woman, Katherine Kennedy, who seems to be their annoyingly perky spokesperson and played it like an airhead debutante, I guarantee there are lots of naughty ghosts in her lingerie drawer."

He paused for another toke and sip of bourbon from his coffee cup, as a speed rush flooded through his brain and flexed every muscle in his body.

"But none of that should detract from the fact that there's a huge chunk of the working population in this country who are suffering brutal humiliation and hopelessness at the hands of the elite. Those bastards in Washington are destroying the middle class, sending jobs overseas, and the meager menial leftovers are going to thousands of criminals and vagrants streaming across the border!

We have to save American jobs in manufacturing, mining, energy, and construction. We have to toss out our ridiculous trade agreements that screw America's workers and institute training programs to prepare for the revolution that's coming. We know, if we all stick together, stand up for our rights, and defend the American dream, there's hope for every one of you, it's right out there on the horizon waiting for you to seize the future!"

He paused to chug and puff, "The folks who lost their jobs to robots or down-sizing or businesses moving someplace else, don't care why. They care about being able to provide for their families, keeping a roof over their heads and food on the table.

I say it's time we clean out the deadbeats in Congress, who fight and squabble and make fools of themselves and still can't seem to get anything done. Let's elect real patriots to support the next Republican president. We need a real American to lead this country, an independent rabble-rousing crusader, who doesn't owe a debt to anyone and doesn't give a damn about what people think, because he has the vision of what America should be and how we're going to get there.

We sure as hell have had enough of immigrant presidents, who came from who knows where, running a government that favors the rights of people of color at the expense of those of our majority, or plays pansy-kiss-ass with Wall Street to finance their campaigns. We need a badass who scares the crap out of our enemies and allies alike, because they won't have any doubt that our guy will defend this great country first, last, and always! So, put up, shut up, or get out of the way, because this country is about to relaunch the glory days. Our people will rise up to claim their rightful place in our society, to rebuild a roaring economy and insure the future for real Americans!"

He paused for another long snort and a deep tug on the stogie, "I'd like to thank so many of you, who have written, offered support, and contributed to my exploratory committee. I want you, all of you, who have given me a thousand good reasons to think long and hard about making a commitment to the salvation of this great nation and the sacrifices demanded by a national campaign.

I use the word salvation because I believe that our nation is under attack from within. There's a conspiracy to restrict our freedoms, brainwash our children, confiscate our weapons, and remove any reference to our Lord Jesus Christ from our society.

Hell, when I was a kid, we used to say the Pledge every morning and our principal, Mr. Edwards, would read a prayer over the intercom. No one was embarrassed because we all did it together and the grownups called it our civic duty. That doesn't happen anymore!

To all of those people out there who are struggling to get by, who have lost a job, or a home, or your dreams of a better future, I promise to do everything I can to bring attention to your plight and to force our useless government to step in to do what's right!

We know that Joe Casey, the boring socialist Senator from the great state of Wisconsin, has thrown his hat into the ring for the Democrats, along with sad old Vice-President Morton, who should have been put out to pasture decades ago. Then there's Governor Billy Estes from South Carolina - who just barely got re-elected by his own people, chubby Charles Garner from Florida - who's got scandals of his own, and Sam Trippet - an up and coming loudmouth junior representative from New Mexico, lining up for the Republican nomination. We all know there will be dozens more playing with the narcissistic notion that they have the right stuff to lead this nation to glory, when the rest of us already know they haven't got a snowflake's chance in hell, no matter how much money they've got backing their crusades.

Most of them, no, all of them have proven time and again that they don't have a clue or give a damn about what's ailing this country and haven't the faintest idea of how to fix it. They haven't experienced the tyranny and repression people are up against out here in the real world. They've never worried about feeding or clothing their kids. They've never been fired, laid off, disgraced, humiliated, passed over in favor of someone who fills their boss's demographic standards, or been kicked out of their homes.

It's going to take a big dog in Washington to force these bastards to rescind all their stupid rules and regulations that discriminate against regular people, real Americans, in favor of worthless minorities and filthy immigrants. It's going to take someone with vision to fight for America's place in the world, to stop throwing billions of dollars away on allies who won't stand up for us in the United Nations. Let's eliminate, so called, 'humanitarian aid' for places we've never heard of, in favor of using that money to reduce people's taxes here at home or investing in rebuilding our infrastructure. Our roads and bridges are falling apart, our ancient railroads are a joke, and our airports are decades out of date.

We need someone who doesn't give a damn about what the establishment thinks, someone strong enough to force them to do the business of government for the people they represent...or resign! We need someone who truly possesses authentic patriotism to lead this great nation back to pride and purity, to being the country we all believe in, the country we'd fight and die to protect, the country we want to hand over to our children!

So, with great humility I'm pleased to say that, after long consideration, I think I'm your man!"

Even in the soundproofed studio, he could hear Milly Clark, who was supposed to be covering the phones out in the front office, running down the hallway screaming, "Holy Shit! Jack Hannah get your ass out here before these callers melt every piece of wire in this building!"

A grinning Murphy leaned back, took another big swig from the bottle, and exhaled a huge plume of smoke, "I'm ready to jump into the battle for all of you. So, if we're going to turn this into a real campaign to go after all these nitwits who couldn't find their own butts in a dark closet, then we're going to need your help and support.

We're going to need people to organize meetings and rallies, go door-to-door to convince their neighbors that there is hope in this great land, and for everyone to send what you can to finance our campaign, so we can hire good people who know how to turn a dream into a presidential crusade. I'm not going to accept PAC money or big corporate contributors who want to own their candidates, so, I'm counting on all of you, every one of you, to put your heart and soul into changing the future. I appreciate every contribution you send to Murphy for President, at WBFK, P.O. Box 1040, Cincinnati, Ohio.

For all you patriots out there, I believe that, if we all join together to stand up for our traditional values, we can take this thing all the way to the White House!"

Jack Hannah managed to run the jingle, while juggling multiple phone lines, and add his announcer's voice, "This has been Mac Murphy broadcasting unfiltered truth to the world from WBFK in the heartland of America.

Send your contributions to Murphy for President, at WBFK, P.O. Box 1040, Cincinnati, Ohio, and we'll send you a first edition 'Murphy for President' bumper sticker by return mail!

Tune in tomorrow night for your next dose of reality from our presidential candidate - Mac Murphy! I'm producer Jack Hannah, thank you and good night."

~

Milly Clark answered the phone in the office, "WBFK, how may I direct your call?"

Murphy's voice was raw and gravely, "Morning Milly, it's Mac. How're things?"

"Well, I quit at midnight, put the phones on the answering service, and went home exhausted. Last count was twenty-one hundred calls, messages, and pledges for contributions, and they're still coming. These people are nuts about you, even if you do sound like you smoked three packs of Lucky's and swallowed a flaming frog."

"That's wonderful but, if Hannah was doing his job, it would be twenty-thousand!"

Exasperated, she snapped, "Hang on and I'll put you through."

The line clicked and Hannah picked up, "Rough night?"

"Where the fuck is our coverage? Nothing in the Times or the Post, hell, all we got was a two-inch column on the back page, behind the obits, in the Enquirer! The editors are pissing all over themselves, mooning over Sam Trippet, and we get nothing?"

"You rushed into it before I had a chance to get some pro's on board to organize our media and spread the word. I'm drafting a press release that will go out today and, oh by the way, you did get some time on the news channels this morning, as the closing joke."

"Who was it that said there is no such thing as bad press?"

"If you're going to run a campaign, then we have to at least make it appear that it's a real campaign with paid workers who know what the fuck they're doing, who know how to plant a story that sticks, how to twist an arm for public support from people who count, and how to cover up your bad habits and nasty disposition."

"You're a son of a bitch, you know that?"

"For the moment, I'm your sonofabitch, now get a grip. You decided to do this, so either do it right or shut up. Get sober, work on tonight's program and don't talk to anyone about anything until I have time to get at least a few wheels rolling. Are we together on this? 'Cause, if not, I've got a radio station to run."

"Yeah, man, I'll get my shit together and you do your job!"

The phone went dead and Hannah looked up to find Milly leaning against the door jam, "Are you sure he's up to pulling this off?"

"We both know it's all a show with him, he doesn't believe half the nonsense that comes out of his mouth, it's just a part he's playing and, who knows, maybe he'll con his way into the White House."

"I'll believe that when I see it."

"Stranger things have happened," laughed the studio manager. "I need to make some calls. Would you see if you can figure out some way to organize and respond to all those calls and messages?"

"Sure boss, I'll just snap my fingers and have that for you momentarily."

"Hey, I don't know shit about running a political campaign, let alone a campaign for President of the United States. Are you kidding me?"

"It's more than just kind of bizarre," replied Milly. "This could be a riveting ride but you've gotta put a leash on that bastard or it's all gonna blow up in our faces."

"Roger that," replied Jack, dialing.

~

Murphy poured two fingers of Bourbon into his coffee and a little cream to grease his organs, which were not responding after a rowdy night of overindulgence. He tottered out onto the tiny deck overlooking a barren thatch of woods standing guard around a few Junipers whistling and moaning in a relentless northerly gale, and wrapped his thin bathrobe around his soft body, his hand shaking violently as he lifted the cup to his lips and sipped.

He coughed and spat and sipped again, *"Whose idea was this anyway and why would any sane person even consider wasting a vote on a sleazeball like me?"*

The wind buffeted his loose robe but offered no resolution to the quandary.

"It's your own damned fault, your ego's bigger than your brain. You better figure out how to lasso this stallion before it heads off at a full gallop or you'll kill yourself through your own stupidity."

He slugged the now cold coffee. *"You're never going to get through this performance, keep the stream of consciousness flowing with endless bullshit to charge up the nutcases and the press, and appear to be the smiling energetic all-American candidate they expect you to be…unless you find a doctor to schedule the ups and downs to coincide with being in character, being that Martin McClintock Murphy, instead of a schmuck hiding out in this hovel."*

He had hoped that a blast of frigid air might rekindle his sparking brain but, instead, tremors wracked his body and he dropped the cup, which shattered into tiny white shards exploding across the dark cedar planking, as he staggered inside and across the room to collapse on the couch amid a slow-motion avalanche of food sacks, pizza boxes, discarded newspapers, a minefield of empty bottles, and a half-dozen overflowing ashtrays that had ejected their contents across the grimy Persian carpet.

~

Jessie reeled in his line and placed the rod across his knees, watching Johnny's lithe body react to the tiniest ripple or splash, his concentration totally tuned to the environment but nothing was biting. A pair of gulls swept effortlessly across the water, the orange sun's radiance transforming them into golden flames sweeping against an indigo sky above the barren moonscape that once was The SunnyBreeze Resort.

A stubble of fuzzy tufts sprouted from beneath the desolate sandy key into patchy carpets of the faintest green, first hint of nature's ability to erase all trace of human blunders by reforesting the wounded land with new life. He spotted a pair of bobcats bounding across the vast emptiness and pointed, "Bobcats!"

Johnny relaxed and turned to watch them play, "Nothing biting."

"Nope, but it sure is beautiful out here. This is the magic light."

"How come you're not painting?"

"Actually, I've started a couple of paintings in the studio. The first is going to be our alligator friends, George and his family in the little cove, because that's a very special memory I share only with you."

The boy blushed, as he tucked his rod into the clips along the inside of the hull. "What's the second?"

"The second one is my recollection of all those thousands of hopeful faces looking up, while Mayor Turner was talking at the Capital in Atlanta. They were transformed from being terrified and desperate victims when they arrived, to being empowered to rebuild the country we all believe in and they're willing to fight for it."

"Yeah, I couldn't believe how many people were out there, all sorts of people, and they were all together because they were scared about how they're gonna survive."

"You've been talking to your mom about this, huh?"

"Yeah, can't help it, the phone's ringing all the time, the dining room table's covered with stacks of paper, and she's been up to work with Miss Kennedy twice in the past two weeks."

"There's a lot going on and she's right in the middle of it."

"Yeah, I know," laughed Johnny, "but I'm pretty sure she's having the best time she's ever had."

"That's good, she deserves to be valued for the person she is, besides being a great mom."

"Yeah, you're right."

"Tell me about what you found, when you rascals escaped into the crowd at the rally?"

"You're not mad?"

Jessie hugged him, "I care what happens to you and I'm protective of you. That was a dumb stunt, but you already know that, so I hope you'll consider including me or your mom, before you go wandering off again."

"Okay."

"Hey, I'm not mad but I am curious about how you interpreted what you saw. That has to be the biggest crowd you've ever seen."

"It was way bigger than the crowd in the square downtown and scarier too."

"Why?"

"Because, there were some pretty strange people out there, everyone yelling really loud, jumping around, and waving signs. I felt like a midget caught in a huge wave, when they started fighting and we got carried along with the crowd and lost sight of the little kids. I was so scared that we'd never find our way back to save them, that they were going to get trampled or someone might try to steal them."

"There are consequences to our choices and disaster can strike in a flash," said Jessie. "A long time ago, I was involved in some demonstrations, while I was in college, and I learned that the first rule of being in a large crowd is knowing where the exits are and how you're going to get yourself and whoever you're with to safety when the trouble starts."

"It was scary."

"Yeah, but you haven't answered the question, did you feel the energy?"

"Before they started fighting, I felt like there was some kind of really strong connection between all those people, when everyone was packed together listening to the speeches and dancing to the music."

"You noticed that there were lots of weird people, all kinds of people gathered together to find help and support in each other, to find hope for the future of their families. That's what this is all about," said Jessie.

"Why are the bad guys trying to stop it?" asked Johnny.

"They work for some very rich people who want to own everything and don't want to be forced to pay their fair share to keep the country running. They're selfish jerks but we're going to show the people a better way."

"That's cool, but I don't think I'm ready to jump into those crowds again without you."

"Deal. What'd you think of Sissy and Sam and all the other kids?"

"I liked them a lot. I'm pretty sure the Spratlins are rich but the girls are just like my friends at school."

"You and Sam are pretty close to the same age."

"She's five months older than me."

"You like her, I can tell," laughed the artist.

Johnny blushed.

"We'd better head home before our girls start worrying about us."

"Yeah, my mom always gives me that look, when we're going fishing," said the boy, pulling the rope on the little Johnson.

"Well, we did kind of push the limits on that one, didn't we?" He laughed, "On the other hand, there really was no other choice and a lot of people are alive today, because we did something completely crazy together."

Johnny dropped Jessie at the dock and headed around the point and across the bay to his family. Gracie bounded across the lawn, as the artist traipsed up the steps, prancing around and around, yelping. He leaned the rods into a corner next to the back door and knelt down for a hug and a slathering. "How's my girl? Have you been looking after Kate for me?"

Gracie cocked her head and nuzzled the screen door open. They had acquired some new furniture to replace the remnants of Jessie's bachelor days, destroyed in the bogus police raid, shopped for new kitchenware and replenished the staples, and repainted the room a deep dusky gray with warm rust doors and molding while it was empty. The most glaring reminder was the plywood covering the empty spaces on either side of the front door, where two stained-glass floral panels were shattered. Jessie claimed to be thinking about designs for new glass panes but she had yet to see the sketches.

Kate turned from the sink for a kiss and a hug, "Did you guys catch anything?"

"Naw, it was pretty quiet."

"Get a chance to talk?"

"Yeah, he's got a very mature view of all of this, although he admitted that being caught up in the crowd scared him big time."

"You just want to hug them to be sure they're safe."

"He's special and so is whatever you're cooking, smells like garlic."

"My mom's lasagna and a big salad."

"I'm not worthy."

"I'll agree with that," laughed Kate, offering a glass of Merlot.

"How was your day?"

"Oh, you know, nothing spectacular…just trying to write three different articles and a half-dozen press releases for All People Matter, a meeting with Tabitha, and an hour on the phone with Mavis and Katherine. I have to fly up there for a day or two next week to meet the Public Relations people."

"Weren't you the gal who was just going to come back to cover a rally back when?"

"I was the gal who was dumb enough to give you a second chance and you get us kidnapped and locked up in a disgusting abandoned jail on our first date!"

Jessie burst out laughing, "At least it was memorable."

"Yeah, pretty much everything with you is memorable, if not terrifying!"

He kissed her and Gracie whined. "Are you jealous?"

The Shepherd rubbed against their legs. "Or are you just hungry?"

"I spent way too much time on the phone too and I'm pretty sure they want to try to have at least one major protest every couple of weeks in cities across the country, through the summer and into the fall, culminating with a gigantic rally in Washington right before the election." He paused, "And a sudden realization that real life continues in spite of our preoccupation! Planning sessions for my Art's Important camp start next week and I'm going to have to figure out how to schedule all of this."

"Can't some of the other artists fill in when you need to be gone?"

"Yeah, I'll work it out but I can't neglect the kids, they're what this is all about."

"It's about people deserving better," replied Kate, with a smile. "I get the symbolism of that last rally but I'd be voting for someplace warm and symbolic, November can be cold as hell in D.C."

"But you grew up in Wisconsin!"

"Yup, and I'm never going through another one of those winters ever again. Twenty-four of them were more than enough."

"Yeah, there were some days walking to class when I wondered whether they'd find my body frozen in midstride climbing Bascom Hill, in the spring when everything thawed."

She picked up Gracie's bowl from the counter and set her dinner on the floor, with a pet, then walked over to the open back door. "I don't think it gets any more beautiful than this."

He wrapped his arms around her, "It's far more beautiful since you got here."

"You're gonna have a hard time getting rid of me."

"Good."

Nellis fixed up an office in Nanny's bedroom for Katherine and had two telephone lines installed, along with high speed internet and computers. She considered using her office at Stanton Oil but the very idea seemed awkward on so many levels, with Spratlin's political affiliations in Washington and, after working in the executive suite for so many years, the chilling realization that a fair percentage of the workforce were far more sympathetic to the white-nationalists than All People Matter.

They held full administrative gatherings in the hotel downtown but most of the crucial plans or agreements were drawn up over coffee on the porch or long walks through the early spring gardens and the pecan grove. Nellis' steel gate, an emotional barrier against the outside world for too many years, stood open, welcoming activists from across the country.

He cooked delicious feasts for all who happened to be in attendance and it was not unusual to find people sleeping in the guest room, on the couch and floor in the living room, even folks curled up on the lounge on the porch with a passel of dogs.

Nellis stepped over several bodies on his way to the kitchen to start the coffee, fed a couple of logs into the wood stove, and strolled over to a small shed standing on the barren pad of his barn, surrounded by a herd of chatty dogs, bleating goats, meowing cats, and a flutter of clucking chickens, to fill and place bowls, separated by discreet and well-practiced boundaries to eliminate competition.

He pondered whether the invasion of guests might subside in the fall, before harvest time, and whether he'd have a new barn to cure his crop. They might be trying to save millions of people but there was a smaller audience, who depended on his product and others who benefitted from the profits. It was getting close to planting time, as soon as the last chance of a freeze passed by, and having folks wandering in and out unannounced might prove awkward.

Kate strolled across the driveway and Gracie whined and wagged her tail, trotting over to circle around her legs. She gathered a lavender sweater around her body against the chill and raised her cup, "Good coffee and a beautiful morning, what more could we ask?"

Nellis laughed, "World peace, good will to all God's creatures, and all that crap."

The other dogs gathered around for a pet and she knelt to greet each in turn, gazing around at pale purple redbuds, pink and white dogwoods, pockets of quince amid waves of yellow daffodils blooming in beds around the drive, Saucer Magnolias sprouting creamy magenta spikes, and black walnut and pecan trees showing tiny green pips peeking from bare branches. "I'm entranced with this glimpse of your paradise waking from winter."

"I'm always behind but somehow I keep it going. Nanny, my deceased wife, saw it all in her head long before anything ever got planted and we kept adding stuff, year after year, until it matured. My kids are the fourth generation to grow up on this land but Nanny was the first to transform it into a garden."

"She had quite a talent."

"Many."

"I'm sorry you lost her."

"Cancer, long story that didn't end well." He looked across the gravel to a golden beam of sunrise setting the porch aglow, "But now, in spite of my cranky disposition, Katherine's made the old farmhouse a home again and it feels right."

She hugged him, "What's happening with the barn?"

"Well, the insurance company is dinking around but we all know they haven't a chance in hell of finding the bastards who did this, let alone making them pay, so they're just wasting time and treading water. I've got to get things rolling in the next couple of weeks, before storm season gets started."

"Maybe we could do an old-fashioned barn raising. I'm bettin' we could get all the help we could ask for."

Nellis laughed, "Actually, Spratlin sent his construction crew over the last time it fell down and he's offered their help again, as soon as I get the money from the insurance for the lumber, just to keep everything on the up and up."

Kate's eyes twinkled, "Does this happen often?"

"Well, the last time was a direct hit by a tornado, which is how I got to know Sissy and Samantha, and then there was the Representative who was pissed off because I exposed his racist past, so he pulled out this huge gun and put a round between his own eyes right outside the gate, and a midnight raid by a bunch of chicken-shit Klan guys, who beheaded Chester, my pet pig, and impaled him on that post over there. Guess they figured I hadn't got the message when we hooked up with y'all, so they came back to burn down the new barn, just to make sure."

"Before Jessie dragged me, kicking and screaming, into all of this, I flew around the country writing articles about exclusive resorts and ostentatious private homes, which paid me a nice living but left me feeling…not envious really, more…empty and appalled by the disparity of outrageous opulence against the crushing reality that the other ninety-nine percent are facing. It never dawned on me that the rich megalomaniacs, who owned those palaces, planned the destruction of the middle-class, until I got involved with hundreds, no, thousands of families in Dolphin Bay."

"Then add the next step – that they have an army of loyal enforcers, who don't mind getting their hands dirty, and they're everywhere. We caught a bunch of good 'ol boys, who planned on murdering Maybelle Brown and her children," he pointed to the lane, "because that Representative raped her again and again for years. I can guarantee they were replaced before they had their rights read to 'em in jail."

"You want to believe that we're past all that but we're not." She shook her head, "We got kidnapped by a bunch of fake cops, when we were just getting the protest organized, and it turned out that those bullies were taking orders from a construction oligarch. Since all that happened, I've been reading about how fascist and communist regimes in Europe employed private armies to eliminate the competition and create chaos in all the key assets that allow a society to function - like freedom of assembly, freedom of movement, an unbiased court, and a free press."

Nellis grinned, "Combined with an avalanche of propaganda blaming every problem and failure on the opposition or a minority group, while promoting the glories of maintaining the purity within their culture or race that's threatened by hordes of inferior people invading the country. When all the pieces are in place, they'll dummy up some fake calamity and postpone elections, so they can take complete control.

There's nothing new in any of their moves, our ignorant voters don't care about history, so they don't understand what's really happening, because it hasn't happened in this country since Joe McCarthy commandeered the great Communist scare in the Fifties. These gangsters just picked up where he left off."

She took his arm, "I need more coffee."

"Well, you're a cup ahead of me. Let's go see if there's any left on the stove before these freeloaders drink it all."

The dogs perked up and bounded across the yard to greet a parade of children marching up from the little red bridge. Sissy ran to hug Nellis, "I've missed you."

"Me too! We've all been doing grown up things, which is a terrible excuse for neglecting my favorite girlfriend, but I propose a game of chess this afternoon after school."

"You don't stand a chance," replied the little sprite with a gleam and a smile.

"We both know, I've just been letting you win," snickered Nellis.

"Oooo, now I'll have to make you suffer, before I force you to concede," laughed Sissy.

"Are you that good or is he that bad?" asked Kate.

"It's not that he's a bad player, he's just predictable and that makes him easy prey."

"Well, just from being around him, I know that Nellis is an extraordinarily intelligent man, so that means that you must be a prodigy."

Sissy curtsied, "Most grownups don't give little girls much credit."

"Oh, I think we all notice," said Nellis. "It's more a matter of trying to keep you from letting your many gifts go to your head! Aren't you late for school or something?"

"Has he had his coffee this morning?" asked Samantha, "He seems kind of grumpy."

"Actually, I was on my way to find my first cup, until you children interrupted."

"Then, maybe we should go," giggled little Hubie.

"But I'll be back this afternoon to take my revenge," added Sissy with a hug.

Nellis kissed the top of her blond head, "You children be careful on your way to school and work hard at your lessons. I promise you'll find most of it useful, when you get to be an adult."

"Does that mean it's completely useless until we get old?" asked Daniel, with a wry grin.

"You're just way too quick this morning, now git before you're late!"

"Yes, Sir," moaned the children, as they trooped down the lane.

"They're a brilliant bunch," said Kate. "You're lucky to have them around to keep you young and honest!"

"I think I lost both of those a long time ago," laughed Nellis. "Now, can I please have a cup of coffee and five minutes to read the front page of the paper?"

"Come along."

Sammy was propped up on the lounge, wrapped in a blanket, cuddling Momma Betsy and her brood of rambunctious kittens, and offered a groggy, "Good morning."

"Good morning to you," said Kate, leaning into the rolling tangle to pick up a gangly gray fur-ball for a nuzzle.

"Sleep okay?" asked Nellis.

"Yeah, I have a porch like this that looks out over Dolphin Bay and there's nothing more soothing than falling asleep to the sounds of nature."

"Roger that. There's supposed to be coffee inside, if y'all haven't drunk it all."

"I'll take a cup, if you find some."

"Can do."

Nellis found Benny, Althea, and Amy hunkered around the dining room table with printouts of the morning's headlines, which were far more timely than the thin Cameron Gazette he plopped on the table. "Fine morning."

"That remains to be seen," said Benny, yawning and rubbing bloodshot eyes.

Kate laughed, "You have no one to blame for your misery but yourself."

"Amen, sister, amen."

"Did you see that right-wing blowhard, Mac Murphy, has announced that he's running for president?" Asked Althea.

"He's a crank with lots of fanatical opinions but no credentials to run anything."

"Sounds like he's in it for the fame and glory," said Kate, "not serving the country."

"Ah, he's a joke. He'll get a little bump from the announcement but, without major donors, he'll be history in a month," said Amy.

"Who's for real?" asked Nellis.

"So far, it seems like Governor Grant, from North Carolina, Senator Willis from Texas, but the big money's behind Creighton Steil – handsome, charming, sleazy, sadistically homophobic and reportedly gay, radical evangelical former governor of Indiana," said Althea.

"Other than being a closet queen, he's everything the far right could want in a candidate, totally dedicated to the nutcase fringe and obsessed with reducing everything about the federal government to ashes," added Benny. "He's the personification of the looming threat that All People Matter is fighting."

Nellis grinned, spying Katherine in the doorway of her tiny office, the yellow nail polish on her slender toes peeping beneath the hem of a long blue gown, "There's fairly strong evidence that the cabal behind the destruction of the economy are placing heavy bets on him."

"Why would they take a chance running a gay person? If we know, everyone knows," said Althea.

"Good question but he voluntarily and enthusiastically spouts the party line, and he's famous for signing the most brutally restrictive anti-gay legislation in the country, even if it was overturned by the courts, so we can be fairly confident that he's more than an ambitious soldier taking his marching orders from on high. Either way, we need to research every facet of his life," said Katherine, "and every other plausible opponent."

"Anyone stepping up for the Democrats," asked Nellis.

"Vice-President Morton but he's so buttoned up and boring, I don't think he's got a chance," said Kate. "Governor Davidson from Massachusetts is making exploratory noises and Vincent Paul from California seems to be everywhere these days."

"Any movement from Mayor Turner."

Katherine shook her head, "I called him last week to see if he wanted to participate in the rally in Chicago next month. He seemed interested but dismissed being a candidate out of hand."

"He'd be good for the country," said Nellis.

"That's why he won't run," said Sammy, still wrapped in the blanket. "He understands the game and how vicious our enemies will be."

"I love President Gonzalez," said Amy, "but he never had a chance to move any major legislation through the Republican logjam. We need someone strong enough to bulldoze the far right."

"I'm fairly sure other candidates will surface," said Nellis, "there's still time to mount a campaign."

"Name one major personality who'd be dumb enough to waste a run against a stacked deck. The Republicans hold all the cards, for the moment, and they're on track to elect their guy, unless hell freezes over first," said Katherine. "We have to be smart enough to emulate their model and concentrate our efforts on building up from the grass roots and that means being active in every district in the country."

"You sound like you've got a roadmap all laid out," said Nellis.

"We're getting there, steadily moving towards a consensus," smiled Katherine, "and we're not going to let millions of citizens fall into poverty without a fight."

~

Stanley French stood at the massive window looking south across Long Island Sound through fog and drizzle from Conrad Blaho's magnificent estate on Field Point, south of Greenwich. He sipped fine scotch from a heavy crystal tumbler, "Is that Great Captain's Island out there with the faint light blinking in the mist?"

"Yes, it is," replied his host, COO and heir to the vast holdings of Lebanon Steel. "There's a lighthouse and keepers lived out there from 1829 until 2003, when the structure was deemed dangerously dilapidated and outdated. The light you see is automatic and solar powered."

"There's something romantic about a couple or a family living out there for years, surviving treacherous storms, man against the sea," said John, French's eldest son. "Yet another industry that's eliminated overhead through automation."

"It can't be that many workers," said his younger brother Michael.

"You'd be surprised," replied Will Terry, genius behind the massive propaganda campaign. "There are lighthouses all along this coast, because these were treacherous waters for sailing ships arriving from England. Even if the lights are unmanned, most of them are still warning sailors to avoid the dangers."

"How'd you know that?" asked Ethan Tomlinson. "You're a California boy."

"Actually, I was born in Massachusetts and didn't head west until I went off to college, so this is home to me."

"I'll be damned," said Tomlinson, "you never cease to amaze me."

"Let's keep it that way," laughed the cinematic mastermind.

French turned back to the small group gathered around an octagonal table before a roaring fire in the native stone hearth that warmed the great room against the chill. His grown sons, John and Michael, and a well-groomed group of peers were being trained in strategies to guide the campaign to maturity. After a half-century of zealous diligence, spawned at that first meeting with Blaho and Tomlinson at the ranch to hatch a strategy, they adhered to a ruthless allegiance to fulfilling the goal of complete deconstruction of the government in order to re-institute the natural social order, established at the dawning of civilization, where the masses serve at the pleasure of their Aryan masters.

Modern democracy evolved as a unique form of government to embrace equality and universal civil rights during the past hundred years or so, but, as their campaign approached the brink of ultimate triumph and absolute control, it would appear that over the course of history, this would prove to be a minor interruption in the tradition of domination by the few.

He was amused that the profits from his firm, Dynamic Devices, which had grown to become the single largest defense contractor for the United State Military, had financed the crusade against the status quo. Within the next few years, the Defense Department would be taken over by private contractors, his private contractors.

He walked over to the table and lifted his glass, "Gentlemen, I believe that success is within our reach, if we can find and promote a strong, dedicated candidate to become our next president. Do we have a consensus?"

"The polls have Willis, from Texas, as the early leader," said Michael.

"That bastard is stupid enough to believe his own evangelical bullshit," replied Conrad. "He's an idiot."

"Well, second is former Governor Jeffrey Grant from North Carolina," added John. "He's a traditional conservative and he's got solid credentials and a broad following. In fact, he won sixty-seven percent of the vote in his second election."

"Are we forgetting that he refused to sign our abortion bill because he wanted women who were raped or carrying dead babies to be exempt," blustered Blaho. "He can't be trusted."

"Then we're down to the third choice, Creighton Steil, who's proved his loyalty time and again, while he was Governor of Indiana. We made a lot of progress with his help," said Tomlinson.

"But he's a fucking faggot! Everyone knows that," yelled the steel magnate.

French took a sip and smiled, "I think that's the point, we control him, we own him, and he'll do as he's told."

Will Terry added, "He's great on camera, not afraid to spout unfathomable horseshit with that pious look of sincerity. Middle America will eat that up and, even if the truth comes out, we'll have a deflection campaign ready to go. We can cover that."

"Is there anyone else, who's willing to run and worthy of consideration?"

Michael volunteered, "There are lots of people running or making loud noises about running and almost all of them have been through our courses, but each is flawed in one way or another. Whether it's weird sex, questionable investments, or awkward associations, they all have something to hide that could sink a campaign."

"What about that loudmouth radio guy, Mac Murphy?" asked French.

Tomlinson started laughing, "That guy's a drunk speed-freak who makes his money by keeping the crazies totally charged up over complete bullshit. There's no way he's going to appeal to a broad spectrum of the electorate. He's a delirious loser, a flash in the in the pan, who'll be dismissed and forgotten before the ink's dry on tomorrow's first edition."

French shook his head, "That's the kind of guy who builds a grass roots following that could prove inconvenient, if he can keep it together."

"We'll make sure he can't," said Terry. "I can have a series of ads ready by next week and I'll make sure they make him look like a horse's ass."

"How about a horse's turd?" asked Blaho.

"Done."

Chapter Seven

Murphy stumbled across the living room, shielding his eyes against blinding sunshine slashing through gaps in the disheveled curtains, a terminal hangover in a tattered plaid bathrobe with every intent of murdering the moron pounding on his front door. He fumbled with the latch and pulled the door open to find Jack Hannah, with two other men. "What the fuck could you possibly want at this hour?"

"It's ten-thirty and you were supposed to meet me at the station at nine," replied the studio manager, grabbing his robe to push him back into the muddle piled knee-deep throughout the house. "You smell like shit and this place is disgusting! What the hell do you think you're doing?"

"Just getting primed, brother, getting the juices flowing."

"Bullshit!" shouted Hannah. "If we're going to do this, then you have to be on board twenty-four/seven. I can't see any reason why any sane person would even consider running a campaign for a complete loser, a total fraud, knowing that he's going to self-destruct and we're gonna lose before we get started. Why should I or anyone go through hell trying to keep you in line, while pundits and comedians get laughs at the travesty you'd make of the presidency."

"But I…"

"No 'but's', either you're in all the way or we're out of here."

Murphy gazed around the once fine room, now trashed beyond recognition, eyeing an open bottle of Bourbon on the mantle with two fingers of whiskey in the bottom. He licked his lips, "Fine, you win."

He shuffled through the debris, "Who are these bums you brought with you?"

"This is Shepherd Stone, political operative from Boston, who's going to run the campaign."

Stone offered his hand but Murphy ignored it and stepped closer, "Why would you want to work on a campaign of a drunken bum like me?"

"Because I think you know how to strike a tone that resonates with a huge audience that's never voted as a block, because they never had anyone with the guts to address their grievances or say what they're thinking. You might be a nutcase but you're their spokesman, you reinforce their belief that they've been left behind by international corporations and 'progress' that eliminates their jobs. They worry about keeping their guns, defending their church, and preserving their Angloheritage and you give them common enemies to blame for their problems."

Murphy looked up at him, "We both know I'm just a con artist spouting bullshit."

"It's bullshit to people who actually have a clue about what's going on in the world but you don't seem to realize that your people take great pride in the fact that they live inside a rural bubble and you're one of the only sympathetic links with an outside world they believe threatens their very existence. That's powerful stuff."

"What's your politics?"

"I have the singular goal of exposing and embarrassing the corruption of the status quo. That's not left or right, really, it's just that modern society has always been governed by the same elite class of arrogant gentry pulling strings from their mansions and penthouses. Our leaders conspire to look after themselves and their sponsors, they toss out programs to help the poor or provide minimal health care or cleaning up the environment but those are just social band-aids to prolong the charade. The working people of this country are being systematically eliminated from the economy by those same oligarchs and they're ready to revolt."

He fixed on Murphy's bloodshot eyes, "The All People Matter movement is just getting started but, in spite of the fact that, ultimately, we share a common enemy, they definitely don't appeal to your audience. They might speak for some angry voters but I think you could lead a political revolution, if you're willing to take on the character of white crusader defending all that America used to stand for…God, guns, and the Constitution."

Murphy turned to the other man, without responding, "And who's this?"

"This is Dr. Theodore Billings, who's going to help you to be ready when we need you and resting when we don't."

"Dr. Feelgood, huh?" replied Murphy, with his hands on his hips, his robe hanging open, looking the man up and down. "What you got in your little black bag."

"From the looks of you, I'd guess that you couldn't survive a short sprint, let alone the marathon that we're going to have to endure between here and the convention. I'm going to help you maintain your edge through the months ahead and we're going to depend on modern science to transform a drunk second-rate radio personality into a presidential candidate."

"I like your attitude and I'm feeling kinda run down, Doc. Got anything to help?"

"You're feeling a hangover, made worse by the fact that you're a pile of old bones held together by blubber and motivated by, I would guess, a smorgasbord of addictive substances that you appear to consume in absurd portions. Now, go take a hot shower with lots of soap, find some clean clothes, and let's go someplace to find you some food that doesn't have green mold growing all over it."

~

An hour later, the candidate appeared, clean shaven, dressed in khaki slacks, a white shirt, and a blue blazer with a red and white striped handkerchief peeking from the breast pocket. The whites around his blue eyes resembled red country roads winding through jagged mountains on a faded map but the pupils were dilating.

The doctor produced a small leather bag and withdrew a stethoscope, "Open your shirt."

Murphy started to protest but fumbled to unbutton the starched shirt and Billings pressed the cold stethoscope against his flabby skin, firing a tremor through his entire body. The doctor moved the frigid disk around his chest, instructing him to inhale and exhale, looking away at some fleeting phantom as he listened intently.

Next, he checked his blood pressure, felt the glands around his neck, blinded him with a laser powered penlight, before moving on to invade the inside his nose, throat, and ears, and tapped two fingers on his back and his abdomen, inspected his fingernails, and finally said, "Thank you."

Mac buttoned his shirt and looked up at the tall slender physician, "Well?"

"Well, according to my initial examination, you should probably already be dead."

"That bad, huh?"

"You're a mess. Your blood pressure's through the roof, your heart's racing when you're standing still, and I'm betting your cholesterol count is somewhere outside the stratosphere. What do you eat?"

"Pure crap. If it tastes good, I eat it."

"What about drugs and alcohol?"

"Yes."

"Yes?"

"Yes."

"I see. We'll have to work up a regime."

"Doc, I'm not looking for redemption and I have no intention of sacrificing my self-destructive habits just to chase some ridiculous dream of residing in the White House. What I need from you is to keep me in prime form for every appearance, interview, or show and figure out how I can get some sleep between gigs." He paused and looked from one to the next, "And, in case you boys haven't got the picture, I have no intention of winning this damned thing."

"So, what's the point?"

Murphy burst out laughing, "To have some fun, raise some hell, crash the Republican Party like drunken teenagers, upend and offend the status quo, and stash away every dime, every influence or favor, and jump every good-looking piece of ass that comes our way. This is going to be a rolling circus until the grown-ups catch up with us."

The three men looked at each other and all spoke at once, until Stone raised his hand, "You're joking, right?"

"Gentlemen, I propose that we run a campaign that's a flaming dart honing in to demolish the reputation of every straight-laced fraud who's running for office, one that's a complete embarrassment to the 'conservative' pansies who bow and scrape to the greedy assholes who've doomed this county to ruin, and provide a soapbox for the working poor. We're selling a product...me...and the idea that the little people actually do matter, they do have opinions and hopes and fears like everybody else, and they're tired of being looked down on as the deplorable and insignificant ugly cousins of American society.

As crazy and ignorant as most of them are, they built this country with their blood, sweat, and tears, for the bastards who're screwing a huge chunk of the population for fun and complete domination. They're the first to sign up to fight our wars, to defend our democracy with their lives, expecting nothing more than a little respect for their bravery and dedication. They might live in an alternate universe but it's their reality and they've always gotten screwed every which way by the government and big business and the unions. They're easy to pick on because they're a faceless nameless invisible and irrelevant culture and no one will stand up for them, except a bunch of redneck preachers scrambling the words in the Good Book to make personal fortunes by making things worse."

Stone asked, "Are you actually for all the stuff you spout off about on your show?"

"Hell no! I don't believe most of the crap that comes out of my mouth. I'm just a messenger, a character who represents what those people believe and isn't afraid to say so."

"So, this is all just a…sham, a performance?" asked Dr. Billings.

"Yup. Has been from the very first broadcast, when I invented this charming persona, and I've been totally fucked up for every show since. I plan to stay in character and in this groove until we're finished in November."

"It does pose an interesting opportunity to run a campaign on instinct, instead of worrying about building a path towards trying to grab a nomination. That's a platform for experimentation with delivering our message through multiple avenues. If we can actually raise some money, we could dispatch carefully crafted ads to specific groups and localities. We just need to identify what they hate the most and keep 'em riled up."

"That's easy, they hate anyone who doesn't look like them, doesn't sound like them, and doesn't believe fervently in their bizarre form of Christianity, even if it doesn't have anything in common with the kind of religion I grew up with," said Murphy. "Southern Baptists are passionate and pig-headed about what they're for and what they're against, but these folks are way beyond that. They believe every breath of ecclesiastical nonsense that pops out of their perverted preacher's mouth and they aren't afraid to act on it."

Hannah grinned, "The other thing is that we've received a steady stream of contributions since Mac did that first show and it's been accelerating since he announced."

"How much do you have to work with?" asked Stone.

"More than a half-million."

"That's a start. I could get some research going and bring in a couple of ad guys to build us an image."

Billings rubbed his chin, staring at Murphy, "That's the most ridiculous, outrageous scheme I've ever heard but, from my perspective, the biggest problem is how to keep you from complete physical collapse or losing your tenuous grasp on reality or both."

"Doc, I was a thespian, the golden child of the University of Georgia's drama department. I even played a crazed and desperate Lear to a standing ovation in my final performance and I've been doing variations on the same shtick ever since. If the machinery's properly oiled, I can turn it on to do a radio show five nights a week but it's going to be a different deal, when I have to appear in public or on television five or six times a day for weeks on end. That's where you come in."

Twenty minutes later, the car pulled into the parking lot in the glow of the sputtering neon chicken towering above the entrance to Katie's Chicken House. Katie's daughter, Sara, led them to a round table next to a large window overlooking a gully meandering down a hill through a forest of bare trees just beginning to show hints of green.

The four had remained virtually silent on the drive to the restaurant and Stone waited, until Sara had filled their water glasses, taken drink orders, and provided menus, to say, "I've had several thoughts about all of this. First, I'm fairly sure your fantasy would end up getting us all arrested and thrown in jail at the very least but...if you ignore that very real possibility, I think I know how to do this without playing the traditional game."

"How's that?" asked Hannah.

"Well, Murphy's got a solid platform with his show and, with a little promotion, I'll bet we could get it carried on even more stations, reaching a far larger audience, which would bring more supporters and more contributions."

"And?"

"And then we get real selective about where we make public appearances or allow media exposure."

"That doesn't make a lick of sense," said Murphy.

"Actually, it does," said the political pro, "and I'll tell you how we're going to do it. We're going to coordinate a daily media blitz built on scripted subjects you're talking about on your show. We'll release carefully edited videos of the most contemptable moments of your broadcasts to every news outlet in the country, stuff they can't resist running in prime time, so they can say, 'Can you believe he just said that?'.

Sending out digital information doesn't cost a dime, other than having the right crew of techs to handle production and distribution to blitz the news cycle. With really talented people, our whole media presence could be handled from a small office.

Second, we stage large rallies, starting in those markets right in the middle of the country, where you can draw big crowds of true-believers ready to tear down the fences to get at their oppressors. If we have to hire 'fanatical' stand-ins to post up on the stage, as your cheering section, and move them around the country from one gig to the next, fine…that's a cheap investment, but these events need to be like a political version of Woodstock, so big, so loud, and so outrageous that it's an entertainment draw that dazzles audiences and mocks every tradition we can mangle."

"I think you're on to something," said Hannah. "I could see rallies that follow the tradition of big rock festivals, with lots of music and entertainment, leading up to an hour of Murphy's take on reality. Think big screens with dramatic scenes that provide a visual backdrop for the speech – soldiers marching, flags waving, cheering crowds, everyone's fantasies about the glories of our democracy played off against a dystopian future wrought at the hands of every other candidate in either party, all accompanied by a killer soundtrack to enhance the emotional reactions."

"We'll make every appearance into a four-hour extravaganza."

"And you'll only have to participate for the last scene of the play," laughed Hannah.

"There ya' go," said Murphy. He paused, "I'm remembering Leni Riefenstahl's film, 'Triumph of The Will', where she made Hitler look like a god standing in a single spotlight high above enormous crowds of adoring supporters, assuring them that together they could bring glory to the fatherland again, if they could defeat and destroy the enemies that created the country's problems in the first place."

"What about All People Matter?" asked Dr. Billings.

"I think Murphy's got a lock on millions of ultra-conservative evangelical bigots who have never voted in their lives. They're the folks the polls completely ignore, which works to our advantage," replied Stone.

Hannah added, "I think we'll pillage the more radical people from them and they'll pick up some of the light-weights from us, and, oh yeah, they're appealing to the traditional Democrat pitch of one for all and all for one, which is exactly opposite of our supporters, who want to end immigration, deport everyone who isn't pearly white, speaks another language, or worships another religion. Mac's listeners might reluctantly vote Republican, if they can't vote for a fascist, but they'd never be caught voting for a liberal."

"Everything about All People Matter gives me material to make them out to look like candy-ass rich folks trying to tell poor people how to overcome their poverty," said Murphy. "And they don't have a charismatic leader, except that gorgeous brunette with the long legs. I'd like to have a long slow political discussion between the sheets with that bitch."

"She's out of your league, sucker," laughed Stone. "I met her at the rally in Atlanta and I'd suggest not underestimating her, her name's Katherine Kennedy and she's intelligent and completely dedicated to their cause. I didn't get deep inside the organization but I'm sure they've got some pros working behind the scenes, because they pulled a hundred-thousand people together on a couple of weeks' notice."

"She's just another rich bitch trying to make up for her inherent bigotry by leading a worthy cause for the underprivileged. I'll take her down a notch or two before we're finished with this."

"I have no doubt, but use some tact."

"Tact is for losers, I want to smash 'em in the mouth with outrageous bullshit that gets everyone pissed off and us on the front page of every paper in the country and the top of every news program all day, every day," replied Murphy. "That's the only way we survive past next week."

~

Kate poured coffee into her mug from the carafe on the stove and padded out to the back patio overlooking the bay, greeted by a lick and a rub from Gracie. Tangerine rays of a low morning sun raced through the palms, banyans, and scrub oak, etching trunks and branches into sculptures reaching for red hibiscus blossoms and clusters of Oleander.

Jessie looked up from the Dolphin Times, "I like your story about Tyrone Turner, he comes across as a compassionate down-to-earth intellectual who could run our country for everyone's benefit."

"Yeah, I really enjoyed getting to talk with him again. He said he's going to be speaking at the rally in Chicago."

"Cool," replied Jessie, squeezing her hand. "The big stories about Senators and Governors jockeying for position in the primaries are all over the front section but, did you see the article back here on page nine, about that right-wing nutcase, uh…Mac Murphy, who's tossed his hat into the Republican race?"

"Who's he?"

"Evidently, he's got a huge following on his ultra-conservative radio talk show out of some little burg near Cincinnati. From the way the article's written, the reporter kind of writes him off as a joke, but some of the quotes are just outrageous, like, 'Government regulations destroy jobs', and 'Criminal immigrants are surging across the southern border to murder, rape, and pillage and the liberals are welcoming them with open arms', and this one, 'Congress should deny every judicial nomination made by our lame socialist president until the next election, when the people can decide what kind of judiciary they want'." He took a sip of coffee, "Is that a choice between open impartial justice or Gestapo kangaroo courts?"

"We hear a lot of that kind of nonsense coming from presumptive Republican candidates trying to appeal to the radical fringes but, maybe, not quite that direct."

Jessie looked up, "They might be writing this imposter off as a joke but there are millions of ignorant people who believe this shit, millions who would actually vote for a totally unqualified blowhard just because he isn't afraid to voice their twisted version of truth."

Kate sat down to sip and gaze at little whitecaps rippling across the water in the warm breeze. "Those people are getting screwed by the Republicans just like every other working class stiff and they'd be better represented by All People Matter."

"The difference is that a fairly large part of their population is profoundly evangelical, fanatical about guns and abortion, and totally racist – those are the issues they put before their own impending doom. Joining forces with any group that isn't white, even against a common enemy, is beyond impossible."

"I was raised in a home where you were expected to be polite and respectful to everyone, period. So, I don't understand how a culture of hate can exist in this country in this century." She paused, "Well, I do, it's everywhere…"

"It used to be that we didn't acknowledge it, society didn't admit the dirty little secret, but bigotry and racism never disappeared, hell, it probably never even diminished, it just became invisible and unmentionable."

"It isn't going to change until voters stop electing fat white guys, who are far more interested in lining their pockets by denying rights and benefits to those who need them most, rather than making the world a better place."

"Amen to that, sister," he raised his cup to toast. "Have you talked to Tabitha lately?"

"Yeah, she and Mavis are organizing strikes all over the country and putting a PR firm together in their spare time."

"What?"

"Yeah, they interviewed a whole slew of companies and finally decided that it'd be easier and cheaper if they just hired the key people they wanted out of all the interviews."

"That's fairly brilliant."

"And far more secure having it in-house than in someone else's office a thousand miles away."

"Benny, Sammy, and Eddie took off for Chicago yesterday, to set up the arrangements. They're meeting Amy and Althea, Beal and Sheldon, and Brad and his guys from Cameron."

"Katherine wants the rest of us up there by Saturday morning and Mavis's daddy is providing a plane."

"I could get used to this."

"Then paint some paintings, so we can survive our volunteer work!" laughed Kate, leaning to kiss him tenderly. "I like what you're doing in the studio."

"How so?"

"Well, the lagoon is feeling kind of magical, as if shafts of warm light are flowing through the trees to make the gators seem real and animated. I keep waiting for one of them to swim closer."

Jessie waved a hand, "This is the same light."

She looked up, "You're right, it's got that same quality, shafts of warm light creeping through long dark shadows."

He smiled, "That one has to go to Johnny's house."

"It's a beautiful rendition of the secret place you two shared. After all the stories you two told me, I can see the connection in the eyes of the alligators."

"What about the painting on the other easel?"

"That one really moves me because I looked out across that plaza at all those hopeful faces looking up at us and you've captured that feeling.

I gave up counting but you must have hundreds of faces in the painting and every one of them is a unique character."

"I was overwhelmed by the humanity of the moment, the shared sense of community and common purpose, and I tried to capture the transformation of the look in their eyes, from terror and anxiety to pride and confidence."

"I think it should be a poster for the campaign and you should call it 'Hope'."

"I don't have any problem with that, as long as it's reproduced to my standards, but I don't know where the original should hang and I don't want to sell it. I guess that will reveal itself when it's finished."

"How do you know when a painting is finished?"

"Sometimes it's the fear that if I add just one more stroke of paint, the entire canvas will rip away from the frame and end up in a puddle on the floor."

Kate laughed, "No, really?"

Jessie kissed her, "It took me a long time to learn to trust my eye to recognize that anything more would be too much. Mother Nature's a messy artist, she's leaves clutter and disorder behind and that debris is what makes my rendition of perfection seem real to the viewer."

"You know Derek Rangle's feeling neglected because you haven't replenished his gallery with new work."

"Yeah, he called a couple of days ago and I told him that I want to get these two finished and then I'll get into production. I'm afraid when I get going, I'm selfishly focused and totally boring for days and sometimes weeks."

"There's so much going on that we both need to strap on our roller skates and just go for it."

"I actually used to be a pretty good skater."

"Ice or wheels?"

"Ice, played hockey on a lake with the local guys."

Kate laughed, "And you've still got your own teeth? You must have been good."

Shepherd Stone's public relations team and their media specialists expanded into every nook and cranny in the cinder-block building that housed the studios of WBFK, piling the halls with everything that had filled all those spaces for the past twenty years.

Milly Clark staked out her post behind the reception desk but was completely bewildered by the new phone system the tech guys installed, with rows of flashing buttons and calls going unanswered.

Adam Bell, the technical guru, knelt next to her chair, installing a module under the desk, "You really do need to stop worrying about this phone system, it takes care of everything and routs calls to the proper person. We've got people covering Murphy's fans, so the only time you have to answer is when this phone rings. It will be a call for you."

"What about calling out?"

"Just pick up the handset and dial," laughed Bell.

"I feel like I'm being automated."

"You are, isn't it fun?"

"No, I like working."

"Well, now you'll have different chores to attend to, instead of wasting time saying 'WBFK, how can I help you?' With all that's going down, we're counting on you to keep us grounded!"

Murphy's gold Cadillac squealed through the parking lot, spun sideways and came to rest with a tailfin implanted in the scraggly hollies down the side of the building. Moments later, the service door slammed open, silhouetting the tardy host in a flood of golden light with seven minutes until airtime. He clamored through the tumbling gauntlet down the dark narrow hallway and burst through the soundproof door into the studio, dazzled by enormous lights, four guys in black shirts setting up cameras and reflectors.

Shephard Stone was sitting in Mac's chair behind the desk, making notes on a clipboard, "I've got some talking points lined out for you and, as you can see, we'll be taping your show to cull your most outrageous comments to pass along to the media."

"Great! Get the fuck out of my chair!"

The campaign manager stood up as the host dumped a pile of clippings on the mountain of paper and debris on the table, tossed his coat on a side chair, loosened his tie, popped a handful of pills with a slug of Bourbon, lit a cigar and leaned back. "What's our theme?"

"National pride and how we've lost our international standing, our economy is getting ready to fart, our military is a shadow of the dominating force that once commanded fear and respect around the world and, obviously, morale is low, the Democrats want to give away the farm to the big banks, and Hispanic and Muslim immigrants are storming our shores to rape and pillage our country!"

Murphy's eyes rolled back in his head, as he took another huge swig of whiskey and capped the bottle with a satisfied sigh. "Sounds like standard procedure to me."

"You can do this in your sleep. Speaking of which, have you slept?"

"Yeah, the doc put me on some sleeping pills that knock my right out for eight straight hours and I wake up like someone flipped a switch, which is totally weird."

"So, where is he?"

"Oh, he had to take care of some business and said he'd be back tomorrow."

"Good, I'm not comfortable with you...self-medicating."

The host laughed, "I've been mixing the same cocktail five nights a week for the last four years and I'm not about to break precedent now!"

Jack Hannah clicked on the intercom, "We're two minutes to air."

"I'm ready when you are, boss." He tapped the ash off his cigar, looking around at the video crew, "You guys ready?"

"Yeah, we're tied in to your mike and the video's looking good."

"Damn well better get what you need quick, before I melt under these damned lights."

"You give us lines we can use and these guys will be gone in a hurry," said Stone.

Hannah tapped on the window and Murphy put on his headphones and pulled the mic closer. "Quiet on the set, and four, three, two, and…"

"Good evening folks, this is Mac Murphy broadcasting unfiltered truth to the world from WBFK in the heartland of America on this beautiful evening. I welcome all my listeners because this is going to be a special show, just you and me and this film crew that's taken over our studio to preserve our love affair for posterity. Say hello guys!"

The four men bellowed, "Hello America!"

"True patriots, one and all. Ladies and gentlemen, I'd like to talk about pride tonight, national pride, because I fear we've lost something precious.

I watch the news and read the papers and all I hear is doom and gloom. We've got international troubles, we've got economic problems, crime's up and employment's down, our military is weak and our borders are as porous as a sieve. The Democrats blame the Republicans and the conservatives blame the liberals and nothing gets done.

It's hard to hold your head high when your country, my country, our country is headed for the trash-heap of history, going out not as the most powerful country that ever existed but with a whine and a whimper.

The purity of our heritage is being sullied by a swelling tide of dirty immigrants, inferior human beings with no skills or education, criminals who infest our cities with crime and disease, peddling drugs and prostitution to turn God-fearing citizens away from the path of righteousness. They expect us to feed and house them, provide education for their mongrel children, and medical care for illnesses they bring with them from who knows where. They don't want to work their way up, like everyone else, they want to steal jobs from American workers. They don't pay taxes, they don't learn the language, and we sure don't want them to become integrated into our society or change our national language to Spanish.

So, my question is, why don't we send them all back where they came from? Round 'em up and ship 'em out, all of them, right now!"

He took a slug from the WBFK coffee cup full of bourbon and a toke on his fat cigar, and jumped out his chair, screaming, "We all know why immigration is out of control, because those damned politicians in Washington are too busy talking big, lining their pockets with kickbacks, and taking orders from the fat cats to get funding for the next election. They don't have time to deal with the real issues that are destroying this country!"

He turned to the camera, fists raised above his head, "It's not just whimpy President Gonzalez, the first president in history who can't speak English, who's gotta go! It's the Republicans who control Congress and can't get anything done because they're squabbling amongst themselves and blaming the Democrats for their own ineptitude! We need a real leader in the White House, supported by true patriots replacing these arrogant swindlers.

Give me your votes and a Congress of our people, ready to work, and I promise to give you a country that you can be proud of, a country that is the undisputed king of the world, with military strength that fosters fear in our enemies and respect and loyalty from our friends, a thriving economy that drives the markets across the globe, and a safe haven for all of you, by unleashing police power to rid our cities of violent ghettos and the scum who live there.

Together, we can rebuild our great nation, by erasing the laws and regulations that enrich the greedy tycoons and hold the rest of us hostage! Our only hope is clearing out inferior elements, confronting the lies and corruption that have become institutionalized in our government, and incarcerating all the people who contributed to the demise of our democracy. There can be no mercy, if we are to survive as a nation, as a people, enshrined and protected by our belief in the Constitution and the word of God."

The lights clicked off, as the station went to commercial, and Stone yelled, "Now that's what I'm talking about!"

Murphy pulled off his headphones and took another gulp of his bourbon, "That what you need?"

"Hell yeah!" laughed the campaign director, turning to the crew, "Did you get that?"

Thumbs up, "You bet. That last rant is going to be a classic!"

"That's what's going to keep you in this race," said Stone. "Keep it up."

"I'll see that the best of this is all over the morning news shows," said Hayden Crawley, first cameraman and video director.

"I'll bet we just pulled in another fifty grand in contributions and I'm just getting started."

~

Murphy fumbled for the phone, glancing around the living room in confusion. Somehow, Stone and Billings sent a clandestine cleaning crew to sterilize his house, removing a large truckload of clutter and debris, stocking the refrigerator with real food, and shipping all his clothes to the dry-cleaners to be disinfected or destroyed, while he was out. The change was transformative and disturbing, the first step in acquiescing to being handled.

Cleanliness did not seem to offer any relief for his hangover. He spied the jangling phone lying innocently on the coffee table, thought about pitching it into the fireplace, but reluctantly picked it up. His throat was dry and raspy but he managed to croak, "Hello?"

"Murphy, it's Stone, have you seen it? Turn on your television, you're on every channel and they're not just playing a few lines, they're playing the whole damned thing!"

"No shit?"

"No shit, go turn it on."

The candidate dropped the phone on the couch and started to get up to turn on the set but realized that the remote had mysteriously reappeared and it actually responded by lighting up when he touched it. He hit the button and a beautiful buxom blond woman appeared, "I think the Republican candidates better sharpen their messages and get their campaigns in order, because we now have a solid conservative favorite in this lead up to the impending primaries. Martin McClintock Murphy is a radio host who has something to say."

The beautiful face dissolved into Murphy raging at the camera and played all the way through to the end. The blond's cohost said, "Whether you agree with his message or not, that's the most powerful and direct delivery of a concise and coherent policy from any candidate in the race and it's sure to find support with a giant swath of the population."

"Ladies and gentlemen, I believe we're witnessing history today and I expect to hear a lot more from our new leading candidate for the office of President of the United States." Her face lit up with a smug emotionless smile, "This is Cindy Hawkins, American News. We'll be right back."

Stone's muffled voice screamed from the telephone stuffed between the cushions of the sofa, "Now we've got a real campaign!"

"No shit?" Murphy gazed around the neatly arranged room. Antiques, once tastefully beautiful and valuable for their age and impeccable craftsmanship, looked worn and abused in spite of being soaked with gallons of lemon oil, which covered the acrid scent of rotting drapes and decaying carpets.

He missed the shifting piles of paper and garbage that insulated him from everything outside his inebriated bubble and provided a poor man's security system, if someone was foolish enough to enter the unlocked front door.

If he allowed this whole charade to start rolling, there would be no refuge, no isolated death-defying overindulgence to slake the wicked demons raging inside his head or the ogres of the barren wasteland, who snuffed the fires that once burned in his heart during his foggy long-forgotten youthful naïveté. Once he accepted the role of presidential candidate, the challenge of assuming this character would consume his whole persona, just like most of the endless adaptations he substituted for being a real person in real relationships for more years than he'd care to admit.

He took a long, slow deep breath and spit out a cloud that fouled the whole room, "So, what do you need from me now?"

"The crew will be set up for your show tonight and I was thinking you ought to take some carefully screened calls and give the audience your take on some of the things that are bothering them."

"Yeah, I take calls to fill time, once in a while."

"Well, let's use that to show that you're in touch with the plight of the working people and you have, not only, opinions but solutions too."

"Who's screening the calls?"

Stone laughed, "You won't believe it but we've got five people answering the phones twenty-four seven and we're going to have to add more."

"What's the reaction after last night?"

"Oh, how about eight-thousand callers and a quarter million in contributions?"

"Shit."

"Bet it'll be more by tomorrow, if you're on your game."

"First, I need to see the doc, and, second, I want Milly filtering the calls that come through to me."

"We've got people to do that."

"What don't you understand? Milly filters my calls, period."

"Fine, done. Dr. Billings will be here an hour before you go on."

"Great, I'll be there."

"On time?"

"On time."

Stone pressed the button to end the call and looked up at Hannah, Billings, Haden Crawley, and Milly, "Believe that when I see it."

Milly giggled, "He has actually been on time more than once."

"Maybe twice," added Jack Hannah. "If he doesn't come busting through that back door half-crocked, I worry."

Stone looked at Billings, "Do you really think you can keep him on track? This is going to be a long slog and it's all for naught, if he goes off the rails."

"While I was gone, I spoke with a colleague of mine, who deals with unusual personality disorders. After listening to the show last night, he suggested that, in layman's terms, our candidate is completely off his rocker, unconstrained by morals or conscience, absolutely egocentric, and his entire presentation is that of a stage actor working without a script in a dark-comedy club, totally adlib and unrestrained. If you track how he moves from one subject to another, it's all triggered by one good line. When he hits the note that completes the thought, he's ready to move on to new territory. That's why he's so engaging to the audience, he leads them along to a rowdy conclusion, then heads in another direction and off they go."

"So, you're saying he's a typical presidential candidate who spouts patriotic bullshit without believing a word of it?" asked Hayden Crawley.

"That's far more succinct than my description but, basically, yes. Except there's no telling if or when that controlled explosion will ignite into fireworks or he'll just run out of gas."

"That's where you come in," said Stone. "The question is whether you can keep him in prime fighting form when we need him and out of the way when we don't…without killing him."

Milly raised her hand timidly, "I hope you're not going to kill him with overwork or with kindness because I know there's a good person underneath all that brash bluster and hateful nonsense. He's just shooting his mouth off and we're all getting paid for it."

"Well, now he's going to have to work with the team to engineer a real campaign," said Stone. "We've already had several calls from big donors who want to know if he's the real deal and I'm pitching him as hard as I can but, if truth be known, I don't think any of us knows for sure and I doubt we ever will, unless he explodes in a supernova or wins the White House."

"This looks like the ultimate money machine," said Crawley, "and, if you asked me, I say go for broke until it breaks."

Chapter Eight

The twenty-hour drive, fueled by caffeine, amphetamines, and a few brews to mellow things out, left Lincoln Todd and Roger Stanislawski ripe and edgy, as they parked the rental Chrysler behind the 'Banners R Us' hangar at Aurora Airport, thirty-five miles west of downtown Chicago. The two men crawled out of the car and stretched their aching bodies, before striding into a large open barn housing two Cessna's, a yellow Stearman biplane, and a sleek little kit-plane with stubby wings and a cockpit canopy pushed back near the tail.

A scruffy man in dirty jeans and a saggy American flag tee-shirt checked off every item on the preflight form for the Stearman with a large 'X'. The two men walked across the gleaming gray floor, "You Lorton?"

"Yeah, you must be Lincoln Todd and Roger Stanislawski," said Henry Lorton, fumbling his clipboard before offering to shake. "I'm pleased to meet two legends."

"Aw, we're just cogs in a machine that's trying to save this country from itself," said Roger.

"And we're nothing, without enthusiastic volunteers like yourself. You guys do the heavy lifting."

"Hell, this is nothing, I love to fly and I believe in the message. What more could I ask for?"

"Well, the big guys wouldn't get too upset if we at least paid for your gas."

"Gentlemen, you've got yourselves a deal."

"Are you cleared to circle the site?" asked Todd.

"Actually, flight control is making me run up and down just off Lakeshore Drive but I'll make sure everyone sees our banner."

"Cool, just make sure you're there about one o'clock for maximum exposure."

"Can do."

"How long can you stay up?"

"Aw, with the extra drag, max is probably a couple of hours, maybe three but, if they don't scramble the fighters to blow me outta the sky, I could probably refuel for another run. Hell, Matty said a bunch of ace mechanics just installed some new gear, sorta like power steering, so this should be a blast."

Lincoln Todd reached to shake, "You're a patriot and I'll make sure that everyone knows what you've done for the campaign. It's time to untangle the legal knots the Democrats used to destroy the rights of white Americans and it's not going to happen unless our people join together to demolish the liberal doctrine that promotes the rights of brown illegals, who are pouring over the borders."

Stanislawski added, "Two-thirds of that crowd are wetbacks trying to game the welfare system and the rest are lily-livered nigger-lovers who need to understand that we're going to bleach this county by deporting every last one of those animals and we'll gladly send their protectors along for the ride."

Lorton grinned and hooked a thumb over his shoulder, "Like the sign says, 'Free White America!'."

"That's the goal, isn't it?" chuckled Stanislawski. "We just have to make people understand that this is a war for the future of our country and there's no turning back until we've conquered the liberal elite."

"Amen to that."

Todd handed Lorton a wad of cash, "This should cover your expenses."

"That's way more than enough."

"You're going to embarrass the leaders of the 'All People Matter' rally and you'll be on every news broadcast in the nation by dinnertime. That's mega-publicity for the cause and you'll be famous!"

"I'm on it," said the pilot.

"Great, we'll call you after you get back."

"Cool. Glad to help."

"Thanks," said Stanislawski, as the two men sauntered across the hanger.

They climbed into the rental and Todd headed for the exit, squinting his eyes against brilliant sunshine and scratching his stubble. He popped a couple of Black-Mollys with a swig of warm beer, "I need food and a shower before we hook up with our people."

"Yeah, you smell like shit." His partner reached behind the seat to grab a metal briefcase, set it on his lap, and flipped the latches to open the lid revealing a pair of joysticks, a panel of gauges, and rows of knobs and switches. He pressed a button and lights flashed before the machine beeped.

The driver glanced over, "What's that?"

"Insurance."

~

A tangle of police cars and firetrucks formed a protective barrier at either end of the block, as a fleet of white limousines pulled to the curb on Balbo Drive to discharge dozens of speakers and advocates just behind the stage in Grant Park. The driver hopped out and trotted around to open the door for Standler, who offered a hand to Mavis, looking chic in a fitted pink leather military jacket with a matching beret, fashionably tilted to hide her healing wound.

She in turn helped Tabitha from the car. The publisher had recovered her balance and, with it, a fierce passion for exposing the traitors and rebuilding the middle class. A crisp breeze off the lake buffeted the fabric windbreaks on either side of the stage, stirring the soaring temperatures of an early sweltering siege, as a small parade of activists and dignitaries passed through security into the restricted backstage arena. Standler escorted the ladies up the few steps to hug Katherine and Kate.

Tabitha peeked over the rims of her big round sunglasses, chic camouflage hiding fading purple bruises around her eye, to scan a tremendous crowd packing the field, "How many are we expecting?"

Katherine tapped her clipboard, "I'll be disappointed with less than a hundred-thousand."

"Way to go, girl!"

"We're expecting folks from as far away as New York and the West Coast," added Kate, as Nellis and Spratlin wandered over in deep conversation.

"What's up?"

"Oh, nothing," said Nellis.

"Nothing my butt," snapped Katherine. "Let's have it."

"Brad and Beal have picked up rumors about a counter demonstration trying to make a showing during the speeches this afternoon."

"Any sign of people congregating?" asked Standler.

"Not yet but the city police are aware of the threat and we've got massive security in layers for blocks in every direction," said Spratlin.

"Have you noticed that yellow plane flying back and forth with that 'Free White America' banner?"

"Yeah," said Beal, "we pointed it out to the cops and they said that he's within his rights and he has a permit but they'll be sure to have someone waiting when he lands."

"Good thing," said Katherine. "It's hard enough getting these people to join up without someone nitwit trying to intimidate them with that huge racist billboard!"

A band cranked up the first song of the day and Nellis trotted off toward the stage, "I've got to sit in for a couple of tunes and then you guys are on for the introduction."

Mavis blew a kiss and asked Kate, "Where's Jessie?"

"Oh, he and Sammy and Benny are organizing the speakers, over in the guest tent."

"Did Mayor Turner show up?"

"Yes! He's in there talking with Chicago Mayor Anthony Wythe, plus mayors from Indianapolis, Milwaukee, Pittsburg, Detroit, and Cleveland, and sympathetic Senators and Representatives who are all facing an unprecedented surge in unemployment back home," replied Katherine. "Plus, we're starting to pick up some major-league donors, who want to help out."

"Good, because I can attest that funding a national movement is expensive!" said Mavis.

Kate hugged her, "We wouldn't be here without you and Tabitha and all your friends who have been so dedicated to making this happen. We have associates in all fifty states begging for help in organizing their own protests and strikes. People are starting to realize what's going on and they're pissed."

"Let's hope we can channel that anger into votes," said Spratlin. "We need to get everyone organized for the big welcome."

Katherine tapped the schedule on her clipboard, "Here come the troops from the tent. The entire lineup should be accounted for momentarily."

The campaigners converged behind the stage, as the final strains of a psychedelic rendition of the "Star Spangled Banner" shattered eardrums for blocks, while the plane with the banner flew back and forth, lower and slower on each pass.

Nellis stepped up to the mic, "Ladies and gentlemen, how 'bout a hand for 'The Windy City Blues Band', these guys know how to cook!"

Huge applause.

"We'd like to take a short commercial break to introduce you to some of the folks who have worked so hard to bring all of us together on this beautiful day to express our unity and determination in exposing and decommissioning the conspiracy that has forced so many Americans out of work and into poverty."

Boooo's and whistles.

"Well, I've got news for you. Look around, every one of you hundred-thousand or so people are in the same boat. Your neighbors are suffering the same anger, disillusionment, and frustration as you are, and they're the folks who are going to help you change our world. Get to know each other, set up networks to share information, and find ways to help each other out. We're all in this together!"

The crowd roared, as nearly a hundred guests trooped up the steps and spread out across the stage.

"Ladies and gentlemen, may I introduce the organizers of this incredible event, starting with the Reverend Jimbo Combs, with a benediction."

The enormous former basketball star strode up to envelope Nellis in a bear hug. He lifted the microphone, "Y'all know me, but I'll bet you don't know that I always wanted to play for the Bulls instead of trying defend against them!"

Chicago's basketball fanatics erupted.

"If you know about my roundball career, then I'm sure you've all heard about my ministry. We built a glass temple in Tampa several years ago that can seat ten-thousand worshippers but, you know what I discovered? It can sleep and feed fifteen-thousand needy citizens every day, so it's been converted into a magnificent homeless shelter."

The audience cheered.

"Ladies and Gentlemen, I believe in my Lord Jesus Christ and I hope that you believe in your God as strongly and as surely as I do, because I want to ask him or her to bless everyone here, to relieve the pain, the burdens we all carry with us every moment of every day, since our own personal nightmares replaced the lives that were stolen from us.

I want to ask God to give us the strength, the unity of purpose, and the determination to destroy the conspiracy, reclaim our democracy, and give everyone here the opportunity to contribute to rebuilding this great country for all of us, not just the privileged few. In His name, Amen and Hallelujah."

The crowd turned to a loud bang as the yellow Stearman backfired and, with only a momentary hesitation, Katherine stepped up to the mic with a radiant smile, "Hi! I'm Katherine Kennedy and I'm the coordinator for All People Matter!"

Cheers.

"I want to thank all of you for coming out to support our grassroots campaign to take our government back from the radical right-wing conservatives, starting with your local school board and city council, your state legislature and governor, your representatives and senators, and, finally, the person you will elect to sit in the Oval Office. The next president will decide who we are and what direction our country will take for the next four years. Will we allow hate and bigotry, greed and corruption to dominate our lives and our future?"

"NO!"

"Then, all of you need to understand that the greedy families, who planned and executed this treasonous coup, have every expectation of convincing you to support and vote for their lackeys, unqualified white-nationalists who will spout scripted right-wing gibberish blaming the Democrats for all the problems our country is facing, even though the Republicans control the vast majority of state governments, statehouses, the House of Representatives, and enough seats in the Senate to block the president's legislation and judicial nominees.

They'll blame immigrants for stealing jobs, they'll blame minorities for imagined conspiracies, they'll blame women for refusing to accept less pay for equal work or demanding the right to determine what we do with our own bodies, or anyone who insists on an end to the senseless killing that has taken the lives of nearly sixteen-thousand innocent people in the past year. Rather than enacting stricter gun laws, Republican state legislatures across the country are passing laws that allow any fool to buy and carry a gun without training, a license, or a background check. How many more will die from stupidity, in addition to those who die as a result of anger?"

The crowd was still and nearly silent, as the plane puttered by, the white lettering fluttering against a blue sky.

She pointed, "They're trying to intimidate us with that racist billboard behind that plane."

"One for all and all for you," shouted a stout black man, holding up his baby girl.

"They blame their enemies to cover their crimes, conjure new scandals to deflect attention from their systematic campaign to destroy our democracy, repeal more than half the Amendments, and make the Constitution irrelevant by stacking the courts with radical judges, who will make judgements that favor the rich at the expense of everyone else.

They'll blame you for needing help to feed your children or finding shelter or job training and they'll mock you for being unemployed without admitting they closed the plants and moved the jobs to Singapore! They'll blame you, while they're eliminating programs to help the poor, like affordable health care, educating our children, and protecting your voting rights!"

"Amen sister!"

"I'm here to tell you that all people matter! You might not be rich but you have a right that is far more powerful than money, you have the right and the responsibility to vote! So, join the All People Matter coalition and visit our blue booths, that are all around the park, to register to vote in the primaries and the general election in the fall. We need your help! Thank you!"

Cheers and applause, as Jessie hugged Katherine and took the podium. "Hi! How about another round of applause for Katherine Kennedy, who's in charge of coordinating our whole campaign?"

The enormous audience responded with another raucous round of revelry. "My name's Jessie Cotton, you might have heard about the first rally we put on in the middle of hurricane Dot in Dolphin Bay, Florida."

"You guys are crazy!" yelled an elderly Hispanic man with a large straw hat.

Jessie laughed, "You're probably right but I think what you saw was absolute desperation. Everyone who attended that protest faced the same challenges and problems that you're dealing with right here, right now. What sets them apart is that they were brave enough to go first! The question is, are all of you brave enough to fight for your rights, for our democracy, and the future of our country?"

"Yes!"

"Damn right!"

He scanned the endless sea of hopeful faces, "We're going to have more than a dozen of these rallies from coast to coast before the election next fall and I can guarantee that every one will draw at least this many people, because the pain and suffering is universal. There is no community anywhere in this country that's immune to the misery, the loss of hope and dignity, that's been spawned by this tiny group of wealthy traitors and the only way we can take our country back is by voting their hand-picked candidates to embarrassing defeats in every race for every office in the land. You have the power the make that happen and I believe that together, we shall overcome this nightmare."

The plane sputtered and the crowd turned. "Some people, like the pilot of that plane, believe this country would be better off if the government deported everyone who doesn't buy into their racist nonsense but what they don't seem to understand is that they're just white stooges to the Republicans who are paying big bucks to buy this election and, after they convince enough of those ignorant bigots to cast votes for their guys, they're going to screw them too."

The crowd cheered.

"I could go on but there are a lot of people who would like to address you this afternoon, so I'd like to bring out someone I admire and respect without wasting another moment, Atlanta's Mayor Tyrone Turner!"

The park exploded with applause and cheers, as Turner marched across the stage to take Jessie's hand, whispering, "Y'all already covered most of the bases."

The artist laughed, "None of us could say it quite as eloquently as you will."

"Thank you." He stepped up to the podium facing a sea of humanity, people who needed to see a vision of hope and salvation beyond doomsday rhetoric and political confrontation. He waited patiently for the crowd to settle, his physical presence and his intellectual prowess demanded the respectful attention of the audience.

The mayor watched thousands of heads turn to the sound of the engine of the Stearman biplane growing louder, as it traced along Lakeshore Drive at two-hundred feet, trailing that intimidating banner.

He waited until the sound faded, "Ladies and gentlemen, I'm delighted to see that so many of you could join us on this sultry afternoon and, hailing from a southern city that regularly exceeds temperatures conducive to human survival, I want to remind you that there's plenty of cold water available and four medical tents for anyone who might become overheated. Keep an eye on each other and stay ahead of heat stroke."

"Amen and thank you brother," yelled a tiny little black woman in a white dress and a floral hat under an orange parasol.

"Now, the disgusting banner trailing behind that beautiful biplane just reinforces the reason that I chose to be here today, because I believe in the Constitution and the Bill of Rights. I believe in the very simple premise of equality, inalienable rights, and the sanctity of our democracy. And I believe in all of you!"

Massive cheers.

"Katherine and Jessie gave you the big picture, the overview of the people who planned and enacted this campaign of social demolition, electoral manipulation, and the deconstruction of our government. I don't know about you but I read several newspapers of various political persuasions every day, I watch local and national news reports on the television, and I occasionally sneak in a peak at sports programs, particularly our local teams – The Braves, Hawks, and Falcons!"

Cheers, jeers, and whistles.

"My point is that it's still possible to find reliable information, reporting based on actual facts by qualified journalists, as opposed to the avalanche of opinions, misleading propaganda, and outright lies that has become standard messaging for the Republican party.

I believe that it's time for the press and concerned citizens to call out every single lie in the constant barrage they try to slip through the filters of common sense and moral decency. If reporters were more concerned with establishing and demanding truth, rather than landing a splashy story or a front-page headline, we wouldn't be in this mess. Lies can't stand up to the challenge of cold hard facts and liars can't broadcast their deceptions and denigrations without assistance from media empires more interested in ratings and profits than their ethical obligation to publish the truth."

He could feel the profound reaction erupt from the massive audience. "Here, here!"

"Right on!"

154

"Several weeks ago, I led your brothers and sisters on a march through Atlanta to call out our racist governor and his posse of ignorant legislators. We were confronted by a menacing mob of more than a thousand armed white-nationalists, who were paid by those very same people driving their campaign to attack our leaders to create a televised spectacle of mob violence to prove their political dominance. They won't be satisfied until they can eliminate anything or anyone who stands in their way with impunity, especially anyone who promotes a general strike that shuts down their money machine and draws attention to their greed.

In the process of sharing the truth with the America people, we recruited more than twenty-six thousand volunteers to run for office, canvas the state, and pound on every door, in every town or village in every county, to personally deliver our message to everyone. We need to use that as the template for protests and rallies across the country, to send our emissaries to talk one-on-one with every voter in the nation about our responsibility to seize this final desperate opportunity to put a stop to this madness…before the pinnacle of freedom and democracy becomes an autocracy of tyranny and repression and Reagan's 'Shining city on the hill' will be reduced to ashes."

Thousands booed in an angry chorus.

"You're suffering the result of their greed, their inhumanity, and treasonous amorality and, at the same time, you hold the power to doom their conquest by electing officials who believe in our democracy and all that we stand for, those same ethics and principles handed down by our Founding Fathers and defended by our brave soldiers through centuries of assault. It all starts and ends with your vote in your precinct on election day."

He paused, as the growl of the yellow plane, puttering south along the shoreline, rose to a piercing wail that slowly faded into the clamor of the crowd. The passing pause revealed growing chants of "White Power", "Deport the Immigrants", and "Death to Liberals" from clusters of agitators waving signs, scattered in pockets amongst the vast sea of faces, their defiance overwhelmed by a roar rippling through the crowd, primal anger overflowing the fragile restraint of communal compassion to pummel the invaders in growing eddies of chaos and mayhem driving fluid streams of protestors racing for refuge and protection from the riot. Brad and Eddie's mates gunned the engines of their choppers, attempting to clear paths through panic and pandemonium for the security forces to get to the scuffles but regimented and well-armed squads of intruders pushed the brawls towards the exits.

"They're all about blame or deporting their enemies or denying our right to protest peacefully or challenging the right of every citizen to vote. Everyone matters and we don't care about your ancestry, your spiritual beliefs, or the color of your skin. We value the content of your soul and the depth of your character. We care deeply and sincerely about what's in your heart, about the creative spirit that drives you to survive, to succeed, to triumph over an enemy that won't stop their assault until they've taken your job, your home, your place in society, your children's future, and, finally, your dignity."

The rumble of the airplane engine grew louder, closer, and he looked out across thousands of terrified demonstrators, churning in multi-ethnic swirls and denim vortexes, to spot the tiny yellow streak lining up on Soldier Field.

"We'll know they've won, when the vast majority of our citizens bow down to their authority..." Unsure, unbelieving, Mayor Turner struggled to continue, fixated on the sun glinting off the spinning propeller and the pilot scrambling out of the cockpit, as the plane dropped over the Fields Museum and leveled off at fifty feet aiming directly for the stage. He pointed and waved his arms toward the sides of the field, shouting above the raucous surging crowd and the snarling whine of the approaching airplane, "Run for your lives! Save yourselves!"

He froze in place, mesmerized by the sinister shadow of the plane rippling across waves of panicked protesters parting like the waters of the Red Sea and a partially opened white parachute fluttering after the pilot, as a stout southerly draught carried him over the stage towards the eternal jets spouting from bronze seahorses in the Buckingham Fountain at the far end of the park. The plane dipped and rolled but maintained course, a brilliant golden smudge tracing a spinning silver specter skimming just above the writhing blanket of humanity slumped on the ground.

Benny streaked across the stage, tackled the mayor and tumbled off the edge, while luminaries and the stage crew scattered. He covered the mayor with his body, overwhelmed by the growl of the engine and the buzz of the propeller fracturing the air, before a pair of fat spinning tires bounced on the edge of the stage. The yellow belly of the plane seemed frozen in the moment, suspended above them, blocking the cloudless sky, until the wheels crushed the podium and plowed two long black streaks to the back of the stage.

The gleaming propeller tore through the scaffolding supporting the flapping fabric roof and girders bearing suspended struts of theater lights, with a deafening screech of mangled steel and massive eruptions of sparks streaking through the chaos. The yellow wings ruptured, spilling gas across the plywood platform as the dented and fractured prop chewed through the background at the back of the stage and the plane slowly nosed over into the VIP arena, scattering petrified dignitaries into the street. It tottered there, tail up, for a long silent moment, before a thundering orange explosion blew shards of shredded airframe and flaming staging after the fleeing elite, dropping dozens in the VIP arena.

Benny rolled Turner over, "Are you alright?"

"Yes, thanks to you," he replied, wiping dirt and grass off his face, "I think."

Before Benny could lift him up, Brad and Eddie appeared, grabbed both of them, and hustled them around the side of the stage. "Are you okay?"

"Yeah," replied the mayor, "shaken and definitely stirred."

"You've got my vote," said Eddie.

"I'm not running for anything."

"After images of you, standing up to that plane on that stage without missing a beat, hit the airwaves, you'll be drafted to run for president."

In shock, the mayor's face sagged for a moment, unable to grasp the gravity of the attack or focus on the consequences or the injured, let alone his political future. He gazed across the park, bearing witness to the impossible, a stampede of tens of thousands of patriots fleeing a blatant attack by the iron fist of American fascism.

Brad slapped Benny on the back, "That was a world-record sprint across the stage. Next time we're picking up sides, I want you on my team."

"No problem," replied the landscaper, as pairs of medics raced through the carnage to treat the wounded. "Anyone else hurt?"

"I'm hoping the plane didn't actually hit anyone but I saw people falling after the explosion."

"Any of ours?" asked the mayor.

"I don't know, we were more concerned with getting you guys out of the line of fire."

"Yeah, about a minute late," cracked Benny.

"Hey, you're the hero, not me."

"Let's go see who we can help," replied Benny, taking the mayor's arm to guide him around the side of the stage, where a haunted crowd huddled together, watching firemen douse the flames and medical personnel scrambling to tend to the wounded scattered across the walkways.

Spratlin trotted over, glanced at the confusion in the mayor's darting eyes and said, "Let's find you some help."

Four ambulances roared through the roadblocks and screeched to a stop at the bottom of the steps, while howling sirens approached from all directions. Their crews pulled out gurneys and raced across the pavement to evacuate the most seriously injured.

Brad ran after them and knelt next to a doctor treating Amy for a jagged tear on her shoulder. "Are you okay?"

She looked up and winced, "Why is the initiation to these secret clubs always so painful?"

"I think you passed with flying colors back in Atlanta, so you didn't really have to show off here." He took her hand tenderly and kissed her fingers, "I'm sorry you got hurt."

"It was so weird, like the moment everyone realized what was happening, it all slowed down, like in the movies. I could see Nellis wrap his arms around Katherine and push her out of the way, along with three or four other people, Mr. Standler grabbed Mavis and Tabitha, and everyone was helping everyone else run away from the middle of the stage. I don't know what happened to Althea."

"I'll find out," said Brad, gazing around at dozens of people down. He squeezed her hand and stood, focused on a small round bundle lying on the ground on the far side of the burning plane. "I'll be right back."

He charged through a growing troop of rescue workers and raced through tangles of debris to kneel next to Sammy, who had a nasty gash above his left ear. The little man looked up at him, "It's worse than it looks."

"It's just a scratch, brother," replied Brad, glancing at the female medic pressing a dressing into the wound to stem the bleeding, while she dug through her medical bag with her other hand.

"We need to transport him."

"I'll get a stretcher," said the former marine, running to an ambulance crew just entering the fray. "I've got a guy who's critical over here. He needs you now!"

The team hurried to Sammy, lifted him onto the litter, and started away but the woman ran along beside them, holding the compress on his head. "Where are you taking him?"

"Northwestern Memorial's easiest to get to."

"But Mercy's got the trauma center! Take him there."

Brad grabbed his hand, "You hang in there and I'll have someone at the hospital by the time you get there."

Sammy winked as they whisked him away.

Benny ran up, "Was that Sammy?"

"Yeah, nasty gash on his head but I've been in combat and seen worse survive. He's in good hands. I told him I'd send someone to look after him, if you want to go?"

"But what about all of this?"

"We've got a thousand people working on it, go where you're needed. He's at Mercy Hospital and check to see if Amy's over there too."

"Thanks," said Benny, heading down the steps to hijack a limousine.

His radio crackled, "Brad, you got your ears on?"

"Yeah, man. What's the latest?"

"Pilot's dead. Impaled himself headfirst into the top tier of the fountain," replied Nellis.

"And?"

"Next question is, how'd the plane stay on course after he jumped out?"

"Either it's the most balanced airplane ever built or remote control."

Brandon Beal's voice interrupted, "Yeah, we want to check what's left of the controls on the plane, after they put the fire out." He paused, "Cops and our guys caught a few of the troublemakers trying to blend into the pandemonium and I swear some of them look like the thugs who caused the trouble in Atlanta."

"Wouldn't surprise me to find that they're paid enforcers, sort of the low rent version of Hitler's Brown Shirts without the uniforms?" asked Nellis. "Hell, after how fast they replaced the first bunch in

Cameron, I'll bet they've got squads of goons they can move around the country as needed or, worse, eager volunteers in every town in the land, invisible to anyone who isn't paying attention."

"Sure bet. We're working with the police and sharing intel, so I'll let you know what we find after the interrogations."

"Cool. How many down?" asked Brad.

"Still counting but I'm guessing an easy hundred, maybe more."

The biker turned security manager scanned the little plaza, "I've got at least twenty casualties back here. Listen, I'll buzz you back in a minute."

Kate and Katherine moved from one injured person to the next, until they both knelt down next to a woman. He ran to find them hovering over two medics who were attending to Bobbie Warmington, who had taken a blow from one of the metal lighting struts across her back, as she scurried off the stage just ahead of the plane shredding the 'All People Matter' banner that stretched across the background.

He dropped to his knees between the women, "How's she doing?"

"She got whomped by a big chunk of steel," said the young doctor. "I don't think anything's broken but she might get away with one giant painful bruise."

"Didn't hit your head?"

Bobbie turned awkwardly, "Probably would've been better, I've got a thick skull."

"You're a mom," laughed Brad. "Moms have to be tough."

"Especially with three kids."

He turned to Katherine, "I sent Sammy to the hospital with a head gash, Amy with a laceration to her shoulder, and then Benny to look after them. Mayor Turner was showing signs of shock, so Spratlin took him to find help. How 'bout the rest of the crew?"

"Well, first, I have to say, thank God we didn't allow the children to come along on this trip."

"Amen to that," said Kate. "Little Johnny was pissed he didn't get to come."

"Same with our troops," replied the coordinator. "Fortunately, we moved most of the dignitaries back to the air-conditioned tent, so they were out of the direct line of fire. Eddie's packing them into escorted limos and sending them to the hotel for safe-keeping, until we're sure this is over."

Kate looked up, as a video news crew swept through the carnage, "Oh my god! This whole thing is being broadcast live across the world. Everyone already knows what happened."

Bobbie Warmington winced, as she looked up at Katherine, "I know we're both in shock but you need to get out ahead of this right now, before the propaganda machine turns this to their advantage."

Katherine squeezed her hand and stood up, tears smearing her mascara, "How can the people we're trying help on so many fronts believe in us, when we keep leaving dead bodies behind?"

Nellis hustled through clusters of the stunned and frantic, to wrap his arms around her and lead her to a calm corner. He held her close and let her cry until she pulled away, "I'll never outlive the guilt."

"You can't take that on, sister, your shoulders ain't broad enough and you don't have the luxury of letting this slow you down. Our people are counting on all of us to keep going until we beat these bastards. They're not gonna quit and neither can we."

"But...?"

"No but's, go find someplace with a mirror, fix your makeup, and get ready to fight back. You're the voice of reason and compassion defending the helpless...with fire and rage and venom!"

She pulled him close, "We need a couple of days at the farm, with the gate closed."

He kissed her tenderly, "Amen to that, darlin'. And, in case anybody's askin', I sure am proud of you."

Brad approached, "I hate to interrupt."

"Then don't," said Nellis. The former marine turned away, "Wait, I'm just joshin' ya'. What's so important?"

He looked at Katherine, "I'm sorry we let you down."

"No one could have imagined a suicidal pilot flying his plane into the stage, in spite of weeks of preparation and hundreds, maybe thousands of police and security people all over this event."

"But we should have stopped it," said Brad. "Listen, I just got a call from Abe Sheldon, who's down at the police interrogations, and he said that the rioters they arrested are claiming that 'All People Matter' paid them to stage the unrest to stir up sympathy."

"That's bullshit!" snapped Nellis.

"That's how committed these bastards are," replied Brad. "And how coordinated their whole operation is."

"What do you mean?" asked Katherine.

"Right-wing media is already calling it a conspiracy by the 'liberal cabal' that tried to gain sympathy with the suicide truck at our 'secret' meeting in Houston. They were running with the story before the guys down in lockup had a chance to start talking."

Katherine made no attempt to clean up the black smudges around her eyes or run a brush through her tangles of auburn hair, before she walked up to a cluster of microphones before the blackened hulk of the smoldering wingless plane, standing upright with its demolished nose implanted in a shallow crater ground through the concrete by the mangled propeller, balanced by the wheels implanted in the smoking skeleton of the splintered stage.

She hesitated for a moment, blinded by a barrage of flashes and brilliant video lights, while, one by one, the other members of the executive committee, tenacious volunteers, and rescue workers lined up behind her.

"My name is Katherine Kennedy, I represent the 'All People Matter' movement and the tens of thousands of people who support our cause of the repatriation of our rights, our liberties, and our democracy.

Most of you had the luxury of watching videos of today's tragic and demonic attack on a peaceful rally, here in beautiful Chicago, while all these people were struggling to survive it. The unofficial casualty count is three-hundred and sixty-two injured and one-hundred and twenty-seven dead." She hooked a thumb over her shoulder, "Including the pilot who flew this plane into a crowd of over one-hundred thousand citizens of our country. This certainly qualifies as one of deadliest acts of terror in American history!

And that's exactly what this was, an act of brutal barbaric terrorism, and the fascists who planned and paid for this mass assassination will be brought to justice!" Katherine waved her hand, "Pan your cameras around this little plaza, where your viewers can see countless victims, who have yet to be moved to the hospital or taken to the morgue. I can promise you that none of them set out this morning intending to be murdered. They came to fight for their rights as human beings, the rights guaranteed by the Constitution and the Bill of Rights, by our Founding Fathers and all the soldiers who fought and died defending those basic ideals.

I've been informed that the nationalist propaganda machine is cranking out conspiracy theories and I would suggest that they look no further than the people behind the companies that buy advertising and sponsor their networks.

These are the same people who have been buying our elections for decades, with the sole purpose of dismantling our government and our democracy, so they can run the economy to maximize their profits without the worry of regulations or paying taxes that will just be wasted on 'the little people'.

I've got news for them, the little people might not possess the oligarchs' wealth and power but they do possess a remarkable weapon in their own defense. They have to power to vote and I promise you, they will be out in droves for the remaining primaries and the general election and they will put an end to this depraved and demented campaign for the destruction of our democracy.

This country was founded on the belief that government should be of the people, by the people, and for the people…and, rest assured, the people are about to take back the reins of power and then we're coming for the traitors who are deconstructing the very foundations that make the United States the envy of the world. Take my word, we've reserved an orange jumpsuit, some shiny silver bracelets, and a tiny cell for each and every one of you!"

Katherine turned and walked around the side of the stage into shadows, followed by the core of the movement. Stanton walked up the microphones, "I really don't think there's anything to add to Miss Kennedy's statement. We'll have updates for you, as we receive them."

The lights swiveled and the pack of reporters spread out to produce a monotone hum, as they all faced the cameras and frantically attempted to share the details of the tragedy and Katherine's response in respectfully subdued voices, in two minutes or less.

Chapter Nine

Katherine's speech was the top story across the nation and probably the world Almost every station showed it from start to finish, followed by taped replays of a resolute Tyrone Turner standing calmly above thousands of people fleeing the plane, as it flew just above the crowd to crash into the stage, with live voice-overs from solemn reporters on the scene.

Will Terry threw a wadded-up ball of tentative campaign slogans at the television, "That black bastard's going to be the Democratic nominee!"

"That ten seconds of tape will win him the nomination. He looks proud, steadfast, and courageous. Hell, it's got to be ninety plus in the shade and he didn't even break a sweat before that kid swept him off the stage." Ethan Tomlinson took a slow sip of his Scotch, "I'm going to suggest that, forget the rest of the field, we need to lob everything we can find squarely at him right now. I'll put research on churning up dirt, while I start working on 'our side of the story' and you need to put your team on finding every scrap of film that was ever shot of him. I want to have something totally devastating running in twenty-four hours."

"We've already got our networks churning out conspiracy theories and the Republican candidates are picking up the message. Hell, Willis is demanding a Congressional investigation of their whole movement and the political machinery behind it. Grant's claiming he's about to receive documentation that will prove the pilot was paid by someone inside the All People Matter executive committee!"

Ethan grinned, "I wonder where he's going to find that?"

"Did you set him up?"

"He's not the first chump stupid enough to fall for the fake. He's a Republican!"

"We should have the contenders down to a reasonable count within ten days," laughed Terry.

"The big guys think that Creighton Steil is their man."

"He does have the sincere pious pose down to a science and that incredible voice but he'll probably self-destruct when the voters figure out he's a faggot."

"What about that radio guy, Mac Murphy?"

"He spouts off on his radio show every night and he's claiming the phone banks are busy day and night. He's been picked up by four or five conglomerates and they're showing really campy videos of his rants on cable channels and the internet, so he's reaching a bigger crowd, but he still hasn't done a live gig."

"Did you get those ads produced?"

"Yeah! Dynamite, and I do mean explosive material but there are two reasons not to run them. First, because he doesn't have a specific geographical footprint and second, because negative ads would only call attention to his tiny little campaign. We've got 'em in the can, if and when we need them."

"I'm hearing rumors that his people are lining up a speech at the Bridgestone Arena in Nashville next week," said Tomlinson, "right in the heart of redneck country."

"We'll want to have some of our people in attendance."

"Can do."

~

The pilot's warm baritone interrupted a heated argument between Stone and Hannah about how Murphy should handle the tragedy in Chicago, as the Gulfstream circled over a shimmering lake to line up with the runway at Smyrna/Rutherford County Airport, home to the plane which was donated for the occasion by a Nashville sympathizer. "Ladies and gentlemen, buckle-up, we're on final approach into Smyrna-Rutherford. The temperature is seventy-two degrees and we're going to see a beautiful sunset. I hope you enjoyed the flight and we look forward to returning you to Cincinnati this evening."

"You can argue all night but we all know that Mac's going to play to the crowd and his rap's going to go where they lead him," said Milly Clark, nudging Dr. Billings. "Isn't that right?"

Murphy toasted Hayden Crawley, who was pointing a video camera at him for background scenes to edit into the final publicity release of the first Martin McClintock Murphy for President rally, "Just want the folks to know that this is the genuine Mac Murphy, what you see is what you get and I hope everyone comes out to join us tonight, 'cause we're gonna kick some ass."

"Keep in mind that we're on the ballot in the next round of primaries."

"We sure as hell aren't going to win California or New Jersey," replied the candidate.

"But I have hope for Iowa, Montana, and South Dakota because you actually have a sizable audience in those states," said Stone. "Hell, you could actually win one or two of those."

"How am I going to win any of them, if I've never been there?"

Hannah grinned, "Because, with today's technology, you are there. People hear your voice every night and can't wait to see the clips on the morning news and the internet. You're a phenomenon."

"You guys are in charge of all that, I just show up when ordered."

Billings handed Murphy a small paper cup containing two black capsules and a large blue tablet, "We're ninety minutes from show time, time for your vitamins?"

The candidate downed them with a final swig of bourbon from a crystal tumbler and wiped his lips with the back of his hand, "You just keep me on the edge Doc. That's your contribution to the success of this campaign."

Billings smiled and settled back in his seat as the wheels touched tarmac with a gentle bump and the plane motored along the runway, turning onto a taxiway and then into a large hanger. The pilot opened the hatch and assisted Milly down the few steps to pavement where Austin Crouch, world famous country music producer, was leaning against a waiting white limousine in a starched white western cut shirt and a black Stetson.

He stood up and touched the brim of his hat, grinning with a practiced smile, "You must be Milly Clark, I've been looking forward to putting a face to the voice."

Milly reached a hand, "We've talked so many times. I'm very glad to meet you and I hope you know how much we appreciate your generosity."

"Not a problem," laughed Crouch. "I don't know whether your guy's for real or not but I'm damned sure he's going make things a whole lot more entertaining than those old drunken cows, who keep repeating the same old crap over and over without ever saying anything!"

"I can guarantee you won't be bored," laughed Milly, turning to the candidate. "Here, let me introduce you to Mac Murphy. Mac this is Austin Crouch, world famous record producer who donated the plane.

"I sure appreciate you letting us ride on the Gulfstream, it was a treat," said Murphy with a grin, as he shook the producer's hand. The actor shifted into countrified nationalist mode, "I heard what you said to Milly and I want to say that I'm not gonna guarantee that we'll win but I'll damned sure keep the bastards honest."

Crouch laughed, "That's about all we can ask and probably more than enough to make people think about the issues and then act on that knowledge."

"We're both playing to the same audience – hard-workin', beer swillin', gun totin', girl chasin' patriots!"

"We speak the same language."

A driver in a black cowboy suit opened the back doors of the long white car, "Can I give you a lift to the Arena? It's about a half-hour drive."

Everyone piled in and their host passed around crystal flutes of cold Champagne, toasting as the limo eased out of the airport and headed northwest on Highway 41, "Here's to a rousing speech and cheering crowds."

"Here, here!"

He turned to Stone, "You must have a machine running the advertising, because it's been building everywhere for the past two weeks. The whole town's buzzing."

"Yeah, we've had a crew on the ground lining up promotions for the program but we've never tried a scaled blitz like this before."

"I'd say you're right on the money, lines have been forming since they opened the doors at noon." He lifted his glass to Murphy, "You're only a legend at the moment but I've got a feeling that, by the end of this evening, you're gonna be a rising star in presidential politics!"

~

Stone handed a list of bullet points to Murphy, "Here, I've put your tag lines in order, I trust you'll expand and expound on these?"

The candidate scanned the list, "Basically, the same shit I talked about on the show last night in the same order."

"Well, it worked on the show, it ought to be twice as powerful when you lay it on ten-thousand cheering fans," added Hannah.

"It works because it's organic, it's pure improvisation and it comes to me in the moment so I don't need your damned list!" screamed Murphy, tearing the list into tiny little pieces that fluttered to the floor as the warm-up southern country band blasted into their latest hit, 'Give Me Freedom or Another Shot of Whiskey'.

Portly Clancy Hamilton, retiring United States Senator, spent his entire career sponsoring legislation promoting the rights of wealthy white citizens at the expense of everyone else, particularly people of color. His broad face lit up with a publicity smile as he lumbered into the wing and reached to shake Mac's hand, "I am so very honored to have this opportunity to set up the crowd for you and promote your maverick campaign. If you win, you can pick up where I'm leavin' off and I'll look forward to serving in your Cabinet."

"I sure appreciate the support of like-minded patriots like you," replied Mac.

The video crews tightened their perspective as the MC's voice echoed around the enormous arena and the crowd shuffled towards the stage, partially filling the orchestra seats, as he started the introductions and credited the sponsors. He pointed out celebrity guests and finally, introduced Hamilton. "Ladies and gentlemen, our very own Senator Clancy Hamilton!"

Three-hundred pounds of shrewdly ignorant blubber stretching the seams of a seersucker suit hiked up the professional smile and waddled out to the podium under a huge red and white 'Pride and Purity' banner, amid tepid applause. "I'm so pleased to see so many loyal patriots here this evening to welcome the man I believe will become the next President of these United States! We've all been fans of his show for years and we know that he's opened his heart and bared his soul, so we might grasp the depth and dedication of his principles and convictions, his righteous moral character, and his brazen patriotism and dedication to constructing a future for real Americans.

I'd like to introduce the only man running for the presidency who can lead our troubled country, mired in partisan conflict and pig-headed inaction, to enact a new beginning, a resurrection of the basic principles of the Founding Fathers that our nation be governed of, by, and for our people. Once he's elected, we can begin to reclaim our democracy by exposing and convicting the traitors who've rigged the system, destroyed our freedoms, and sullied our reputation around the world.

He's a candidate who can rally working-class Americans to stand up for our rights, defend us against the assault on our freedom to worship, the Second Amendment, and the liberal lies being drilled into our children in the public schools."

He played the moment with sad eyes and droopy lips that made his flabby jowls sag like an old coon-dog, until he turned and winked at Murphy and his handlers standing behind the curtain at the side of the stage, "There is only one candidate who will stand up for real Americans! Let me introduce the next President of these United States, Martin McClintock Murphy!"

Thousands of rabid fans jumped to their feet, strutting true Southern hospitality with piercing hoots and bellowing hollers, hoisting Confederate battle flags and waving hundreds of placards reading – 'Mac Murphy for President', 'Free White America', 'Deport the Immigrants', "Abolish Abortion', and 'End Public Education'.

The Senator waited for Murphy to stroll over to the podium, waving to the cheering fans with a huge smile, and lifted his arm in a victorious salute. "Ladies and gentlemen, Martin McClintock Murphy!"

With a nod and a wink or a thumbs-up, the candidate walked back and forth, clapping and pointing to people he'd never seen before, before settling behind the podium, where he waited patiently for the crowd to settle and then he waited for them to quiet and then he waited a full minute longer staring straight ahead, while they stood silently still and totally absorbed in the pudgy man with the silver hair in the blue suit, commanding the spotlight.

He started slowly, softly, "I'm so pleased that all of you and millions of enthusiastic patriots, scattered across this great county, have chosen to listen to my voice every night, to visualize the truth about very real threats to your very existence, and to believe that there's hope for our nation in these trying times.

I know in my soul that I must reveal the truth for you, so you can to take it into your hearts and we can begin rebuilding the glory of our democracy, the strength of our military, and our absolute domination of the other nations of the world.

Our schools are a complete failure, refuting the basic tenants of our Christian society with warped history and unprovable scientific postulations, while test scores continue to fall far behind many other inferior countries. Our roads and bridges, railroads and airports are crumbling and decaying out of neglect and incompetence, our rights and freedoms are under siege by the liberals who are still running most of the agencies of our government and the judiciary and, until we change that, the future is bleak.

Our Republican Congress can't agree with itself and alien imposter President Gonzalez wants to expand government giveaways to thousands of illegal immigrants, who are pouring over our borders looking for a handout, and you can bet your bottom dollar he'll protect them with executive orders until they have time to steal the jobs of hardworking Americans!"

While the audience jumped to their feet with a cheering ovation, he paused and gazed around at thousands of faces radiating hope and allegiance to the bogus cause he was creating. He realized that, since his collegiate acting career, he had never quenched the need to be in the spotlight at the center of the stage with everyone's eyes following his every move and expression, their ears tuned to the melody and cadence of his voice, their moods and emotions subject to his interpretation of the script. Except he had every expectation that the heat of this performance would burn through the history books.

"I have absolute distain for the All People Matter movement, because I've seen evidence that their elite central committee is getting rich off the very people they're pretending to help and represent. Sleazy Mavis Sloan, ancient Victorian publisher Tabitha Hall, temporary and corrupt Representative Stanton Spratlin, and their willowy airhead spokeswoman, Katherine Kennedy, who's got plenty of ghosts hiding in her closets, are raking millions off the top from donations being sent in by desperate people just like you.

So, although I don't support anything about the group, I am terribly sorry for the hundreds of innocent people who died in the tragedy in Chicago. The authorities seem ready to suggest that there was a conspiracy behind the attack by that sad sick pilot and we're seeing plenty of stories in the media about this being just another disgusting demonstration of the desperate extremes that the All People Matter consortium will resort to, to generate sympathy and increase donations leading up to the elections.

I, for one, don't know what to believe...the corrupt official investigation or journalists who don't seem to have any facts or proof to back up their allegations. You can't believe any of them, they can twist anything into the latest 'Breaking News'!"

Thundering applause!

"I'll tell you what I believe. I believe that most of the blame for the coming depression should be targeted on the corporations who are closing factories and laying off hundreds-of-thousands of American workers, so they can open new facilities in Singapore or Mexico or China, where labor is cheap and they don't have to put up with shady unions or ridiculous over-reaching government regulations. Most of those companies are owned by a handful of people on Wall Street, who worry about profits and margins and couldn't give a damn about folks like you losing your job, your house, your family, and your life!"

Whoops and hollers.

"They own the stock market! They control every agency in our government, and they're part of a tight little clique of billionaires and trillionaires who want no responsibility for anything or anyone who doesn't make money for them. Either you serve or you starve and they don't care which you choose. I know that every one of you knows exactly what I'm talking about! How many of you have lost a job or been demoted or had your pay or hours cut in the past year?"

Hundreds of hands shot into the air with a bellowing chorus of cat calls.

"I want to rebuild our economy to include all of you. We'll start by making renegade companies that pull up stakes and ship out, compensate the workers they're leaving behind, not for a couple of months but a couple of years! And they should be forced to pay for technical schools to retrain their personnel for new jobs!"

"Yeah! Right On!"

"And we'll reward companies that expand their American workforce with incentives and tax breaks."

"Alright!"

"And we'll tax the shit out of those greedy bastards in the ivory towers, who are trying to screw the country, before they destroy everything that hardworking people like you have built for generations!"

The whole building trembled with a deafening roar.

"This is a war! A war between real Americans and the elite liberal clique on Wall Street, who've been rigging the vote for years and they damned sure don't want to face someone who isn't intimidated by their wealth and power! Someone who isn't impressed with their snotty aristocratic arrogance! Someone from outside the reach of their corrupt political machine!" He paused, his beady blue eyes twinkled and his thin lips curled into a grin, "Someone like me standing up for people like you!"

The crowd exploded with cheers and applause, stamping their feet and waving their signs. The band started playing 'Happy Days are Here Again' and the audience danced in the aisles as a shower of red, white, and blue balloons tumbled from the ceiling.

"You have the power to rebuild our nation, to rebuild the glory of our democracy, and rid our society of the freeloading spawn of criminal immigrants flooding across our land to steal our jobs, our security, and our future. You have the power of the vote and I'm the only candidate who speaks for you!"

He stepped away from the microphone, waving to the adoring crowd pressing against the edge of the stage, reaching to shake hands. One woman unbuttoned her blouse to expose enormous breasts, another handed him a room key with a fetching smile and yet another a pair of black panties which he stuffed into his pocket as their fingers parted and he marched off the side of the stage.

The arena vibrated with a roaring chant, "More! More! More!"

Stone and Hannah patted him on the back and the doctor looked into his eyes as he wiped perspiration from his forehead with a handkerchief. "Are you alright?"

"Yeah, I'm buzzing right along! That was intense!"

The doctor handed him a glass of ice water and two pink tablets. "Here, take these."

The candidate followed orders and strolled back out to wave and blow kisses to the crowd for a few minutes, before his handlers motioned him back to the wing. By the time, they walked through the complex and out the back door to the limousine, the charge was wearing off and his knees felt weak.

He slumped into the back seat, tilted his head back and started to snore.

"Is he gonna be alright?" asked Austin Crouch, as he sat down beside the sleeping candidate.

The doctor smiled and leaned to check Murphy's pulse, "When Mac Murphy goes out to talk to his people, he gives it everything he's got and he's totally wasted when he's finished. He'll sleep for a couple of hours and be ready to go again."

"That's amazing!" said the producer. "I'm always drained after putting on a show and I sure wish I could conk out when I'm done, instead of fighting the adrenaline rush until the sun comes up."

"I could help you with that," said the doctor.

Stone interrupted, "What'd you think of the show?"

"I think, with some polish and professional production, you could sell out stadiums," said Crouch.

"Ever worked on a political campaign?" asked Hannah.

"No, I've done some big shows for big stars but nothing political."

"Well?" asked Milly Clark. "Why don't you sign on to help us with our next show in Indianapolis in three weeks?"

"I've got commitments…"

"Bullshit," said Stone, "I checked your published schedule, you've got nothing going on, period! Your list of stars is shrinking to wishful thinking and you're up to your ass in debt. I think we need each other and you've gotta believe that this is going to be the rowdiest, rudest, and crudest campaign in history. We're all going to make a fortune and cause as much trouble as we can before the grownups figure out what's going on."

"Are you in?" asked Hannah.

Crouch looked at dowdy Milly's blushing smile, "Is this for real?"

"Yes, it is. Nobody thinks he can win, including him, but I guarantee he'll upend the political applecart and make those arrogant bastards talk about issues that matter to the people in that arena and that's about as patriotic as anyone's gonna get in the next election."

"His show is pulling in hundreds-of-thousands of dollars every week and it's only going to grow, so we can make it worth your time."

"Fine, I'll do the show in Indianapolis and then we'll see but I'm going to need a fat budget to make this work."

"You got it," smiled Stone, leaning back into the plush leather seat, sipping very cold Champagne from a crystal flute, as the long car headed out to the airport.

~

Nellis closed the gate, as the last of a tense and wounded executive committee disappeared down the dusty lane on their way to the airport. He knelt to cuddle and pet the dogs and nuzzle with Gracie, "I'm sorry we've been gone so much but from the looks of you, Sam and Sissy didn't under-feed anyone."

He reached into the mailbox and pulled out a stack of bills, a pound of advertising brochures, and an oversized envelope from Academy Insurance. He shoved the mail under his arm and tore the flap open, pulling a formal letter and a big fat check that would more than cover rebuilding the barn. "Hot damn! Just in time."

Katherine, Kate, and Jessie were sipping iced tea at the picnic table, along the side of the house near the Hasty Bake, and looked up as he skipped up the path. "What are you so chipper about, sunshine?"

"I got the check from the insurance!"

"Cool! I know it's been a long wait," said Jessie, reaching under the table to scratch behind Gracie's ears, whispering to the dog, "You know that I've been well trained, don't you? We'll have to get you two girls together."

"Yeah, well, it's here, that's what counts."

Katherine kissed his cheek, as he sat down on the bench, "I know Stanton's guys are ready to go, whenever you say the word."

"How 'bout now?"

Kate grinned, "So, what ya' cookin' for dinner, chef?"

Nellis scratched his whiskers, "Well, I was thinking about smokin' some salmon, if you kids wouldn't mind taking the truck into town to pick up the package I ordered at the fish market?"

"Are you sure you trust me to drive that priceless vintage hunk of junk?" laughed Jessie.

"Hey, now, she's sensitive," replied Nellis. "You hurt her feelings and she might have a mind to quit running on some lonely stretch of highway in a thunderstorm in the middle of the night, just to teach you some manners."

Kate was inspired by the prospect of smoked anything, "Plus, the longer we dawdle, the longer we'll have to wait for that luscious salmon."

"Fine! I can smell it now!" Jessie glanced at Nellis, "You drive a hard bargain."

"I've got a great dill sauce to go with, if you'd let me make it?" said Kate.

"Sure," said Nellis, "I don't mind sharing the duties or the bounty and I've got some growing in the garden."

Twenty minutes later he opened and closed the gate after them and gathered the dogs to find Katherine, who was still sitting on the bench, chin in hand following butterflies lingering around the first red and yellow milkweed blooms. She looked up as the pack trotted into view, "That was pretty smooth."

"What?"

"Getting them to leave for a little while."

He sat down next to her and wrapped an arm around her shoulders, "They're good people, who've become good friends and comrades and I'm glad they're staying over until tomorrow but we haven't had any time to talk about what happened." He kissed her cheek, "I was real proud of how you handled that press conference and how you kept everyone else going, even though I knew you were screaming inside."

She leaned her head on his shoulder, "I don't know how I survived before I met you."

He laughed, "Things were neat and tidy and boring. Now, you can expect someone to try to kill you at least every couple of months."

She punched him in the ribs, "If you hadn't pushed me into talking to the press, I think I might have tossed in the towel that night. I'll never outlive the guilt for the eight dead in Houston and a hundred and fourteen in Chicago, plus all the other people who got hurt. How can we put on the rally in Philadelphia next month, knowing that the gangsters are going to keep gunning for us and our people?"

"You left off, 'until we quit'," replied Nellis, "and we don't get to quit. That would disgrace the legacy of all those dead and injured people who believed that, together, we could change the world…and we haven't changed much of anything yet."

"Damn you," said Katherine, tears running down her cheeks, "I want to go crawl into bed and pull the covers over my head until the election's over but you push that responsibility button somewhere deep in my gut and haul me back in."

He kissed her tenderly, "I understand exactly how you feel but there's no quittin', so we'd best figure out what needs to happen to make the next one safer while we've got Kate and Jessie here. We already know it's going to be bigger."

"What the hell are you going to be doing?"

"Well, this place is feeling neglected and I don't see anyone stepping up to take over my chores, so I'm way behind. I'll be around to do whatever you need done but I've got crops to plant and a barn to build before our next shindig."

She kissed him passionately, "You think you could put off getting started until after our guests get back?"

Mavis and Tabitha convened a meeting of the directors of their secretive effort to build miniature self-contained communities around manufacturing or fulfillment centers that she and Standler were shepherding along. Reverend Combs supplied his splendid board room in the offices of his Crystal Cathedral in Tampa for the conference.

From the balcony, they watched thousands of homeless people moving around the gleaming sunlit chapel like ants on a hill of crystals. Tall curtains divided the enormous space into dormitories, a counseling corner, and a spiral of pews for gatherings, meetings, and services. The complex also contained a school for the children, a commercial kitchen and cafeteria serving free meals all day every day, with a basketball court and playing fields out back. Reverend Combs was most proud that the folks who were making it all work were members of his congregation, who gave up their grand and glorious Sunday services to turn the Bible's teachings into genuine empathy.

Mavis stood, her blond hair brushed back to cover the fuzzy patch around her fading scar, "I'm sure you're all familiar with the tragedy in Chicago and I want you to know that we're working overtime to make sure that the next rally in Philadelphia will be as safe as the experts can make it. But...I should add that the size of each gathering is growing exponentially. We had well over a hundred-thousand in Chicago and we're projecting more showing up next time."

"How can you guarantee their safety?" asked Harvey Sacks, Harvard graduate and CEO of the country's second-largest financial group.

"We can't," replied Mavis, "but we can't keep them away either, because what they're going through is worse than dying for a cause they believe in…their future."

"Besides, there's no one else who'll stand up for them," said Tabitha. "The future of the nation has no meaning, if it doesn't value and enable more than half the population that's being jettisoned into poverty. Our greedy brethren view them as worthless and expensive castoffs, better to destroy their dignity and let them die in desperation."

"You've all seen the people downstairs. They're not some alien race, they're the people who make our world run smoothly, they do the invisible but totally necessary jobs that make our society function and every one of them is willing to fight all the way through the election to get back even a little of what they've lost," said Reverend Combs. "I believe that this nation was born of compassion and common decency and we, all of us, can't bow down to anything short of overturning the fascist coup and restoring hope."

Ancient and lecherous Bernie Baker nodded, "It's no secret that Stanley French, Conrad Blaho, and their comrades spawned this conspiracy decades ago and their countless political foundations and committees make it very easy for their closest conspirators to contribute vast sums in untraceable donations, targeted to specific and strategic races across the country. The chosen candidates are bound to protect and promote their sponsor's interests or face being replaced in the next primary."

"We all know many of them," said Ned Flint, his sad stare fixed on Mavis for a moment. Neither had managed to escape the guilt or loneliness since the death of her late husband, Tate, but in spite of the circumstances, they shared their grief tenderly. "And I must say that most of them make every effort to maintain the illusion of being honorable benefactors in their communities, while they're creating a dark future at very private conferences that tout patriotism, economic conservatism, and defense of a feudal tradition. Their closed-door discussions center around the fortunes to be made by rounding up, housing and deporting immigrants. Tighten up sentencing mandates to keep private prisons packed with prisoners to maintain staggering profits, repealing EPA regulations that inhibit their industries, and legislative proposals that will eventually eliminate taxes and all social programs. They're trying to build a world where they'll no longer be required to finance the maintenance of benefits or privileges for the worthless parasites who consume so much and contribute so little."

"To counter all of that, we now have thirty-four villages up and running and a dozen more on line," said Standler, "Of the original seventeen projects, we are massively profitable in all but two, and the workforce has taken ownership of running the enterprise and refining their communities in every case. They maintain the properties, make improvements, and tolerate no crime. Zero."

"My hat's off to you," said Flint. "It's hard enough to run a commercial property, let alone training an unskilled population and then handing over the keys to the city. That's amazing."

"Thanks, but we've employed thousands of experts to create and intertwine social and work environments for thousands more. It's self-perpetuating," replied Mavis. "The flip side is the growing support for the All People Matter movement, in spite of the vicious attacks. We've purposely avoided publicity about our housing projects, because we're not geared up to care for all the unemployed who need help, but there's no denying the demands of a hundred-thousand pissed off people who are willing to fend off brutal assaults to make their point."

"How many are you registering?" asked Erwin Nash, pharmaceutical whiz-kid and youngest of the group.

"We got more than thirty-thousand in Atlanta," said Tabitha, "We haven't seen the numbers for Chicago but every signature represents a committed voter and a high percentage become volunteers."

"We're supporting Democrats in races across the county," said Harvey Sacks, "but I still don't have a clue who we should support for president, they're all dumber than dirt."

"Sad old Vice-President Morton, the poor man was born without a soul. Governor Davidson from Massachusetts has the Kennedy look, charm, and the women problems too," said Tabitha. "California's young entrepreneur, Vincent Paul leans hard left but lacks experience and maturity, and then there's Joe Casey, truly one of the most boring human beings on the planet."

"Dull choices," said Bernie Baker. "Hell, even dour tricky Dick Nixon was more exciting than these jokers."

"The Republicans are in a scramble," said Mavis, "and not every candidate is willing to march in lock-step with the mandates of the inner circle. No one has any idea of who's going to come out on top, when we head into the conventions and then the elections. Their media machine's propaganda is lethal to any candidate who stands up to them. Their disgusting videos are as deadly as that damned plane!"

"Speaking of which, did the cops or your security guys ever figure out how the plane hit the stage without a pilot?" asked Erwin Nash.

Mavis shook her head, "The experts found a control mechanism in the plane and the cleanup crew at Grant Park found a suitcase with an electronic flight training system inside. They think someone else was flying the plane like a toy."

"Bet that freaked the pilot out," said Sacks.

"And thousands of innocent people who happened to be in the way," added Baker.

"What about that nationalist bigot, Murphy?" asked Standler. "Did you see the videos from his rally in Nashville? It looked like a rowdy rock concert for white nationalism."

"Yeah, but he managed to rile the racist base without sounding like Adolf Hitler," added Nash.

"He might be a nutcase but he's smart, a master of his audience, and he's building a grassroots campaign that might not need to kowtow to French and Conrad and their buddies," said Duffy Timmons. "He's talking for the people who live out in the middle of nowhere. The people who didn't just lose their jobs and their factories, they lost whole towns and cities in the process. The farmers can't compete against giant agri-corporations buying up every available acre and using robots and satellites to plant and harvest. Nobody's ever gone after that vote before and you have to admit that he might be on to something, if the Republicans can't get their shit together and he finds a few sponsors to pay the bills."

"That's a totally terrifying prospect," said Tabitha. "That man represents everything this country never was and, we can only hope, will never be. He's a disgusting fraud, a charlatan, and I wouldn't be surprised if he isn't out-ted for some twisted predilection before this goes much farther."

"And what if he slides through unscathed?" asked Mavis. "What if he's the last man standing?"

"Then we better find someone of quality and intelligence to carry our banner, before the party throws their support behind one of those losers," said Erwin Nash.

"Mayor Turner could march into the convention without a challenge, after his performances in Atlanta and Chicago. The videos made him look like he's a man who doesn't flinch in the face of impending catastrophe and the public's reacted to it."

"Like it or else, he became part of the executive committee of All People Matter," said Mavis. "He claims he's not ready for national office. Whether that means that he's watching the polls or has other plans, I know not."

"If he runs, we're all in," said Standler. "He's what this country needs, even if most folks haven't figured it out yet."

"We can't put our money and our efforts behind wishful thinking, we need to push forward with a focused strategy and a concrete plan," said Flint.

"Then we continue to support expanding the communities that you're building, get behind progressive candidates in every precinct in every race in the country, and put more money into All People Matter's media message to expand our visibility and our voter base," said Harvey Sacks. "The message is out there and millions are sympathetic, if not gung-ho supporters, and our propaganda needs to support the simple truth that the future is in the hands of those who are willing to work to get out the vote. If they shirk their responsibility, the consequences for everyone will be most dire."

Everyone stared from one to the next before Bernie Baker interrupted, "Not to change the subject, but what's happening with SunnyBreeze?"

Mavis smiled that magazine cover smile, "Honey, you're so rich, what's a hundred million here or there?"

The old man's face flushed into a brilliant shade of crimson but before he could speak, Mavis laughed, "The fund containing the owners' payments should cover most of our initial investments but our mortgage company will absorb some of the losses for the facilities because none of the insurance companies are anxious to pay market value for empty sand dunes, and in the end, I'm sure the buyers will suffer."

"Have you given any thought to rebuilding it or starting another?"

"I can give you a thousand reasons why not," replied the beauty, "but, even though Tate and I conceived it together, it was his baby and he played it brilliantly."

"What about the school?" asked Duffy Timmons.

"That's another story. We've found a location on the mainland that might prove even better than the original site and we're definitely going to try to open a space for the first classes by this fall. Reverend Combs keeps reminding me that training the next generation is not something that can be postponed."

"Amen to that, sister," smiled Jimbo. "The future doesn't happen without the kids."

A warm westerly breeze carried a few gulls across the bay, above a pair of pelicans coasting on a cushion of damp air a few feet above gentle ripples scattering the amber rays of the setting sun. The fish were down deep and none were biting. Jessie shaded his eyes, as he glanced at the melting sun, "I'm pretty sure it's getting close to dinnertime and our ladies will be looking for us."

Johnny reeled in his line, "Yeah, I know but I hate getting to the end of our afternoons because we don't get to go fishing as often as we used to."

"I know, I wish we could go backwards in time. for a lot of reasons, but your mom and I have to try to help these people. Sometimes you do what you have to do because there really is no other choice. Sort of like our rescue mission, it was totally insane and foolishly dangerous but there was no other way to save those people, so we did what we had to do. I hope you know how proud I am of you."

The boy turned to pull the rope to start the little engine, "And I'm proud of you. I wish I could go to Philadelphia with you. I've never been there and I'd like to see the Liberty Bell and Independence Hall."

"And the steps outside the Museum of Art, from the Rocky movies?"

"Yeah, for sure."

"I think we should play it safe, until the security people get us through one rally without anyone getting hurt. You already know how fast a crowd can turn dangerous."

"Yeah, I know, but…"

"Be patient, time will come." Jessie reached to pat his knee, "How's your mom doing?"

"The bruising on her back is turning weird colors but the doctor told her that's good. She's moving around a lot more and she's jabbering on the phone all day."

"She's an amazing lady and a good mom."

"I guess I'm pretty lucky."

"Yeah, you are. Hey, do you know where you're going to school in the fall?"

"Actually, mom said that Mrs. Sloan told her that they're going to try to begin classes in a temporary building, until they get a new campus built. So, I guess I'm going there."

"I think I have a lot more faith in what Mrs. Sloan is trying to do for education, than I did before all the stuff we've been through. She might be an independent thinker but I have faith in her intent."

"She seems really smart and…she sure is pretty," blushed Johnny.

Jessie laughed, "Yes, she is extraordinarily beautiful. Did you know that she's a celebrity and that smile's been on just about every magazine cover in the world?"

"Really?"

He looked at the confusion in the boy's eyes, "You've got a crush on her, don't you?"

"What's a crush?"

"You'd like to spend more time with her, just to look at her gorgeous eyes and that curvy shape, maybe get close enough for a whiff of the expensive perfume she wears."

"Naw, I just think she's pretty," stammered Johnny.

"Hey, I'll tell you a secret."

"What's that?"

"We male people spend a great deal of time gazing at female people. We're mesmerized by their eyes, their smiles, the curves of their bodies, the way they smell, and the subtle wiggle when they walk. We can't help it but the trick is not being obvious about it, glancing instead of staring."

"I think being a grownup is going to be confusing," said Johnny, easing the boat into the slip in Jessie's dock. "I kind of like girls but when I try to talk to them, I can't think of anything to say."

"I know what you mean and I'm pretty sure they conspire together to make us feel awkward but I've found that if you can't come up with anything bright to say, ask them a question, like, if they're a classmate, what's your favorite subject or how'd you do on that test? It's easier if you already know something about them, like do they ride horses or play sports or have a dog or a favorite song. Keep it simple, let them do the talking."

"Okay."

Jessie gathered his gear and leaned to hug Johnny, "The other thing you'll find is that sometimes when you get a girl talking, you can't get her to quit!"

"Kinda like my mom on the phone, since she's been stuck at home."

"Yeah exactly. I've got to get some work done in the studio or Mr. Rangle is going to disown me, so how about I call you on Wednesday and we'll figure out our next adventure?"

"Cool."

He pushed the little boat out into open water, "You be careful going home, say 'Hi' to your mom, and know that I love you."

"I love you, too." Johnny gunned the engine and the aluminum runabout putted along the shoreline around the point.

Gracie bounded down the lawn to prance around him, as he trudged up the rise, "How are you, girlfriend? You taking good care of Kate?"

They reached the porch and Jessie leaned his rods against the house and knelt to hug Gracie, who slobbered his face with kisses. "You're my best girl."

"I guess coming in second best is okay," said Kate, peeking out the kitchen door. "How was the fishing?"

Jessie walked over to kiss her, "They're hiding down deep but it was nice to spend some time with Johnny. He sure is growing fast."

"Yeah, you're good for each other."

"Funny, thing…"

"What?"

"Oh, he thinks Mavis is beautiful and I'm pretty sure he's got a crush on her."

"Hell, I think she's beautiful, sexy, dynamic, and incredibly intelligent!"

He put on his soulful look, "So, if I wasn't as wonderful as I am...?"

"Don't think you're out of the woods yet, buster. You're still in training."

Jessie kissed her again, "Does training ever end?"

"No, it pretty much goes on forever. You're in the 'putting the toilet seat down' phase and that's just the beginning."

"Johnny said he thought growing up was going to be confusing and I'm thinkin' he's right."

She kissed his cheek, "Go wash up, I've got cold lemonade and a tuna salad in a cantaloupe."

"Yum."

Kate walked over to prepare the plates, "I talked to Katherine earlier."

"And?"

"The first Republican debate is tomorrow night and the Democrats get together on Thursday and we don't have a candidate to throw our weight behind."

"As far as I'm concerned, there's only one guy capable of taking over the Democratic Party and that's Mayor Turner."

"Yeah, but he's being hedgy, doesn't want to commit to anything but making appearances at our rallies."

Jessie sipped the cold lemonade, "Ah, that tastes good, it was hot out there."

"Come sit."

They carried their plates outside and sat down in the shade at the picnic table. "I think you ladies should go pay him a visit the day after the Democratic debate."

"Friday? Why?"

"Because, I'm fairly sure the 'debate' will be a snooze and most viewers will switch to reruns at the first ad. None of them have anything new to say, it's the same old spiel they've been touting for the last three election cycles. No matter how loud they say it, it's still just insincere drivel. And, oh yeah, he's going to have a completely different attitude, being confronted by three gorgeous ladies than a couple of wisecracking dudes like Nellis and me."

"I'll agree the current candidates have no energy."

"None, and no personality either. Hey, this tuna salad is wonderful on a warm evening."

"Thanks. You know, you might be right. If we could hit Turner, after a dismal showing the night before, maybe he'd go along."

"Never know until you try but, if you girls are going to do this, you'd better set it up quick, before someone has to be somewhere else."

"I'll call Katherine and Mavis after dinner."

"That's a dangerous trio, he doesn't stand a chance!"

~

Murphy skidded the Cadillac across the parking lot, burst through the back door with a deafening bang, stumbled down the hallway, and crashed through the sound proof doors into a studio blazing with television lights shining down on a half-dozen people watching the end of the Democratic debate on a large monitor.

Sloan turned, "My God, you're ten minutes early. What's wrong with you?"

"I need to see the doc before I melt down," sneered a moderately plastered candidate, flopping into his chair to prop his red, white, and blue cowboy boots on the desk.

A gorgeous makeup artist from the film crew tucked a towel under his chin, pushed his head back to wipe the sweat and grease off his forehead and nose and doused him in a cloud of powder to dull the reflections and hide the gray bags under the slits that masked everything but a mischievous glint in his dark blue eyes.

Dr. Billings walked over to hand him a small white paper cup containing two black capsules, "Here's your pregame vitamins."

"Thanks," replied Murphy, pulling the bottle of bourbon from the bottom drawer for a long swig. "You seem to have me sort of stabilized."

"You hired me to help you recover between gigs, so you can make the long slog to the convention."

"Hell, we'll be lucky if they don't lynch me before then," laughed the host.

Stone walked over and leaned across the desk, "Did you watch any of the debate tonight?"

"Yeah, about the first twenty minutes. Those idiots have no presence, no ideas, nothing. I'll tear them down to their skivvies, real quick."

"Great," replied the political director. "Hey, Austin Crouch is coming in tomorrow. Think you could be sober enough for lunch?"

"Yeah, man, no problem."

Jack Hannah's voice rattled over the speakers from the control room, "We're at a minute and counting."

Murphy pulled on his headphones, arranged the microphone, leaned back in his broad black chair, and lit a cigar. His eyes blinked rapidly and his thin lips curled into a cheeky little grin, as he morphed into character.

"And we're live in five, four, three, two, and...we're on the air."

"Good evening folks, this is your next president, Mac Murphy, broadcasting unfiltered truth to the world from WBFK in the heartland of America.

I don't know about you, but I lasted about twelve minutes into the Republican debate the other night and less than ten with the Democrats tonight. I couldn't decide whether to watch a black and white rerun of 'Gunsmoke' or sit down at the kitchen table with a bottle of Jack to dull my sheer frustration at their lack of...character or personality, conviction or vision!

Something, anything beyond those polished coiffed cookie cutter humanoids spewing the same tarnished bullshit with gleaming smiles. It's all scripted! It's all fake! None of these imitation candidates has the brains or the balls to stand up for these United States of America against friend or foe.

Now, I've taken a lot of flak from my supporters, demanding that I take on those losers in the debate but, after careful consideration, I decided that it wouldn't be fair to make them look like a flock of chickens scattering in panic on their first charge out of the chute. Hell, as far as I could tell, they all stumbled from the git-go and did their very best to shoot themselves right in the foot on their first answer to the first question, and then everyone took turns convincing the audience that he had no clue about what was coming out of his mouth. No wonder both debates garnered the lowest ratings in the history of potential presidents getting together to shoot the bull!

None of 'em could chew gum and walk at the same time, let alone offer any solutions to solve the problems of filthy migrants pouring into the country and jobs flowing out like water over Niagara Falls, the deficits we're running with every trading partner in the world, or the disgraceful state of unready-ness of our military, or fixing crumbling roads and bridges, deplorable railroads and antiquated airports. They didn't talk about how inept and incompetent Congress has been since the Republicans took control. Our Senators and Representatives make lots of speeches but they can't seem to get anything done and our lame lame-duck president hides in the White House and signs executive orders that are countermanded by his own staff, because there's no chance of support to put them into action.

When's the last time anyone actually saw his face or heard his voice? Hell, the newscasts don't even bring him up anymore, he's like number thirty-seven on the potential top-story list and then only on the late-late news as filler. He's irrelevant, a ghost of the brash loud-mouthed liberal champion spouting plans to nationalize healthcare, offer free college tuition, and universal preschool for the little tykes." He paused and puffed, staring into the video camera for a long moment before jumping out of his chair to scream, "He didn't accomplish a damned thing! Nothing! Not one item from his to-do list, when he took office seven years ago! And, rest assured, he's going to slink out of town after the election to hang out in his big expensive and empty presidential library, which we're paying for, and no one will notice or acknowledge his passing."

He sat down, took a slug of Bourbon from the coffee cup Milly Clark prepared before every show since they started taping, and exhaled a cloud of cigar smoke, "Ladies and gentlemen, I can't imagine any of the contenders from either party as President of these United States, Commander-in-Chief of the most formidable armed forces on the planet, and the most powerful and feared statesman on the world stage. Think about it. Can you imagine any of them giving a serious speech on your televisions about dealing with some calamity or threat, or backing down an enemy, or reassuring the nation after a natural disaster? Really? Can you?"

He sat there, puffing and sipping, gazing around at his collection of racist relics lining the walls, for more than a minute, letting those images settle in. "America needs a real patriot running the show, someone who has nothing to gain by accepting the job, the calling, or the responsibility to defend our country, our beliefs, and our future as custodian of the Founding Fathers' dreams and intentions.

We've strayed from the path of righteousness! Hell, we can't even find common sense anymore. There's no turning the ship around without a whole new crew and an admiral at the helm who understands the churning currents of world events, where to find allies and safe harbor during a storm, and how to galvanize his men into a domineering force to be reckoned with by any enemy foolish enough to try.

We need to be the biggest, baddest, most unforgiving son-of-a-bitch on the block. Anyone who wants to screw with us better understand that we carry a grudge and we'll make their lives miserable until it's redeemed with clear and cruel consequences. Back in the days before the wimps took over the White House, our military made sure that our influence extended to the far corners of the Earth. If you elect me, I'll resurrect our military's prowess and rekindle decaying morale, rearm our troops with state-of-the-art technology that will make our enemies quiver and our allies fall into line to salute the real balance of power.

There can only be one boss of bosses and I plan on using every means at our disposal to dominate the world stage and offer our trading partners new rules for the world economy. The days of American giveaways are over! We paid for rebuilding Europe and Japan after World War II, we turned a medieval frozen turd into a manufacturing giant, after the Korean War, we've supplied trillions of dollars in aid to almost every country on the planet and I ask you, have any of them paid us back? Hell No! They've got their grubby hands out for more!

My fellow Americans, it's time for us to take back our country, to right the ship and set a course for the salvation of our place in history, before another batch of morons gets sent to Washington D.C. to spend the next couple of years cozying up to fat-cats for help topping off their re-election funds, instead of doing the work of the people who sent them there.

Join the Murphy for President foundation! Send in those contributions to help spread the word! Listen to my show tomorrow night and come see us in Indianapolis in two weeks. The show's free, so bring your friends for great music, inspired speakers who understand who we are and where we're going, and, of course, yours truly for an unscripted off-the-cuff conversation that will scare those other candidates right out of the race!"

Jack Hannah's baritone erupted from the speakers, "This has been our next president, Martin McClintock Murphy, broadcasting unfiltered truth to the world from WBFK in the heartland of America. Send your contributions to Murphy for President, at WBFK, P.O. Box 1040, Cincinnati, Ohio, and we'll send you a first edition 'Murphy for President' bumper sticker by return mail!

Tune in tomorrow night for your next dose of truth from our presidential candidate - Mac Murphy! I'm producer Jack Hannah, thank you and good night."

Chapter Ten

Katherine, Kate, and Mavis accepted iced tea with lemon rounds impaled on the rims of delicate glasses from the slender co-pilot, who was acting as steward.

"Ladies, we'll be serving salads and an assortment of sandwiches shortly and we're a little more than an hour from touchdown in Atlanta. I have to run through our checklist but I'll be back in a few minutes. If you need anything, please press the attendant's button."

"Thank you."

The handsome blue uniform slipped back into the cockpit, with three pairs of eyes following his feline flair until he disappeared. Mavis held her glass up, "Ladies, a toast to convincing our quarry to jump into the race."

"Nellis said he couldn't resist the three of us," said Katherine.

"Jessie said the same thing," laughed Kate. "He made it sound like we're dangerous vamps ready to pin him down with our stiletto heels until he gives in!"

"Or worse, seduce him!" laughed Mavis, sipping her tea. "Most guys trip over their tongues, as soon as any of us walks into a room. Might was well use it while we've still got it."

Katherine smiled, "I had to kiss Nellis the first time, because he was so hung up on trying to play the country gentleman."

"Jessie and I met at a frat party, which is funny because I got dragged in there by a friend who didn't mind flirting for free beer. I was a little hippie chick who didn't hang out with jocks but it just seemed so natural, as if we'd known each other forever."

"Tate was all gung-ho, slam-bang-thank you ma'am until I flew him to Paris for dinner and a weekend in a quaint little hotel. Didn't take a second night before he realized that there might be more to life than jumping every sorority chick on campus."

"I'm sorry you lost him," said Katherine.

"Me too, but in hindsight, we both knew that we couldn't keep the fantasy couple thing going much longer and we'd been faking it for the scandal rags and the gossip columns for years. I was bound and determined to help him make SunnyBreeze a monumental success before I let go of him but he beat me to it."

"I know you still love him, I can see it in your eyes, hear it in your voice."

"You're right, there will never be another moment when he isn't in my heart, but we have work to do, so let's get on with our strategy."

Kate squeezed her hand, "I think we ought to make Katherine our spokesperson."

"Why me? Mavis could make him drop his false teeth with that fabulous smile of hers."

"Because you come across as the business person, the one who can make him see the bottom line," said Kate.

"That's the point, isn't it? We want to convince him that there's no one in the field better prepared to lead the country out of this quagmire," replied Mavis. "We don't care whether his pecker is inspired, we want his conscience, his intellect, and his heart to commit to saving those thousands of desperate souls who show up at every rally."

"And the millions more who haven't had the chance to share their fears and anger and desperation. We already know that every one of them is going to vote for change," added Kate. "We need to challenge his perspective on the effect that he can have, as opposed to the damage that will be done, if the Republicans take both Houses and the Presidency."

"The nation is at a tipping point where it could pull itself out of the darkness or the ignorant masses could get behind some racist pig with a big ego who wouldn't hesitate to trash our democracy for the oligarchs who are trying to buy the election," said Mavis.

"Maybe that's the other point," said Katherine, "that we need a leader who can have an effect on the balloting all the way down to the local school boards and he's the mayor of a huge city, where he's dealt with all sorts of people and overcome all sorts of problems. The opposition already has a lock on organization, so we have to use mass to pull voters to the polls."

"Even with the growth we've seen since we started all of this, we're never going to connect with enough people unless we have a star out front and, even though you ladies are beautiful, intelligent, and totally committed, we're not going to carry the day without his help."

Mavis smirked, "He's in serious trouble."

~

An hour later, the pilot's warm tenor filled the cabin, "Ladies, we're on final approach to Hartsfield-Jackson, so please buckle up. Touchdown in six minutes. The temperature is 84 degrees, with partly cloudy skies and a moderate breeze from the southeast. The local time is 12:41 PM. We hope that you've enjoyed our flight and we look forward to serving you later this afternoon."

The ladies applauded and minutes later they morphed into a feline posse strutting across the tarmac to a waiting limo. The driver tipped his hat as they climbed in and ran around to take the wheel. "Where to?"

The trio chimed, "City Hall!"

The long car slipped into traffic on Highway 75 and the ladies stared out the windows at residential districts and sprawling apartment complexes nestled into the hilly forest for a few minutes of contemplation.

Mavis glanced at her watch, "Looks like we'll be right on time."

Kate rubbed her arms, "We've been through a lot of weird stuff but I get chills just thinking about that confrontation at the Capitol. The white-nationalists waiting in ambush were so angry and hateful, as if beating up poor unemployed people would solve their problems or prove their superiority."

"They weren't there to rough up the protesters," said Mavis. "They were there to terrorize all of us into giving up the movement."

"Seems like every time they come at us, it gets more violent and bizarre," said Katherine.

"I don't know why this one freaks me out. I mean, Sammy, Jessie, and I were kidnapped, locked up in a gross abandoned jail, and left to starve. I guess I can't shake seeing the fury in their eyes, the ferocity of their taunts…and maybe because there were so many of them."

Mavis pointed out the window, "Hey, there's the Capitol and it all looks fairly calm today."

Kate rubbed her arms again, "I keep having these dreams of each of the attacks and it's always the same people coming after us. The savagery in those faces never changes."

"Have you let it out?" asked Katherine, rubbing her shoulders.

"Not really."

"It's hard to let go but please remember that we're here to help, console, listen, tease, and taunt," said Mavis. "I've lost it more than a few times and I'm bettin' you did too."

The lanky brunette nodded, "Nellis held me for hours until I got it all out one night and after I got myself under control, he basically told me that I don't get to quit and I'd better get my shit together so it doesn't happen again."

"Were you pissed?" asked Kate.

"With anyone else I would have been but he said so gently, so compassionately, that I just accepted it as the obvious truth that I didn't want to hear."

"I always feel like he's restraining his primal instincts," said Mavis. "Ever seen him pissed?"

"Let's just say, you don't want to be the person standing in front of my old man when he's pissed off." Katherine grinned, "And don't cross him, he's like a ghostly archangel delivering a cruel version of Karma where it's most deserved and, half the time, his targets don't even know he was responsible for whatever happened to them."

The limo pulled to a gentle stop in front of the curved concrete entry to City Hall. The driver opened the door and offered a hand to help each of the ladies out of the car. He handed his card to Mavis, "I'll find someplace convenient to park, just give me a call when you're ready to go."

The famous blond smiled that smile, "This could be a long discussion or we could all be heading back to the airport with our tails between our legs in nothin' flat. I guess we'll just have to see how it plays out."

The driver looked confused, "I hope your meeting goes well but I really don't see how any man-person is going to say 'no' to the three of you."

"Thanks, we'll call you," said Kate, as they turned to stroll inside, where a matronly woman in a gray dress, with a starched white collar, smiled, "You must be Misses Sloan, Kennedy, and Crockett?"

"Yes, we are," replied Mavis, offering her hand.

"I'm the Mayor's personal secretary, Phyllis Crane. If you'll follow me?" said the woman, with a knowing smile. "I can see why the Mayor is looking forward to this meeting."

Katherine said, "We thought we might have a better chance of him being receptive to our proposal!"

Their heels clacked a dissonant rhythm, as they marched around a circular fountain and across a magnificent atrium, up an elevator, down a hallway past the public entrance to the Mayor's office to a side door with a touchpad. Mrs. Crane punched in a code and they turned into another corridor where she opened the third door on the left into a small library, with bookshelves to the ceiling, heavy drapes behind a beautiful antique desk, and comfortable chairs around a glass coffee table with a bouquet of pink roses in a crystal vase.

"If you ladies will have a seat for a moment, I'll tell him you're here," said the secretary. "May I get you anything to drink?"

"Water would be lovely," said Mavis.

The woman disappeared through another door and before they settled the mayor strolled into the room with a big smile, "How are all of you?"

"We're fine," said Katherine, "better since we got here without having to fight our way through a mob!"

"I'm fairly sure they'd part ways if the three of you were leading the march," said Turner. "Please, have a seat. I know that your crew wouldn't have sent out the big guns unless it was important. How can I help you?"

The women glanced from one to the next, before Katherine said, "After watching the dismal debates, you already know why we're here and I'm sure you've considered all the reasons we could list why you should consider embracing a run for the presidency."

"You don't beat around the bush, do you?"

"That's why we chose her to be out front for the movement," said Kate.

"From our perspective, which includes those millions of desperate people who need us to succeed, there isn't anyone else who could galvanize a vast majority of the population into a political tsunami and that's what it's going to take to beat back the threat to our democracy. The thought of the tyrants buying both Houses of Congress, the presidency, and ultimately the judiciary is terrifying."

The Mayor smiled, "I hope you don't mind if I string you along for a while, I'd like to take you to dinner tonight. It's not often that I get to escort three beautiful, intelligent, and famous women at the same time!"

"We'd still go to dinner with you, if you said 'yes'," replied Mavis.

"Ladies, my first hesitation is that I might fail and I say that with a bare heart. The notion that a black man might be elected to our highest office was inconceivable not too long ago. Now that it's possible, we have to assume that those racist bastards will do everything and anything to prevent history from repeating itself, including assassinating me. You'll forgive me for admitting one of my fears."

"I don't blame you at all," said Mavis, "and, considering our security failures, you have every right to be concerned. On the other hand, as soon as you declare your candidacy, you'll have Secret Service protection."

"Why else?" asked Kate.

"I've spent my entire life fighting for the right causes, for the poorest people, the most oppressed among our citizenry, and I will go to my grave proud to have served my fellow man. I believe that part of my reluctance is that I might, in some way, not live up to the expectations of people who so desperately believe that I can make a difference for them.

We all know that, even if I survive the campaign and get elected, a Republican Congress will bend over backwards to block everything and anything that I propose. The chance of advancing meaningful legislation is slim at best if the Democrats don't carry a lot of down-ballot races."

"Mayor Turner, win, lose, or draw, those people believe that they can defeat the bastards who caused this nightmare and they need a champion to lead them into battle. You know and I know that you are that man," said Mavis.

Before he could respond, Kate added, "Independence Hall in Philadelphia would make the perfect background for your announcement."

The Mayor's eyes were stern, piercing, "You've already decided how this is going to go down."

The corners of Katherine's red lips curled into a grin, "And, if I'm not mistaken, so have you."

$\sim$

Ethan Tomlinson was contemplating the fog rolling over the point outside the broad windows of his office at ImageSculptor in Malibu, focusing on tactics and messaging heading into the primaries and a contested convention when the buzzer sounded and his new secretary's breathlessly sexy voice said, "Mr. French on line two for you."

"Thank you, I'll take it," replied the boss, picking up the receiver, "Stanley, how are you?"

"I'm as fine as can be expected at my advanced age but, more important, I'm excited about the prospects for the election. We might finally triumph in taking control, if our people don't screw things up."

"We'll have to see which candidates survive until the convention, looks like four of them are still stroking. Whoever claims the nomination will clean up, the Democrat's bullpen is full of has-beens who talk like they've got a mouthful of porridge."

"We're putting a lot of money behind all of them but, of the current crop, Steil's the one who's been most loyal to the cause."

"Duly noted."

"I need to know what you've got planned for the All People Matter rally in Philadelphia this weekend?"

"Actually, we decided that violence or confrontations on the steps of Independence Hall would make for bad visuals and besides, the logistics suck. There's no way out of there, so we cancelled our plans for this one."

"Good. Sullying the cradle of The Revolution and our democracy just erodes the common illusion that Republicans are the party of flag and country. I'll deny it until my very last breath, but we both know that we're the party of greed and division, lies and distortion, big promises and measly returns."

Tomlinson chuckled, "That only works if you've got a brilliant public relations manager building the brand and being anal about the details!"

"Pat yourself on the back for being right on this call," replied French. "What's happening with that blabbermouth from Ohio?"

"Even though the crowd was kind of thin, he was a hit in Nashville and his rant got plastered all over the media for twenty-four hours before he disappeared into a crowded field flooding the airwaves. The audience for his nightly show is growing rapidly and he's got a rally coming up in Indianapolis. We're planning to have some of our people in the crowd to make sure things get rowdy and Will's putting together some ads to expose him as a drugged out alcoholic."

"What's the play?"

"Whether his followers vote for him or not, we need them to vote for our candidates in all the other contests. We're fighting for the same core constituents to get behind state and local races and we've got a ton of promos going out across the country to back our people and reinforce our message."

"What about the primaries?"

"Well, with the new format crowding them all together, he's got a shot at a hefty chunk of the Midwest and the rust belt, if he can figure out how to rally his core supporters. Our guys are gonna take the South and the West, and a few of the mid-Atlantic states."

"What's the final pitch?"

"Take Back Our Country."

"Simple, clean, nebulous, and amorphous."

"It shows strength, determination, the righteous fighting a common enemy in defense of God and country...and guns...defense of the unborn and quashing the heathens, and all the other mantras and tag lines we've been promoting for years. We'll make it the party slogan at the convention."

"And it plays to every tiny group in our coalition of haters – the evangelicals and the pro-lifers, the racists and white nationalists, isolationists and protectionists who want to renounce treaties and agreements, and the folks who believe that our country reached a peak in 1850, when unrestrained white men owned their women and their slaves. For them, it's been downhill ever since."

"That's who we cater to," replied Tomlinson.

"Until after the elections," said French, "when we finish dismantling their world."

"Hate is more powerful in uniting people than any other bond. Give them a common enemy and they'll fuse into a crusade every time."

"We're counting on it, in spite of the fact that we're the elites they're all complaining about."

"We've been hearing rumors floating around about secret construction projects on abandoned military bases. First, is it true and, second, how do you want us to handle it if it gets out?"

"Deny, deny, deny!" shouted the industrialist. "No one can know!"

"But it's out there, people are whispering about massive arrests and disappearances."

"DHS is coordinating with our private contractors to build and service detention facilities in remote parts of the country to house a roundup of illegal migrants, until they can be processed through our special courts and shipped back across the border. They've also developed a highly secure form of transportation to transfer detainees anyplace in the country."

"How's that happening without Democrats raising hell?"

French laughed, "It's all paid for in the nine-thousand page budget our Republicans rammed through last year without allowing the opposition to see one word of it, let alone make objections. Hell, the president had no choice but to sign the damned thing without ever looking inside but, buried within the DHS budget is a brand-new department called ARC – Alien Relocation Command, and it won't be long before it ramps up to capacity."

"How come I'm getting visions of old black and white newsreels of the Gestapo rounding up Jews and shipping them off to Auschwitz in cattle cars?"

"I'd say it's more like Hitler's Brown Shirts, the political Storm Troopers, who enforced the will of the Fuhrer before he took control of the government."

"We're talking billions of dollars...thousands of employees...sprawling facilities to hold them, food to feed them, guards to guard them, and customized transportation to move them."

"We all know the government is totally incapable of running an operation like this efficiently or expeditiously and private enterprise has every right to make a profit. Works out best for everyone."

"Except the illegals," said Tomlinson.

"That's the point, isn't it?"

"Take Back White America!"

"Exactly."

~

Sissy shifted her king's bishop halfway across the board to pin Nellis' queen in the corner of the antique game table set up in a cool breeze wafting through the porch, with a passel of dogs and the mewing of a tumbling ball of feline fluff on the lounge.

Nellis sighed, "You know you're very cruel for such a young age. You might grow up to be criminal."

The girl stuck her tongue out at him, "You're just beginning to realize that I'm going to have you in check in two moves."

"Ah, I see, you're going to add your queen to this little mix of bishops and knights to plug up my escape," replied Nellis, stroking two-day's growth on his chin before skipping a knight to block her line on his king. "That ought to hold you for a couple of moves."

"I'll just pick off your defense one man at a time, before you figure out that there's no escape."

"Not my rook!"

"Tell me something?"

He pushed a pawn, "What?"

"What's a primary? My dad was talking about them."

"Most states have a primary election, meaning before the final one, people vote to select their favorite from a bunch of candidates for different offices and those, mostly Democratic and Republican choices, will run against each other in the fall to see who wins the office. We broke up Brantley's candidacy in the last primary and your dad got himself appointed to Congress until the governor decides to hold a real election. The biggies are the presidential primaries coming up over the summer for the big election in November. Does that make sense?"

"Yeah, I guess. He said that there are a whole bunch of them coming up all across the country."

"Well, used to be that they'd stretch them out from February until early summer but, sometimes, someone running for president collected enough delegates to lock up the nomination way early, so it was kind of frustrating for people to vote when they already knew the outcome. Now, nobody knows who's going to win until the very end."

"Is that supposed to make it more exciting?"

"I think you're on to something, they're trying to draw more people to the polls but I'm not sure that this works any better than the old way," said Nellis pulling his other knight out to fight the onslaught of white pieces. "Actually, I think they changed it so the public relations companies that crank out all the advertising for the candidates can continue to make an obscene fortune right up until the end of the campaign without interruption.

"Is this election more important than the ones before?" She ran her other bishop two spaces to take a pawn that was protected by his queen in the corner. The question was whether he'd sacrifice his queen to her rook to begin a cascade of ferocious moves that would leave his king exposed and vulnerable."

"Like I said, you'll probably grow up to be a criminal." He pushed a pawn to block the rook but the damage was done. "Yes, I think this election is more important than most because, if a Republican wins the White House and they hold majorities in the House and the Senate, they'll have absolute power to pass or repeal any laws they want."

"And people who disagree won't have any say?"

"Exactly."

She paused and looked up from the board, "Are the bad people trying to get these guys elected?"

"Yes."

"Is that why they're trying to stop you?"

"Yes."

"They should go to jail."

"Not that I disagree with you, because a lot of people have been hurt or died, but we're fighting to keep the rules fair and that doesn't mean much, if we don't follow those rules ourselves."

"I'm proud of all of you," said the adorable chess shark, taking his queen to set up his doom.

"Well, thank you!" His grin sagged into a dejected scowl.

Katherine stepped out onto the porch, "Beat him again?"

"Always," beamed Sissy. "He did put up a pretty good fight, until I got him cornered."

"Don't gloat," growled Nellis. "It's embarrassing enough."

The girls burst out laughing and patted him on the back, as the herd of dogs got up to rub against their legs. Gracie put her head in his lap and looked up with sad brown eyes.

"You're just making fun of me too, aren't you?"

The dog yelped agreement and trotted out the screen door.

"You women are all in cahoots."

"Pretty much," said Katherine, kissing his forehead.

"Where are you going?"

"I've got to meet Stanton at the plant to go over the quarterly financials with the board, then a little conference at the hotel with a half-dozen activists from the West Coast. They're headed to Philly to help coordinate for next week."

"You sure are busy," said Sissy.

She leaned to kiss her on each cheek, "I keep trying to blame Nellis for getting me into this mess but I wouldn't trade it for anything.

We're trying to help millions of people who are scared and desperate and I won't quit trying even when the last vote is counted."

"I wish I could help."

"You just pay attention to how it's done," said Nellis. "Someday, we're all going to be counting on your generation to save the world."

"Gee, no pressure there, especially after your generation's screwed it all up."

~

The cross streets were blocked off by police cars and firetrucks and entry to the park was limited to pedestrians, who were screened as they entered. A sea of eager faces packed shoulder to shoulder, generating a cloud of communal heat against a late spring wind blowing in off the Delaware. Humanity stretched from the tiny podium in front of the Washington statue outside Independence Hall to the National Constitution Center and Franklin Square around the corner.

Brad and Eddie's bikers cordoned off the small plaza in front of the famous building with gleaming chopped Harley-Davidsons parked nose to tail with a burly rider in between. Police and Eagle Security personnel covered the five blocks from rooftops to basements.

There were no banners or signs, no bands or music, just a single podium on the brick pavers but speaker towers with video screens would permit tens of thousands to see, hear, and interact in the surrounding parks.

Nellis strolled up to the microphone with his vintage Martin six-string, "I hope y'all can hear me because I want you to sing along. Come on now, we all know the National Anthem!"

O say can you see, by the dawn's early light,
What so proudly we hail'd at the twilight's last gleaming,
Whose broad stripes and bright stars through the perilous fight
O'er the ramparts we watch'd were so gallantly streaming?
And the rocket's red glare, the bombs bursting in air,
Gave proof through the night that our flag was still there,
O say does that star-spangled banner yet wave
O'er the land of the free and the home of the brave?

The crowd picked up the tune from the second line and sang along through four verses, ending with a rousing roar,

And the star-spangled banner in triumph shall wave
O'er the land of the free and the home of the brave.
Francis Scott Key 1814

"Now that's the spirit! I'd like to welcome you to The Philadelphia 'All of You Matter A Whole Lot' Rally and I'm glad you all agree that we can make a difference. I'm Nellis Gray, from Cameron, Oklahoma. You might have heard about a little tussle we had with some rednecks trying to hijack our elections. Well, we put a stop to that conspiracy and I'm hoping we can all get together to do the same with the upcoming elections. Are you with me?"

Thousands cheered.

"I'm known for going on and on, so it would probably be best if I introduced our spokeswoman, Katherine Kennedy, who'd like a few words with you before we get on to our featured guests."

Katherine strolled across the brick pavers and kissed Nellis on the cheek. She hesitated for a moment to stare up into George Washington's eyes, eyes filled with aspirations of independence and the wisdom to fear the coming revolution, unleashed by a gathering of men in this building to become the greatest democracy in the history of the world. She turned to the microphone, "I don't know about you, but I'm feeling awfully humble standing in front of this historic building and all it symbolizes, with George Washington's eyes staring down at us. Do you think he'd be proud of what we're trying to accomplish?"

The crowd roared.

"I do too! We started out fighting a little band of redneck racists long before we realized who was behind them, a gang of greedy families waging open warfare on our society and our way of life. These people think they have the right to oversee the transformation of our country into a two-class autocracy, where they're free to take until they've sucked every resource out of the ground and destroyed the environment. They won't stop until there's nothing left and they don't care who suffers to satisfy their gluttony."

A deep groan rumbled through the mall.

"I'm here to tell you that we have the power to stop this rush to madness, to reclaim our rights and our dignity, to purge our government of their lackeys, and send the conspirators to prison for treason! I can guarantee that the patriots who fought and argued to produce the Declaration of Independence in this building would be proud of what we're trying to do!"

The mob started chanting, "Freedom Now! Freedom Now!", moving and swaying as one.

"We have the power to change the future but that only happens if every one of you is registered to vote in the primaries, because our whole population is counting on you!"

"Yeah!"

"If you haven't registered, please sign up at the blue kiosks on every street corner in the park. Please don't hesitate, don't put it off. We need every vote to count and yours could be the vote that changes an election." She paused, scanning the mass of humanity, "If we don't get this right, it could well be the last real election we ever get to vote in."

The audience was almost silent, swaying back and forth together.

"That's not just some line out of a political promo, that's what I believe, that's what I fear the most…that if we allow the Republicans to control all three branches of government, we will never again be allowed to gather together to express our views or protest injustice. They'll strip away the first Amendment to dismantle our free press and replace it with the truth according to White Nationalist sensors. You'll be allowed to worship any religion you want, as long it's the version of Evangelical Christianity that's approved by the government and paid for with votes. Actually, they'll just call the Constitution and the Bill of Rights null and void and everyone will be subject to the will of the state.

You've already seen the first wave of fascism, where they eliminate your job, force you out of your house, confiscate all your belongings, and destroy your dignity. Am I right?"

The crowd yelled and jeered, the anger and the fear driving desperation and rage.

"I'm sure many of you have witnessed people, particularly immigrants, disappearing from your communities. We've all heard reports of roving bands of black uniformed government enforcers grabbing people off the streets. Prominent immigration lawyers tell me that they can find no arrest warrants and no trace of charges, trials, or incarceration…but they never come back."

A thousand voices shouted eyewitness stories.

Katherine bit her lip, "I think that's all the more reason that I should introduce our first speaker, an institution of courage and honesty, strength and decency, a defender of all that's right and true! Please welcome Atlanta's Mayor Tyrone Turner!"

The former Falcon's linebacker strolled across the brick plaza and hugged Katherine, with a smile, whispering, "You could have brought me in on a high note."

"Nothin' but the truth, so help me God."

"Amen, Sister, amen."

He stepped up to the tiny podium and waved to the cheering crowd, adjusting the microphone as high as it would go, which was about level with his tie clasp. He shouted, "Thank you, thank you!"

The ovation continued without pause for almost five minutes. "I've got to admit that I'm excited to see all of you too, but how about we have a conversation and then we can get rowdy!"

The thunderous roar erupted again.

"Ladies and gentlemen, I'm pleased to be here with you on this fine sunny day, in front of a statue of one of my heroes, George Washington, who helped shape an agreement and a famous document inside this building that set our nation on the road to independence and her people to freedom.

Our forefathers exhibited enormous courage and fortitude, forging a rebellion with a ragtag militia, comprised of farmers and untrained volunteers, against the regimented and well-armed troops of the most powerful empire on the planet. It would have been easier to bow to the will of King George but the men who gathered in this building had a vision of a nation built on freedom, dignity, and justice and they vowed to fight for their beliefs until they triumphed or died trying!"

"We need our own general!" shouted a slender black woman in an orange shawl near the front, spinning around with her arms in the air. "We already have an army!"

"Darlin', wherever you're going, I'm going too," replied the mayor, with a hardy chuckle.

"Ladies and gentlemen, Miss Kennedy revealed the truth about what's happening in our country - the lies, the manipulation, and the oppression. Our ancestors fought an enemy that was arrogant, brutal and dumb enough to wear bright red coats, but our contemporary persecutors want to remain anonymous, hiding in the shadows of their villas and penthouses where they can direct the destruction of our democracy and the dismemberment of our society."

Boooo's.

"They'll go to any lengths to avoid exposure, to protect their privacy and their shady connections, so I suggest that we start calling them out, one-by-one. I propose that we put their names and their stories on the front page of every paper in the nation, on every news program, on every talk show, or media news feed for all the world to see.

We hold the super-rich up as heroes, as pillars of our society and examples for our children, when in reality a fairly large group of them are really enemies of the state - traitors, collaborators, and criminals. They control sprawling international empires, have famous names, fabulous holdings, and well-managed images that will be slightly tarnished when they're publicly tied to this treasonous conspiracy."

The crowd chanted, "Freedom Now! Freedom Now!"

Turner held up his enormous hands, "Ladies and gentlemen, I am here today because I believe in all of you. I believe in the future of this nation. I believe that the Constitution and the Bill of Rights apply to every citizen, not just the few, that justice is the great equalizer, that honesty and courage will overcome lies and deceit, and that, together, we can take back our country, our democracy, and our future! Are you with me?"

The roar reverberated through the neighborhood, "Turner, Turner, Turner!"

He waited patiently, until the chaos died to a sustained wail, "I believe in the vision of our founding fathers, their intent to establish the foundations of a nation, by and for the common people, through the documents they produced right here in Independence Hall. So, I can think of no more fitting moment, no more historic setting to announce that I will run for the nomination of the Democratic Party for the office of President of these United States and I hope you will support my candidacy!"

Jessie and Nellis escorted Katherine, Kate, and Mavis, followed by all of the coordinators, staff, and members of the executive committee to surround Turner, as the crowd exploded with cheers and applause.

Mavis leaned to kiss his cheek, "I'm very proud of you."

He turned to say, "You ladies drive a hard bargain."

"You were easy prey!"

"I'm going to feel very vulnerable every time I face the public."

Kate pointed to four men in dark suits and sunglasses, scanning the crowd as they approached the steps of the building, "I believe your security detail has arrived."

"How did you…?"

"Tabitha made a few calls."

"Remind me to thank her for her foresight."

"She sees, we do," replied the writer.

Murphy sat back in his chair, sucked down a swig of bourbon and toked on his cigar, observing Hayden Crawley and the video crew scrambling to finish setting up lights and cameras, Stone in a clutch of advisors and assistants pouring over the latest polls on a desk at the back of the studio, and Jack Hannah standing in the window to the control room tapping the watch on his wrist. The doctor rifled through his black bag to produce a little white paper cup, which he carried through the mental bubble that walled off the candidate from the chaos like a sacrament in a silver chalice, an offering to the gods of madness and lunacy.

"Here's your vitamins. Sorry I was late getting here."

Murphy took another nip and downed the pills, "It's alright, they'll kick in just about the time I get to the important stuff. Just be prepared to reel me back in when I'm done."

"I'm your man."

Hannah's baritone voice erupted from the monitors, "We're counting down, two minutes to airtime. Places everyone."

Penny Baker, the makeup girl tossed a towel over Mac's chest, wiped the sweat from his brow, frosted his face with powder, and brushed his hair back. "There's no saving you."

"You should know by now that what you see is what you get, darlin'."

"Thirty seconds."

"If you weren't so old and ornery, I might think you were kinda cute."

He scanned her voluptuous curves and patted her bottom as she scurried away. "If you weren't so young, we'd both be in serious trouble."

"Ten seconds…five, four, three, two…we're on the air."

"Good evening folks, this is your next president, Mac Murphy, broadcasting unfiltered truth to the world from WBFK in the heartland of America."

New patriotic theme music swelled and faded, "I'll tell you what, I think we've finally got a real contest for the race for the presidency and the soul of America, after the slate of candidates from both parties worked so hard to convince the nation that none of them have the brains or the brawn to take on the duties and responsibilities as our Commander-in-Chief.

If you want America to be a second rate also ran, a fading glimmer of our former glory, snuffed out by an inept bungling fool on the international stage, vote for one of those morons. I'll guarantee you that they'll give away the farm before they're sworn in!

And, while I'm on a roll, did you see that jackass from Atlanta spouting off at the All People Oughta Matter Rally in Philadelphia this morning? African-American elitist liberal aristocrat announcing his candidacy for the highest office in the land, standing beside a statue of George Washington in front of Independence Hall?

Hell, most of the signatories of the Declaration of Independence kept and traded slaves and I'm pretty sure this travesty is not what they had in mind, when they drafted our sacred documents. They'd be outraged at the audacity, the blatant disrespect for the sanctity of the office. His election would tarnish the honor of the White House, adding yet another stain to an unblemished and unbroken chain of command going back almost two-hundred and fifty years to the birth of our nation.

Throughout our history, each president championed the hopes and dreams of our people by setting an example for everyone else. We've fought our way back since the advent of civil rights but, I think you'll agree, this is a step too far!

The executive committee of the All People Matter movement are transforming themselves from their fake commitment to defending the desperate and dispossessed against the greed of international corporations. Now they're trying to manipulate presidential politics to insert their impostor, so they can institute the ultimate socialist welfare state through government handouts to illegal immigrants, criminals, freeloaders, and ghetto trash."

He jumped out of his chair, screaming through a haze of cigar smoke, "All you people of color, step to the front of the line! White citizens don't have rights anymore! We're handing over our heritage, our dignity, our pride, and the purity of our nation to an ignorant and illiterate tribe of mongrels, who have no respect for history, for the rights of patriotic families that go back hundreds of years, for the integrity of our social order, or the economic collapse that their incompetence and charity to their brothers and sisters will ensure.

Ladies and gentlemen, there is only one way to stop this impending disaster." He paused, staring into the camera, "You and I have to stand together to defend our great nation from this menace. We have to march in lockstep through the remaining primaries and into the convention, where we'll raise hell until we take the nomination, and then, we'll bury All People Matter and the Democratic party in an electoral landslide!"

The entire crew stood in awestruck silence, while the lights on the multiline phone across the studio lit up like fireworks.

"Ladies and gentlemen, I don't think I can say it any clearer than I have tonight. I'm your candidate and I'm the only one who can defeat the dancing bear and save our country from disgrace. I need your help and support. God bless America, thank you and good night."

The soundproof room exploded in cheers and applause that drowned out Jack Hannah's closing plea for donations. Stone walked over to pat a sweating Murphy on the back, "That was excellent! The contribution spigot just opened full blast. We're going to roll into Indianapolis and the crowds are going to bust down the doors to get in!"

The limousine passed rowdy crowds heading for the entrances arguing with noisy protestors lining the sidewalks and waving signs - 'Murphy's a Moron' 'No Racist Presidents' and 'Deport Murphy!' - as it slipped down the ramp into the bowels of the Lucas Oil Stadium, home of the Indianapolis Colts. Several agents surrounded the car before giving the driver permission to open the doors. Stone leaned over and patted Murphy's knee, "You've reached the bigtime."

"What do you mean?"

"You've got Secret Service agents for your security detail and the ultra-conservatives have been flooding the airwaves with negative ads about you for two weeks, so you are now a serious candidate!"

"Hell, someone got the wrong message, that's for sure. The badder they make me look, the more appealing I become! How many folks showed up for the party?"

"Capacity is sixty-seven thousand and we've already got fifty-thousand inside with more outside waiting to get in."

"Hell, this could be our first sellout!"

Raucous country music echoed through the hallways from the main stage at the end of the stadium and Austin Crouch was waiting with an extended hand and a huge country smile, when Murphy climbed out of the car, "Man, these folks can't wait to see your act. You won't believe the vibe, man. It's intense!"

"I'm thinking you're the man I need to thank for making this into an extravaganza."

"I'll take all the credit you'd care to offer but I'm pretty sure the crowd upstairs would riot if you didn't show up. They start chanting 'Murphy, Murphy' every time a speaker takes the stage." He shook hands all around, "Let me take you up to our suite, where we can relax until you go on."

They packed into an elevator which rose rapidly and opened into a carpeted hallway, lined with large graphics of football heroes, leading to a lush private suite. Crouch guided Murphy to the windows overlooking the field, where thousands of fans covered the floor and filled every seat in all three decks.

The candidate gazed around the huge arena and smiled, "We're going to party tonight!"

"This is just the beginning. We'll get bigger, bolder and louder at every stop, until we get to the convention."

Stone walked over with a rotund little man in a silk suit, who held out his hand, "I'm Milton Graves and I'm very pleased to finally meet you."

"I've heard that name," replied Murphy, shaking his hand, "oil, isn't it?"

"One of my companies owns a few wells, pipelines, refineries, ships, fleets of trucks, and gas stations that sell my products."

"One of your companies?"

"Well, I do have mining interests on five continents, processing plants, steel mills, a diamond concern in the Netherlands and South Africa, and real estate in most of the major capitals. I guess you could say that I have diverse interests." The entrepreneur's dark eyes twinkled and his puffy lips curled into a smile. "I'm sure that if you were elected to our nation's highest office you might become a champion for the rights of business and commerce."

"I'm campaigning on my opposition to governmental over-reach on regulations and I want to completely revamp tax policy to promote growth and investment."

"Then I think we have common objectives and I look forward to forging a mutually beneficial relationship."

Murphy grasped his hand, "Climb on board brother because this train is gaining speed and it's going to be one hell of a ride!"

Stone engaged their first mega-contributor, while the doctor handed a small white paper cup to Murphy along with a coffee mug full of bourbon. "Time for your vitamins."

The candidate glanced into the paper chalice, "How come there're three?"

"You seemed a little draggy earlier, so I upped your dosage."

"I'm flyin' on two of those suckers, you sure I can handle something else on top of that?"

"Don't worry I'm your doctor, remember?" replied Billings, with a pat to the shoulder. "I can reel you back in as soon as you're finished."

He downed the pills with a chug of whiskey and shook his head as the fire raced down his gullet to incinerate his stomach. "How soon do we go on?"

Crouch glanced at his watch, "Twenty minutes. Band's about to finish up, Indianapolis's wimpy local mayor will introduce Indiana Senator Ted Sherman, who will introduce you."

"How's that bastard going to introduce me if he's never met me?"

"He's one of us," laughed Crouch. "He knows his lines and his place."

"Wants to be in the Cabinet?"

"Absolutely and I'm pretty sure Commerce is his first choice."

"Hell, guys like Graves want to gut the EPA and the Internal Revenue Service."

Stone leaned close to whisper, "He can have whatever he wants, he just handed me a check for a million dollars."

"No shit?"

"No shit."

~

A tall lanky former baseball pitcher with an unruly tuft of salt and pepper hair, a furrowed brow over dark dancing eyes, and a perpetual cockeyed grin, Senator Sherman played a tough country bumpkin persona that masked the cagey political shark, who defended his turf and his sponsors with absolute fidelity and resolute tenacity. The baseball legend was famous for brushing players away from the plate with stinging fastballs that curved inside at the last moment, the Senator made a reputation for removing opposition with insults and bravado wrapped in lies and innuendoes. His patrons financed his campaigns and lined his pockets because he routinely slipped last-minute amendments promoting their agendas into must-pass bills in the chamber.

He ambled across the stage to shake moderate Mayor Phillip's hand, with a grimace and a nod of momentary tolerance. A two-handed wave brought the crowd to their feet, "Good evening Indianapolis! How y'all doing tonight?"

Raucous cheers.

"Any night I get to spend with my people is a good night and I know tonight's going to be extra special because I get to introduce a rising star in the party, a man of depth and courage who isn't afraid to stand up for what we all believe in, a man who, with your help, could very well become the next president of these United States!"

Whistles and applause.

He turned and pointed to a giant banner, reading, 'Pride and Purity', "You know and I know exactly what that means. Our flag has been soiled, the very fiber of our society tarnished, our military neglected, our status in the world weakened to the point of embarrassment, and our rights and liberties threatened by an administration that's afraid to enforce the laws on the books, afraid to confront our enemies, and too timid to force our allies to pay their fair share for the defense of their own failing governments.

Why should our citizens pay taxes that are used to prop up corrupt leaders in other countries, when our roads are crumbling, our schools are pathetic, and we're being invaded by illegal immigrants bent on stealing our jobs, defiling our women, and jacking up our kids with drugs?"

Booo's and whistles.

"We have to stand together to take back our country, our place in the world, our pride, purity, and dignity before the liberal elite destroy this great nation. The past eight years have been a ridiculous waste of time. Nothing has been accomplished because Washington's tied in knots and the Democrats refuse to compromise on anything. I know, because every bill that I've proposed has faced absolute opposition and a presidential promise of a veto before they even know what's in it. Our nation can't function this way. It's time for a change, a big change, a transformation from fading influence to reclaiming our rightful place at the pinnacle of sovereign power.

We need a leader who aspires to unquestioned and unchallenged domination and we need you to help him get there! Let me introduce my good friend and the next president of our United States, Martin McClintock Murphy!"

Murphy's heart was racing, his hands shaking uncontrollably, and his vision fading in and out of focus with crackling flashes. Consumed by the amphetamine rush, the primal energy of the crowd, the band playing 'Good Times Are Here Again', and the challenge of the most daunting part in his theatrical career, he took a deep breath and released it with a slow whistle as he transformed into character. His body projected a regal arrogance as he straightened his spine, threw his shoulders back, thrust his chest forward, and lifted his chin imperceptibly, so he appeared to be looking down on everyone else.

Stone leaned to whisper, "Go get 'em, tiger."

He nodded and marched out of the wing to deafening cheers and applause. The audience oozed like molten rock, pushing the first ten rows into a crush at the edge of the stage with hands waving and hundreds of faces distorted into primeval screams that melded into a wretched wail careening around the stadium, gaining strength from thousands of fans stirring the darkness in waves of fanatical zeal. Sharp spotlights illuminated and video cameras captured his every move, projecting his blazing image on enormous screens like a god descended from the heavens to lift his chosen people to the rapture of venting their tribal hate without fear of derision or retribution.

He finally got to the Senator and shook his hand, lifting their arms together in a triumphant display of unity and fraternity. Sherman patted him on the back and disappeared, while Murphy stood perfectly still behind the podium, his arms at his sides, his eyes focused on an exit sign in the darkness on the second balcony at the far end of the field, and he made no attempt to speak for more than three minutes while the rowdy crowd slowly settled to virtual silence.

He stepped forward and began slowly and softly, "Our nation and her people are suffering and exhausted from years of infighting and incompetence by the leaders of both parties. None of them have the brains or the guts to rise above petty bickering to take the reins and move our country forward. They're too worried about cozying up to their corporate bosses to get money to finance the next campaign, never mind that they didn't accomplish a damned thing during this session or the last or the one before that.

Never mind that corporations are closing factories and sending your jobs overseas, where they can hire cheap labor and avoid job-killing regulations. Never mind that governmental agencies are systematically erasing your rights and your future, destroying the spirit that allowed patriots like you and me to build this nation from the ground up with our bare hands. They're filling the press with mumbo-jumbo propaganda to hide the truth about their real agenda of supporting the elites on Wall Street with tax cuts and lazy immigrants with handouts that come out of our pockets. They want to take our guns away, limit religious freedom, and fill our children's brains with fake science and their twisted revisionist version of history."

He paused, waiting for the roar to die down, "We all know what they're doing but no one is willing to confront them, to throw them out of office, to start a revolution to restore our freedoms and our pride, to take back our country and finally fulfill the dreams and ambitions of our founding fathers.

Ladies and gentlemen, tonight, we're going to begin putting an end to their greedy games. Tonight, together, we're going to convince your family, friends, and neighbors to become true-believers and join our ranks to take over Washington, D.C. to right the ship of state and set a course for our promised land!"

Cheers and applause.

"We're going to take back our school boards, our city councils, our state legislatures, the House and the Senate, and then we're going to seize the White House!"

The roiling arena of angry zealots exploded into pandemonium, the roar reverberating through the churning crowd, dancing and waving

'Murphy for President' posters, and surging to the edge of the stage. Four Secret Service agents raced to protect Murphy from the screaming fans trying to scramble onto the stage, amid a torrent of women's underwear dropping out of the darkness to litter the floor.

"Ladies and gentlemen, would you do me a favor," asked the candidate, eyeing several bare-breasted women being squashed by the crush of bodies. "Would everyone please take one step back? I'm afraid some of these folks up front here might get injured by your enthusiasm. C'mon, move back just a little."

A deep groan drowned out the cheers, as the crowd eased back a step to relieve the pressure but the partially dressed women shifted to the center, right in front of Murphy, who blew them a kiss. "You've heard all the reasons why I shouldn't be running for office, all the lies and made-up stories, but I know in your heart of hearts you understand that I'm the only person in this race who's going to tell you the truth tonight and tomorrow and always. I'm just a regular guy with problems and bad habits just like every one of you but I'm also the guy who isn't afraid to stand up to these bastards and I won't be afraid to show them the door!"

The audience let out a deafening snarl, as bodies piled up on the lip of the stage and four security guards appeared from the wings to march back and forth, stepping on fingers and shoving fervent fans back into the chaos on the floor. Fights broke out and the agents tightened their ring around the candidate.

"I know you have to get this frustration out of your systems but I need every one of you to stand together with millions of your brothers and sisters across this great nation to vote these traitors out of office and replace them with patriots who believe in the grand scheme of our revolution. We need people who understand that the cure for this disease that's infected our society for decades won't be easy and it sure won't be pretty, people who won't shy away from tackling the hard problems with brutal dedication to the goal of taking our nation back from the weasels and the vermin.

Our time has come and with your help, I'll march through the remaining primaries, we'll take the nomination at the convention, and then we'll take the White House in November! Are you with me?"

The arena erupted with cheers and the thunderous rumble of stomping feet, pounding chairs, and thousands chanting "Murphy! Murphy! Murphy!"

The candidate raised his hands above his head, shouting, "You are my people and I'll lead you to victory, reclaiming your dominance and restoring your pride by rebuilding our democracy to serve our people and our beliefs! God bless you and God bless America!"

Murphy stepped away from the podium and the agents closed around him before he could move to the edge to shake hands and get a closer look at the topless ladies who were reaching up to offer room keys and phone numbers. Overwhelmed security guards resorted to kicking enthusiastic fans who attempted to scale the platform pitching them into the crowd without mercy. Blood splattered across the shiny stage and flailing bodies clashed in a brawl that spread into the darkness, as agents escorted Murphy into the wings.

Stone reached to shake his hand, "Man, that was fantastic! Did you see how crazy those fans got? It was like one those films of a Beatles concert!"

"You're too young to remember the Beatles…but I do."

Austin Crouch patted him on the back, "I wish some of the 'stars' I work with could play a crowd like you do, they went nuts!"

Dr. Billings looked into his eyes, "How are you feeling?"

"Like the top of my head's going to spin off and zip into space."

He held out a white paper cup and a mug of Bourbon, "Take these vitamins and things will seem a bit more calm."

"As you order, doc," replied the candidate, downing two pink pills with a big gulp of whiskey.

Milton Graves and Senator Sherman waited in the tunnel behind the stage with congratulatory smiles and the three gushing women. Graves took his hand, "The reaction of your supporters makes the rest of the field look like amateurs. I believe with a little help from our friends, we can find you a path to the convention."

"The convention's just a congratulatory party for the worker bees, I'm aiming for the White House!"

"You keep producing reactions like that and we'll get you there," said the Senator.

Graves added, "I'll be in touch with Mr. Stone in the next few days."

Murphy shook his hand, eyeing the tall buxom brunette, "I appreciate your support and look forward to a mutually beneficial friendship."

Graves stepped out of the way, slipped the three women hundred-dollar bills, and pushed them into Murphy's arms, "Enjoy your evening."

Chapter Eleven

After being awakened a third time, as Jessie slipped out of bed and wandered out to the studio in the dark, followed by the click-clack of Gracie's nails on the floor, Kate asked, "Are you alright?"

"Yeah, I'm just anxious that everything gets off as planned for the first day of camp tomorrow. We've got almost twice as many kids and a whole bunch of new instructors this year and it's all got to flow like clockwork."

"Relax, you've done this how many times before? It's just gotten bigger and you've got some great people organizing it. It's going to be fine."

Before he could respond, the telephone rang in the kitchen. Gracie cocked her head inquisitively, as he picked up the clock, "It's almost four in the morning, do we know anyone who's been kidnapped lately?"

Kate moaned, "Been there, done that."

The artist padded into the kitchen and picked up the receiver, "Hello?"

"Jessie, this is Police Chief Trapper Johnson. I'm sorry to wake you."

"You wouldn't be calling at his hour, unless there's something going down."

"I'm really sorry to inform you that someone torched five of the six tents that you had set up over in the park for Art's Important. The fire department responded immediately but there was nothing they could do."

Jessie's brain burst into overdrive, "Was anyone hurt?"

"No, I'm pleased to say that no one was injured and I've taken the liberty of calling Henny Wilbanks, the owner of Baywater Tents, and he'll have replacements here ready to set up day after tomorrow."

"I can't believe this happened and that you took that upon yourself. Thank you."

"Mr. Cotton, you make a difference in the lives of so many kids and, because they're valued at the camp they come away with confidence and self-esteem, which means that most of them aren't going to go out and get into trouble. So, in the end, you make my job easier."

"I never thought about it that way."

"Most people wouldn't," replied the chief. "What about supplies? What was in those tents?"

"Just tables and chairs. We always bring in supplies the first morning and then replenish them as we go, keeps theft and waste down. Once camp starts, we always have security patrolling day and night. Too many little people to worry about."

"I'll see that the city has crews out to clean up the mess first thing in the morning and we'll increase our patrols to make sure this doesn't happen again."

"Thanks."

"I'll see you over there tomorrow."

"I'll be there." The line went dead and Jessie trooped back the bedroom.

Kate asked, "Who was that?"

"The Chief of Police informing me that five of our tents were torched. No one was injured and fortunately we're moving supplies in tomorrow morning."

"What are you going to do?"

"Well, the Chief took it upon himself to call the owner of the tent company who will have five new tents set up day after tomorrow."

"But you've got hundreds of kids coming in the morning?"

"We'll go back to how this all started, by having class in the shade of the trees in the park. I'll call Megan Payne, head of the Parks Department, and see how many picnic tables we can round up. It'll be totally crazy but we can pull this off."

"Do you think this was done by the white nationalists or just some drunk arsonist?"

"Considering Nellis' barn, I'm taking it as a personal warning, but they just pissed me off. Don't mess with my kids!" replied Jessie, leaning to kiss her with a grin. "Art's important but all people matter."

"God, you get even more clever when you're pissed," laughed the writer. "Time was that I was totally petrified by all of this but, after riots, hurricanes, and airplane crashes, I know we'll get past this."

"It's all about the kids."

"I'll write a story for the paper but I'm supposed to head out to meet the girls in Atlanta for a conference with the mayor. He's put a campaign committee together to get his name on the ballot in as many states as possible and added to the candidates' debate before the next batch of primaries. We want to hold a rally in St. Louis, that same day, so we can have a mass showing inside and outside the arena that night."

"You go, we'll handle this."

She wrapped her arms around his neck, "Have I reminded you that, in spite of running out on me, getting me kidnapped, trying to sacrifice me to a hurricane, and being a lousy date, I still love you?"

"I'm glad," replied the artist, with a passionate kiss. "I was starting to worry that you might be getting bored."

Somewhere far away in the sodden recesses of Murphy's brain, he was aware of a rhythmic pounding, like the deep round tone of the mallet striking the skin of a kettle drum, thumping air inside his eardrums, a sonorous timbre rumbling through his core to rouse his consciousness from a near-death state of coma.

After Friday night's radio show, he started off with three more of Doc Billing's Black Molly's, so he'd be primed to consume the better part of a bottle of Jack with Penny Baker, the curvy makeup girl from the video crew who brought over a gram of fine coke and a seductive smile. Finally, as the sun was coming up, he popped a handful of those pink pills he usually took after the show to drop out of orbit.

His right arm was dead, his fingers completely numb, buried under something soft and heavy. Painful waves pounded inside his skull and a strong sweet scent of drug store perfume overwhelmed his nostrils, as he opened his eyes to downy mounds of smooth white flesh caressing his cheeks, accompanied by a full-throated snore. He rolled back and stared for a moment, while struggling to focus on Penny's pretty face, although not quite as young as she first appeared under studio lighting, with lipstick and makeup smeared on the pillowcase and her mascara and eye shadow smudged into deep gray pools around her eyes.

He lifted the sheets to inspect a tangle of naked bodies, hers a sculpture of voluptuous curves lying next to his embarrassingly ignored and abused assemblage of misplaced fatty deposits where the taut muscles of his youth once resided. The incessant hammering jarred his brain into sluggish motion and he placed his feet on the carpet, holding his head in trembling hands until the room stopped spinning and consciousness staunched the acid bomb in his stomach long enough to stumble to the bathroom to throw up in the toilet.

The mangy vagrant in the mirror looked angry and afraid to even consider the possibility of inebriated impotence, because he had no memory of the hours since he left the station. His face was pale and puffy, his eyes buried behind dark slits, his thinning hair snarled in a rat's nest, and a stream of syrupy sputum dribbled down his chin. "You look like presidential material to me, bub."

He swished his mouth with cold water, pulled on a thin bathrobe, and staggered through the living room to unlatch the front door, intending to beat the person on the other side into silent submission. He found Stone and Hannah grinning from ear to ear. "What the fuck do you want?"

"You're going to be center stage at the debate in Miami Beach next week."

The contender rubbed his bloodshot eyes and squinted against the sun, "I'm surprised those losers let me in."

"Didn't have much choice because none of them have enough momentum to demand much of anything," said Hannah. "They're a bunch of peacocks strutting around trying to impress naïve voters but it's all for show."

Stone put on his sincere campaign chairman look, "Having guys like Milton Graves running interference doesn't hurt."

"When and where?"

Hannah grinned, "Fillmore - Miami Beach, Tuesday night, and it's going to be broadcast live."

"So, the Party's making a play for the Florida vote right out of the gate," mused Murphy. "How fast can you get me the dirt on the other Bozo's who are running? I can start picking them off on my Monday show."

"I can have it printed out in an hour, with bullet points, if you want 'em," replied Stone.

"Can you have someone drop them off?" He looked down at his naked body protruding through the gap in the open bathrobe and pulled it closed. "I'll get cleaned up in the meantime."

"Can do."

An hour later, a bedraggled Penny was banging around the stove, pretending to know how to fry bacon, when a clean-shaven Mac answered a knock and let Milly Clark into the foyer. She looked around the reasonably orderly living room with approval until she noticed the partially clothed makeup girl at the stove. "I'm sorry, I didn't realize you had a guest."

"Oh, don't worry about her. Did you bring the files?"

"Yes, they're right here," she said, handing over a stack of paper. "I'd offer to help you get organized but I can see that you're busy."

"I won't be busy after I get some protein in me, you're welcome to stay," replied Murphy.

Milly turned to leave, "Just give me a call later and I'll come back."

"Alright, thanks for bringing them by. I'll call you after I have a chance to look through the material." She hurried outside and he closed the door after her.

"I definitely don't understand women," muttered the candidate, dropping the pile on the table, as he settled into his lounge chair.

Penny peeked out of the kitchen, "That's easy, everyone knows she's in love with you."

"Really?"

"Really! I've got bacon and toast, do you want eggs with this?"

"Can you cook fried eggs?"

"I could try."

"Don't bother, bacon and toast might save my soul," said Murphy, absently, as he picked up the top folder labelled 'Governor Jeffrey Grant'.

His date brought a plate of slightly burnt bacon, two limp pieces of toast, a jar of strawberry jam, and another mug of coffee. Her breasts escaped her loose blouse, as she leaned for a kiss, "You need anything else? Coffee, tea, or me?"

He brushed her aside, "I'm gonna be busy for the next few hours. You might as well grab your stuff and go."

"Gee, thanks a lot," whined the makeup artist.

"We had a good time, now I've got work to do, simple as that."

"You had a good time," replied Penny, marching to the bedroom to gather her things. He barely looked up as she stomped through the house, slamming the front door as she left.

He munched bacon and sipped hot sweet coffee, as his eyes scanned the pages. "Well, I guess she answered that question."

On page twenty-seven, he found a note about a rumor suggesting that the governor had fathered a child with an African-American cheerleader from his high school nearly forty years ago. Although there was no further information, the research staff could search for a year book from their school and birth records from local and surrounding hospitals.

Page eighteen, in South Carolina's former governor, Billy Estes' file, revealed that his father was a Grand Wizard in the Klan and that the old man's four brothers were implicated in a mysterious lynching in the tiny burg of Sandy Springs just north of Lake Hartwell in the late Fifties.

Chubby Charles Garner of Florida appeared the bumbling fool who got elected Congressional Representative on a fluke. His opponent died. Sam Trippet was a loudmouth who took his orders directly from the cabal that was financing the Party, but Creighton Steil, former governor of Indiana, was known for being a radical evangelical homophobic sleaze-ball, who passed the most repressive anti-homosexual bill in the history of the county. A half-dozen lawsuits rattled around the courts for nearly three years before the law was finally deemed unconstitutional. There was also speculation that he was controlled by a domineering wife, who held the purse strings and his bravado against the LGBT community was cover for his secret identity as a closet queen.

Each and every file exposed his fellow candidates as shallow political impersonators, lacking any personal accomplishments or commitments to anything beyond their own egos and serving their paymasters, who financed their meager careers. Every other candidate on that stage was receiving scandalous amounts of money from three shadowy political action committees that shared a post office box in Detroit. Tuesday's event should prove to be easy-pickings but he had to wonder what they were reading about him.

~

Shepherd Stone leaned close to Murphy's ear, as Penny Baker dusted his face with a pale blue powder puff to mask the testament to overindulgence wrinkling his jaundiced skin. "I know you've got all this in your head but I want you to come across as being worthy of claiming your place on the panel, knowledgeable instead of arrogant, aggressive without being a bully. Whether they like it or not, you're the guy they're chasing, it's yours to lose, so act accordingly."

"I'll take 'em apart before the first commercial."

"That's what I want to hear," replied the campaign manager. "We need to tune your message to reinforce the fringe without scaring off all those undecided voters who should gravitate to you instead of the Democrats."

"Everyone has something or someone to hate and I've got the right bait."

"You do realize that this will be your biggest audience ever. Networks are predicting twenty-million plus!"

The stage manager bellowed, "Five minutes, five minutes everyone!"

"Good thing I got great training in drama school at the University of Georgia," said Murphy, running his hand up the inside of Penny's thigh, as Stone walked away. "I've been preparing for this show since I was a kid."

The makeup artist reached into her kit to grab a pair of scissors, which she held above Mac's face, "I'll drill a hole in your eye socket if you don't get your hand off of me right now!"

"It couldn't have been that bad, you stayed the night and cooked me breakfast."

"So? You have all the class of an unwiped asshole. Do you expect me to jump your bones or give you a fast blow job in front of all these people?"

"Neither, just get my juices flowing. I like to be primed when I go into battle with an angry mob of mental midgets."

Penny sighed, dropped the scissors into her case, and took up a brush to smooth out the bags under his eyes, as her left hand slid under the towel to inspire his limp member.

The audience settled as the announcer introduced the candidates, "Ladies and gentlemen, welcome to the Republican Debate, featuring the leading candidates for the nomination for the Presidency of the United States. We're coming to you tonight from The Fillmore Miami Beach, famous for decades of stunning performances by stellar musical artists from across the world and the generations.

On our left, let me introduce Tar Heel Governor Jeffrey Grant, from North Carolina, next to him is Longhorn Senator Saul Willis from the great state of Texas, beside him - radio host Mac Murphy from Ohio, to his left is Governor Billy Estes of the Palmetto State, South Carolina, Representative Charles Garner for the Sunshine State, Sam Trippet, representative from New Mexico, the land of enchantment, and former Governor Creighton Steil from the Hoosier State of Indiana. Welcome to all of you."

The audience responded with applause and muted cheers.

"Now, please welcome our host and moderator, Paige Phillips!"

The stunning blond newscaster, with the reputation for masking brutal honesty and loaded questions behind a disarming smile and a soft Virginia accent, acknowledged the audience and turned to the camera. "Thank you and welcome to our audience and the candidates, who are contesting the Republican Debate with us tonight. Our distinguished challengers will be asked questions that were drawn from an overwhelming volume of submissions by voters from every district in the country, thoughtful questions that have been kept under lock and key until just a few minutes ago.

The order was determined by the luck of the draw and each of these gentlemen will have three minutes to answer to your questions, before another will be given the opportunity to respond for two minutes. Each candidate will also be given two minutes, at the end of the program, for a summation. We have requested that our audience refrain from reacting to the answers, so the viewers at home can form their own opinions and make up their own minds."

"So, let's begin." She turned to the panel, "Governor Grant, let me start with you. I don't think that anyone would argue with the fact that our country has a problem with immigration, what do you see as our greatest challenge and how would you deal with it?"

The governor, a tall fit former football star, brushed back bushy salt and pepper hair and switched on a toothy grin for the camera, "I want to thank you, Miss Phillips, Independent Broadcasting, and the Republican Party for sponsoring this event. It's an honor to be up here with these extraordinary candidates and I look forward to hearing their positions on the challenges that face this great nation.

We all know that we have a flood of illegal immigrants assaulting our borders every day, many of them running from the law in their home countries, hoping to disappear into our population, where they get handouts from the liberal government, until they can steal a job from a hardworking American.

The current administration has shown complete incompetence in their attempts to stem the flow or remove these leaches from our country, so I think we should empower each state to deal with the problem through whatever means works best for them."

Murphy interrupted, "As a matter of fact, there's a secret branch of Homeland Security that's doing just that. I'm told that they're rounding up more than ten-thousand illegals a month and shipping them back where they came from."

An indignant Paige Phillips said, "Mr. Murphy, you're interrupting Governor Grant's time."

"Governor Grant ought to spend some time learning something more than the pat lines that his handlers drilled into his head. I'm sure the rest of these idiots would have responded the same way!

No one seems to want to admit it, especially our lame illegitimate president, but the government has a clandestine army called the Alien Relocation Command and they're building gigantic detention centers on mothballed military bases out in the boonies all over the west and, if I'm elected president, I'll be right up front in expanding this force to round up every last one of them and ship 'em out, until we resolve the problem once and for all! I want the illegals to be so scared about what we're going to do to them, that they turn tail and head back home."

The conservative crowd cheered.

Phillips turned, "Ladies and gentlemen, please!"

Murphy couldn't resist one more comment, "Aw, let 'em cheer for the truth!"

The moderator tried to ignore him, "Governor Estes, do you have a reply?"

Before he could speak, Murphy said, "Hell, this is right up your alley, Billy." He turned to the camera, pointing, "His daddy was Grand Wizard of the Klan back in the day."

The audience gasped.

"Mr. Murphy, that was not only out of line but uncalled for. Please refrain from interrupting the other contestants!" said Phillips sternly.

"Let's make this a real debate, let's talk about truth, because every single one of these dimwits has been run through training programs put on by the cabal that's trying to buy this election."

"Mr. Murphy!"

"Hell, Sam Trippett and chubby Charles, went through it up in Jackson Hole last month. Estes and Willis are classmates from a program in Houston paid for by ultra-conservative Casey Buck, who owns Global Oil, the largest privately owned oil company on the planet.

These morons have been drilled on how to respond to these questions with cookie cutter answers to promote the agenda of their sponsors and we can be damned sure that Buck and the other members of his fraternity don't give a damn about the folks out there in television land, who are losing their jobs, their homes, and their place in our society. You want to have a debate? Let's talk about helping them instead of making the fat cats richer!"

"Mr. Murphy, we expect a certain level of decorum in this debate and if you can't respect that then I will have you removed!"

"Lady, the American people don't care about your decorum, they want to know how these losers are going to solve the problems of unemployment, jobs leaving the country, affordable health care for their kids, or getting our troops out of stupid wars!" He stepped out from behind the little lectern and pointed at the camera, "You people know who's speaking for you and it sure as hell isn't one of these comedians!"

He held his hands up, as two security guards took his arms and escorted him off stage to ecstatic supporters in his entourage, while the crowd booed and jeered.

Hannah wrapped him in a bear hug and Stone patted him on the back, "You couldn't have played that any better! You're the outlier, the defender of the little guys, and now, everyone in the nation knows you're for real!"

"Bet I don't get asked back," snickered the candidate, eyeing a smiling Milton Graves, blocking his exit with a blond on each arm.

~

Ten identical white limousines, escorted by more than a dozen black Suburbans turned off Cole Street, easing through a gauntlet of security to roll down a long ramp into the barren concrete bowels of the Convention Plaza in St. Louis.

Coveys of staff and an impatient press pool greeted each of the five candidates and their entourages as they unloaded at the back-stage entrance to the Ferrara Theater, an intimate fourteen-hundred seat venue with four broad balconies, stacked one atop the other to bring the entire audience close to the performance.

Aides and advisors surrounded their contestants to push through reporters, photographers, and video crews who shouted questions to which Massachusetts Governor Jimmy Davidson flashed a confident smile and a wave. Sad old Vice-President Tippin Morton, who should have sauntered off years ago, managed a tired grin as he shuffled past without a word.

Joe Cassidy, the passionately boring socialist Senator from Wisconsin, stopped to say, "I think the American people will see a clear choice for the nomination and the path to our future after tonight."

Vincent Paul, California tycoon and CEO of Twyxys, a revolutionary software company, added, "It's time to reinvent our stagnant government to be more responsive to the needs of the people and I think everyone in America will understand why that's so important to our future."

Finally, Mavis, Kate, and Katherine, wearing matching rainbow patterned pantsuits, escorted Mayor Turner into the scrum. He stopped to say, "I hope the American people take advantage of this opportunity to hear each candidate, to judge our intelligence and our character and decide whether any of us possess the capacity to lead our nation out of the chaos that we've been enduring for far too long. Everyone out there needs to make a commitment to vote because the coming election will determine who we are, what we stand for, and what kind of world we want to leave for our children and grandchildren. The choices we make will personally affect every citizen in the county, not only during the next four years but for decades to come. Thank you."

Security led them to an elevator up to dressing rooms along a hallway beneath the stage and as the crowd dispersed to their assigned spaces, Katherine took the mayor's arm, "How are you feeling?"

"I'm fine," smiled Turner. "This is old hat but it's a pleasant change to be able to say that I respect each of my competitors, they're all good men with good intentions."

"Sad that neither party put up a woman," said Mavis.

"I agree absolutely, especially in times like these, but can you imagine the Republican reaction to a ticket with a black man and a white or Hispanic woman? They'd sell that as apocalyptic!"

"Their white base is terrified that they'll lose the status that they still believe they possessed in some fictional long ago, like before the Civil War." Kate pointed to blotches of pastel colors, blending one into the next on her rainbow suit. "But we've all seen the color of the crowds that show up at the rallies."

"Yeah," laughed Mavis, "Denim!"

The stage manager strode down the hall yelling, "Five minutes, places everyone!"

"Do you have your copy of the closing statement?" asked Katherine.

"I don't need it, we all know what I need to say," replied Turner.

The candidates trooped up a short flight of steps and through a door onto the stage taking their places at the five podiums as the crowd cheered and applauded. The house lights dimmed and a single spot flashed through the darkness to illuminate Trevor Hobbs, renowned news anchor for International Public News.

An announcer counted down, "Five, four, three, two...and we're live."

Hobbs's weathered reassuring features and a sterling reputation for taking no prisoners in interviews, projected the impression that he had been everywhere and experienced everything worth reporting over the past forty years. He smiled into the camera, "Good evening and welcome to the National Democratic Debate being broadcast from the Ferrara Theater in beautiful St. Louis, Missouri. We'll follow the usual rules of three minute answers to each question, two minute responses, and a thirty-second follow-up, if we decide it's appropriate. Each candidate will close with a short statement. Our audience has been instructed not to applaud or react to anything that happens on stage, after our introductions, until the completion of the debate.

"Now, allow me to introduce Massachusetts Governor Jimmy Walker, Senator Joe Cassidy from Wisconsin, Vice-President Tippin Morton, Atlanta Mayor Tyrone Turner, and California's Vincent Paul, CEO of Twyxys Software.

Let me start with you, Mr. Vice-President, with all due respect to our president, who has been frustrated by a resolutely immobile Republican Congress, why do you feel that you can win them over to support your programs and pass your legislation, if you were to win the election?"

Tippin Morton, an aging political pro, his puffy eyelids drooping under the weight of age, his lower lip quivering ever so slightly, looked directly into the camera, "Mr. Hobbs, I'd like to thank you, the League of Women Voters, and the city of St. Louis for inviting us to talk with the American people tonight.

To answer your question, as a Senator, who also served several presidents in cabinet positions and as vice-president, I believe that I bring years of experience in working with the opposition to create compromises that moved the country forward. President Gonzalez has done everything in his power to advance his agenda but political and social resentments have driven the parties to extreme opposition. I'll bring us back to an equitable center, where old foes can find new allies."

"Mr. Vice-President, you are the deciding vote, should there be a tie in the Senate, and yet in two terms of service, you have never been required to cast that vote and there has never been a tie in the House because only Republican legislation reaches the floor. If the Republicans can maintain a majority in each chamber, why would anything change?"

"Because the voters, Democrat and Republican, are sick and tired of the stagnation in Washington. If they vote change, then change will happen."

Hobbs shook his head, "Governor Walker, do you have a response?"

"Yes, this election is not just about keeping a Democrat in the White House, it's about changing the balance of power in Congress. We need the voters to support progressive candidates who are promoting great solutions for the broad spectrum of problems this country is facing. I've seen polls that suggest that we're closing the gap."

"Thank you," said the moderator. "Mr. Paul, here's the perfect question of our tech savvy candidate, "How would you improve, not only voter turnout but the security of the whole system of voting?"

The suave confident, if not quite arrogant, CEO replied, "You're right, I'm the only one who can give you an intelligent response. I've always thought that we should tie Social Security, our driver's licenses, voter registration, health insurance, and banking into one identification card that follows every individual throughout their lives. With the integration of everything into the internet, it would be easier to carry one electronic card that you could use for everything. With the advances in technology, it won't be long before we won't need to carry any form of identification besides our faces."

"It would also be easier to completely erase our right to privacy," added Joe Cassidy.

"Do you own a cell phone?" asked Paul.

"Sure."

"Then, someplace out there in the cloud, there's a server that's recorded everything you've bought, every place you've spent money, every trip, every phone call, email, or text that you've sent or received. You might be able to close and lock your front door every night but the computers start recording everything, as soon as you interact with anyone anywhere through any communications device. In that way, privacy is an illusion in our world."

"That's totally frightening," said Hobbs, "to wonder who's watching from the other end?"

"That's the new reality," replied the CEO.

"There are some traditions that we may regret losing." The moderator turned to the camera, "As a reporter, I must ask Mayor Turner a personal question. Sir, I think every American wonders what you were thinking as that airplane dove on the stage in Chicago?"

"You know, there are those critical moments in life where everything slows down and your perception speeds up, that heightened awareness enables you to take in every detail in your surroundings all at once. When I realized that the airplane really was lining up to strafe the crowd and crash into the stage, my first concern was to warn the people in harm's way. I'm afraid I was a bit awestruck by their response, because they parted like the waters of the Red Sea, scattering to the edges of the park in two great waves of humanity that saved thousands of lives. Unfortunately, most of the dead and injured were close to the stage when the plane hit.

I think the last figures I heard were three-hundred and sixty-two injured and one-hundred and twenty-seven dead and all of those brave souls came together to demand an end to the oligarchs' campaign to destroy the middle class for the benefit of the wealthy few.

Our nation suffered a coup, several years ago, when the conservative party handed over their consciences and their entire philosophical foundation to the radical racist fringe. Their new leaders have set about the task of dismantling everything that makes this country the envy of everyone in the rest of the world, while justifying their programs with a blizzard of nonsensical lies and propaganda."

"I believe," he glanced at his fellow contestants, "no, we all believe that we the people expect better than this. We the people demand an end to the corruption, the oppression of the working class, and the limitless corporate funding that allows those wealthy few to buy votes and throw elections. They've been doing it for decades, starting with your school board and your city council and the only way that things are going to change is for each and every one of you to march into the polls and cast your vote for a return to sanity and common decency!

This is it, there is no next time, because I truly believe that we must win this election decisively or the next Republican administration will find an excuse to cancel the elections four years from now.

If you want to stop the destruction, silence the madness, and restore our democracy, vote! Take you mother and father, sister and brother, your neighbors, your best friends and your worst enemies, get them all to the polls before the American dream becomes a sad memory. You have the power, now is the time to use it wisely!"

The crowd roared their approval and rock-steady Trevor Hobbs could only nod his head in agreement. The other candidates had no choice but to applaud enthusiastically, in spite of realizing that one unscripted question just changed the poll numbers dramatically.

∼

Mavis strolled to the back of the Gulfstream to offer a flute of cold champagne to Mayor Turner, who was sitting on a couch with Jessie and Kate. "No thanks, the doctors put an end to that a long time ago."

"Well then, let me toast you just the same," replied the cover-girl, lifting her glass. "Network polls suggest that you just moved to the front of the pack."

"Here, here!" added Kate, hugging Jessie. "With honesty, intelligence, and sincerity, you've given the first real hope of redemption to millions of terrified Americans. All People Matter!"

"I'm proud to represent them and to have all of you in support. Perhaps together, we can make a difference in the future of our country."

"I'm fairly sure that you'll be tomorrow morning's lead," said Tabitha, applauding with Standler, Benny, Sammy, Sheldon, and Beal, and a pair of Secret Service agents, who attempted to remain inconspicuous in the last pair of seats in the cabin. "The networks will want interviews."

Bobbie Warmington paged through her notebook, "We've got you on the ballot in next week's primaries in Iowa, California, and New Jersey. We didn't make the cut in Montana or South Dakota."

"It feels rather odd, asking for votes without having a chance to visit these places, to talk with the people, to understand their concerns, one-on-one, in person," said Turner. "The rest of the candidates have all been campaigning but, despite sophisticated media machines and organization on the ground, none of them seem to have struck a spark."

"Let's not worry about starting an inferno in this first batch," said Kate. "We'll make time for you to rub shoulders with your constituency during the next few weeks. We don't have much of a ground game going yet but we'll have the first round of television ads up tomorrow."

"I don't think there's any doubt that you'll face that crude racist Mac Murphy for the general election, it will certainly be a battle for the hearts and minds of the downtrodden majority in this country. The most insignificant of us will decide whether they can put aside their anger and frustration to help rebuild our democracy or hand over the nation to racism and hate," said Tabitha. "It's a struggle between the little guys and the wealthy few, those who are in this for the common good, as opposed to those who lust to rule by destroying anything that might impede their gluttony and greed."

"You've already set the tone for the campaign, the strikes, and the rest of our rallies," said Mavis. "Everyone can relate to common sense and common decency over chaos and lies."

"Anyone who can't see the looming darkness on the horizon is either blind or a fool," said Benny. "The working poor understand the stakes and you have the presence to bring them on board."

"Thank you, young man, I appreciate your honesty."

"Primaries on Tuesday, our rally in Denver on Saturday," said Bobbie.

Chapter Twelve

Ethan Tomlinson's phone buzzed and the young receptionist's sensual voice whispered, "Mr. French on line one, shall I take a message?"

"No, I'll take it, thank you." He hesitated, then pressed the button, "Stanley, how are you?"

"Murphy and Turner stole the damned debates! Most of our entries never got a chance to speak before that asshole turned the show into a three-ring circus! What the hell are you doing about it?"

"Will Terry's releasing a flurry of ads across the country that blast both of them."

"We've spent billions of dollars to seize control of the electoral process and my associates in The Forge are up in arms!"

"Every candidate has their first teams working the primary states, we own the airwaves, and the latest polls still show a tie between Grant, Steil, and Trippet in Montana, Iowa, and South Dakota. Steil's ahead in New Jersey and Trippet's got a slight lead in California. Estes got bumped by the Klan comment in the debate and Charles Garner's self-destructing. Murphy is a distant sixth in all five races."

"The press is intrigued with him. His headlines sell papers and spice up the news programs on television. He's got nothing going for him, other than a big mouth and crazy conspiracy theories, but with stunts like that, he's still dominating the field!"

"He's an outlier with no budget and, if he doesn't make a decent showing on Tuesday, he'll probably disappear."

"I don't want to hear 'probably', I want an action plan to solve the problem!"

"We could try to buy him," replied Tomlinson, gazing at golden whispers of sunlight dancing through wispy fog outside.

"A little mouse told me that Milton Graves is putting money behind him."

"Is he one of us?"

"No, he's a renegade who's looking out for his own ass," replied French. "He's making a chancy personal bet that could pay huge dividends."

"So, if we can't beat 'em, maybe we should join 'em," laughed Ethan. "Hell, we haven't had a political assassination in years.

"Turner is a bigger problem than this little rat. Their PR people are setting him up as the wise old father figure the voting population so desperately wants, instead of the crazy uncle he really is."

"We'll be ready, if he starts gaining momentum."

"He's already got the nomination sewed up and he hasn't received a single vote!" cried French.

"I'll make sure it's all-hands-on-deck and they're mustered for battle. Let's see how things work out on Tuesday and go from there."

"Blanket those states with ads and get your volunteers out in droves. We've spent decades to reach this point and we can't let it slip away."

"We won't, we've already got our people inside his campaign."

The line went dead and he dialed Will Terry's number. It rang twice before the video guru answered, "Will, Ethan. Listen I just got off the phone with French, who's all lathered up about the debates and losing control. What's happening in the polls?"

"Everyone's talking about Murphy and Turner but we still haven't seen any reliable numbers."

"It's time to release those Murphy ads you've been sitting on."

"You sure that won't just give him more momentum?"

"I don't think we have any choice, nip this in the bud before it has a chance to take root. In the long run, Turner is a bigger problem."

"I've got legions who are eagerly awaiting the chance to remove that obstacle."

"Let's not get ahead of ourselves. Smother the markets with ads, make sure your people are everywhere, and let's see what we can make happen on Tuesday."

~

Trevor Hobbs turned to his cohost, beautiful raven-haired anchor, Melanie McQuade, "Today's a big day for both parties, what can you tell us?"

"We're getting reports of a dramatic increase in voters in all five states. New Jersey polls close in about two hours and our initial tally points toward Steil and Turner but it appears that dark horse Mac Murphy might slip in for second place in the Republican race."

The producers cut to a video of Murphy ranting about his competitors at the debate, "These morons have been drilled on how to respond to these questions with cookie cutter answers to promote their sponsors' agenda and we can be damned sure that Casey Buck and the other members of his fraternity don't give a damn about the folks out there in television land, who are losing their jobs, their homes, and their place in our society. You want to have a debate? Let's talk about helping our neighbors instead of making the fat cats richer!"

Miss McQuade had to smother a grin, "The Republican National Committee is looking into Mr. Murphy's conduct, as well as his allegations, but no one suspected that exit polls would show him with fairly strong support, particularly among working-class people."

Hobbs added, "His delivery might be raw and unconventional but, to his constituents, his message comes across as honest outrage about their concerns. Our journalists haven't had time to investigate or reach any conclusions about his accusations regarding a secret coalition of the wealthy trying to buy elections but it smacks of old-fashioned conspiracy theories that usually lacked any proof to back them up."

"The wealthy have tried to exert their influence in almost every election, since we inaugurated our republic, and there have been legends and rumors about secret societies for generations, but we have no reason to believe that an elite league of the very richest Americans is conspiring to take down our democracy."

Hobbs's features sagged into a practiced expression of sincerity and concern, "The working people of our nation need someone to blame for the slow grisly deconstruction of the middle class - the loss of jobs, incomes, homes, and families. Mr. Murphy wants them to believe that he's their fearless defender, that he's willing to stand up to the greedy gentry who seem to have caused their misery.

It's a brilliant bit of political posturing, Murphy's David trying to take down a gluttonous Goliath and his chums, or Robin Hood commandeering the disposable wealth of the aristocracy to provide for the desperate and destitute."

Melanie McQuade smiled into the camera, "On the other side of the race, Atlanta Mayor Tyrone Turner appears to be leading his four closest challengers by double digits, which is fairly amazing, considering he's a late entry and hasn't visited any of the states in contention today. Other than a smattering of television advertising, he's relying on his dramatic appearances at the gigantic All People Matter rallies over the past few months and his overwhelming performance at the debate."

"There's another rally in Denver over the weekend and rumors that Murphy has scheduled several stadium events," added Trevor Hobbs. "I'm sure primary victories will encourage even more people to get involved in the election process, before we all converge on the conventions."

Mavis shouted at the reporters on the television screen, "Damned right there's another rally and we'll keep on rallying until we put our man in the White House!"

Tabitha snickered, "My dear, between the two of us, we've no chance of overturning decades of treasonous manipulation in the next few hours of conversation but, with proper cerebral stimulation, we might strike upon some ideas to move our campaign just a wee bit closer to triumph for our people."

Mavis raised her glass, "I'm sorry, I'm just frustrated on so many levels…"

"I'm reminded of the period before the revolution, when our founding fathers…and mothers…conspired in secret about their dreams of freedom from the yoke of the most powerful and oppressive force on the planet. The English maintained robust support from a fairly large portion of the population of the colonies and many were eager to stifle the mutineers to sustain their own promising fortunes. Through years of fear and frustration, those patriots focused on their vision of a nation governed by and for her people, rather than bowing to the whims of some distant noble elite, and adjusted their strategies to suit ruthless adversity.

We started with a tiny rally in a hurricane and now we've got millions of supporters and a legitimate candidate for President of the United States, who has taken up our standard of freedom and equality that has been dragged through the mud for years. If it all fell apart tomorrow, we'd have a lot to be proud of, but we know there's more. It goes on until all these wonderful people get their lives and their dignity restored and we can take pride in being Americans again."

"I know you're right, you're always right," said Mavis, "but so many things shifted in my life, after SunnyBreeze was washed away and Tate died. From knowing exactly how I was going to help the cause, with our expanding campaign to build self-contained economic oases for thousands of unemployed souls to conducting massive re-education with legions of true-believers convincing their neighbors about the righteous path to fixing the problems that plague the country. I couldn't recognize that truth is only valid if folks are willing to accept it. I believed that we're all in this together and everyone should naturally jump on board but there are lots of people who would rather blame someone else for their troubles than stand up and fight back!"

"Many of those people are raw, emotionally drained, and open to believing the disgusting propaganda blanketing the airwaves. They have no idea of what truth really is but they'll follow anyone who offers hope."

Mavis stared at Jessie's brilliant sunset firing through a violent storm charging the beach with towering surf and howling winds assaulting battered palm trees. The painting's vivid colors were enhanced by a very simple driftwood frame over the massive fireplace in Tabitha's salon. "I want the rest of this campaign to feel like Mother Nature's power in that painting, so fierce and relentless that our enemies will opt to get out of the way before we cut them down!"

"I like your spunk but someone has to ask, what happens if we lose?"

Hannibal Davis, Tabitha's houseman and faithful friend, leaned to refill their glasses with a splendid Chardonnay, "Knowing you two, the answer to that question is obvious, you'll continue with this quest, regardless of whether Turner and the Democrats win or lose, because it's taken decades to make this mess and it's going to take decades to put things right."

Tabitha smiled, "That's certainly astute and succinct, the election is merely the end of the beginning…"

Mavis interrupted, "But certainly not the beginning of the end."

"Unless Murphy wins," laughed the publisher.

"Banish that horrible thought before someone hears you!" shouted Mavis.

An hour and another bottle of Chardonnay later, the newscast started reporting the first returns out of New Jersey. Trevor Hobbs stepped up to a monitor with a map of the state, divided up into districts that were beginning to change colors. Light blue blotches for Creighton Steil clustered around the northern counties, as well as Princeton and Trenton's suburbs, with sprinkles of various shades for the other candidates speckling the state like glitter glimmering sparsely on a growing rusty tide, representing Murphy districts, expanding around the industrial centers of Newark and Edison, with more swelling across the agricultural corridor and up through the middle of the state.

Tabitha answered a telephone on the end table, "Hello?"

"Tabitha, it's Katherine. Are you watching the news?"

"Of course, dear, I'm sitting here with Mavis and we're getting quietly stewed."

Mavis leaned close to listen, "Can you believe Murphy's strength in New Jersey?"

"I'm astonished and afraid that the trend will continue in the other states."

"That's why we're getting drunk," laughed Mavis. "If it comes down to a one-on-one debate between Turner and Murphy, our guy's gonna make him look like a piker."

"We can only hope," replied Katherine. "We'll have to see what the voters decide through the rest of the evening. Have you talked with Kate?"

"Not since this morning," said Tabitha. "She said that she's working on a couple of stories for the papers. We'll check in with her after we finish this call."

"Good, because I didn't get an answer earlier."

Gracie stood on the raised foredeck, her tail wagging at the sight of Johnny, before Jessie could pull his new rebuilt Crestliner Sportfish into the second slip in the dock.

Kate tossed the boy a line and he tied it off to a cleat, before jumping onboard to check out the features. "Wow, this is in perfect shape and I like the flat decks, and I really like the Merc one-fifty, I bet she really moves along."

"I haven't opened her up yet but she seems pretty stable in this light chop. Thought I'd bring her by to show you, before I took her to her new home for the first time."

He smiled, "I approve!"

"Think there's room for three, once in a while?" asked Kate with a peck on his cheek.

"You're welcome anytime, even in hurricanes."

"Well, there aren't any on the horizon, so how 'bout I pick you up on Thursday afternoon and we'll see if we can find some fish."

"Deal," replied the boy.

"Great, because we need to head for home but I wanted you to see her first."

"I'm honored."

"You should be!"

Johnny untied the rope from the cleat and tossed it to Kate while Jessie eased her out of the stall, waving as he pulled away from the dock, "See you on Thursday!"

An orange sun oozed into jagged palm trees along the key, casting golden streaks to illuminate the little boat skipping across the whitecaps on the run up the bay. Kate held his arm, "I'm so glad you got this boat, I know you've missed the old one since we lost her in the storm."

"Had to find Johnny's first but I'm glad I waited for this one, she's a beaut!"

"Have you come up with a name yet?"

He pursed his lips, gazing out across the water, then turned to her, "The last one was 'Kate', so, maybe this one's 'Kate too'."

She squeezed his arm, "I'm honored but you can come up with a better name than that."

"How about 'People'?"

"That's a weird name for a boat."

"Yeah, but it's kind of what this part of our lives is about, a reminder of our involvement with all of this, when she became part of the family."

"It's your boat and you can name her whatever you like." She kissed him with a flirty smile, "I wonder what's happened in the primaries. I'm feeling kind of guilty for not being on the watch team but this was far more important."

Jessie hugged her and nibbled on her neck, as he slowed the boat to slide into the slip, "Not that watching talking heads on television could change anything."

"True that," replied Kate hoping onto the dock to tie her off, "and it'll be a few hours before we get returns on the western states."

Gracie trotted up the path to the porch and stopped short, sniffing the deck.

Jessie said, "C'mon girl, let's go find you some dinner."

The shepherd mix walked over to block the door, as Kate reached for the doorknob to insert her key, but the door swung open. "I know I locked this when we left."

Gracie darted into the kitchen, skidding across the floor to point at the front door. Jessie followed her, "What's wrong, girl?"

The dog barked once, staring into the entry where a taut trip wire dropped from the door knob to a blinking detonator impaled in a white brick. Jessie reached for her collar and backed into the kitchen. "Call Chief Johnson and tell him to send the bomb squad. His number's on the pad."

Kate dialed, "Chief Johnson, please. Yes, this is Kate Crocket, I'm at Jessie Cotton's cottage and he asked if you could send the bomb squad. We have a suspicious package on the inside of our front door."

"Thank you, we're leaving by the back door now."

Jessie stroked Gracie's ear and pulled on her collar as they crept outside, gently pulling the door closed, and circled around to the lane out in front of the house. Within minutes, a large van rumbled down the drive, with blazing red and blue lights flashing in the twilight shadows, and four men jumped out, "Where's the explosive?"

"If it really is a bomb, it's wired to the inside of the front door," said Jessie. "The back door is unlocked."

"Alright," said the policeman, donning a heavy helmet and a thick protective suit. "We'll take a look."

A second officer suggested that they move up towards the main road, while the squad investigated the threat. Flashlight beams flicked across the inside of the windows, before the interior lights clicked on one by one. After anxious moments, the front door opened and the padded explosives expert appeared carrying the white package out in front of his body. Two men opened a bin in the back of the truck, while the first man placed the bundle inside and stashed the trigger in a separate container, then sealed the heavy doors.

Jessie released Gracie and took Kate's hand as they slowly walked towards the house, to talk with the officers, "What was it?"

"C4" replied the officer, as he pulled off his gear. "That was enough to blow your house across the bay and leave a nice crater in its place. Any idea of who would plant something like this in your home?"

"Sure," said Jessie, "we're both on the executive committee for All People Matter and I can guarantee there are lots of people who'd like to stop us. After kidnapping us to stop the rally downtown and their attacks in Houston, Atlanta, and Chicago, this is amateur stuff."

"I'm sorry, I should have known - Jessie Cotton and Kate Crocket. I've admired your art and my kids went to your camp this summer, Mr. Cotton, and you write the terrific articles in the paper."

"You're right," replied Kate, "and this episode totally freaked me out, so tomorrow's story should be about the heroics of the city's bomb squad. I want your names and personal information."

"Aw shucks, we don't want to be famous, in fact it's better if folks don't know who we are. This is just part of our job."

"I understand exactly how you feel, so I'll write an article that talks about how helpless a common citizen feels in this situation. I could feature the squad as a unit, not as individuals, if you can give me some background. Would that work?"

"Sure," replied the officer, "and we could always use a bigger budget for more protective gear!"

"I'll mention that," laughed the reporter, "but I do want to thank all of you for coming to remove that horrible thing before someone, like us, got hurt."

"You're welcome and I'll tell the Chief to station a car in the neighborhood in case the bombers come back to try again."

"We'd appreciate that," said Jessie offering his hand.

"You're hometown heroes and we all appreciate everything you're trying to do."

The second officer added, "We're just working guys like everyone at your rallies and, if the Council cuts the budget, we're out of a job too."

"Did you guys get a raise after the city caved to Mrs. Hall's shutdowns?" asked Kate.

"Yeah, we did and we appreciate every little bit to take care of our families but it sure wasn't enough."

"The only way it's going to change is for everyone to get involved in the movement and make sure everyone you know goes to the polls in November to cast their votes for the right people in every race from school board to the presidency."

"They have the money but you have the power," said Kate.

"And we're all supporting what you're trying to do," said the officer, tipping his helmet. "We'd best be heading out of here to dispose of your oversized firecracker."

"Hey, could you take a picture of it before you blow it up," asked Kate. "I could use it in my article."

"Sure, I've got a long lens on the camera!" laughed the man, picking up his heavy gear to stow it in the truck.

They waved, as the armored van turned around and lumbered up the lane, and followed Gracie's wagging tail down the path to the house. Kate took Jessie's hand, "So, now it's not only dangerous to go on a date with you but coming home might be dicey too!"

"You are a cruel woman, you know that?"

"I guess I've come to grips with the idea of dying with you but getting blown up is kind of messy, don't you think? We should send them a secret message demanding that their next attempt will leave me glamourous enough to look good in a coffin."

"I'm thinking about keeping you just the way you are, until we're suddenly old."

"Ooo, there's another horrifying thought. Why can't we just be youngish forever?"

"With all the stress we go through, I'm surprised we're not showing more symptoms!" laughed Jessie, holding the door for his girls to enter.

"Quick, turn on the television and let's see what's happened," said Kate.

Jessie clicked on the set and the handsome pair of anchors popped onto the screen. "Well, Trevor, it's going to be an interesting night, what's your take on it?"

"Melanie, I wouldn't go so far as to say it's historic, but I will say that it is unusual for two late entrants, with modest budgets and no national campaign organizations, to make a dent in so many reliably loyal establishment districts across the country. Atlanta Mayor Tyrone Turner is shutting down his middle-of-the-road opponents and, while he doesn't appear to be taking first in any of the contests, Mac Murphy could collect more votes than any other Republican candidate and that's got to rile the dark money PAC's and big-time contributors who had this election all planned out."

"I'm sure there will be plenty of heated late-night evaluation sessions attempting to identify the errors and weaknesses and plot out new strategies for the foundering campaigns of everyone who didn't win big," said McQuade with a radiant smile. "We have several more rounds over the next few weeks and then we'll head to the conventions."

"There are going to be a lot of operatives in the hot seat tonight."

"Do you honestly think we'll have anyone in either party who can walk into the convention and take the nomination?"

Hobbs stared into the camera, "I think today's elections are exposing chinks and cracks in the agendas of both major parties. No one can predict what's coming next and the American people have the power of the primary vote to decide who will represent them in the fall elections. We can only hope they choose wisely."

"On that note, we'll pause for a commercial," said McQuade.

Kate picked up the phone and dialed, "Hi, it's Kate. So, Turner took New Jersey and might take California?"

"Yeah, it looks like he's basically tied with Walker and Paul in the other three and it's possible he could collect most of the delegates," replied Katherine. "Where have you been? I've been trying to call you for hours?"

"Well, that's kind of a long story. We went to pick up Jessie's new yacht…"

Jessie leaned in to interrupt, "It's a little fishing boat."

Kate laughed and continued, "But when we got back, Gracie went on alert in the entry and we've spent the last hour watching the bomb squad haul a brick of C4 out of here."

"Shit, I thought they'd move on to bigger, more creative demonstrations of their anger and outrage."

"Well, the locals seem to have a laser focus on us, with the burning of the tents at Jessie's kids camp and now this."

"Do we need to set up protection?"

"We're going to call Eddie and see if he might have some guys who can keep an eye on us, until we head out to set up the next rally. Is everything on track?"

"It's gonna be after tonight's results. Money's already starting to roll in and volunteers are lining up."

～

Murphy pulled off his headphones, leaned back in his chair to rest his calfskin ropers on the desk, while the staff applauded his outrageous banter and the video crew killed the lights. He took a big swig of Jack Daniels and lit another cigar, watching Stone and Billings escort a late fifties-early sixties suit, with gray hair and an arrogant grin, across the cluttered and crowded studio.

The doctor inquired, "How you feeling? Your show was inspired."

"Hell, it ought to be, considering I'm kicking ass across the country, we're picking up a shitload of delegates!"

"No, I mean how are you feeling?"

"I'm flying in the ozone, which is good because it looks like I need to be on top of my shit," replied the candidate, pointing.

"I'll bring your meds when you're finished," said Dr. Billings, quietly.

The suit said, "How'd you like to organize those delegates you picked up into a nomination?"

"How are we going to earn enough to push everyone else out of the way? And who the hell are you?"

Stone interrupted, "I'm sorry, allow me to introduce Casper Wein political organizer extraordinaire. Mac Murphy."

Wein reached to shake but Murphy grunted and took another swig, "What irreplaceable talent are you going to bless this campaign with…cosmic yoga or delegate deliverance?"

"I've listened to your show, watched your theatrics at the rallies, and followed your progress with the voters and I think you have a charisma and strength that resonates with the working class and the unemployed, two immense pools of votes that have never been tapped. You're showing well in the middle of the country but taking second in New Jersey proved that you can steal precious votes from blue states and I believe that's a winning combination."

"So, all that's old news."

"I've talked with Jack and Shepherd and we all agree that there's a valid path to the nomination and I know how to organize your people at the convention and pull the right strings to make it happen."

Murphy took a deep drag on his stogie, "You got a sense of humor?"

"As in funny ha-ha?"

"Obviously, you don't, so besides promises of success, what else you got to offer?"

Wein replied without hesitation, "I think I could convince the cartels to throw some support behind your campaign to hedge their bets against Steil getting exposed for what he is and the other three fighting to be dead last in the race. I thought I'd start the discussion at fifty-million."

Murphy whistled a stream of smoke, "That'd get someone's attention."

"It'd buy a lot of delegate votes, if you're willing let me work on it."

"I said at the very beginning, I don't give a good god-damn about winning this thing, I'm the voice of the people, in it for the money and every piece of ass that gets close enough to grab. We're out to raise some hell, tear up the Republican Party, and have a good time doin' it. If you can get hip to that and you can actually produce truckloads of cash, you're hired."

Wein stuck out his hand, "Deal."

Lincoln Todd rolled out of a soiled bed in the seedy motel room to grapple for the grimy phone on the nightstand. The mouthpiece bore the lingering scent of cigarette smoke and stale beer. He mumbled, "Hello?"

"Todd, it's Roger, just checkin' in to see how things are linin' out?"

"What time is it?"

"Well, hell, it's time to get moving, son!"

He glanced at the plastic clock, "It's six-thirty in the fucking morning. Nothing's going to change between now and, say, nine o'clock or even ten, you asshole!"

"Our folks want some reassurance and they don't sleep in."

"They don't stay up all night getting our people set up and ready to drop into place."

"So, what do you know?" snapped Stanislawski, scratching his chest, his eyes darting, sweat dripping through his sideburns.

"We've got a team of eight on the maintenance crew for set-up, we've got another eight on security, and a dozen working in the beer stalls and food concessions around the arena. Hell, one of our sponsors owns the concession on all the food service in the center!"

"I don't know shit about that," replied Roger. "Did you get the gear?"

"Yeah, man, along with a complete breakdown of the system - how to transport it, where to place them, and how to arm these suckers. These babies are going to light things up."

"How many?"

"Sixteen. We've been going over the floorplans of the convention center and it looks like we can have maximum impact by taking out the primary exits.

"Do our guys know what they're doing?"

"Shit yeah, they're all committed, ready to rock. The maintenance guys will deposit the goods in plastic trash barrels under cover of our security detail and our food service crew will seal the exits when the fireworks go off."

"Perfect," replied Stanislawski. "I'll be there, with several dozen of our friends, ready to help heat up the panic level."

"There's a truck ramp on the south corner of the building, point your people that way, if things get out of control."

"If we do our job right, they will!"

"This is going to be better than Chicago!"

∿

Nellis leaned over the table, tracing the floor plans for the Colorado Convention Center. "This is our first indoor rally, so it's a different critter than being out in the wide-open spaces."

"I'm not sure I'd want to be right dead center in that hall with tens of thousands of bodies between me and the doorway," said Jessie. "The biggest problem is getting our folks out if there's another attack."

Beal pointed, "There are sixteen exits to the hall. We'll confine the flow in but, once the show starts, we'll have everything open in every direction and we'll be maintaining walkways through the crowd."

"We're bringing all your guys and our guys, plus local police and the facility's hired on an extra thirty-six off-duty officers. Hell, we might outnumber the audience if you have an off night," chuckled Abe Sheldon, chomping on the stub of an unlit cigar.

"We're going to have our guys and Eddie's mixed in with the crowd, looking for troublemakers," said Brad, without acknowledging the joke.

"They keep sending the same crew to lead their attacks," added Eddie. "They ought to be familiar by now."

"I'll know the boys who led the assaults in Houston and Atlanta on sight," said Brad. "and we've got to assume that they were in attendance at the other raids too."

"I wouldn't be surprised if the news crews didn't get some nice portraits of those guys," said Nellis, turning to Beal. "Think you could sweet talk your connections into loaning us some tape that the feds haven't already confiscated?"

"I'll see what I can do."

"Seems like their investigation is taking a really long time," said Jessie.

Sheldon looked up, "They won't say anything to anybody, including us, until they have solid evidence and they've narrowed down the suspect list."

"We know Turner is going to have personal Secret Service protection, so our concern has to be looking after our guests," said Eddie.

"Hell, they could send some guys in for this show and pick up some likely participants while they're here," laughed Nellis. "We ought to suggest that during our meeting with them tomorrow."

"What's the perimeter?" asked Brad.

"Other than necessary vehicles, delivery and limos bringing in the talent, we're not going to allow anything near that building. There's plenty of parking and the protestors proved they can walk a block or two to participate in their futures," replied Beal. "We didn't have the gear to shoot down the plane but we can sure as hell keep a car bomb out of range."

"What about Stout Street, it runs right through the center?" asked Jessie.

"It'll be closed off, as well as the ring of streets around the arena, plus we've got a first-class fire station right on the property."

"We're putting our faith in you, brother," said Nellis, "'cause we need to keep our people safe."

"We're working every angle with everyone who can help," said Sheldon, "and we're all going to be wired in to the same frequencies, so we all know what's happening."

"Right on."

~

Nellis walked into the Exhibit Hall of the Convention Center and whistled, "This is ginormous! How big is this place?"

"Nearly six-hundred thousand square feet," replied Jessie, jogging across the endless floor towards the stage on the west end of the hall.

A huge 'All People Matter' banner stretched across the backdrop, illuminated by a lighting system suspended from the ceiling thirty feet above the stage. Giant portraits of Turner flanked either end and the band's amps and drums were set up and ready to go. "I'm getting' spoiled playing to gigantic crowds," laughed Nellis. "I spent most of my life playing smoky honky-tonks in little burgs with funny names at the very end of the two-lane. Hell, some of them were at the very end of a dusty cart track, but the crowd always looks the same from up here. And, even at these gigs, there's always a cute little blond down front with dreams of some rock star whisking her out of her hellhole and some immature gawky dude hanging on to her for dear life."

"Yeah, they packed eighty-thousand screaming fans into Camp Randall Stadium in Madison, so I know what you mean. A crowd that size cheers and it knocks the wind out of your lungs!"

"Tell you the truth, I always felt way more comfortable up here than down there in the middle of the crush of humanity and I always made sure I knew how to find the back door."

"Let's hope we sail through this one," said Jessie, as Kate, Katherine, Mavis, and Bobbie trooped through the vast cavern. "Everything cool?"

"Yeah, doors don't open for hours but the crowds are already gathering outside."

"We do know how to throw a party," added Mavis, with her magazine grin, trotting off to rein in the press crew and position television cameras.

Katherine kissed Nellis' cheek, as he strapped on Lucy, his 1959 Goldtop Les Paul guitar, to tune up. "Looks like another sellout."

"You have everything under control?"

"I'm always a nervous wreck until everyone is on site and ready to go."

"What's the lineup?"

"You and Jazz can play until we get most of the crowd inside, then Althea and Amy will get things rolling and I'll come out to talk about the movement and introduce Tabitha. Then Stanton will bring out Wally Jenkins, Denver's Mayor, to present Tyrone. We could parade a dozen other speakers but I think we need to keep this one short and to the point so we can get everyone out of here before something bad happens."

"Sheldon and Beal seem pretty confident that they've got a handle on this one. Brad and Eddie are going to have their people cruising through the crowd to put down any rabble-rousers and there's a Secret Service presence too. We've been through all the planning sessions and I'm not sure that there's much more they can do."

"Forgive me being nervous."

"Hell, you're the star of the movement and I get anxious just watching you," said Nellis with a hug.

Twenty minutes before the doors were set to open, Sheldon handed out mugshots of Todd, Stanislawski, and three other hired thugs to Brad and Eddie. "These were matched to images from the first confrontation in Atlanta. They showed up again in the crowd outside the governor's office and again in Chicago."

Jessie scanned their rap sheets, "Yeah, these guys fit the mold — violent crimes, affiliations with gangs and hate groups, and no legitimate source of income. We'll keep an eye out for them."

Brad pointed to the photographs of Todd and Stanislawski, "These two for sure. The skinny guy tried to take me out with a club in Atlanta."

~

Lincoln Todd wore a floppy pink afro wig and red-rimmed plastic sunglasses with large round lenses. He carried a placard that read 'Peace, Love, and God Above', and melded in with a group of stony college kids under a sea of signs being carried along by a wave of eager protestors.

The crew was in place and ready to provoke as much havoc as possible, as soon as the first incendiary surprise ignited. He fingered the remote trigger in his pocket, noting two of his men in a food concession and his maintenance workers placing yellow trash barrels inside the primary entrances to the arena.

He pushed through the crush to find Stanislawski leaning against a pillar, decked out with a bushy moustache, fleece lined jean jacket, and a dusty beige cowboy hat. "You almost look authentic."

"And you look like you're confused about your heritage with that nigger hair. All you need is blackface!"

"Sometimes, standing out in the crowd is the best way to become invisible. People are looking at the get-up instead of the person inside the costume."

"Not that I give a shit, unless you get us busted, but where do we stand?"

Todd nodded toward a uniformed security guard watching over two maintenance workers, who were moving the last two yellow barrels into place at the exit on the far side of the room. "Those should be the last of them."

"Sixteen armed and ready?"

"Yup and my guys are in position and ready to rock. How 'bout yours?"

"I've got them split up in packs between the entries, so, when the fireworks go off, they can start a ruckus that pushes the panicked crowd into harm's way. Our signal to pull out and head for our exit is your last blast."

"I'll set off fourteen at thirty second intervals, with an extra thirty second delay on the second last one, so they can anticipate the last," replied Todd. I'll wait for Turner to begin his speech, unless something goes weird and I have to start sooner. We've got enough people in here to go for it right now but we'll wait for the appropriate moment, when the video will show the Democratic nominee in a panic."

"I'll tell my guys and we'll be ready," said Stanislawski, ambling off into the roiling mass of humanity.

~

Nellis scanned the animated protestors flooding into the enormous room from three directions, rushing streams of bodies jammed through the broad entries, swelling to blot out an endless sea of gray carpeting. The crowd was edgy and enthusiastic but orderly, eager to join thousands who shared their desperation. His eyes searched the room sensing something out of place, something...

He turned to Jazz and the band as Jose, the percussionist, counted off and they jumped into the wailing introduction to 'For All That's Right and True'.

Courage and devotion define us
Lift that banner for all to see
Fear and lies can't stifle truth
Raise your voice against tyranny

Brothers and sisters
I stand with you
For every generation
For all that's right and true

Come together
Let no one refrain
The people's voice has been betrayed

March into morning
Let's seize this day
Lead, follow, or get out of the way

Raise your voices
Let them feel our rage
The lines are drawn, we're here to stay

March into morning
Let's seize this day
Lead, follow, or get out of the way

Dare to dream of what might be
When compassion and liberty
Replace shadows and mysteries
With the promise of humanity

Brother and sisters
I stand with you
For every generation
For all that's right and true

The band powered through a short set of rocking protest songs to pump up the energy before Amy and Althea appeared from either side of the stage. Nellis turned to the audience with a grin, "Ladies and gentlemen, I want to thank each and every one of you for coming out to make your voices heard! You are the soul of this country, inspiring us with your strength, courage, and determination, the heart of the nation, keeping us focused on who we are and who we ought to be, and I hope that y'all know that you're a force to be reckoned with because you hold the power of the vote. You can change the world by taking the time to vote for candidates who'll work to make things right!"

The crowd cheered.

"And make sure you take your mom, your dad, your sister and brother, your in-laws, your outlaws, and uncle Jimmy's second cousin's niece's daughter's boyfriend when you go to the polls! I'm Nellis Gray and this is Jazz Taggart and his Band of Merry Men."

Rowdy cheers and applause.

"We're going to turn things over to Althea Dodson and Amy Martin, who started the Worker's Union of the Unemployed in Atlanta, to get things rolling. We'll be back later to finish up the program."

The spectators were charged up for Amy and Althea, who bellowed, "How y'all doing?"

Spattered applause and a few shouts and wails.

"We said, HOW Y'ALL DOING?"

Their roar shook the building.

Amy yelled, "Hi! I'm Amy!"

Thousands answered, "Hi, Amy!"

"And this is my cohost, Althea. And I've gotta say that we've got a ton of people jammed into this room, so look after your neighbors and let's keep everyone safe."

Althea jumped in, "We organized the Worker's Union of the Unemployed in Atlanta to help coordinate tens of thousands of folks just like you, workers who have suffered the same indignities, the same frustrations, the same nightmares."

Amy added, "People are losing their jobs, their homes, their place in their communities, and finally their dignity, and it's happening in just about every town or city from coast to coast. Am I hitting a chord here?"

Massive boos and jeers.

"The only way to fight the conspiracy is for all of us to join together to vote these criminals out of office in November and take our democracy back!"

Nellis stashed Lucy in her case in the dressing room and marched through the lounge behind the stage, greeting Spratlin who introduced Denver Mayor Wally Jenkins. He patted Tyrone on the back, kissed Katherine on the cheek and headed down the broad hallway where he found Brad talking into a walkie-talkie.

"Any sign of the goons?"

Eddie's voice crackled over the radio, "Negative. I'm walking the perimeter and we've still got tons of people trying to squeeze in."

"I'm pretty sure the Fire Marshall's keeping tabs."

"No trouble on this end, so far."

"Roger." He turned to greet Nellis, "You guys sounded good."

"Thanks. Listen, I was watching the folks flood into the auditorium and there's something out of place or not right or something. I can't put my finger on it."

"One of your hunches?"

"Yeah, something like that."

"After rescuing the kids from the kidnappers, we all trust your instincts. C'mon, let's take a walk and see if anything pops out at you," said Brad, strolling down the hallway to salute a security guard manning the backstage passage. They leapt into a human tsunami surging from the exits and muscled through the flood of bodies to the relative calm between two exits at the back of the room. Video screens and speakers mounted on pillars brought Amy and Althea to everyone in the arena and the crowd reacted to their spunky energy with rolling waves of applause and cheers.

Amy yelled, "We don't want handouts, we want opportunities!"

Nellis folded his arms across his chest and turned to watch the people pouring in from every direction.

Brad leaned close, "See anything that rings your bell?"

The guitarist surveyed the parade of protestors, embodying every size and shape, ethnicity and background. They all trooped in with the weight of the world on their shoulders, some despondent and desperate for comradery and support, most anxious to find hope and promise and purpose. His eyes followed three old black ladies in their Sunday best with little hats and veils, marching in with determination accompanied by two younger women in stylish jogging suits striding after them, followed by a middle-aged woman with graying hair herding three teenagers for a lesson about real democracy, four sailors in uniform who seemed totally out of place despite the bevy of infatuated girls tagging along, and a young couple pushing a pink stroller with oversized wheels, their eyes full of worry and hope.

Every individual has a unique and tragic story but each is a variation of the same nightmare, a terror common to everyone in the room…a scourge devouring the working class. His eyes scanned the endless rush of despair until a pretty blond teenager in a yellow rain slicker charged through the entry and, almost in slow motion, tossed a drink cup with a red straw into a shiny new yellow trash bin just inside the doorway as she passed.

He turned to young Spratlin, "I played a lot of arenas and every one of them had the trash barrels on the outside of the door, so people didn't trip over them trying to escape in an emergency and, probably more to the point, it's easier for the maintenance guys to pick 'em up."

The former Raider cocked his head and walked over to the barrel, pulling it aside to pitch a pile of trash onto the gray carpet until it was empty. "Damn, nothing."

Nellis grabbed the handle and flipped it over to find a thick red plastic disk and a small metal box taped to the bottom. "That looks like trouble to me."

Brad grabbed his radio, "We've got explosive devices taped to the bottom of the yellow trash barrels just inside the entrances. Remove them as quietly as you can and get the fire department and the bomb squad in here now!"

Lincoln Todd leaned against a pillar near the center of the crowd, biding his time until Turner took the stage for maximum impact. He noticed security guards upending trash barrels inside the lobby entrance on the southeastern wall of the room and swiveled in place, spying another bin being hoisted and carried out the door. Searching for the tall fake cowboy, his fingers clutched the remote in his jacket pocket and clicked the safety switch to 'arm'. He hesitated, scanning the activity around the exits, before pressing the button to detonate the first bomb just inside the eight doors at the back of the room.

An intense concussion shook the building, a half-a-heartbeat before a brilliant yellow flash spewed clouds of flaming fog, igniting the carpeting, walls, and clothing of hundreds of stunned and frightened people engulfed in the blaze. Most collapsed on the melting rug or staggered back into the crowd, desperate for help and medical attention.

Amy screamed, "Head for the nearest exits!" while the Secret Service cleared the stage and ushered the dignitaries to safety. The planted agitators abandoned their temporary duties in the concessions and blocked the entrances, fighting with police and security and pummeling anyone trying to escape. Panicked protestors surged forward, stumbling over fallen bodies writhing in a growing heap jamming the doorways while the tormenters disappeared into the melee heading for the next target.

Todd counted to thirty and hit the button again. A security guard, carrying a trash can on his shoulder, was decapitated by the blast as he dashed out through the west exit. The fireball scorched hundreds fleeing the blinding inferno in a sizzling shower that raised a fiery curtain across the corridor, igniting a gas line feeding the griddle and fryer in a concession stand with a violent whoosh, loosing a leaping blue flame that bobbed and swayed like the tongue of a serpent scenting prey. Flocks of frantic people gave a wide berth to avoid its bite as they scampered towards an exit.

He stopped to stare up at a giant video screen. Althea was back at the mic shouting through smoke and flames for everyone to remain calm and move to the exits and the bomber chuckled, "Eat this nigger bitch!"

His finger pressed the button again and again, as he turned to wade through the ruckus towards the supply entrance in the south corner and stumbled over a smoldering legless torso in a yellow slicker. Desperate screams of pain and horror echoed through the enormous hall and terrified droves stampeded through billowing smoke, some carrying the injured and the dying, drawn to any wisp of daylight, only to change direction as each successive blast ignited with mind-numbing impact, blocking another escape route with tangles of scorched and dismembered bodies. Two or three of the bombs exploded outside the arena but Todd grinned as number eleven detonated, collapsing the left side of the stage and tossing Althea off the edge, as flames clawed up a large portrait of Mayor Turner.

Nellis and Brad fought through a roiling human torrent, struggling towards the rostrum through chaos and a desperate agonizing din, when the guitarist slammed into a guy in a heavy coat with a floppy pink afro and huge sunglasses, who tumbled to the floor. "Excuse me," said Nellis, grabbing the man by the collar before he was trampled under roiling waves of stampeding feet.

The man's glasses slipped down his nose as he struggled free of the coat and started running towards the back of the hall, evading one of the sailors carting the pink pram over his head followed by his partner carrying the limp blistered body of the young father, the hysterical wife tagging along behind.

Nellis yelled, "Hey, that's him!" before he was swallowed in the pandemonium but Brad charged after the escapee as he tossed the pink wig over his shoulder and plowed through swirling throngs scattering to escape the searing fires flaring around the perimeter. The ceiling lights flickered through thick black smoke swirling up to the ceiling of the gigantic room where acrid clouds curled through emergency sprinkler showers to engulf the victims in stifling darkness. A tall cowboy stumbled into the former marine, as the bomber disappeared into the crush and another blast ignited a blaze on the right side of the stage, a brilliant barrage of red and yellow flames felling the mother who brought her children to learn about the promise of the power of the people.

Spratlin turned to the dazed cowhand, his battered Stetson askew and half the fake moustache peeled off his upper lip, and reached to grab his jean jacket, just as another bomb detonated with a deafening roar and a blinding flash that drove terrified souls scrambling ahead of the rushing wall of flame. A surge of smoldering victims engulfed the two men, dragging them along in a raging current that swirled into jostling eddies searching for salvation and oxygen.

He lost sight of the tall cowboy, as an aging black woman grabbed his hand in desperation. Her curly hair was singed and melted beneath the shredded remnants of a small green hat covered with smoldering skin peeled from her forehead, where a stream of flaming gel splattered across her face. "I lost my daughter Becky, she's in there someplace. Oh, Lordy, please keep her safe."

He could see her lips moving but he couldn't hear her words.

One of her companions looked stunned but fairly normal from the front, but the back half of her clothes were blown off in the explosion, leaving her spine and shoulders covered in black ash and ruptured blisters.

Blazing sunshine flooded the hall as the south service doors rolled open and firetrucks pulled inside with lights flashing and sirens blaring. Hundreds of people dashed to daylight through tumbling clouds of smoke as two more bombs detonated at the exits on either side of the stage. Brad guided the women out of the arena to a concession stand, doused towels in ice to cool their burns, screaming, "Medic! Medic!" in a flashback to being pinned down in an ambush during the war.

An ambulance crew appeared out of the chaos and he turned the injured over to the experts, before sprinting down the service lane outside the building to push through dense black haze and tormented turmoil to gain access to the restricted area behind the stage as one more brain rattling concussion and a fearsome flare roared above the screams somewhere in the far corner of the hall.

Eddie and Beal organized the evacuation of most of the speakers after the detonation of the first blast, while the Secret Service hustled candidate Turner, Representative Spratlin, and the mayor into an armored limousine. Brad barreled down the hallway to Katherine, "Did we get everyone out?"

The spokeswoman coughed violently, "Yeah, most of them didn't argue, well, except for your father. Have you seen Nellis?"

Her words were muffled and distant but he watched her mouth form the word 'Nellis', "He got swallowed up in a flood of panic after we almost caught the bomber."

Brad watched Standler's lips, "You almost caught him?"

"Nellis crashed into him, helped him up and just as he realized who he was, the guy fired off another bomb about twenty feet away. He ran into the crowd and disappeared when his partner blind-sided me with an open-field block. Two more blasts went off and everyone surged away from the fire," replied Brad. "I lost my radio in the scuffle and I can't hear much of anything other than a constant roar, anybody got any idea of how bad it is?"

Nellis stumbled down the corridor holding his hands over his ears and hugged Katherine, mumbling, "It's horrible, I saw piles of bodies blocking doorways, body parts everywhere along with lots of dead and injured still inside and medical crews working on hundreds of casualties outside…and that doesn't cover all the folks who are wandering aimlessly under our toxic indoor thunderstorm in shock."

Beal lowered his walkie-talkie, "They don't have a count yet but the cops and our security guys caught some of the goons who were ambushing people trying to escape. They've got them locked up downstairs but they're not talking."

"Doubt they will," said Nellis, "they're true believers willing to sacrifice for the cause. Bet some of them will show up in footage from the other rallies."

"Wouldn't be surprised," said Katherine. Her hands fluttered to her lips and her eyes darted through the dense smog to thousands still staggering to the exits, "They're pathologically persistent."

"And deadly," said Nellis, staring at the blood on his fingers. "Everyone was on top of every possibility, except them infiltrating the crews that already worked in the building."

"How do you know that?" asked Mavis.

"I bought a drink at one of the concessions earlier and the smilin' guy behind the counter was one of the terrorists fighting with the cops and beating people trying to escape. He and four or five of his troops almost knocked me flat when they ran down the corridor."

Katherine wrapped her arms around him and buried her face in his shoulder, weeping. "What have we done?"

"We did everything we could think of to keep these people safe but it's hard to defend against a well-organized hit-squad that's determined to kill as many innocent and unsuspecting victims as possible. This is on the Republicans and if you don't say so, I will."

"Don't," said Katherine, "it won't do any good. Their media circus will just use it as ammunition that they can twist around to point the blame at us…and maybe rightfully so."

"You can't take this on…"

"How many times are we going to allow this to happen? How many times are we going to call a rally with every good intention, only to see hundreds of innocent people murdered by tribes of political muggers for expressing their desperation?"

"Then we'll coordinate a national campaign to organize people to register and vote to snag Turner the nomination and then the White House. There are ways to do that without bringing hundreds of thousands of folks together."

"Fine, but we're done with this." She waved her hand at the carnage, "I won't do this anymore."

Mavis appeared with Kate and Jessie, "We got everyone evacuated and Tabitha's waiting in the car."

Kate and Mavis embraced Katherine and guided her towards the exit, "C'mon, it's time for you to go. The cops and the feds are already sealing off the site and the press won't be far behind."

"I need to make a statement."

Mavis kissed her cheek, "Nothing you can say is going to make things better. Let's work on a statement that we can control."

Nellis grabbed her hand, "You really do need to leave, we'll take care of coordinating with the cops."

"There's nothing you can do here," added Jessie. "Go with the girls and we'll catch up with you at the hotel."

Katherine allowed herself to be maneuvered through putrid smoke laced with the scent of burnt flesh, down two flights of stairs to a limousine, flanked by two police cars, waiting in the underground labyrinth with motors running.

Nellis turned to Jessie, "This whole thing was being shown live across the country, so it's all out there. Someone's going to have to talk to the reporters to bide time until they get a statement together."

The artist turned as a film crew pushed past security into the hazy hall, with hundreds of injured wandering through the fog and medical crews checking charred bodies strewn across the floor amid smoldering piles of discarded signs and banners. The cameraman clicked on his light and pointed the camera at Nellis, as the reporter shoved a microphone in his face, "Can you tell us what happened here?"

He glanced at Jessie, "The Republicans sent their assassins to slaughter more innocent people."

"How can you blame the Republicans?"

"Because the guy who was firing off the bombs was also in Houston, Atlanta, and Chicago. I had him in my grasp until he set off another explosion but I'm absolutely sure he wasn't just some yahoo taking out his aggressions on people of color. When the authorities get finished with their investigation, there will be no doubt in anyone's mind that he and his crew are paid executioners."

"That's a heavy charge."

"Sonny, turn that camera out into the room and take some shots of the hundreds of mutilated bodies lying amongst the severed arms and legs all over the floor, bits and pieces of men, women and children struck down for expressing their belief that their plight was manufactured by the same tyrants who financed this slaughter. Medics are hauling the injured to hospitals and federal investigators are already beginning to collect and analyze evidence. This is how the Republicans win elections. If they can't keep opposition voters away from the polls through shady voting laws and blatant intimidation, they'll kill anyone who organizes against their candidates."

Jessie stepped in front of Nellis, "That will be all for now. You can see that we've been through a lot and the All People Matter movement will have a statement for you within the hour."

He hustled Nellis out the side door, "What are you nuts? Are you trying to start a civil war?"

"Everything I said was true, so it might be time for one, because I'm sick of these rich assholes using money and power to grind down the little guys. It's time to stand up and tell the truth."

"Let's get you out of here before you cause more trouble than we've already got."

Chapter Thirteen

Murphy accepted his traditional campaign coffee cup of bourbon from Milly Clark and leaned back in the chair, so Penny Baker could wrap a warm moist towel around his face before she applied his makeup. "Thank you for the coffee."

"You need anything else, just let me know," replied Milly, ogling Penny's curves with a sniff, as she marched away.

Jack Hannah, Shepherd Stone, Milton Graves, and Casper Wein pulled up chairs for a final discussion before the rally at Cincinnati's Great American Ball Park. Murphy peeked from under the warm towel and whispered, "I think they've caught us, Penny, could you give us a few minutes?"

"Certainly," replied the makeup artist, as she stood and sauntered across the plush carpeting with a hypnotizing rhythm.

Doc Billings handed him a small white cup full of pills, "Here's your vitamins. You should be in prime form tonight."

He looked into the cup, "There's more than usual."

"I've rearranged your cocktail to smooth things out. I think you'll be more comfortable."

The candidate tossed down the pills with a slug from his coffee cup, looking from face to face, "This looks like they called out the big guns to tell me someone died."

"No," said Stone, "but this is the last and, perhaps, most important rally of them all. We're heading into the final primaries and the convention."

"If we can get more than a third of the delegates next week, we can march into the convention with momentum and a good chance of taking the nomination on the second ballot," said Wein. "We're working every vote that isn't nailed down and I think we can pull this off."

"That's all well and good," replied Murphy, lighting a stogy, "I'm in this 'til it's over but I don't see beating Turner in the general election."

"Don't worry about that, we'll take care of it. We've got a long way to go before we have to worry about him," said Graves, glancing at Wein. "You just do your thing tonight for your home town crowd and we'll stage the convention."

Stone added, "The video crew is going to use tonight's stunts to build a series of ads to motivate your voters and convince the doubters that you're the real deal. You speak their truth from your heart and no one else is willing to stand up for them."

"You might tread lightly on All People Matter, considering what happened in Denver. Their supporters are mad as hell and scared shitless that the bad guys are taking names, so they're looking for a candidate who can protect them from wonton violence," said Jack Hannah. "We could use their support."

"Hell, if we invite people of color into the circle, half our true-believers won't be believin' anymore!" shouted Murphy. "We represent a class of citizens who take pride in being ignorant evangelical bigots, clutching their guns to defend their women from the butchers, who are coming from Washington to murder the unborn white children of America, so dark-skinned immigrants can take control!"

"We're going to have to refine your message a little bit to pick up center-right voters who claim to be undecided," said Graves. "You've convinced your audience, now broaden your message, give them permission to jump on our train because with their help we're going to roll right through the convention. All the candidates have big money backing their bids but those deep pockets don't waste their precious profits backing chumps who might not provide a huge return on their investments."

"So, I'm supposed to invite Tom, Dick, and Mary to join the party, so their moms and dads will contribute to the campaign?"

"We all know that underneath your crude schtick, you're a very bright and creative actor who's in this for your own entertainment and enrichment but the people who can buy you an election want to see some assurance that the winning candidate is capable of becoming presidential, that he can roll up an election victory and drag the rest of the party along on his coattails."

Murphy sat up very straight, his shoulders back, his skull tilted ever so slightly to lift his chin, as if he was looking down on his advisors. In a clipped London accent, he said, "M'Lord, I can be anyone I need to be, from the stodgy Lord Mayor to the chipper Indian cabby, from Hamlet to Othello. Give me a juicy role and I'll make you giggle and weep."

Wein laughed and applauded, "If this doesn't work out, I'll connect you up with some theater people in New York. You'll be a smash!"

"It's all the same business," replied the candidate, settling back into his chair. "Now, if you gentlemen are finished, I have to prepare for a performance."

His handlers wandered away and Penny Baker appeared with another hot towel, "I bet you were something in the theater."

"That was fun but so is this."

She readied her pallet and brushes, draped a towel across his chest, and laid another across his crotch to hide her left hand unzipping his pants.

~

Monty Gibbs and the Rough Hands finished a rousing set of patriotic nationalistic country barn burners on a massive stage constructed to resemble a 1920's art deco cityscape decked out for a tickertape parade, behind a collection of vintage Duesenbergs, Cords, and Rolls Royces lined up just beyond the infield in the Great American Ball Park for a rowdy crowd, who were cranked up and ready to get crazy.

Gibbs yelled, "Thanks Cincinnati, you're the best audience in the country and I know you're anxious to welcome the star of the show, so here's former Four-Star General Trent Crosley to introduce him."

The general, more famous for being drummed out of the Marine Corps for berating a hospitalized soldier suffering from post-traumatic stress disorder than any battlefield accomplishments, marched across the stage, ramrod straight, bulldog jaw, squinty eyes, salt and pepper buzzcut, wearing a dark blue suit with seams and buttons straining to contain his broad chest and thick biceps. He stood for a long moment, gazing out at the cheering crowd that nearly filled the forty-two thousand seats, and waited for them to calm.

"Good evening America!"

The crowd erupted with a flutter of signs promoting Gibbs for vice-president.

"It is my great honor to stand before you tonight to introduce the next president of these United States!"

The audience cheered.

"Our country is in peril, being destroyed by a cadre of incompetent, treasonous liberals who have no business managing our government, let alone our nation! They made a mess in Washington that's spilled over to infect every state and every community in the entire country and it won't get better until they've been booted out the door!"

"We want Murphy! We want Murphy!"

"We need a president who will take the reins of power and lead us to world domination. We need a president who will support and defend our military from relentless interference from Congress, whether it's squeezing the Pentagon budget or ignoring the needs of the warriors on the battlefield and under the care of the Veterans Administration. We need someone who understands how hard it is in today's horrible economy for American workers, someone who's willing to stand up to the manufacturers because they're boasting that their products are made in America, while they're shipping jobs overseas and refusing to bring profits back to this country from tax havens like Ireland. The only part of the company that actually resides inside our borders is their corporate headquarters, so why shouldn't they be taxed just like every other American manufacturer?"

He paused for waves of cat calls, boos and jeers echoing around the ball park.

"We need a leader who won't hesitate to tell the big banks to stuff it, the elites to quit hording their enormous profits, curb their greed, and share the wealth, someone from outside the party system to tell the Democrats to stop whining and get with the program or ship out! We need a guy with big brass gonads to defend real Americans just like you against our enemies, foreign and domestic! America needs Mac Murphy!"

Jack Hannah leaned close and waved his hand around the stadium, "All these crazed people and millions more watching television in their shabby living rooms believe everything you say, everything you preach and everything your promise. It might be bullshit to you but they've elevated you to god status and, if you can close the deal, they'll take you all the way to the White House."

"That's total bullshit."

"No, that's what the latest polls say and our own numbers suggest that we're going to win several of the final primaries on Tuesday."

The candidate stared for a moment in disbelief then smiled and shook his head as the other handlers patted him on the back and offered encouragement, while Penny Baker buffed his forehead with powder and massaged his crotch, "Go get 'em tiger."

Doctor Billings tipped Murphy's chin to look into his eyes, "How are you feeling?"

"Like I could screw ten women and still be ready for more."

"You're in prime condition, go do your thing and I'll be waiting when you get finished."

"You better be waiting with at least a couple of blonds," replied Murphy, "and some more of whatever's in your cocktail. I don't ever want to come down from this."

The crowd rose to their feet with a roar that carried across the Ohio River into Covington, as he took his time emerging from the bullpen to stroll across the outfield. A dazzling white spotlight tracked the solitary figure, who appeared to float over a perfectly a manicured lawn glowing like a floating lime-green cloud in the darkness. He grinned and nearly stumbled, flushed by a massive heatwave that energized his body, charged his brain with pyrotechnic inspiration, and hoisted a throbbing erection as he waved to his chanting fans wallowing in the adoration.

"Murphy! Murphy! Murphy!".

The general bellowed, "Here's the man we need! Ladies and gentlemen, Martin McClintock Murphy, the next President of the United States of America!"

Signs and banners waved from three tiers of rabid fervor. The crowd egged on by paid and well-trained agitators, who traveled for hours on buses from across the nation to shake up the amateurs at the last big Murphy extravaganza before the convention and provide the networks with a sordid spectacle that would keep viewers riveted through countless news cycles.

Hours of raucous music and reactionary speeches, solemn prayers that glorified the white race and radical Christianity, while denigrating everyone else, and a constant patter of subliminal messages, buried in the white noise hissing through the speakers, molded sympathetic strangers into a dedicated army ready to march into battle against the elitist liberals, sub-human African-Americans, parasitic Hispanics, bloodthirsty Muslim terrorists, and any other minority who could be blamed for destroying everything that sustained their twisted fantasy of maintaining white male dominance despite changing demographics and cold hard reality.

The candidate marched up the stairs and across the expansive stage for a vigorous shake with the general, then patted him on the shoulder dismissively before settling into character. The self-anointed savior stood alone at the podium under blazing lights, backed by a vintage cityscape decked out in red, white, and blue bunting, flashing marquees, and neon signage as if a parade was about to appear, marching down Main Street under clouds of confetti. He gazed around at thousands of people jumping and screaming, a torrent of lady's undergarments showering down over the dugouts, an arc of blue uniforms carrying truncheons to dissuade overzealous fans from rushing the stage, and a woman sitting in the first row behind third base with her spikey black high-heel shoes propped up on the wall to expose her bare thighs spread wide.

He shook his head, stepped back, and waited. After five minutes of deafening pandemonium, the noise settled to just this side of a jet engine running at full throttle. "Ladies and gentlemen, my fellow Americans watching from across this beleaguered country, allies, friends, and supporters…and even those who have yet to endorse my candidacy, I say join all these patriotic Americans who support my campaign to take back our nation from the traitors who have tried so hard to destroy everything that makes America the leader of the free world.

For generations, the right and left, Republicans and Democrats, have taken turns raping our economy, obliterating our rights and liberties, dragging us into senseless unwinnable wars that only benefit the folks who own the war industries and the cemeteries. They've flooded our nation with dirty immigrants who come here expecting handouts that we pay for, until they can steal our jobs, our homes, our women and our future!"

The stadium reverberated with a raucous response from worshipping fans, freed to expose their pent-up rage and frustration, to blame the 'others' who caused all their problems or stole what they thought they deserved, and to hate openly with thousands of comrades ready to join in mob violence given the slightest incitement.

"Why should we send our troops all over the world to defend foreign countries that don't give a damn about helping us out, when we need our military to repel the thousands of illegals who are storming our borders every day, like disease-infested rats fleeing a sinking ship. Too many countries owe us billions and we all know that we'll never see a dime of that money back, let alone be able to count on them to act like a trusted ally. They disappear when we have a tough fight in the United Nations or disputes with bullies like China, or when we need to renegotiate rotten trade agreements to save our own workers and the world economy.

They want us to defend their sorry-ass countries from their enemies, while they laugh at us and take advantage of our generosity, and I say it's time to tear up all of our treaties and agreements and renegotiate them on our terms! Not just some of them, all of them! One-on-one, none of this multilateral nonsense that makes everyone else rich at our expense!"

Tens of thousands of voices chanted, "America! America!"

"We need to demand that companies who want to profit from all the advantages this country offers, allow our citizens to make their products instead of thousands of little Chinese guys stuffed inside dangerous factories in some god-forsaken hellhole across the ocean, working for nothing and expecting no benefits.

I can absolutely guarantee that many of you have been screwed by big international corporations who buy up American companies so they can close down domestic manufacturing and ship it somewhere else. And they sure as hell don't care about the workers who got dumped out on the street in communities all over this county - moms and dads and kids who lost everything because they believed in the American dream!

Well, as long as we've got these assholes running Washington for their rich buddies who own those big corporations, things are not going to change! They care about their profits, about keeping their investors happy, and they sure as hell don't give a damn about you! It's time to take America back from this conspiracy of rich tyrants."

"Murphy! Murphy! Murphy!"

"We all know that the liberals want to open the borders to filthy criminal immigrants and if we don't stop that right now, they'll send out their goons to take away your guns and your freedoms. They'll challenge your right to religious liberty, the right to worship your god your way without being forced to accept profane laws that contradict everything we've learned from the Bible. Every life is precious from the moment of conception until the day we meet our maker, so you can count on me to defend your right to embrace your beliefs!"

A brilliant flicker lit up the far corner of the third tier behind first base, where a large white cross burst into flames, followed by another past third. Murphy pointed, "See, I promised you I'd protect your rights and those folks up there are just reinforcing the energy, the solidarity we've got going here tonight! Hallelujah and God bless every one of you for coming out here to show the country what we really believe!"

The audience bellowed.

"We're going to win the nomination in Detroit and then we're going to win the presidency. I believe in our dream because you know and I know that together we can take back our rights, our government and our nation! Are you with me? Are you willing to rise up and fight for what you want, the pride and purity we all believe in? Then let's start right now! C'mon show the world that we're coming to take our country back and we won't take no for an answer!"

The whole stadium reverberated with a raucous chant, "Murphy! Murphy! Murphy!"

Signs and banners fluttered in every section on every level of the stadium and fanatical fans poured over the walls around the infield to race for a chance to be close to their spiritual leader, to bow down to the father figure who vowed to right the injustices and dispense revenge for the cruelty doled out by their enemies in Washington and Wall Street. Police and security swarmed onto the field to dissuade waves of passionate supporters with battering batons and brutal force.

Giant screens displayed gory images of flailing truncheons, blood splattering, and writhing bodies piling up among the chrome hubcaps and immaculate veneers of the elegant antique automobiles arranged as a glimmering barricade around the stage.

Murphy yelled, "Hey! Stop that! Those are my people! We all know the Democrats and the All People Matter mob are behind this! They slaughter their own people and now they're trying to kill ours!"

But hundreds, then thousands ignored the video bloodbath and stormed the field in waves of overheated zeal, panicked by random shots piercing the persistent primal roar of carnage surging around the stadium. Brawls erupted in every section, sprawling into panic and pandemonium with petrified patrons jamming the exits and tumbling down stairways and over banisters onto people fleeing the seats below. The candidate's voice rose to a scream, "Stop this right now!"

Secret Service agents charged the stage from behind the stylized backdrop under heavy flurries of confetti, wrapped Murphy in a human cocoon and hustled him down the steps and across the outfield to a waiting limousine in the service tunnel that removed him from the scene with screeching tires and little concern for pedestrians on the streets outside the stadium.

Four agents knelt on the floor of the car with guns drawn, while Murphy brushed himself off and turned to find Penny Baker sitting next to him with a mischievous grin that melted when the agent at their feet turned to ask, "Are you alright?"

"Yeah, I'm fine, why'd you yank me outta there? I was just getting warmed up."

"When shots are fired, we don't wait around to ask who's shooting at who. We contain our package and secure an exit as fast as we can."

"What shots?"

Another agent moved to sit on the bench seat, "I counted seven from four different directions. If they'd been snipers, we'd be transporting a corpse to the coroner's office, instead of a candidate to safety."

Murphy wrapped an arm around Penny, "Then I guess I should be thanking each and every one of you for saving my life, even if those morons were shooting at each other."

Unimpressed, the agents turned away to check in with the rest of their teams on secure radios, while four motorcycles and a convoy of Suburbans, with lights flashing and sirens wailing, escorted the long car onto the highway through Mount Adams, past Hyde Park, Mount Lookout and Ault Park heading for the sanity and safety of the radio station.

Murphy placed Penny's hand on his terminal erection, "How'd you end up in this car at just the right moment?"

"Actually, I was hiding out in here and all of a sudden the doors opened and these guys threw you in."

"Who were you hiding from?"

"Actually, I wasn't hiding. Hayden suggested that I spend a little time with Milton Graves to make sure he's pleased with our work. He wants to ride this gig all the way to the White House and, if I can help that along, then it's just part of my job."

"So, you take care of Graves' jollies and everybody keeps the gig?"

She smiled and rubbed his crotch, "But you're first on the list."

"I should be and, after tonight, I'm ready." With a brutal kiss and a sinister smile, he grabbed the back of her neck, unzipped his fly, and shoved her face into his lap.

~

Only a few lights twinkled in the darkness of the farmyard, as Ned Perkin's old panel truck slowed to a stop in a cloud of dust. He blinked the headlights, flashing Gracie and the pack of dogs prancing around the drive yelping and whining, until Nellis popped out of the barn to wheel the steel gate across the gravel, while Ned eased the truck around the side of the barn, then rolled it back.

He climbed out of the cab and hugged his old friend, "Seems like you've been going through more than your share of shit lately."

"Yeah, man, we've seen some bad stuff. Katherine's devastated and we've cancelled the rest of our rallies until the Feds finish their initial investigation."

Ned knelt to pet the dogs, "Have you heard anything yet?"

"Forgone conclusions, brother. We know who's behind it, question is whether the G-men can get the bastards we nabbed at the rally to talk, so they can pin it on the oligarchs. Who else has the money and the motive to put up the bucks to hire roving bands of assassins?"

"Endless blitz on the radio while I was driving, the Republicans trying to blame All People Matter for killing their own supporters, which is totally bizarre," said Ned, grabbing his bag from behind the seat.

"Truth has no meaning in their world. The ultimate goal is to dismantle the government and destroy our democracy, so the rich can quit wasting their dirty dollars on taxes that might benefit the little people."

"I saw your rant on the tube. Couldn't quibble with a single word you said."

"Yeah, well, you might be the only person on the planet. I caught a bunch of flak from everyone, including my ol' lady, who banished me from getting anywhere near the press for speaking my mind with billowing smoke and raging fire. More than a hundred dead and nearly a thousand wounded wandering through chaos and destruction in the background."

"I don't blame you. It's about time someone stood up, stopped being politically correct, and told the truth about these fascists. The country I believe in doesn't tolerate terrorism and mass murder."

"Amen, brother. You hungry? I saved you some smoked chicken but considering you showed up in the middle of the night, I'm not claiming it's hot and fresh off the grill."

"Hell, anything you cook is way better than the crap I've been eating on the road."

Nellis clapped him on the back, "Well, I'm glad you're here, so I can save your innards."

"Gotta admit, I was surprised to get your call. What's happening with your crop?"

"Actually, we had a hot dry spell, then days of heavy clouds, and some of our girls couldn't wait another moment for harvest. I've got a shipment ready to go."

"Is it your Jamaican Blue?"

"No, this one's Dancing Dreamer but the Blue's looking good, probably two or three weeks. It ain't fast but it sure is pretty."

"I can't believe you're getting away with growing and harvesting with all these official types hanging around."

"I had to work some scheduling magic to make everyone go someplace else at critical moments, which is about the only time we don't have security hanging around, but it all seems to be working out."

"Just so they don't wander off to admire your crop of sunflowers or tour the barn while you're curing."

"Once an outlaw, always an outlaw? Actually, it's been all about timing, besides, we've both got people who are counting on our success, so there ain't no other choice. C'mon and I'll feed ya'."

The dogs herded the two men up the walk and through the porch, "I noticed that the ol' place is kinda dark. What's that about?"

"Actually, for the first time in months, we're alone in our humble abode. Everyone's gone off to testify or arrange or organize or lick their wounds but they're all in a holding pattern until the big meeting in Atlanta with Turner. The girls talked him into running but everything changed in Denver."

"So, the whole movement, millions and millions of people are holding their collective breath until he decides whether he's in or he's out?"

"Yeah, if you think about it, it seems kind of obvious that he's been the prime target since the first big rally in Atlanta. With all the death and destruction, nobody really zeroed in on the 'why'...until I started ticking off things about each attack and it dawned on me that our confrontation with that armed mob on the steps of the Governor's office could have been the end of it, if they'd succeeded in keeping him from jumping into the race. That riot changed All People Matter from a fringe movement into a national campaign."

Ned sat down at the table in the kitchen and Nellis brought him an Olympia. "I'm sorry I couldn't be there and I don't mean to be insensitive to all the folks who were killed or injured but their half-assed attempts kind of backfired on them."

"Yeah, and they had to up the ante each time they missed. In Atlanta, all they had to do was instigate a big mob to fight with the protestors as a cover to take out Turner but Chicago was highly coordinated and the attack in Denver had to involve lots of people who were trained, put in place weeks ago, and assigned to specific tasks."

Ned scratched his beard, "That takes time and money."

Nellis fired up the oven and pulled a tray of smoked chickens, a covered dish of roast potatoes, and a handful of thick green beans from the refrigerator. "Give me twenty minutes and I'll have you a meal."

"I don't know whether I can wait that long, my belly's been talking to me for the last hundred miles."

"Yeah, it's complaining about too many black Molly's, gallons of shitty coffee, and all that fried crap you eat when you're on the road."

"Can't argue with that. Hey, where's Katherine?"

"Oh, I think she's asleep. She's the strongest women I've ever known but Denver kicked her ass. She's in a deep depression and even my sweetest, suavest, most compassionate and understanding shtick doesn't make a dent, so, it's going to take some time to work through it. Hell, Mavis and Tabitha hovered over her for a couple of days, until she told them, in no uncertain terms, to go home."

"I know she's the kind of lady who feels responsible, even when she had nothing to do with the attack."

"You know and I know, brother."

Katherine appeared in the doorway, barefoot, in a long pink robe. Normally statuesque, tangles of auburn tresses draped sagging shoulders, her deep brown eyes were bloodshot slivers adrift in gray pools, and her voice was a deep whisper, "I know too but that doesn't bring them back."

Ned got up and walked over to hug her, "You can't take responsibility for paid assassins."

"My brain agrees, my heart is another matter."

"You want something to eat or drink?" asked Nellis, pushing a pan into the oven.

She looked up, "A full bottle of really good Scotch sounds like a terrific idea but I think I'll settle for a glass of ice water and pass on the self-pity and the hangover."

Ned shook his head, "I'm living proof that you can't drink your guilt away. Took me a while to realize that cheap booze does the same damage as the expensive stuff but none of it takes away the hurt inside."

Nellis patted him on the back, "I'm with ya' brother."

"I keep going over our preparations for everything in minute detail - from scheduling to layers of security, every moment of the program, from the giddy excitement as the crowd charged into a room that transformed into mayhem. I can't shake the smell of melted carpeting, burning flesh, and death, or the brilliant flashes just before the mind-bending concussions, or the screams of terror and panic, or the look of shock and fear in the eyes of thousands of our people running for their lives through blinding clouds of thick black smoke billowing through acrid showers from the fire sprinklers," sobbed Katherine. "It just keeps playing over and over and the end is always the same."

Ned sat down and wrapped an arm around her shoulders, "I haven't been on the inside of all of this but I've been watching from out there in real America. I've been talking and listening and I know that you have an enormous following of people who need a spokeswoman like you - intelligent, dedicated, and unyielding – to tell their story, to reassure them that they're not alone in this fight to stand up against the gangsters who stole their lives. They follow you because you've convinced them that if everyone sticks together, we might actually win. They need your voice, your spirit, and your spunk to guide them through the elections as a unified movement, knowing that – win, lose, or draw – they stood together against the enemy of the people."

Katherine buried her face in his shoulder and wept.

"The bad guys can't win if we refuse to quit, if we're willing to defend our democracy despite the intimidation. If we show up at the convention and win the nomination for Turner, and then help him win the election - they lose," said Nellis.

She looked up, "Right now, that seems like a fairytale ending to this nightmare and I'm not sure I have the strength to carry this whole movement across the finish line."

Nellis smiled sadly, "We're not carrying them, they're carrying us."

She took his hand as he rubbed her aching neck, "There's something else."

"What's that?"

"Nanny's been with me since we got back from Denver."

"What do you mean?"

"I mean I can feel her empathy, her caring nature surrounding my spirit. She's been right next to me every second, with me when I pulled the covers over my head, when I cried myself to sleep, when I wake up praying that it was all just a horrible nightmare. She's here now."

"Where?"

Katherine closed her sad swollen eyes and inhaled deeply, exhaling very slowly. "She's inside me, she's warm and calm, compassionate, concerned about me but still...strong, determined, unyielding..."

Nellis grinned, "That's my girl...both of you."

Phyllis Crane smiled and greeted each of the distinguished guests spilling from three limousines lined up in the circular drive of City Hall with heavy security and City Police cars blocking access.

Mavis shook her hand with a brief hug, "I feel like we're invading you, considering the last time we came to visit there were just three of us."

"I've heard him mutter in his darker moments, 'I never should have listened to those damned women'."

"Considering what's happened since, I don't blame him," said Kate.

The Mayor's secretary scanned the crowd, "Looks like we've filled our quorum. So, if everyone will follow me, I'll show you to our conference room."

Nellis squeezed Katherine's hand, "Are you okay with this?"

"I'm worried that he'll listen to the angels that protect him and drop out of the race...and, at the same time, I'm afraid he won't."

Bobbie Warmington couldn't help gawking as the herd trooped through the atrium but opened her notebook, "Of the twenty-four members of our entourage, nineteen think he'll pass, but every one of them believes the movement will impact the next election, one way or the other."

Jessie and Stanton escorted Tabitha to the elevators and she turned to touch Katherine's sleeve, "The movement is bigger than any of us or all of us, for that matter. If we all disappeared tomorrow, our people would carry on because they don't have any other choice, this is about their survival and the future of our country. Having the ear of a sympathetic president would make our mission easier but it won't solve the problems or end the fight."

Katherine leaned to kiss her parchment cheek, "You are a wise old owl but you'll have to admit that the guilt we carry for the deaths of so many changes the calculation."

The elevator doors opened and they stepped inside without interruption. "This is a war and our enemies have chosen violence and intimidation. We've opted to defend our democracy, the sanctity of our rights and our beliefs, and the dignity of the middle class. We have to uphold those values, no matter the cost, because they can't win unless we quit."

Jessie chuckled, "Say that to the mayor and he'll have to keep going."

The doors opened on a sundrenched balcony and Mrs. Crane walked with Stanton into a hallway, "I'm glad you've all come today, he's been looking forward to this meeting with you, all of you."

"I'm...we're all honored...hopeful and anxious."

They turned into a large airy room with rich golden burl paneling, sliced from the broad trunks of Georgia's ancient Live Oaks, punctured by tall slender windows casting luminous fingers across a broad rug milled from fine Georgia cotton, with the outline of the state surrounding a bulldog and a blue panther resting beneath a peach tree at the center. The carpet extended from a large conference table at one end, covered with sandwiches and light refreshments, to comfortable furniture casually arranged facing five chairs behind a coffee table at the other. She looked up and said, "I honestly don't have any idea about what he's decided or what he'll have to say. Your guess is as good as mine."

Brad, Eddie, Sheldon, and Beal peeled off to talk with Barry Clark, head of security for Mayor Turner, while the leadership filtered into fill the room.

Phyllis Crane stood before the conference table, "I want to welcome all of you and thank you for coming. The mayor will be with us shortly and in the meantime I invite you to enjoy food and drink, although

I should warn you to avoid the fudge brownies because as I've proven, it's impossible to eat just one."

Mavis walked over to Amy and Althea, "How are you ladies holding up?"

They glanced at each other, before a dejected Amy said, "Not so well. We both feel like we let all those people down."

"We're supposed to be helping, instead of setting traps so the bad guys can murder all these desperate people," added Althea.

"I know exactly how you feel and to tell you truth when I got home, I climbed into my bed and pulled the covers over my head and cried and whined and beat myself up. But, after buckets of tears, my other voice started scolding me for feeling sorry for myself which wasn't going to bring back the dead, heal the wounded, or dispense unmerciful revenge on the evil forces behind these attacks. The folks who died would want us to move forward and all the survivors and millions more are counting on us to lead the charge so, our job is to organize them to elect candidates who will fight for the martyrs."

"We can't quit," said Amy.

Althea added, "But it will never feel the same. The sheer joy and excitement of everything we've been trying to do will always be tarnished by the hate that drove the attacks on innocent, desperate people. We'll all carry that with us forever."

Mavis hugged the two women as everyone stood and turned to greet the mayor, who entered from a side door to enthusiastic applause. He shook hands and exchanged greetings with everyone he encountered as he marched straight to Katherine and took her hands in his to share kisses on each cheek. "I've been worried about you. Grapevine has it that you've been trying to shoulder the responsibility for the tragedy in Denver all by yourself. Having lived these many years in the crosshairs of controversy and condescension, I can assure you that there's plenty of guilt to share with the rest of us."

Katherine lifted her chin, "I am the spokeswoman for this movement and I feel a responsibility for the welfare of every single person who participates, that goes with the territory. I guess the best way to describe how I'm feeling about everything is that I'm wounded but I refuse to be defeated."

The mayor squeezed her hand and smiled, "They set five places for the 'dignitaries' and I hope that you will sit beside me."

"I'd be honored."

"Would you ask those conniving girlfriends of yours and Nellis to join us?"

"Certainly."

He walked up to the coffee table and tapped a spoon against a pitcher of ice water, "Ladies and gentlemen, would you please enjoy some refreshments and then find a chair, so we can begin."

Nellis followed the three women and shook hands with Turner, "I'm surprised you'd want me to join this discussion."

"I'm grateful for your forthright honesty. You can say things that I feel in my heart but could never reveal," replied the mayor. "Please, have a seat."

The buzz of conversation dwindled as the crowd settled into comfortable chairs.

"First, I'd like to thank you for taking the time to participate in this very private discussion about the options before us." He turned to Katherine, "I've spoken with Katherine about the madness in Denver and I'd like to point out that after speaking with everyone involved with the security arrangements - Brad and Eddie, the police, Secret Service and FBI, I've concluded that the All People Matter movement did everything possible to ensure the safety of everyone involved in the rally. It was a horrifying experience! All the more so for the realization that there are people out there who actually conceive of these despicable crimes and all of us will carry the burden of our guilt for the rest of our lives."

He paused, "But...we, none of us, can allow this assault to end our representation of the millions of desperate souls who have been lifted up by what all of you have been trying to do. The whole country is counting on you to keep fighting for all that's right and true. To do anything less would mean abandoning everything that this crusade stands for. Every hope and dream that we've dangled in front of our people, dreams of reclaiming their lives and their dignity, wresting our society from the grip of fascism, and rebuilding our nation from the middle out. That is our obligation and our duty as patriots!"

The audience applauded.

He turned to scan Nellis and the three women, "I think I should admit that I was reluctant to take on this campaign, until Jessie and Nellis sent these three gorgeous and eminently brilliant women to temp and cajole me into the race. They succeeded without much effort. I mean how could anyone say 'no' to these three?"

Everyone laughed in agreement.

"Considering the attacks, the question becomes am I brave enough to continue, knowing that all of these incidents were covers for assassination attempts that failed? I've talked with Barry Clark, my Head of Security as well everyone involved in security for the movement and they've all agreed that the attempts won't stop until they succeed."

The audience stared, silent and unmoving.

"I could give in to my terror. I could focus on my own mortality, the fragility of life, the frustration of not finishing what I've started because some racist assassin got lucky. But I'll give you two reasons why I've decided to continue." He tarried for a long moment to gaze from one supporter to the next, "I've watched the tapes of the attack in Denver with revulsion. The vision of charred lifeless bodies strewn across smoldering carpeting and the dazed and wounded wandering through acrid smoke in search of help, haunts me…but the look on Nellis Gray's face when he told the nation the unvarnished truth about the Republican party, grounded my conflict.

I'll paraphrase Nellis' words, 'The Republicans sent their goons to murder more innocent people. That's how the fascists behind these horrors win elections. If they can't keep opposition voters away from the polls through racist voting laws and violent intimidation, or destroy the reputations of upstanding candidates, who happen to disagree with them, with carefully crafted lies, they'll wage war on anyone brave enough to stand against their campaign to dismantle our democracy.' It wasn't good politics, but it was a raw honest reaction to the slaughter of innocent people and I applaud him for having the guts to say what we all know is true."

Murmurs rippled through the audience and a few clapped hesitantly.

"This won't end until we, all of us, convince the nation of the impending peril to our republic and the freedoms we enjoy as a nation, should the opposition take control of our government. The alternative is institutional feudalism and a rapid regression through more than a hundred and fifty years of progress to the ignorance and isolation that brought on the Civil War."

He paused, his eyes moving from face to face, each bearing conflicting expressions of hope and apprehension bound up in a universal determination masking their rage and fury. "We've got enough delegates to be a formidable force at the convention but I doubt that we could win on the first ballot. A lot can change between the first and the second or the second and the third vote. So, if all of you are brave enough to see this through to the election in November, I'll continue my candidacy with dedication and devotion to all those who died trying to reclaim our freedom."

Nellis grinned, as Katherine, Kate, and Mavis jumped up to plant kisses on Turner's cheeks and the burl paneling amplified cheers and applause.

~

"Conrad, how are our affairs?" inquired Stanley French, from the secure suite in the bowels of Dynamic Devices headquarters.

There was a pause, "Muddled, yes, I'd say muddled is the best term I can come up with at the moment. Our people have been going through the numbers and dozens of scenarios but the bottom line is that Murphy has managed to secure as many delegates as Steil and Grant, so it's a three-way draw for the first ballot."

"I've got John and Michael embedded in both campaigns and they're reporting modest enthusiasm at their public events but nothing like Murphy's three-ring circus. Do we have any leverage?"

"They've just installed Casper Wein as campaign chairman for the convention, which pushed Shephard Stone out of the limelight."

"They're both our guys, aren't they?"

"Yes, but their primary responsibility is to feed information to our team, after they do everything in their power to get their candidate elected."

"Why?"

"Because anything less than full commitment would tip our hand. They're both pros and they'll do their jobs," replied Blaho. "Whoever it is, the nominee will be obligated to do our bidding."

"That sounds like wishful thinking," moaned French. "Tell me there's an upside to all of this."

"Tomlinson and I both agree that, if Murphy looks strong after the first round, we should throw our weight behind him...as long as he's willing to choose Steil for vice-president and allow his entire staff to be populated with the very finest and most committed people on our list, fill every judicial vacancy with judges who have sworn allegiance to the covenants of our own Freedom Founders Foundation, and nominate our experts to dismantle his Cabinet departments."

"Why would he go along with all of this?"

"Because, we can put up enough money to give him a real shot against Turner in the general. If that doesn't convince him, then he'll be confronted with a dossier that exposes him as a disgusting sleaze-ball in real life. We have lots of film guaranteed to disqualify him from taking any office and probably send him to jail for the rest of his life."

"This is not how this operation was supposed to go."

"I know but there is one more rather curious perspective on all of this and that is that Murphy is a performer who can gin up his ignorant evangelical base into a frenzy with outright lies and utter nonsense. Whoever is elected the next president will depend on the votes of his followers.

Besides, if we were searching for a distraction from the business of deconstructing the government, he's a bright gleaming object who will use the news media as a gigantic megaphone to smother the airwaves with an endless barrage of blather that will outrage the liberals and keep the peasants marching in support."

"I can see your logic but it all depends on execution."

"No matter who wins the nomination, we will own this convention and we'll use it to further our goals."

"Is Tomlinson running those raucous ads exposing Murphy's bullshit?"

Conrad laughed, "Yeah, and Will Terry is a production genius, but our polling shows that instead of being repulsed, the ignorant underbelly of our society reacts positively to our revolting propaganda, they call him a hero who isn't afraid to show his warts or tell the 'man' to shove it."

"Which proves our contention that the uneducated are easily manipulated to vote against their own self-interest."

"That's the point! Embrace their allegiance and back the candidate who can rally their votes."

Chapter Fourteen

From the penthouse suite of the Renaissance Center, the setting sun fired golden daggers skittering along the Detroit River under a sapphire sky, a slender crescent moon floating over Sagittarius, the archer aiming for the heart of Scorpius as the city lights flickered on in a wave of golden illumination rolling west through dusk.

Jack Hannah walked up behind a motionless Murphy, gazing out the enormous windows at the spectacular panorama and offered him a glass of Jack Daniels in a crystal tumbler, "The vote's about to start."

The candidate downed the drink in one swig and pressed the cold glass against his cheek, "I have to admit that I really don't understand how we ended up here, with a shot at the nomination."

"Great handlers," laughed the station manager.

"Yeah, that's it."

"Actually, you managed to strike a note that resonated with millions of people who don't have anyone else to stand up for them."

"I guess I should feel responsible for not offering real solutions for their plight, instead of bullshit catch-lines that seem to justify or excuse their refusal to face their own ignorance and prejudice. The rabid hate, arrogance, and communal victimization I see in the sea of screaming faces at every rally would terrify me if I wasn't flying in the stratosphere on whatever the doc is putting in those little paper cups.

The thought of actually winning the presidency and implementing even a few of the crazy promises that I've made is beyond my own comprehension. Nobody with more than a couple of synapses firing in tandem could believe any of that crap."

"It's religion to them and you're their messiah, they believe that you'll lead them to a better life, where being white guarantees preference at the expense of everyone else."

"Do you realize how nuts that is?"

"Of course, but we all agreed to ride this thing to the end and here we are, watching hundreds of delegates casting their ballots for Mac Murphy to be the Republican nominee for President of the United States. If you thought the pussy was top-shelf on the first part of this ride, just wait 'til you see what's waiting on the other side of the nomination."

"I'll play it out but we both know that there's no way in hell I should be elected to the highest office in the land."

"Look, Wein and Stone are working their contacts, pulling strings, collecting debts, strong arming and bribing delegates to hop on board while they have a chance. Crawley's already got three or four promos in the bag that are going to appear on all the local stations during the event. Austin Crouch has packed the gallery with twenty-thousand rabid supporters who were bused in from all over the county, and Turner Grave's brought in some of his buddies to throw money at anyone who resists the invitation. It's up to the other guys to try to beat you and, to tell you the truth, I don't think any of them's got the balls or the team to pull it off."

"I guess we'll find out," said Murphy, pacing back and forth along the windows, drawn to the chatter of supporters and staff huddled around six giant televisions, covering the roll call at Ford Field, and repulsed by the returns.

Milly Clark toddled over and took his arm, "Are you okay?"

"Yeah, thanks for asking. I'm just kind of blown away that we're standing on the threshold of the nomination."

"Actually, it looks like you're going to come out with more than a third of the votes on the first round and far more than Steil or Grant. The wheels are turning to grab every delegate who has any doubts about their first choice, before the next ballot. If the boys in the back room have their way, you'll be above forty percent."

He turned to her, "You've stuck it out through this whole campaign, in spite of me being a boorish and vulgar asshole. I think I owe you an apology and my thanks for putting up with me."

Milly was short and dumpy, with a cagy tactical mind hiding beneath mousy brown hair and a puffy round face, but her dark eyes filled with tears, "I know who you really are and we both know that you've been tasked with living in this character you're portraying, pushing everything to the very edge, and I've been watching you struggling to keep yourself from falling out of your own reality."

"I think I passed that point a long time ago."

"Maybe, but I believe that when this is over…whether you're a private citizen or President of the United States, the real you will reclaim your soul and your self-respect. That's when the real Murphy will shine through."

"I can't believe that you still believe in me."

"Hey, I knew who you were the first time you marched into the station, sweet-talking and spouting Murphy-isms to keep everyone else at bay, and you haven't changed anything. This is your greatest performance and we're just about to finish up act one with a flourish." She stood on tip-toe to kiss him on the cheek, "Act two is about claiming your place on the world stage and I know you'll deliver."

"As You Like It, if you'll excuse the pun."

"Just keep yourself together, I've got your back."

"I trust you more than anyone else in this campaign."

She smiled, "And rightfully so!"

Doc Billings marched over with a tiny white paper cup, a glass of water, and a big smile. "You embarrassed the chosen few on the first ballot. It'll be a couple of hours before they try again, so I want you to take these vitamins to keep you on an even keel while we wait."

Murphy took the cup, "Are you sending me up or down?"

"Actually, I'm just trying to keep you from having anxiety attacks for the time being."

"No cosmic rushes or unrelenting erections?"

"Promise."

"You're no fun at all, you know that, don't you?"

"I'm just trying to keep you upright and ready for your time in the spotlight."

"I appreciate all that you've done to keep me going through all of this."

"You're the Kentucky Derby favorite and it's my job to keep you in your prime."

Everyone in the grand suite turned away from blaring televisions to assess a commotion in the entry. A small crowd filtered into the suite ahead of Jack Hannah, Shepherd Stone, and Casper Wein clearing a path for Ethan Tomlinson through the suite to Murphy and Doc Billings, who took the glass of water as the candidate crunched the tiny white cup in his left hand.

The candidate stepped forward with a confident smile and extended his hand, "To what do we owe this honor?"

Tomlinson did not smile, "Is there someplace we could talk?"

"Sure, there's a card room just down the hall."

The men walked around the curved hallway into a small room and Jack Hannah closed the door. Murphy smiled, "I'll say it again, to what do I owe this honor?"

"Do you want to win this thing?" asked Tomlinson.

"That's why I'm running."

"No, you're running because you're getting laid by the best pussy we can supply in every town you visit and you guys are pocketing approximately twenty-seven percent of the campaign contributions in several nameless accounts in the Caribbean."

"What's it to you?" asked Jack Hannah.

The public relations guru offered a small arrogant smile, "I'm not here to shake you down but I am here to offer a proposition."

"Which is?"

"I can see to it that you win a majority vote on the next ballot."

"And what do you want in return?" asked the candidate.

"By merging our campaigns, we can take control of the Party and set the agenda for at least the next eight years."

"What do you want in return for this…gift…of your unsolicited support."

"The privilege of supplying the best and brightest true-believers to your staff. We'll have your administration up and running from day one, a slew of bills ready to send to our Republican Congress, and an agenda to assess all our commitments and relationships around the world. It's time to rebuild the world order to fulfill the needs of the United States, instead of the other way around. After reviewing some of your speeches, I'm sure we can find a mutually beneficial path to promote American dominance and independence throughout the world."

"That's very generous of you but it's also the smoothest line of bullshit I've heard all evening. What do you want in return for handing me the Presidency?"

"First, you'll support the nomination of Creighton Steil as your Vice-President."

"That sleazy faggot should be in jail."

"That sleazy faggot is your ticket to the presidency," replied Tomlinson, who pulled out a phone to display a video of a very drunk Murphy groping and propositioning an underage girl in a bar. "I have lots of these clips that will suddenly start appearing on every television station in the country tomorrow morning, unless we reach an agreement tonight."

~

Nellis reached to rub behind Gracie's ear, as she climbed onto the sofa and rested her head in his lap, lifting her soft brown eyes to gaze up at him, "Am I missing something important here?"

The dog groaned and settled in.

"I think she's feeling neglected," said Katherine, squeezing his other hand. "We've been so focused on the campaign, coming and going, while she's holding down the fort."

Nellis leaned to nuzzle and Gracie licked his nose, "I sure hope you'll forgive me, 'cause we both know you'll always be queen of the farm."

Katherine glanced at the television and turned the volume up, "As we approach the halfway mark of the second ballot it appears that if the voting follows the trend, Oklahoma might well be the delegation to top the twelve-hundred and thirty-seven votes Mac Murphy needs to clinch the nomination," said Melanie McQuade.

"The tide changed when the campaign made the surprise announcement that Creighton Steil had agreed to run as Murphy's vice-president, should he win the nomination on this ballot," added Trevor Hobbs, distinguished anchor for International Public News.

The stunning blond anchorwoman flashed a radiant smile, "Every political reporter in the nation would love to have been a fly on the wall for those negotiations! That's a Pulitzer Prize winning story waiting to be written."

"Both political parties have spent billions promoting a public relations blitz claiming that the days of the political machine picking the candidates are long over but I find it hard to believe that a renegade with questionable qualifications and no experience in civil service could grab the nomination on the second ballot without considerable help from the real powers behind the party."

"There have been rumors for years charging a clandestine fraternity of some of the wealthiest families in the nation pouring millions into critical state and national races to promote their extreme agendas but no one has ever produced verifiable proof that those stories are true."

The graying anchor shook his head with a wry smile, "Even if we believe those stories, no one would ever confirm the truth but skeptics might wonder what they gain by supporting a charlatan?"

"Those bastards can rig the elections to promote their conspiracies by remote control and no one can prove the connection," said Nellis.

A tear trickled down Katherine's cheek, "But we know exactly how wicked and vile their surrogates can be."

"Turner will expose this imposter for exactly what he is."

"I think you're right but the big question is whether all the racist morons who voted for him will give a damn whether he's a liar and a fraud, as long as they believe he's willing to justify their ignorant arrogance."

"He's right up front about supporting racial supremacy, trashing treaties and trade agreements, and rescinding any regulation ever written by a Democrat."

"That's about the only thing he's honest about, everyone knows he's a phony."

Nellis boosted the volume as Hector Hennessey, head of the Oklahoma delegation, declared, "The great state of Oklahoma casts all forty-three votes for the next President of these great United States, Mac Murphy!" and the crowd of fifty-thousand in attendance at Ford Field erupted in a euphoric celebration of white dominance and the demise of civil rights. Clouds of glittering confetti poured through blazing lights to envelope ecstatic delegates dancing and cheering to 'Happy Days are Here Again'.

A graphic filled the screen - 'Murphy wins the Republican Nomination' and Trevor Hobbs resonant baritone confirmed the announcement, "IPN has called the nomination for Martin McClintock Murphy on the second ballot. We have a renegade Republican nominee who wasn't even on anyone's radar a few months ago."

Katherine squeezed Nellis' hand, staring at the red, white, and blue tribal chaos on the screen. "How is it possible that a large percentage of our population has no clue about who they're voting for, let alone what he intends to do? Scuttlebutt has it that he's a drug-addled, alcoholic, pedophile, has-been actor who never performed any memorable parts, except this one."

"An ignorant population is easier to manipulate than an educated one and you know as well as I do the Republicans have systematically reduced or eliminated public education in every red state over the past few decades, removed verifiable facts from the nation's textbooks and segregated or decimated as many school districts as they can manage."

"I have every respect for people's right to their religious beliefs but there's no way that public education should be replaced by private evangelical charter schools run by corporations charged with producing a population of mindless robots who believe that the Earth is flat and history started six-thousand years ago."

"They're succeeding because they've nibbled away at the resistance - reducing budgets, eliminating professional educators, and redrawing districts to isolate everyone who isn't a white bigot."

The brunette rested her head on his shoulder, "That bastard is bought and paid for by the criminals who ordered the assassinations at our rallies and, if they manage to put him in the White House, all three branches of government will be in the service of a couple of hundred greedy families who think they deserve to own the world."

"Then it's our job to make sure everyone understands the stakes at our convention, isn't it?"

She sighed, "At least they'll keep a lid on him for the time being."

"Oh, he's going to be doing more rallies over the next few weeks, including one in Dallas the night after the Democratic convention finishes up."

"I'll bet he'll have a lot to say."

"Sure 'nough."

~

Katherine, Mavis, and Kate stepped out of a white Cadillac limousine onto the wet tarmac of the Executive Airport, south of Dallas, as the Gulfstream taxied up to the terminal under tight security provided by Abe Sheldon's team and a squadron of Secret Service agents.

No other planes were parked within sight. Fuel trucks and service vehicles were confined to a hangar on the far side of the field, all gates were sealed and several dozen guards patrolled the grounds and secured the entire airfield from rooftops in full riot gear with automatic weapons at the ready.

Kate gazed around, as the whine of the plane's engines slowly descended from ear-splitting to moderately annoying, "After being hijacked by a squad of fake cops, all these guns make me nervous."

Katherine took her arm and leaned close, "I'd be nervous if they weren't here."

Mayor Turner followed his security chief, Barry Clark, and Phyllis Crane down the short flight of steps, greeting the reception committee with handshakes, hugs, and kisses from Mavis, Kate, and Katherine. He took Katherine's arm, "I've been listening to polling experts all day and I'm fairly certain that their canvasing doesn't represent our people. What do you think?"

"Our biggest problem is having too many volunteers just showing up wanting to help, the gallery is going to be packed with thousands of supporters, we've got more than eleven-hundred All People Matter alumni scattered through the delegations and they're working to convince the doubters to join the cause. We've got traditional crews monitoring the opposition, feeding the media, massaging the platform, entertaining the donors, and chasing down votes."

"So, where do you think we stand?"

"I think we're going to be about three-hundred votes shy of winning the first ballot but we'll get a clear sense of which of the other candidates is growing support and who's not."

"At which point, we'll have to make a final decision on a vice-president."

"That could make it or break it, depending," replied Katherine. "Have you made a decision?"

Turner smiled and winked, "I guess we'll know when the time comes."

"You know I hate it when you do that."

"Of course, it's my revenge for you ladies dragging me into all of this," laughed the Mayor, "but I'll let you in on a little secret."

"What's that?"

"I'd pick you, if I could get away with it!"

The brunette blushed, "I'm flattered but we both know that you need someone who can bring in votes from different parts of the political spectrum."

"So? That's exactly why you'd be perfect."

"Why?"

"Because you're a formidable female with a computer brain and the compassion of a saint. You're an incredible organizer, a gifted communicator, and you're the face of a national movement that represents millions of desperate citizens and appeals to millions more. You're from a red state in the Midwest, while I represent a blue urban dot in the Republican South. You appeal to middle America, while I bring in the liberals, the minority vote, and the suburbs, but we both know that I'm going to have a hard time with the white working class. If I'm going to form a ticket, it might as well be one that, first, I'm proud of, and second, that offends the fascists in every way possible."

Katherine laughed, "I'm proud to be involved in any part of your campaign but we both know that my grumpy roommate wouldn't tolerate Secret Service protection for five minutes, let alone the rest of the campaign and four years after that! You have to understand that Nellis Gray would just as soon hide away at the farm with his pack of dogs and a locked steel gate to keep the rest of the world outside his little piece of paradise permanently."

"He's as honest and upfront as any man I've ever met and I admire that…and that you have any control over him at all," said the Mayor, with a crooked eyebrow.

"Who said I do?"

They climbed into the limousine and settled in with Kate and Mavis, Phyllis Crane, and Turner shook hands with Marvin Standler and Spratlin. He leaned to Katherine, "To tell you the truth, I really haven't decided my preference but we both know that part of that decision will be determined by who's holding the strongest hand."

"Your face is going to be everywhere this week – ads on every television station, billboards, newspapers, and all over the internet," said Mavis. "Hell, they've even got you giving little speeches on screens above the urinals at the airport!"

"I'm not sure that last one's not the most appropriate," replied Turner, as the cars moved into position behind two black Suburbans, with motorcycle cops ahead and a caravan of security vehicles behind.

Kate laughed, "You've got a captive audience for what, an intimate minute and a half of one-on-one."

He looked at Stanton, "I know these women have assisted in your candidacy, so I have to ask whether they caused as much trouble and turmoil for you as they have for me."

Mavis moped and Kate giggled.

"Fortunately, I only had to obey Katherine and my wife during my brief campaign, so I shouldn't complain."

"Besides, even after kidnappings and car wrecks, you hold the office!" mused Katherine.

"And I have you to thank."

"That's much better," teased Mavis, poking Stanton with a bright red fingernail.

"Okay, down to business," said the candidate. "What's on the schedule?"

"We've taken over an entire floor of the Omni Hotel, so we can entertain our guests in the public areas, while maintaining some privacy for you, as well as all the teams – Communications, PR, Convention and delegate coordination and all the rest," said Kate. "The actual delegate count doesn't start until tomorrow night so, we're hosting a small sponsors' party this evening. A prayer breakfast with the minority delegates in the morning, then an hour to get used to the stage, a veterans' luncheon, meetings and last minute coordination in the afternoon, and a private dinner with the president before the count begins."

"By the time you get finished with me, I'm going to weigh three-hundred pounds! Does every function have to include a meal?"

"You don't have to eat," said Mavis with a sly grin.

"Say's the woman who hasn't gained a pound since she got out of college," said Kate.

Turner asked, "Where's Tabitha?"

"Oh, she and Jessie flew in this morning with Bobbie Warmington. We'll meet them at the hotel."

"Good! She's bedrock in a rushing stream and I look forward to her counsel." He turned to Standler, "Marvin, what's the undercurrent with the right-wing financiers?"

He glanced at Mavis and grinned, "They're completely terrified now that Murphy stole the nomination from their hand-picked, brainwashed, and well financed surrogates. They've had an agenda for decades of dismantling the federal government and as far as I know they have no guarantee that he'll go along unless Creighton Steil can manipulate him from behind the scenes."

"Do you honestly think they'll throw their money into his campaign?"

"They've got no other choice and any Democrat would jump at the opportunity to expose their slimy scheme. If they take the House, Senate, and the White House and stack the courts with white nationalist judges, they'll own the nation."

"We all realize that Murphy lacks any leadership credentials…"

"Other than a big mouth and a meager mind," added Mavis.

Turner grinned, "The man might manipulate or ignore real facts but he knows how to rally a crowd of bigots who know even less than he does, by pandering to their ignorant fears and seething prejudices. I've thought long and hard about this and it seems to me that the voters' decision comes down to which vision of the future are the American people going to choose, survival of the working class or handing over their rights and benefits to provide vast riches for the greedy few?"

"If the electorate in Oklahoma is typical, I'm not sure that a large portion of our population understands what's at stake," said Spratlin. "They're going to vote for whichever candidate promises to defend their personal issues and gives them permission to hate someone or some other group who's responsible for their problems. We're becoming a nation of warring tribes."

"I'm afraid you're right," said Turner, "which means that we're going to have to educate the voters, if we expect them to make an informed choice."

"This is for the heart and soul of the nation," said Katherine. "Too many of our people have been martyred by fascist enforcers and in their name, we can't let the tyrants win."

~

Tyrone and Tabitha stood alone together, gazing out the windows at crowds milling around the Kay Hutchison Convention Center on a typically sweltering August evening in Dallas. "There are probably only ten-thousand people involved in putting on this show, all the rest are here because they want to witness the rebirth of hope."

"All it takes is one determined nutcase to change history." The candidate was quiet for a moment, pointing, "I'm aware that Dealey Plaza is only a few blocks from here."

"I'll make sure we don't send you out in a convertible," said Tabitha, taking his arm. "From what Kate and Katherine told me, most of those people are here because they want you to succeed."

"Thanks, I appreciate that," laughed Turner. "I read a lot of newspapers but that's your world, what's your take on their reaction to our campaign?"

"I think they understand that if Murphy wins, freedom of the press will become a quaint memory in a very dark world and if there's no real, honest fourth estate, then our democracy can't survive. On the other hand, a good reporter will follow any story looking for a scoop, so we have to give them more to work with than the endless drivel spewing from Murphy's camp. I'm sure our Communications people are working overtime."

"It's hard to get normal people to pay attention to the real issues, when the Republicans are lobbing Molotov cocktails to deflect attention from the real news of the day."

The matron smiled, "That's all they've got to sell - bright sparkly diversions that get everyone excited for a few minutes before they realize it's all just nonsense dressed up in red, white, and blue bunting."

Turner looked at his watch, "I hate to be rude but I've got to get ready for my dinner with the president."

She squeezed his hand, "I believe that you can lead this country to salvation and I'll do everything in my power to help you achieve that. I read a draft of your acceptance speech, it's honest and it's powerful. I pray that I get to hear you deliver it to this convention."

He kissed her cheek, "That makes two of us."

~

Mavis and Phyllis Crane greeted President Gonzalez's delegation at the elevators with hugs and handshakes.

"I'm so pleased you could come tonight," said Phyllis.

"I'm pleased that your boss is in the running for the nomination," replied the president. "The prospect of the Republican candidate claiming the Oval Office is terrifying at best."

"All we have to do is clinch the nomination and convince fifty-one percent of the voters that Murphy's a crook and we're not," added Mavis.

Gonzalez took her hand, "Mrs. Sloan, although we haven't had a chance to talk since Tate's tragic passing, I hope you'll accept my sincere condolences. I appreciated your friendship and support during my campaign."

"Thank you. I know he felt honored to be able to offer his assistance but I also think he'd like the fact that he'll be remembered as a hero."

"He was a champion for the little guys."

"Mr. President, if you'll follow me, the mayor is expecting you," said Phyllis Crane.

"Lead on dear lady, just so long as they're not serving hotel chicken!"

Turner entered the small conference room just as his secretary brought the president in through the opposite door. He extended a hand to Gonzalez, "Phillipe, I'm honored that you would share this evening with me."

The president held on to his hand for a moment as they took in the celestial view of twinkling lights of traffic threading a tangle of highways beneath a layer of rolling gray clouds glowing orange in the radiance of the setting sun. The room had been magically transformed into an elegant dining salon with linen table cloths, crystal, china, and silver gleaming under subtle spotlights,

"We both hope for the same result but, having suffered through this endless agonizing anticipation in my time, I must ask how you're holding up?"

Tyrone laughed, "We're still maneuvering to take the nomination on the second ballot, with a little help from our friends, so I guess I'd have to say I'm anxious."

"That's about as honest an answer as I'm going to get! My personal pollster prognosticated somewhere close to forty percent on the first vote, with Walker, Paul, and Cassidy bunched up around fifteen percent, and my rickety ineffectual running-mate barely in positive territory." He paused, taking in the room, "I must say, if I'd been blindfolded, I'd have sworn that we just entered some fabulous New Orleans restaurant, because whoever is cooking whatever, it smells divine!"

"I can promise you that it's not chicken," said Turner, leading him to a comfortable pair of easy chairs arranged in front of large windows looking out over the shimmering lights of the city, as the entourage left the room.

"Amen," laughed the president, accepting a Malt Scotch with a single ice cube in a heavy tumbler. "Someone on your staff has done their homework."

"You're famous for your proclivity for Glenlivet."

"And you for your teetotaler abstention."

The mayor laughed, "It's not by choice, political or moral, believe me. There was a time when I indulged enthusiastically, until the doctors decided otherwise."

"If you think they're pests now, wait until the military witch doctors get hold of you at Bethesda. I've never felt so violated in my entire life and they want to check out all the plumbing every three months! Hell, they know everything about every cell in my body and it's all classified intelligence! I've tried to fire the whole bunch of them more than once but it doesn't do any good, they keep hauling me off to the hospital on their schedules."

Turner grinned and sipped his ice water. "Tell me, as you look forward to stepping down, what concerns you most?"

Without hesitation, he replied, "We have countless challenges around the world – China, Russia, the Middle East, and simmering hotspots all over the place. The economy has been bumping along in spite of the shenanigans of the big banks and the financial industry, but I worry about what's just over the horizon. Europe's trying to transform its coalition into a continental basket case and the midget running North Korea thinks he's a big shot because he's got some nukes to rattle, but what frightens me the most are the shadowy international powerbrokers behind the Republican Party. In coordination with fascist oligarchs attacking every democracy in the world, they've got their minions working overtime to dismantle the federal government, eliminate restrictions or regulations that might inhibit their business profits even if it's against the national interest, rescind all the Amendments after number twelve, and pack the courts with radically conservative judges sworn to uphold their sponsors' interests. They're the enemy within and every other adversity pales by comparison."

"You're aware of the attacks on our rallies, leaving hundreds dead and countless injured and wounded. We have no doubt that the assailants were mercenary shock troops but, even though the FBI has a half-dozen of them in jail, not one has spoken a word, other than pleading not-guilty at their preliminary trials. All of them are protecting the real villains and every one of them has top-flight attorneys representing their cases gratis."

"I'm not surprised, they've been smart enough to use a scattergun approach, blasting away over decades, to pick off little bits and pieces of our democracy until they've filled the House and the Senate with obedient lackeys who'll hand the reins of governance to corporations until there's nothing left to govern. To hell with the little people, let them fend for themselves." He slugged his Scotch, "I came into office under the delusion that I could propose and support reasonable legislation to the Congress but it didn't take long to realize that my primary responsibility was to use every device in the arsenal to inhibit their encroachment on the very foundations of our nation. In spite of the enormous power of the executive, that's been a losing battle."

A waiter in a starched white jacket and black bow tie offered a tray with two fresh drinks, "If you gentlemen are ready, dinner is served."

They followed him to a candlelit table and as they were being seated the president said, "That will be your greatest challenge, holding back their repugnant and carefully coordinated campaign to destroy the country. My greatest fear is that if they take the presidential election, they'll be on their way to succeeding uncontested."

Two waiters appeared and placed domed platters on the table, lifting the covers to release a cloud of scented steam, rich with Cajun aromas. "The chef calls this Pappadeaux Snapper Ponchartrain. The fish and shrimp are fresh from the Gulf, the sauce handed down through his family who lived on the Bayou, accompanied by slender asparagus from his garden, on a bed of infused wild rice. Might I offer you a glass of wine to accompany your meals?"

"I think we'll pass for the moment," said Turner, leaning to inhale the fragrance. "Hopefully, there will be cause for celebration later."

The waiters bowed, "Bon Appetit."

They toasted and Tyrone said, "To a better tomorrow."

"I have faith in you," added the president.

Before either could take a bite, Katherine swept into the room and approached the men with a smile, "The voting's starting and you picked up almost half of the delegates in the first few states, including California, which gives you a sizable lead for the moment."

The president smiled, knife and fork in hand, "I'd offer my congratulations but we both know that it's bad luck and a lot can change by the time they get to a final tally."

"Thank you, Katherine, we'll join you when we've finished here, if that's alright."

"Of course," replied the spokeswoman, withdrawing.

Turner took a bite of the fish in the rich earthy sauce, "Oh, my! If I lose, I'm moving to New Orleans!"

The president's eyes followed Katherine's retreat, "I must say, your inner circle is far more attractive than mine ever was!"

"If truth be known those three women conned me into this campaign."

Gonzalez laughed, "I'm having trouble envisioning you saying 'No' to any of them, let alone all three!"

"Each of them and their partners are among the most talented, intelligent, and dedicated people I've ever known. I respect their opinions, their motives, and their sheer unvarnished honesty."

"I was moved by Mr. Gray's powerful and completely frank reaction to the tragedy in Denver on the news."

"He's not afraid to speak the truth and I'm fairly certain that he doesn't give a damn what anybody else thinks."

"Perhaps not your best choice for ambassador to the Vatican?" added the president with a wink.

Turner grinned, "Absolutely not! But, if I'm going into a street fight, I want that guy on my side."

Twenty minutes later they stepped into organized chaos, with dozens of large televisions, tuned to every network covering the convention, surrounding a frenzied crowd of scrambling staffers rushing to distill voting quirks and trends, running scenarios on every possible consequence, shouting into phones to their operatives in the delegations on the floor, cheering unexpected triumphs and moaning through disappointments.

Katherine was writing on a clipboard, when they approached. Turner asked, "How are we doing?"

She glanced at her tally, "We've just suffered through a flock of red states in the Midwest but we're coming up on New Jersey and New York, which ought to boost our count. The computer nerds are promising just under a thousand votes on the first ballot, more if we get a few surprises in the purple states towards the end."

"Who's in second place?" inquired Gonzalez.

"Governor Walker and Vincent Paul are basically tied at the moment, with Senator Cassidy six points back and Vice-President Morton barely registering," said Kate.

"Have you decided on a running-mate?" inquired the president. "I picked Morton, because of his four terms in the Senate. Unfortunately, I didn't realize that he should have been put out to pasture after his first."

"We're looking at someone who might help the cause without dominating the spotlight," replied Turner. "I like and respect Joe Cassidy a lot but he's a self-proclaimed socialist and too many people don't have the intelligence to understand what socialism is, let alone how it already makes their lives more secure through Medicaid, Medicare, and Social Security to name a few."

"How about police officers, firemen, and teachers?" added Gonzalez. "I've had to deal with Walker on legislative measures, and I find him to be abrasive and arrogant, unwilling to commit to anything until he knows he's going to win."

"Paul is intriguing because he's incredibly smart, a luminary in the tech world, and a celebrity in the press but he couldn't have conquered the mountain without creating a closet full of ghosts that might come back to haunt him."

"Pick the right guy now and you could sew this thing up on the next ballot."

"Or we could just win the second ballot and make our pick based on merit instead of political expediency."

Gonzalez patted him on the shoulder, "I do hope you win this thing for all the obvious reasons but also because you're probably the only man in the race who would expose Murphy for the fool he is."

The crowd cheered and Katherine turned to Turner, "You took the majority in Texas!"

"That's got to help!"

Tabitha took his arm, "May I have a moment?"

"Of course." He turned to Gonzalez, "If you'll excuse me?"

They walked out into the hallway, "I've spoken with the campaign managers for Cassidy and Paul. I refused to talk to Walker's guy, Milton Gall, because they're both assholes."

"And what did you find?"

"Either will turn their delegates over to you for the second ballot, in exchange for the vice-presidential slot."

"That's very big of them," laughed the candidate.

"I think you can win it outright," said the publisher.

"I think we can too and I'm inclined to go for it, before we compromise."

"I'll pass it along to the troops."

Katherine joined them, "Well?"

"Well, straight on 'til morning!" said Turner. "We'll have much stronger support in the national election, if the party is unified around one uncontested nominee."

"You realize that it could go the other way?"

"It won't, because the party wants to win in November and I'm their best choice."

It was well past midnight when Virginia cast all their votes to put Turner over the top and staff, friends, sponsors, and press erupted in cheers and applause. Katherine, Kate, and Mavis hugged Turner, leaving lipstick kisses on his cheeks. Gonzalez slapped him on the back and grabbed his hand, "Congratulations! Now the real work begins!"

The nominee took Katherine's arm, "Is your old boss still here?"

"I think so."

"Would you be kind enough to ask him if I might have a moment?"

"Of course," she replied, disappearing into unconstrained pandemonium.

Ten minutes later, Katherine led Spratlin into the temporary dining room where Turner was talking with Kate and Mavis.

"Allow me to offer my sincere congratulations," said Stanton, offering a hand.

The mayor led him to the windows, "I have a question for you?"

"What's that?"

"Would you consider being my running mate?"

"But I'm a Republican and a novice politician."

"Yes, I'm aware of your philosophical shortcomings but I have every respect for your basic principles, your dedication to our old-fashioned values, like right and wrong, and your support for equality and fairness in your campaign in Oklahoma, as well as your involvement with the All People Matter movement."

"I'm not even a first-term representative and I'm just learning the basics of how Congress works. I don't see how I help your campaign?"

"You're a Republican businessman who can draw a fair number of cross-over votes from moderate members of your party who still remember what a traditional conservative was in the pink or purple states. If we can win the vast middle between the extremes of right and left, perhaps we have a chance of building an executive branch that can actually govern."

"I see your point but I'm not sure I'm the best choice."

The nominee laughed, "To tell you the truth, I offered the job to Katherine earlier today and she turned me down flat."

"She would have been outstanding."

"I know but I would be extremely honored to have you on my ticket."

"Can I have long enough to discuss it with my wife and kids?"

"Certainly, as long as I have your decision tonight."

"No problem," replied Spratlin.

"One more question."

"What's that?"

"Are there any skeletons hiding in your closets?"

Stanton hesitated, "My business is all above board and I'm a contributor to my community." He glanced at Katherine, "I'm not sure how many people know that I had an affair with my secretary for seven wonderful years but it's over now and my wife has forgiven us."

"No little boys or dead bodies, drug trafficking or white slavery?"

Spratlin smiled and shook his head, "No, I'm a pretty boring guy."

"Then you are exactly what I need."

~

The jovial crowd rattled the Convention Center with a rousing chant, as Massachusetts Governor Jimmy Davidson shouted, "The next Vice-President of the United States, Representative Stanton James

Spratlin, his lovely wife Marjorie Murray Spratlin, their four children Brad, Bruce, Samantha, and Sissy, as well as Daniel, Hubie, Muriel, and Martin Brown!"

The children crowded around Stanton and Marjorie, waving to the churning crowd wielding Turner/Spratlin placards in a blue and white flutter that rippled through the arena like choppy waves rushing across open water before a storm.

Sissy took Muriel's little hand and gazed through the spotlights to thousands of adults screaming and bouncing, their exuberance reverberating in waves around the enormous room. She knelt down, "Are you scared?"

The little girl's deep brown eyes glistened in the lights and she giggled, "I didn't think they'd be so excited to see me!"

Sam leaned close, "How come we get in trouble for making too much noise at home?"

Sissy laughed and hugged her sister, "I'm glad we're up here and not down there!"

Governor Walker extended an arm to introduce Stanton, "Let's welcome Oklahoma Representative Stanton Spratlin!"

The herd of children moved with him, as he walked to the podium and shook the governor's hand. Turning to the audience, he waved and bowed, and hugged the closest children until the chaos subsided to a brief pause. "Ladies and gentlemen, delegates and guests, my fellow Americans, thank you for this warm welcome for me...and for my family."

Cheers and applause.

"I think we all find it rather incredible that I, a lifelong Republican, am standing here before you tonight but I want everyone to understand that I'm dedicated to retaking the reins of government for you, the people, for our children, for the future of our democracy, and the belief that our Constitution guarantees every human being the same rights and freedoms as everyone else.

I believe that every person has value and worth, that every one of us deserves respect and acknowledgement, opportunity, hope, and dignity. We have to replace the power structure in Washington with real representation that works for every citizen, not just the few, and, if we're all willing to stand together, we can and we will change the world!"

The audience erupted with cheers and rousing applause.

"I would not be standing here if I did not believe that the man that you have chosen to lead the party and the ticket to triumph in the elections in the fall, is not only the best Democrat for the job but the best man to be our next president, Tyrone Turner!"

Tyrone marched out of the shadows, waving to the crowd, as the children all trotted over to escort him to the podium. He hugged each in turn, kissed Marjorie on the cheek, shook Walker's hand, then Stanton's with a big smile, "I think they're sweet on you, even if you are the enemy!"

Spratlin cracked up and patted him on the back, "I'm happy to be here."

The nominee turned to the microphone and raised their hands above his head in triumphant unity, "Thank you, thank every one of you!"

Spotlights raked across thousands of bodies bobbing and screaming with the raucous fervor of teen fans at a rock concert. Sissy and Muriel and Martin covered their ears and squealed.

Marjorie and Stanton guided the children off-stage, while Turner stood silently still for several long minutes, until the commotion idled into a lowly roar, "Ladies and gentlemen! I stand before you tonight humbled by your support, your faith in me and the American tradition of orderly transitions between administrations that started when George Washington handed the reins of power to John Adams on March 4th, 1797.

I promise that together we will move this country from the darkness into the light, from oppression to equality, from repression and depression to opportunity and hope, from a government owned and operated by a tiny group of wealthy fascists who hide in the shadows, to openness and transparency, honesty and integrity, responsiveness to the needs of our citizens by a vast rainbow of talented men and women who will represent your interests in everything we do."

Cheers and appreciation.

"For the past eight years, President Gonzalez has been fighting to prevent the Republican Congress from destroying this country, tearing it apart one law or right or benefit at a time. He has been the lonely sentry fighting relentlessly to keep them from completely dismantling of our government, our democracy, and our future, and I'm certain that he will continue until his final day in office!"

Boos and cat-calls.

"The legislation they've tried to pass, the funds they refused to allocate, and the federal justices who were nominated and ignored are testament to their intent to transform our society to serve a giant corporation that drains the life out of the hard-working people who make this country the greatest nation on the planet!

I've talked with thousands of your brothers and sisters, who made up the vibrant middle class of our society before big business pushed them out of their jobs, their homes, their lives, and their futures all in the name of profits for the investors! As one of my first executive orders, if elected, I will request a special prosecutor to investigate the corruption of the democratic process by the wealthiest few, because it's time to expose the tyrants who have been running the show from behind the Wizard's curtain!"

The massive hall rumbled with the roar of the crowd.

"It's time to take back our nation by installing our people in every office from the school boards to the city councils, from the State Houses to the halls of Congress. We need people who will commit to transparency, inclusiveness, honesty, and a dedication to root out the corruption and bring the puppets and their paymasters to justice.

It's time for real Americans to act like patriots who believe in the Constitution, the Bill of Rights, and the need for the common sense and common decency that have been destroyed by the opposition. It's time for our Democratic administration to clean up their mess, because we believe that All People Matter! Are you with us?"

~

Murphy screamed at the giant screens lined up in the WBFK studio, "You pompous snob, I'll bury you in the first debate! I'll run circles around your black ass!"

Turner's deep resonant voice thundered from the speakers, "My fellow Americans, other than our Revolution and the Civil War, there has never been a time in our history when the challenges have been so dire, immediate, and immense, when the very idea of democracy is being threatened by wealthy villains who live in our midst but not among us.

I believe that we can triumph, if we're willing to march through every city, town, and village in this country, through violent intimidation and vicious impediments, through lies and cheating and floods of fabricated propaganda full of damning stories that have no basis in fact. I believe that we can take the White House and maybe even competitive minorities in Congress, if we're willing to demand the truth, if we're willing to take responsibility for rebuilding our nation, our culture, and our society together, but none of that works unless we're willing to believe and trust in each other!

Thank you for your nomination and may God bless you and these United States!"

Murphy took a slug of Jack Daniel's from the bottle and raised it to the Democrat waving to the cheering audience in Dallas. "I'll whoop that guy, as soon as you can arrange a debate!"

Jack Hannah grinned, "It's already in the works."

"Where, when?"

Casper Wein raised his glass in toast, "Madison, Wisconsin, two weeks."

"Madison's a Democrat town!" shouted Murphy.

"But rural Wisconsin is as red as Alabama, so it could go either way," replied Shepherd Stone. "Win the first debate and we carry the state and maybe Michigan and Ohio too."

"Given the Red and Blue divide, win those three and we could probably win the election," said Milly Clark.

Penny Baker walked over and leaned to put her makeup kit on the table but Murphy grabbed her hips, grinding against her backside, "Bring it on!"

Doctor Billings handed him a tiny paper cup full of pills, "Time for your vitamins."

The candidate looked at the mix of colors, "Any of these fun?"

"I'm trying to get you into 'Presidential' mode before you give your congratulatory statement to the press."

"Doesn't answer the question," washing the drugs down with a big swig of bourbon.

"You'll feel calm and focused," replied the doctor, "and horny as hell."

He spun Penny around and pressed against her crotch. She pushed him onto the desk and covered his shirt with a towel. "Sit your ass down, if you want to look like something more than an escaped cadaver risen from the dead in front of the cameras!"

"You're no fun."

"That limp noodle isn't going to impress anyone until the Doc's magic starts rushing through your creaky old veins. So, sit down and shut up and I'll see if I can cover up some the age lines and blotches on that sorry face."

~

The phone beeped in the cavernous lounge in the back of the black Lincoln limo racing down Broadway towards his penthouse office in the Financial District. Only his secretary and a scant few associates had this number. Conrad Blaho picked up the receiver, "Hello."

"Conrad, French."

"Good to hear your voice."

"I'm concerned about Turner making Murphy look the fool in the debate."

Blaho smiled, as they past Canal Street heading south on Broadway, "It's being handled."

"But...?"

"We'll have to make time to chat when we have access to more secure communications," said the steel magnate. "I'm sure you'll approve of the arrangements and the potential return on our investments."

"I look forward to talking with you soon."

"Yes, very soon."

Chapter Fifteen

Nellis and Jessie, taking a short break from preparations for the first debate in Madison, strolled across the lush lawn in James Madison Park, a few blocks from the Capitol, looking out across an indigo blue Lake Mendota to smudges of reds and yellows in the trees in Governor Nelson State Park on the far shore.

"This is your home turf," said Nellis.

Jessie gazed around, "It's really strange to be back here, so many memories, good and bad. I really loved this place until it didn't love me back and I had to leave."

"My band played here a few times, funky old place down by the university...Marsh...Shapiro was the guy who owned it..."

"The Nitty Gritty! Yeah, I used to go there all the time."

"Small world."

"Yeah," replied Jessie, staring across the water. "What do you think about the arrangements for the debate tonight?"

"I've talked to all our guys and they're all hooked up with the Secret Service, so we've gotta pray that everyone's got their shit together."

"I hope you're right. The university's a liberal island in a radically red state and I wouldn't be surprised to find both sides in prime form tonight."

"There's a fairly strict decorum at these events but there's no telling what kind of folks are going to show up to cheer on Murphy," said Nellis. "I keep getting that prickly itch on the back of my neck when I think about the possibilities...and most of them involve your basic nightmares."

Jessie shook his head, "You blew up an election and we started a riot in a hurricane just to make a point and somehow all of that evolved into us standing here wondering how we can keep our candidate alive long enough to get elected to the presidency."

"To save our country from itself?"

"Exactly," replied the artist. "We've both seen millions of people whose lives and livelihood were stolen or destroyed by rich thugs, who believe that feudalism represented the high-point of human development."

"Those who have and those who serve them."

"That's succinct."

Nellis reached to shake his hand, "I don't believe either of us signed up to defend democracy against fascism but I'm proud we're fighting the desperados together and I hope we're all smart enough to win in the end."

"Amen, brother, amen."

~

Roaming crowds slowed traffic on State Street and jammed the sidewalks on North Fairchild, gawking at limousines delivering the national political elite and celebrity activists. Lucky students and local supporters, who grabbed the few tickets allocated to normal citizens for the debate, streamed into the magnificent theater in the Overture Center for the Arts, a block from the Capitol Building.

Murphy's fleet of limos, escorted by a convoy of black Suburbans, passed through security blocking North Henry to slip into the service entrance at the back of the complex. Secret Service agents ushered the candidate and his entourage through a churning congregate of cameras and reporters jostling for position to shout questions and capture footage of the smiling, waving nominee bobbing along in a flood of bodies disappearing into the bowels of the building.

He leaned to Milly Clark, "I have to ask you, my most trusted advisor, is this shit really happening?"

"Of course it is, and you're about to give your greatest performance to convince the nation that you deserve the people's vote," replied the little woman. "From Lear to Lincoln, we both know you can do this."

He hugged her, as four branches of security guided them through hallways to a luxurious lounge with a bar, comfortable furniture, and large screen video feeds of the audience filing into the theater.

Casper Wein steered Murphy through greetings and formalities with the party elite, and handed him off to Ethan Tomlinson, who whispered, "Your sponsors send their best wishes for a smashing success."

"I appreciate their support."

Tomlinson looked him straight in the eyes, "I'm sure you'll seize the opportunity to put this thing away."

"Anything less than pandemonium would be a total disappointment," replied Murphy, turning to Shepherd Stone and Milton Graves.

His original patron said, "Tonight's your night."

"I look forward to the fight," replied the candidate, shaking his hand.

Stone turned away from the crowd, "He might be a book smart Ivy Leaguer but that doesn't sell to your people. They want someone who's genuinely crass like they are, someone who will stand up for their nationalistic rights and their profoundly weird beliefs, someone who'll preach to the choir and poke the liberals in the eye with a stick."

Graves added, "They think you're their guy and I've got an action committee of like-minded folk who are putting a pile of money behind your campaign, so go out and prove it!"

Doc Billings walked through the crowd to the small conference, "Mind if I borrow this guy for a short checkup before the show begins?"

"We want our thoroughbred in prime form for this one!" said Graves, clapping Murphy on the back.

The doctor led him to an office, where Jack Hannah, Milly, Penny, and Austin Crouch were waiting to prepare him for his entrance. Milly produced a crystal tumbler of golden bourbon and Billings offered a paper cup full of pills.

"What's the cocktail tonight?"

"Let's just say that your focus will be absolute and you'll be charged with enough energy to make your opponent appear to be moving backwards!"

Murphy chugged the pills with a slug of Jack and settled into a comfortable chair, Penny draped a cape across his chest and opened her kit to dust his face with powder to cut the reflections, camouflage the botches, and smooth the wrinkles, add a little rouge to his pallid skin, mascara to his enhance his eyes, and a gloss to his lips.

Jack Hannah sat down next to them, just as she slid her left hand under the sheet. "Are you up for this?"

"As ready as I've ever been," replied the candidate from inside a cloud of beige dust.

"We've run the numbers and public reaction is evenly split, but party loyalty is through the roof on both sides. This is a fight for the middle five percent."

"Did you add in the hundreds of thousands of folks who never voted before?"

"There's no way to track them besides coming and going from your events, because they're not in anyone's databank...not the Democrats, Republicans, voter rolls, nothing. They're an invisible commodity. We've already started saturating the rural airwaves with ads but there's no way to know whether they'll get fired up enough to actually vote."

"That's why traditional polling sucks pond water," said Murphy. "You count sterile numbers but I see the passion, the desperation, and the rage in the crowds every time I go out there to speak. My people are going to knock your projections into the ditch because they believe their own ignorant bullshit is truth and anyone who doesn't is the enemy."

Crouch grinned and patted him on the shoulder, "That's what I wanted to hear. Fuck everyone else, go out there and talk to them in their language and they'll haul you over the line."

Murphy groaned, "That's exactly what I plan to do!", as Penny fondled his budding erection with one hand while she finished applying tinted lip gloss with the other.

~

Secret Service agents, Federal Marshals, and a herd of private security poured out of Suburbans to surround the limos and cordon off a pathway for Turner and his entourage before opening the car doors.

Mavis, Kate, and Katherine strolled through the gauntlet ahead of their candidate, as camera flashes fired in a blazing flutter and reporters shouted questions that melded into white noise. The six-six former Rhodes Scholar and linebacker for the Atlanta Falcons carried himself with imposing strength and reserved dignity, holding his thumbs up and waving to incomprehensible queries from the press as he was swept inside the fluorescent tunnel.

He took Katherine's arm, "Why do they always ask dumb questions about how I'm feeling or whether I have any prognostications about the outcome of the debate? Of course, I do but I'm old enough and wise enough not to share them with reporters! I might be big, black, and beautiful but I am not Muhammed Ali!"

"Reporters have a tough job and I'm sympathetic with their persistence, after being the face of All People Matter, but I've got to admit that I cherish intelligent questions that warrant an informative response. They're always too few, unless there's a tragedy."

"I agree but there's also the theatrics of building the anticipation, the curiosity, and the hope that one of us might screw up and say something boneheaded or, worse, something of value to dominate tomorrow's headlines!"

"I'd bet on Murphy saying something outrageous enough to suck the oxygen out of the room before this night's over," said Mavis.

"He doesn't have policies or facts to talk about," added Kate, "but he does know how to spin a totally absurd yarn to rile up his tribe."

"I won't validate his lies and conspiracy theories," laughed Turner, "but I do believe in the lessons of history learned at such tragic cost. The end of the Second World War offered the chance to confront racism and nationalism but the white population was consumed with the euphoria of victory and wallowing in a raging economy. More than a half century later my opponent has bared the ugly underbelly of our society, so perhaps we'll make an opportunity to address the hate and bigotry that cover for the Republican subversion that's destroying our country."

Katherine kissed his cheek, "You be you and he'll look the fool."

Turner grinned, "That's the plan!"

A stunning young woman with flashing blue eyes, ruby red lips in a pale complexion, and a long thick braid of glistening black hair walked over to him, "I'm Laura Poole and I'll be doing your makeup tonight, if that's alright?"

He shook her hand, "Only if you can make me look ten years younger and ten pounds lighter!"

"I'll do my best," laughed the artist, leading him to a high chair in front of a mirror surrounded by lights.

Nellis squeezed Katherine's arm and kissed her cheek, "How's it going?"

"I think I'm more nervous than he is," replied the beauty, taking his hand. "How's everything out front?"

"They've got this place nailed down and the crowd seems fairly restrained for the moment, but you can feel the static sizzle of pent-up emotional energy oozing through the calm. The hoity-toities are down front and up in the boxes but everyone else is ready to jump out of their seats to start throwing punches."

"Just what we don't need," replied Katherine, gazing at Turner. "We've done everything we can do to set the stage and prime the media, now it's up to him."

"He's spent his whole life preparing for this mission and we both know he's the best man for the job."

"With all that's happened, I'm almost afraid to watch."

"He needs all of us in the wings," said Nellis gently.

"I know," replied Katherine with a little hug.

Hosts Trevor Hobbs and Paige Phillips appeared in the doorway of the lounge and walked over to shake hands with Turner. "We're about twelve minutes from broadcast, so we'll get the crowd under control and make the introductions before we bring you out. Our techs will have you all wired up, so you'll have a bit more freedom of movement on the stage."

Miss Phillips added, "You won the coin toss, so we'll introduce you first and you'll enter from stage left, Murphy will join you from stage right. He gets three minutes to answer the first question and you will have a minute and a half to respond. You will also give your summation last."

"Do you have any questions?" asked Hobbs.

The mayor grinned, "Anyone fact-checking his responses?"

The network anchor shook his head, "We have to appear to be completely neutral in all of this but I won't hesitate to point out obvious deceptions."

Katherine laughed, "How about sounded a big gong every time he lies?"

"That might be a minor impropriety," said Paige Phillips, "but I'm sympathetic to the idea."

Hobbs checked his watch and reached to shake Turner's hand, "The clock's ticking, see you in ten minutes and good luck with the debate."

~

The director counted down, "Five, four, three, two, and we're...live."

"Good evening, I'm Trevor Hobbs of International Public News coming to you tonight from The Overture Theater in Madison, Wisconsin."

His co-anchor smiled, "And I'm Paige Phillips, of Independent Broadcasting, hosting tonight's Suffragettes' Debate between Democrat Tyrone Turner and Republican Mac Murphy and they're both hoping to secure your support with their performances tonight."

"As we've explained to our studio audience, each of our guests will have three minutes to answer questions culled from thousands sent in by our viewers. His opponent will have ninety-seconds to respond and we'll offer a thirty-second rebuttal at our discretion."

"Let me introduce Democratic candidate Tyrone Turner, mayor of Atlanta, Georgia, the Athens of the South!" said the shapely blond with professional polish and Harvard degrees in journalism and political science, walking over to shake his hand and guide him to the lectern on the left to enthusiastic applause.

Trevor Hobbs' baritone reverberated through the theater, "On our right, please welcome the Republican candidate, radio host Mac Murphy from Cincinnati, Ohio."

The spotlight followed Murphy, waving to cat calls and wolf whistles, as he crossed the platform to shake Turner's hand and wandered to the front edge of the stage with arms raised above his head, smiling and pointing to supporters, before he finally settled behind his podium.

"Gentlemen, we'd like to welcome you to the Suffragettes' Debate, on a balmy September evening in Madison, with a reminder that the mission of the Suffragettes is to ensure everyone's right to vote in every election," said Hobbs, with a broad smile for the camera, while the crowd clapped politely. "Now, by a toss of the coin, Mr. Murphy will take the first question from Paige Phillips."

"Mr. Murphy, you've said publicly that you could solve the problem of illegal immigration once and for all. How would you accomplish that and how would you pay for it?"

Murphy smiled, "Our country is being overrun by tens of thousands of dirty migrants pouring across our borders. Certainly, there might be a few who might legitimately claim asylum and protection from violence in their home countries but the vast majority are criminals and terrorists, members of vicious gangs who peddle drugs and murder innocent people, their child prostitutes spread diseases that diminish the health and purity of our society, and their families suck funding out of services and benefits that were designed to help our citizens, not these filthy freeloaders!

I say, it's time to put an end to this invasion by deploying troops to the borders to round up the illegals and ship them back where they came from! We can stave off the invasion and win this war, if we're willing to put the fear of God into these vermin and make an example of anyone foolish enough to try to sneak into our country!

Now, I know that my opponent will scream and shout about the Constitution and civil rights and all that crap but we all know that Atlanta is a sanctuary city that welcomes all comers, illegal and otherwise, with open arms! Hell, their guests enjoy more benefits than real America citizens – welfare, rent-free homes, healthcare, and education for their illiterate kids! And guess who's paying for it? We are!"

The audience had been warned to avoid reacting to either candidate until the end of the debate but hundreds jumped to their feet cheering.

Cameras followed Paige Phillips to center stage, "Ladies and gentlemen, that will be enough. You were warned before our program began that this behavior would not be tolerated, so I will ask the ushers to remove anyone who breaks this rule for any reason during the remainder of our program. Do you understand?"

The agitators grumbled and returned to their seats, while the rest of the audience applauded.

"Thank you."

Hobbs stepped in, "I'm not sure that your response was actually an answer to the question asked, but we'll turn it over to Mayor Turner for a reaction."

Turner stared at the radio host for a long moment, "I'm not sure that any citizen who has even the slightest inkling of how our system of government works or how our immigration laws are written, could react to your rant as anything but ignorant, petty, and racist."

He held up one finger, "I do have one question for you, sir and that is whether you happen to be a descendant of a tribe of Native Americans?"

"No, I do not. My people came over from Ireland during the Great Famine in the 1850's."

"So, you're not really an American either because you're the product of immigrant stock," said the mayor. "What makes you and your kin any different than these poor brown souls who are desperate to save their children from violence and oppression?"

"My people entered through Boston harbor, legally."

"Your people were escaping poverty and oppression. They came seeking the American dream of security and success because anything was an improvement over the slow starvation they left behind. I'm sure you're not a student of history but at that time, there were few impediments to legal immigration, other than being free of contagious diseases. So, help me understand why your ancestors were any different than these people?"

"We didn't come looking for trouble, we fit in with the people of Boston."

"Because you were white?" said Turner, his eyes wide, his voice deep and measured.

The theater was still, cameras glued to the two men. The commentators and audience captivated by the tension that charged the auditorium.

"My people didn't come with the intention of changing the very fabric of American society, if anything we reinforced the heritage that made this country great!"

"What you're really saying is that they fit in because they were white! Brown people and black people and yellow people don't deserve the same rights or opportunities, do they Mr. Murphy?"

Murphy was distracted by a tiny momentary glimmer flashing in the darkness behind the lighting balcony on the right side of the theater near the ceiling, as he glanced past the cameras towards the audience. A yellow burst and a sharp crack fractured the pent-up hostility fuming beneath the precarious equilibrium permeating the magnificent theater, a moment before Mayor Turner's eyes opened wide beneath raised brows, his lips parted to utter a fragmented thought as a bullet bored a tiny round hole in his forehead and blasted a shower of blood and bone from the back of his skull, glittering like molten rubies in the lights as he fell over backwards with a look of astonishment. A second shot rang out, before security could reach the assassin, and a body tumbled into the orchestra seating below.

He stared at the mayor's huge lifeless body for a brief moment, stunned by the violent reach of his sponsors who valued profits and power over any human life, a twinge of humanity and compassion tugging his soul out of character to mourn the murder of a giant...until Tomlinson's instructions ricocheted through his brain, *"I'm sure you'll seize the opportunity to put this thing away."*

Stunned, Hobbs murmured into his open mic, "Oh, my God!"

The stunned silence was shattered as screams from the audience exploded into chaos and pandemonium with panicked patrons charging toward every exit. Secret Service agents stormed the stage, attempting to shield the candidates from further threats, but the cameras followed Murphy as he sprinted to Turner, dropping to his knees to cradle the mayor's bleeding head in his lap. Security tried to wrest the body from his grasp but he hugged the corpse tighter, blood spurting across his shirt. His mic was live and his scream thundered through the auditorium, "No! You're too late!"

Turner's eyes were fixed and glazed with a haunting look of shock and disbelief, as a doctor reached for a pulse and after a moment, shook his head. The guards backed away to form a protective human barrier on alert for another assassin.

Murphy cried out with the tormented grief of his final performance of Lear, "This tragedy is the work of the deep state, a confederation of traitors who will go to any lengths to stifle freedom of speech and destroy any prospect of fair elections.

Now that they've eliminated the real Democratic candidate, they're counting on the sympathy vote carrying their stooge, Stanton Spratlin - a political novice famous for his shady business practices and torrid affairs, into the White House and we can't allow that to happen!

Tyrone Turner and I might have been competing for your hearts and your votes but no one can deny that he was an icon, a national treasure who exemplified dignity, grace, intelligence, and honor and now he's a martyr who died defending his convictions, who died believing that he could make things better for all of you."

He stopped, pointing through the gap between shifting agents into the camera, drenched in the mayor's blood, tears tracing gray fissures through the makeup on his cheeks, "So, in his memory, this is the time for all of us to join together to fight for our democracy! This is the moment to put aside our tribal arguments! This is our chance to restore the pride and purity of our American glory! I call on every American to stand as one united nation to demand a complete investigation into this assassination, beginning right now!"

Doctors and an ambulance crew pushed through the security cordon to lift a flailing Murphy away from the body. His gray hair was tousled, his makeup smeared and caked, and his shirt and suit glistening red with Turner's blood but he rose up, his fist in the air, screaming through a wall of police and Secret Service, "The mayor and I disagreed about just about everything, but we both believed that the hate and killing must stop! We the people demand an end to the confrontation and violence that has seized our culture, strangled our government, and destroyed the middle class! I don't care if you're a Democrat, Republican, or a Communist - we will march, we will vote, and we will restore our democracy…together!"

The cameras pulled back to a wide view as Murphy was led away. Waves of officials pushed through fleeing crowds and Trevor Hobbs appeared on the screen. "Ladies and gentlemen, we've just witnessed the assassination of Tyrone Turner, Mayor of Atlanta, Democratic candidate for the office of President of the United States, a Rhodes scholar, an extraordinary athlete, a dedicated leader, a dignified orator of historic merit, and a fine human being. He will be sorely missed, not only as a politician but as the embodiment of everything that we as a nation might yearn to be. He filled our world with hope and compassion, he made us believe that there is a future for each and every person in this country."

Paige Phillips stepped into the picture, "Trevor, police tell me that they believe a lone gunman fired the single shot that killed Mayor Turner and then turned the gun on himself. They've sealed off the theater, they're examining both bodies, and medics are attending to members of the audience who were injured when the gunman tumbled off the balcony. We must assume that an investigation is well under way by federal, state, and local agencies."

~

Turner's staff and supporters crowded behind the curtains at the side of the stage, mesmerized by their candidate's measured reaction to Murphy's racist rant. Katherine squeezed Nellis' hand with a confident smile and a kiss to his cheek, during a momentary pause, and turned back to the stage with a gasp, as Turner's head snapped back, his eyes and mouth wide in backlit profile, a crimson splatter erupting behind his head, frozen in the moment before he toppled over like a mighty tree falling in the forest.

Her fist covered her mouth, "Oh, my God! No!"

Instinctively, Nellis wrapped his arms around her and moved away from danger but she fought his grip, straining to run to the body on the floor. "I can save him."

"No, you can't. It's too late," said Nellis softly, watching Murphy skid across the smooth planking on the stage to lift Turner's head into his lap.

Kate burst into tears and grabbed Jessie and Mavis, who joined in the frantic hug, as Secret Service and security flooded the stage, while Murphy's voice filled the theater. "This tragedy is the work of the deep state, a confederation of traitors who will go to any lengths to stifle freedom of speech and destroy any prospect of fair elections."

Stanton reached a hand to steady Tabitha, who turned in shock and bewilderment to stare for a moment, "I think they just called your number, dear. Are you ready to run for president?"

Four Secret Service agents surrounded him, before the thought could register, "How about I go out there and teach that asshole some respect?"

She placed a white gloved hand on his chest, "Don't you understand what's happening? You are now the candidate!"

~

The Secret Service hustled Murphy through the underground hallways to a convoy of dark armored Suburbans hemming in three white limousines. Milly and Penny Baker climbed into the car ahead of him, followed by Doc Billings, Milton Graves, and Casper Wein, two agents up front and two in back.

Milly produced a white handkerchief and started wiping the blood from his face, "Are you alright? You didn't get hit, did you?"

Murphy's hands twitched and his eyes darted from one face to the next, until he grabbed Penny Baker and pulled her onto his lap, pawing at her breast. Finally, he settled on Milly's look of concern behind a bloody kerchief suspended in front of his face. After a momentary pause, he blurted, "Before the show, you said this was going to be my greatest performance, how'd I do?"

Her jaw dropped open and before she could react, Casper Wein leaned over, "That was fantastic! You're going to be the next President of the United States!"

"Absolutely brilliant," added Milton Graves. "By tomorrow morning, the image of you holding the corpse is going to be burned into the memory banks of every person in the country. You just became the center of gravity in these turbulent times."

Billings pulled Murphy's groping fingers from Penny's chest, taking a pulse against his watch, whistled under his breath, and flashed a penlight in his patient's eyes. He opened a small black satchel, selecting several bottles to dispense pills into a white paper cup, poured a cup of water from the bar, and handed it to Murphy, "You might be flying at altitude for your performance but you're in shock from the trauma, so I want to get you stabilized. Take your vitamins."

The candidate took the cup, downed the pills, with a gulp of water. "Yuck, don't they have any decent Bourbon in that bar? And where the fuck are the feds taking us?"

The agent on the bench seat to his right replied, "Airport. We want to make sure that any secondary threat can't find a target."

"Like me?"

"Yeah, like you."

~

The Cameron airport tower was overwhelmed with the influx of private jets delivering and retrieving dignitaries from both political parties. Every room in The Great Plains Hotel was booked, there were lines outside the few restaurants in town, and limousines traced an endless procession to and from Spratlin House but so far, none of the luminaries had ventured down the long gravel lane to the old farmhouse with the locked gate.

Nellis carried a tray with hot tea, sugar, lemon, cream, and a plate of tiny sandwiches out to the porch and set them on the table next to Katherine, who was covered to her chin with an heirloom Hudson Bay point blanket. "Here, I thought you might enjoy some hot tea."

She struggled to sit up and replied, "I'm enchanted with your vegetable garden. Autumn's getting ready to stop being colorful and start being brutal, and all those crops are covered with fruits and flowers. You're amazing."

He handed her a steaming cup and offered the tray, "How are you feeling?"

"Guilty for convincing him to run in the first place, knowing…that his assassination wasn't only possible but probable. I'm horrified and heart-broken because he was everything this country needs in a leader for all the right reasons. I respected his bravery, intelligence, compassionate spirit and he was a friend, a real friend…lost in that split second that tore time into before and after, dawn into darkness. Maybe I'm becoming calloused by the violent attacks in Houston, Atlanta, Chicago, and Denver but this is the focal point where every one of those lives lost was just as tragic as Tyrone's and there are thousands of families who have lost someone dear to the fight for our democracy. My heart is shattered by his loss and I've cried buckets of tears but I know I can't sit here moping forever because I can't let him down. Does that make any sense at all?"

Nellis sat on the edge of the lounge and hugged her, "The world seems to be trying to convince you of how cruel and senseless it can be."

"Every time I think we've seen the worst of it, the storm troopers come up with something even more depraved, and…with all the security on that theater, how'd that guy get in with a gun?"

"I talked to Eddie this morning and they think the gun was stashed in a dead space under that lighting grid. Evidently, the assassin had a legitimate ticket, arrived a few minutes late, walked up the stairs, pulled the gun out and shot Turner. Witnesses said that he appeared with the rifle, aimed, and fired without a moment's hesitation and as soon as the mayor collapsed, he turned the weapon on himself."

"That took a lot of coordination."

"Yeah, and they haven't identified the guy yet. He burned his fingerprints off with acid."

"That's fanatical," replied Katherine, tears streaming down her cheeks as she stroked mama cat Betsy and her latest litter of five suckling kittens under the blanket. "I've been sitting here thinking that if Murphy wins, this might just be the final chapter in our national nightmare. There are too many things to be afraid of…"

He turned to gaze around the yard, "You're safe here and you can sit on this porch for as long as you want."

She hugged him back, "I always feel safe when I'm with you."

"I do need to tell you that Mavis and Kate are taking turns calling every thirty minutes to check up on you, and Stanton's got politicians from both parties banging on his door twenty-four seven, so sooner or later, you're going to have to respond."

"Thanks for running interference. I'll call the girls this afternoon and check in with Stanton but I'm not ready to go back to work yet. What's happening with the organization?"

"Sammy, Benny, Jessie, Kate, and Tabitha are out front but Bobbie Warmington's keeping the lines of communication open with our chapters around the country. Everyone's preparing to launch Spratlin's campaign next week, if they can get Turner's people behind him, and the girls say that polling shows broad appeal to the moderate middle. So, if he shows well and picks the right running-mate, maybe he's got a chance."

The dogs perked up and Katherine turned to a knock on the screen door, "Hi, girls, c'mon in."

The Spratlin sisters stepped inside to a frenzy of dogs demanding attention, before Sissy was allowed to hug Nellis, "We just had to escape for a little while. Our house has been taken over by lots of snotty people in dark suits and we can't go anywhere without those guys over by the barn following us."

Nellis glanced over at the agents checking the lane and scanning the property, "They're just trying to keep you safe from crazy people."

"Like the guy who shot Mayor Turner?" asked Sam.

"Yeah, people like that," replied Nellis, with a gentle pat on her back. "I can't tell you why people do bad things but I can promise that there's way more of us than there are of them."

Sissy glanced at Katherine, "It only takes one bad guy to make everyone else sad."

"How old did you say you were, eighty-two?"

The little blond sprite dropped her head and looked up at him, "You know how old I am!"

"You're awfully wise for being so young."

"Let's play chess just to make sure!" She sat on the edge of the lounge, rubbing behind Gracie's ears, as she turned to Katherine, "I'm sorry Mayor Turner's death was hard for you, are you okay?"

"Thank you for asking," replied the brunette, taking her hand. "He was a very special person and I feel honored to have had the chance to work with him…and I will miss him very much."

"I'm sorry," said Sissy.

Katherine wiped a tear from her eye, "How's your dad holding up?"

"Even with his staff, I think he misses having you around to keep everything straight," said Sammy. "Cars keep getting jammed up in the driveway, picking up and dropping people off, and Mr. Charles is out there trying to untangle the mess. Miss Sibble can't leave the front door and Mama Louise and Maybelle are cooking all day long."

"I'll call him this afternoon, promise."

"He needs you," said Sam.

"We all do," added Nellis.

~

The dogs barked and pranced around the yard as Nellis rolled the steel gate across the drive and the panel truck eased around the barn. Ned Perkins untangled a cramped lanky body from the cab and knelt to hug the pack of slobbering dogs, "How are you guys? I sure am glad to see you!"

He stood up and wiped his face on his sleeve before wrapping Nellis in a bear hug, "Man, you guys have been through hell and I'm so glad you're okay."

"Well, Katherine's still kind of fragile, so I'm hoping your smiling mug might cheer her up."

"If you bribe me with something wonderful to eat, I might feel obliged to help you out."

"Then I guess the what we've having might depend on the size of the satchel you're carrying!" laughed Nellis.

Ned leaned behind the seat and pulled out a stout green duffle bag, "Two hundred large ought to make us even."

"Jamaican Blue?"

"Yep."

"Great, I've got the last batch ready to go."

The driver lifted his nose to sniff the evening scents, as the dogs escorted them up the walkway, "So, what's for dinner?"

"Pulled pork, smoked and finished with my sweet sauce, slaw from a beautiful cabbage I picked out of the garden this morning, and fingerling potatoes slathered in butter."

"Eating at your table is like finding nirvana after a long trek through the desert of barely edible road food."

Katherine padded through the yellow living room to give Ned a hug, "I'm glad you made it safe and sound."

"And I'm sorry I don't have anything more than my love and a big hug to offer for all that you've been through."

She looked up at him, tears glistening in her eyes, "Is the real world half as crazy as the world we live in?"

Ned grinned, "Most of the folks I know are hip to what's going on but it doesn't affect them directly because they have real lives to live - bills to pay, kids to raise, and everything that's been happening to you is staged in violent video clips that run over and over on the television until the audience is numb to the reality of what's happening."

"What do they think of Murphy?"

"He was a joke…a comedy act…until the other night and then he became a real candidate and real people started paying attention."

"I'm sorry, c'mon in and let me get you a cold one. You've got to be bushed."

"Nellis' description of dinner revived my hope for survival," laughed Perkins.

"I baked some fluffy rolls for the pork that should be out of the oven in just a few minutes."

She opened the fridge and poured an Olympia into an icy stein on the counter while he hauled his bag to the guest room. Nellis spooned a mountain of steaming pork onto a platter, surrounded it with a ring of gnarly little potatoes and carried it into the candle-lit dining room with the oval wake-table and the wall of books.

Katherine passed the rolls and Nellis offered the platter and a large bowl of coleslaw and Ned grinned, "You can just leave the leftovers and I'll sleep on the table tonight."

Nellis raised his glass, "Glad you're here!"

Ned clinked them in turn, "To old friends."

Nellis chuckled, "I had to keep a straight face today, while the girls were over to visit, along with their contingent of Secret Service agents who posted up over by the barn. I was worried they might smell something suspicious."

"I saw the look on your face," laughed Katherine, "and I knew exactly what you were thinking."

"Yeah, that'd make a great headline, 'Movement Leaders Busted for Conspiracy'!" replied Nellis. "We do live in confused times."

"I was wondering how you managed to grow this year's crop without anyone tripping over the evidence, if you'll excuse a bad pun?"

"I have to believe that it was meant to be, because in spite of being away a lot we didn't have any guests during those periods when I needed to tend to the crops and we were blessed with good weather, solid rains followed by periods of dry heat. I think you're going to like my final crop of Blue, it's sweet."

"We'll have to try some after dinner."

After Ned plowed through seconds and thirds, another beer, and a mellow joint, Katherine excused herself to make some calls from her tiny office.

Nellis said, "C'mon, I've got to shut down the barn for the night."

The dogs burst through the screen door and tore across the yard, before the old friends stepped into a cool clear evening breeze from the northwest. Ned stopped to stare at the stars, "That's Jupiter and Saturn in the west and there's Mars up in the east. You have such a wonderful unobstructed view from here and you're far enough removed to avoid most of the light pollution."

"Yup, but not for long," mumbled Nellis, waving a hand. "With all the construction and new housing developments all around, that won't last. I'm bettin' the faintest stars will just disappear one-by-one until the sky turns that hazy gray color with only the brightest showing through."

"I always feel like the rest of the world doesn't exist when I'm here, at least until I drive out the gate and get slammed by reality again."

"I'm afraid it ain't far enough to prevent civilization creeping in to destroy the best of nature."

They ambled into the barn and Nellis flipped on a light over a shelf with the telephone. He reached into a cubby and withdrew a thick envelope, handing it to Ned. "I want you to keep this, in case…"

He hesitated before grasping the papers. "In case what?"

"We're too far out front on all of this, especially with Katherine being the face of the movement and so involved in Turner's campaign."

"Are you in danger?"

"I honestly don't know. There's something itching around in my brain, sort of like that feeling you get when there's a storm approaching in the distance, even though the sun's shining and the birds are singing."

"I don't understand."

A pair of doves fluttered through the rafters, as the horses whinnied and stomped their hooves on the flooring in their stalls, demanding some grain to top them off for the night. Nellis filled and carried a pair of buckets to his mares, stroking Babe and nuzzling Bessie, while a clutch of chickens clucked through the straw searching for an evening snack. The goats barely acknowledged the ruckus from their sleepy tangle in an empty stall.

"It's as if the fascists behind this conspiracy are immune to interference, even by the FBI and the Secret Service. In spite of massive security, the assassins waltzed right through every prevent and went about their business. Of the half-dozen who were captured, not one has said a word, besides, 'I want my lawyer.' At which point a squad of the finest, most expensive defense attorneys in the country magically appeared to marshal their pleas."

"So, you're saying it's systemic?"

"I'm saying that this election is just a distraction. Gonzalez might be the president but the conspirators took the reins of power a long time ago and their program of destruction from within is rolling right along. They won't let something as insignificant as a vote of the people interfere with their progress. Whoever wins the election will become instantly irrelevant, because the Congress, the courts, and every Cabinet agency is being run by minions of the tyrants."

"So, how can I help, besides taking a sniper rifle up on the roof?"

Nellis patted him on the shoulder, "I want you to hold the receipts from this next shipment, until you hear from me, and I want you to have this information in case you don't. There are people counting on us and I've included instructions on how to take care of them."

"My tummy might be happy but I'm not likin' any of this."

"Neither am I and that's why you're going to be on the road first thing in the morning before anyone even suspects you've been here."

～

Jessie gazed along the shoreline until he spotted a pride of pastel parakeets mingling in the lush foliage of a Banyan tree hanging over the water, as Johnny motored the MissU2 through the narrows into the little Bay. He pulled a pair of binoculars from his tackle box and scanned across little white caps rolling to the south, "Looks like a few gulls diving on some shiners about half-way down."

"Let's go check it out but I want to drag a line down deep, while we're moving, just to see if anyone's hiding out from the chop on the surface."

Jessie rigged a line with a weight and a jiggly shiner and dropped it over the side, while Johnny hugged the shadow of the key as a wind block. "We'll see whether anybody's home."

He throttled back the little Johnson engine, as they breached the end of dense palmettos and the onset of desolation across the two miles where the sprawling SunnyBreeze resort once stood. Jessie raised the binoculars towards the property, "Hmmm, there are green patches starting to spread across the sand where young plants are beginning to emerge."

"Lemme see," said the boy taking the glasses. "I wonder how long it would take for the plants to take over the whole place, if they just left it alone?"

"I bet it will happen pretty fast because from what I hear, no one's interested in developing this property after what happened."

"It's like it's cursed," said the boy.

"You might be right," replied Jessie, grabbing the rod as line whizzed out of the reel, "I think we might have something."

Johnny grinned, "Now, take your time, let him tire himself out and make sure he doesn't try to swim under the boat!"

The artist reeled in the slack, "Where have we heard that advice before?"

"I don't know, it sounds familiar," said the boy, easing the bow around. "Watch out, he's stopped, give him a little slack so he can't pop the line."

"Can do," said Jessie, watching the coiled line slowly disappear into the dark water until the line snapped taut and the reel screamed.

"He's running off to starboard. You play him and I'll follow."

Jessie reeled when the fish slowed and gave line back when it darted away, then reeled fast when it turned back toward the boat and dove deep, pulling and pulling until the line went limp. "Rats, I'd love to know what that was, I'm pretty sure he was big."

"Maybe a snapper. Marty, down at the bait shop, said that a couple of people had reported catching some big ones this week."

"That'd make a fine meal." He hauled his line in and stashed his rod, "We haven't had a chance to chat since I got back but I'm betting you talked with your mom. What do you think about what happened?"

"I saw it on TV and I was worried that Mayor Turner wasn't going to be the only one who got shot but then the bad guy fell out of the balcony and it seemed like the shooting was over, even if all the people were running around screaming."

"Yeah, it changed from high tension to panic in an instant. The world was transformed in those few minutes and I'm not sure that it will ever be quite the same."

"Were you scared?"

"I really didn't have time to be scared, I heard the shot, saw Turner fall to the floor and the guy tumble out of the balcony, and my immediate concern was to protect Kate and the rest of the people who were standing behind the curtains on the side of the stage."

"I was scared for you."

He leaned to hug the boy, "Thanks, that means a lot."

"What's going to happen next?"

"Well, I think Mr. Spratlin will be running for president."

"He seems kind of straight but I liked him and his kids are cool," said Johnny. "Does he have a chance to win?"

"I honestly don't know. It all depends on how he appears in public and how the voters feel about what's happened. Some of them will vote for Representative Spratlin because they like him or think he'd do a good job, some might vote for him out of sympathy for Mayor Turner, but some might vote for Murphy because they're scared and they'd rather have a bully protecting them. There's no way to tell how it's all going to turn out."

"I hope he wins because that other guy seems really nuts."

"I agree with you and I don't think he'd make a very good president."

Johnny looked down at a little puddle of bilge water rolling with the light chop, "Do I still have to be scared?"

"Scared of what?"

"Of something happening to you or my mom, something bad happening to change the country, something...I don't know...or someone taking the way we live...?

Jessie lifted his chin with his index finger, "I wish I could promise that everything will be alright with all of this but I can't. So, I'll say this instead, life is full of scary things - sometimes you have to run away, sometimes you need to stand and fight, sometimes you win and sometimes, believe me I know, you lose. None of it is simple and none of it is easy but one thing I do know and that is that you're smart and strong and resilient, you know the difference between right and wrong, and I know that you're not afraid of the challenge...sort of like our little adventure in the hurricane. It's okay to be scared, fear protects you from danger, but you can't let it stop you from doing what you know is right and true. Does that make any sense?"

"Yeah, I understand what you mean but I still get these weird thoughts running through my mind of all the bad stuff that could happen."

The artist smiled, "Our imaginations can conjure up endless nightmares but hardly any of them come true. I used to lie awake the night before a big football game and I'd go through every mistake I could make, every trick the other team could pull, and everything that could possibly go wrong and one of two things always happened...either none of it came true and we won or, if things did go wrong, it was something I hadn't even considered.

Point is you have to deal with the problem in front of you and forget about all the 'what ifs' until they happen. You can't change the past, whatever's happened is done, and you can't forecast the future. You can plan, you can prepare, you can be the best that you can be but none of us knows what tomorrow's going to bring."

The boy grinned, "That's not very reassuring. What happened to everything's going to be alright?"

"You're just playin' me, you little punk!" laughed Jessie, hugging the boy. "I sure am glad that you're my friend."

"Me too."

Chapter Sixteen

Little Betty Mowery gazed down from the apartment window above Eddie Glover's bike shop on Congress Avenue, as two black Humvees pulled up to block the driveways. Four men in black body armor and shielded helmets, carrying assault rifles, banged on the door and marched inside. "Mom, you better come here."

Gretchen rushed out of the small kitchen, "What is it sweethcart?"

"Some scary looking men just got out of those trucks and went into Eddie's shop."

Her mother looked out the window, as the men dragged a struggling handcuffed Eddie across the pavement and tossed him into the back seat of the first vehicle, before they sped of down the street with blue and white lights flashing.

"What's happening?"

"I don't know, honey, but we'll go downstairs and see if we can use the phone to find out."

They ran down the back stairs, through a dozen bikes in various stages of repair, into the showroom and then Eddie's little office. Gretchen pulled a tiny notebook from her pocket, looked up Kate's telephone number, and dialed. The phone rang twelve times before she gave up and consulted her little book again, finding Alva Thompson's number.

She dialed and, after four rings, an agitated Alva answered, "Thompson residence."

"Alva, this is Gretchen Mowery."

"Oh, yeah, the lady with the wonderful kids who lives over Eddie's shop, yeah, I remember you."

"Well, I was wondering whether you've spoken with Jessie or Kate?"

"I just tried to call them and no one answered, why do you ask?"

"Well, four armed men dressed in black uniforms just walked into the shop and took Eddie away in two big black SUV's and I don't know why they'd want him, he's one of the good guys. He's even buds with the FBI and the Secret Service."

"Those bastards just came by here and asked Benny to take a ride to talk with their boss. Thought he might have some information about an investigation or something."

"Who were they?"

"I saw one of their badges and it said 'Alien Relocation Command' but I don't know what that means."

"I've never heard of them," replied Gretchen, "and what do immigration authorities want with either of our guys?"

"I have no idea and, to tell you the truth, I'm kinda scared about all of this. I told Benny to call the lawyer but he said it would be okay."

"What if it isn't?"

"Honey, you're scaring me."

"Is there someone else we can call?"

Alva thought for a moment, "I'll call Jessie's gallery owner, he might know if they're out of town."

"Good, call me back. This is the shop number, I don't have a phone of my own."

"Okay, I'll call you back as soon as I hang up with him."

She pressed the button on the phone and consulted a slate board on the wall, with numbers scribbled in different pastel shades of chalk, spotting Tropical Paradise Art Gallery in bright pink along the top edge of the frame.

She dialed and Derek Rangle answered, "Tropical Paradise Artistic Masterpieces! How can I make your world more wonderful today?"

"Mr. Rangle, it's Alva Thompson, Benny's sister."

"Oh, yes Ma'am, how is everyone in your family?"

"Well, not so good. Some official thugs from the Alien Relocation Command just stopped by and asked Benny to go down to their offices to answer some questions about some investigation they've got going. I tried calling Miss Kate but no one answers. Do you know whether they're out of town or something?"

"No, I talked with Jessie yesterday about picking up two paintings tomorrow. Maybe they're just out shopping or something."

"I don't know, I have a bad feeling about this. Something's going down and it can't be good."

"Hmmm…let me try and I'll get back to you as soon as I know something."

"Okay," replied Alva. "Oh, I almost forgot to tell you that the same guys picked up Eddie Glover too."

"That does make things a bit more intriguing."

Rangle disconnected and redialed, waiting for it to ring a dozen times before he grabbed his hat and keys, flipped the brass 'open' sign to 'closed', and locked the door. He drove his vintage Hunter Green Jaguar XKE across the causeway, down the Tamiami Trail, turning off on Poinsettia Avenue.

Jessie's VW bus and Kate's old BMW were parked in the driveway and the front door was standing open. He knocked on the screen door and a dog yelped but no one responded, so he slipped inside to find young Johnny sitting in the middle of the studio floor hugging a limp and barely responsive Gracie. "What's wrong?"

"The bad cops took Jessie and Kate again."

"What cops?"

"Four big guys dressed in black armor, with shiny face shields like in the movies, and four more outside."

Rangle knelt down to pet Gracie, "How do you know?"

"Jessie and I were going fishing and he was late getting ready. The scary guys knocked on the door, came inside, one of them showed a gold badge with a shiny shooting star on it and shot Gracie with that dart," said the boy, pointing to a slender silver tube on the floor. "He told Jessie they needed them to answer some questions about the assassination."

"And they went with the bad men?"

"Yeah, they had these big guns and one of them pointed it at me."

"Did Jessie or Kate say anything?"

"Jessie hugged me and told me I could use his tackle box and they'd be back in a little while."

Rangle walked over to the kitchen counter and opened the silver lid where, underneath spools of line, bobbers, and a stout fisherman's stiletto, he found a hefty envelope wrapped in plastic. "Perhaps this is what he wanted us to find."

"What is it?" asked Johnny.

Rangle tore off the wrapper, then the seal, and unfolded a thick sheaf of papers, with a note in Kate's script clipped to the packet.

> *Should you find us missing and you're clever enough to discover this letter, please take my file to Tabitha Hall. She'll understand the contents and know what to do with it.*

He licked his thumb to turn the page, "Let's just see what the first page has to say…"

Gracie groaned and rolled over on her stomach, squinting her eyes and ducking her snout as if she had a major headache. The boy hugged her gently and looked up, as Rangle's eyes scanned the pages. "What does it say?"

"It says that Miss Kate was investigating a secret government agency called the 'Alien Relocation Command', who are responsible for rounding up and deporting people who are in our country illegally." He looked over his reading glasses, "Just about our whole population descended from immigrants who came from other countries to escape oppression or violence or starvation, and everyone who comes here dreams of freedom and opportunity in a land where everyone is equal.

The 'Relocation Command' seems primarily interested in finding brown people, who came from Mexico or Central America, but they're also arresting people opposed to the right-wing plan for to take over the government."

He flipped through a few more pages, "Turns out that they can't just ship these people back across the border. By law, they have to have a trial in front of a judge to decide who stays and who goes and…because there are so many people being arrested, they've…built giant prison camps out west to hold them until their hand-picked judges can get to their cases."

Johnny squeezed Gracie's neck and started to cry, "Is that where they've taken Jessie and Kate?"

Rangle folded the papers and knelt down again, "First, we should call your mother and tell her what's happened. I'd be surprised if she didn't want you at home, until we know what's really going on and, maybe, you should take Gracie with you. I assume you came in your boat?"

"Yeah."

"I'll walk you down to the dock and then I'll take Kate's investigation to Mrs. Hall's house and see what she can find out. Okay?"

"Okay," replied Johnny, helping an unsteady dog to her feet.

"I know that you helped save Jessie and Kate and Sammy Ball, when they got kidnapped, because you told your mom and she told me and eventually we got them back. At least this time, we know what to do."

~

The red and yellow leaves on the sycamores, oaks, and maples fluttered and waved in a cold breeze as Samantha and a giggly Sissy scampered across the bridge over Crow Creek and strolled around the side of the barn, just as the dogs tore across the drive to prance along the gate, barking ferociously, as two black Humvee's rumbled to a stop in a cloud of dust. Eight men, in black uniforms and helmets with mirrored face shields masking their features, lined up along the gate.

The girls ducked behind a stack of hay bales as Nellis marched across the driveway, "Can I help you gentlemen?"

The voice from the helmet of the trooper in the center of the line was tinny and synthesized, refined to sound imposing, if not quite imperious, "We're from the Alien Relocation Command and we've been requested to escort you and Katherine Kennedy to headquarters. The Command is assisting in the investigation of the attacks on your events and the assassination of Mayor Turner. Our Executive Officer would appreciate a few minutes of your time to clarify some details in your official statements."

"Why don't you give me the address and I'll just meet you there?"

The lead officer's gold badge with the graphic arc glinted in the morning sunlight streaming down the lane, "My orders are to escort you and Miss Kennedy. We'll return you when the Commander is satisfied with your information."

"Where is your…office?"

"I'm afraid that's classified."

"What if I deny your invitation."

"I don't think that option is viable," replied the trooper. "Our orders are specific."

"Fine, you guys wait here and I'll go get Miss Kennedy, and don't let the dogs out, they're not friendly." Before they could reply, he turned and strolled across the yard, up the path, and into the porch.

Samantha pulled Sissy into the barn but Babe and Bessie whinnied, their reins tethered to a stall post, waiting to be saddled for a morning ride. The girls spoke softly to calm the horses and pet them gently.

Sissy whispered, "Let's saddle them up."

"Are you planning an old-time get away, like in the westerns?" asked Sam, making quick work of it, after years of caring for their own horses and ponies, before Spratlin sold them off.

"That's exactly what I'm thinking. As soon as they step out on the porch, we throw open the barn door and charge across the drive to pick them up. If we head down into the south forty, we'll be gone by the time those guys get their fancy four-wheelers through the gate."

"We could circle around, cross the creek down at the shallows, and hide out in the stables at our house."

"What if they start shooting?"

"What if we don't do this and they take Nellis and Katherine and put them in jail or something?"

"Okay, never mind," replied Sissy, peeking out through a window to watch the agitated black guards standing ramrod straight in a perfectly straight line outside the gate watching the house and the pack dogs patrolling the driveway with a chorus of growls, while they waited for their prisoners to emerge.

Presently, Gracie spun around as the screen door on the porch opened and Katherine stepped outside. Nellis froze in the open doorway, as the barn door rumbled open and the horses galloped across the drive, to block them from view.

Katherine looked up, "What do you children think you're doing?"

But Nellis boosted her up behind Samantha and climbed on Babe with Sissy, "They're trying to save our sorry asses, let's go."

He smacked Bessie's rump and the horses bolted around the farmhouse, through the pecan orchard, and over the rise into the meadow as two troopers jumped the gate and unwound the chains to roll it back. The dogs barked and growled, until the men jumped into the truck, then ran through the yard and over the rise after the horses. The Humvees sped across the lawn in pursuit which lasted until they got bogged down in the wet muck at the bottom of the hill, instead of following the gravel road along the fence line.

Nellis pulled up, "Did you girls actually have a plan for our escape or were you just winging it?"

Sissy grinned, "We're going to cross the creek at the narrows and hide you at our house, until we can get my dad to stop this."

He kissed the top of her head and reached to touch Sammy's hand, "You girls are amazing! Let's go!"

They could hear tires spinning and people yelling in the distance, as Gracie led the pack to follow their master. Sam and Sissy cantered to the gate in the southwest corner, then back through the Harwood property to walk the horses across the gurgling brook, up through the forest to emerge behind the barn on the Spratlin estate.

"This old barn has been lonely without horses and ponies in these stalls," said Sissy, sliding a broad door open, "even if Bruce has his art gallery upstairs."

Katherine hugged Sam and climbed down, "I'm not sure it was a plot thoroughly hatched but that was mighty brave of you girls. Thanks."

"It was Sissy's idea," said Samantha, leading Bessie and the dogs inside.

"Either way, thanks for being sneaky," said Nellis. "Is there a phone in here?"

"There's one upstairs in Bruce's quarters," said Sissy, pointing to a stairway. "C'mon, I'll show you."

They followed the little blond sprite up a narrow staircase and into a long studio washed in a smooth even glow by skylights in the ceiling. Monochromatically morose and graphically violent paintings were lined up in the shadows against the far wall, while his easels were surrounded with vividly colorful canvases illustrating the fear and anger in thousands of faces looking up at the All People Matter stages across the country - every age, color, religion, background, and heritage…their desperation the great equalizer that allowed their flagrant display of humanity.

Katherine knelt down next to a large painting with hundreds of uniquely individual faces peering up, "I know exactly where that one came from, it's in Piedmont Park in Atlanta."

She pointed to a black woman with spikey purple hair and a red tee-shirt imprinted with the word 'Freedom' in stars and stripes. I remember that woman. By the time we started marching for the Capitol, she'd been transformed from a frightening victim into a dedicated fighter."

Nellis lifted the handset from an old-fashioned rotary dial phone on a table, "How do I reach your dad?"

"Oh, just dial 'one' and Louise will pick it up in the kitchen," said Sam. "She'll get your call through to him."

Nellis dialed a 'one', with a flash of nostalgic memories of operators and party lines. After two rings, Maybelle answered, "Spratlin House, how can I help you?"

"Maybelle, it's Nellis. How are you today?"

"We've been cooking non-stop for more than a week and I'm getting sick of my own food!"

"I guarantee nobody else is!"

"You're too easy! Why are you calling me on this line?"

"Well, actually, I need to talk with Stanton. We're hiding out in your barn because some Alien Relocation Commandos tried to hijack us but Sissy and Sammy rode in on horseback to save us, just like in the movies."

"Are you making this up?"

"No, no, you know me better than that, it's all for real. Could you connect me with the boss."

"Absolutely, when you come out of hiding, I'll have some fried chicken for you."

"Oh darlin', I might even venture out in broad daylight for that!"

She laughed and line went dead for a moment, before Spratlin picked up, "Stanton Spratlin."

"Nellis Gray. Listen, your daughters just rescued us from being detained by the Alien Relocation Command and we're hiding out in your barn."

"You're joking?"

"No, I'm not and if they're after us, they're after everyone else in the leadership of the movement and our friends need to be warned."

"I'm new to all of this but I've never heard of the Alien Relocation Command. Come up to the house and I'll make some calls to find out who's running this operation."

"If they're striking this close to your campaign, you might want to be careful about who you discuss this with…and I'm not sure that your Secret Service detail needs to know we're here."

"I see your point. I'll be discreet and call you back on the house line when I know something. Meanwhile, Bruce is in the kitchen, so I'll see that he brings you some refreshments."

Katherine took his arm, "What'd he say?"

"That he doesn't have any idea which clandestine branch of government is behind this."

"The same folks who paid for the murders of all those people at the rallies and Tyrone too."

"They don't intend to lose at any price, murder's just a messy inconvenience."

"What did those guys want, anyway?" asked Sissy.

Katherine knelt down, "They don't want anyone organizing all of our people to vote for your dad instead of Murphy. It's as simple as that. They want to own the country."

Samantha grinned, "Does that make you an enemy of the state?"

"At the very least, we're fugitives and you two are accessories!" said Nellis.

"What's an accessory," asked Sissy.

"Someone who helps someone else commit a crime," replied Katherine.

"Is escaping a crime?"

"Yup, and you're in deep do-do," laughed Nellis.

Katherine scolded him, "Stop that, they don't put little girls in jail!"

"If they don't throw you in jail, I promise you're going to lose the next ten games of chess," replied a saucy Sissy, sticking her tongue out. "If you're not nice to me, I'll just leave you here and I won't bring you any food and you'll starve to death."

Nellis grabbed her in a big hug, "I'm so glad to have you in my life, even if the bad guys have other plans for us."

The phone jangled with a droning ring-ring from another time. Nellis picked up the handset, "Hello."

"I haven't made much headway with Homeland Security or the Department of the Interior but I spoke with Tabitha and it seems that Benny, Sammy, Eddie, Jessie, and Kate are missing, and she can't get anyone to answer in Atlanta. She said that witnesses said that they were taken into custody by men dressed in black uniforms with shiny helmets, driving black SUV's."

"Gee that sounds awfully familiar. We had eight of them show up at the front gate with automatic weapons at the ready."

"How did you get away?"

"Your daughters showed up with two saddled horses and we rode out through the orchard and my southern pasture before they could respond. If it weren't for Sissy and Sammy, we'd be in the hoosegow by now."

"I can't believe this is happening…well, considering all that we've been through, of course I can, but I'm afraid I never dreamed that the U.S. government had a covert regiment dedicated to taking opposition figures off the streets. Tabitha said that Kate left a file chronicling the activities of the Alien Relocation Command. It seems they've constructed giant concentration camps on abandoned military bases out west to house their captives until they can be tried in kangaroo courts or they die."

"This is a fascist scheme and they didn't start yesterday. Seems they've got troopers all over the country and their primary job is to take lots of brown Hispanic people and toss them in jail or push them across the border in an ongoing effort to bleach the population."

Spratlin was quiet for a moment, "I have to wonder why they would risk exposure by trying to eliminate all of you before the election even happens. Are the powers-that-be really that confident that Murphy will win and go along with their demands, once he's in the Oval Office, or are they terrified that he won't?"

Nellis rubbed his chin, "I think the best way to take the stink out of dirty laundry is to hang it out in the sunshine."

"I agree. I'll draft and make a televised statement tonight but we have to find someplace to stash you so I don't look like I'm setting this whole thing up as a publicity stunt."

Nellis looked at Katherine with that cockeyed grin, "I know just the place if you could get Bruce to run us down there in his cute little VW bug?"

"I'm sure he'd be delighted."

"We'll watch for your speech."

Katherine put her hand on her hip with that look of 'What are you getting me into this time?' consternation. "So?"

"So, he's going to give a speech tonight exposing all of this." He turned to Sissy and Sam, "I'm going to ask you girls to look after our critters for a few days, while we go underground, until we know what's happening."

"Can I ask where?" inquired Katherine.

"Well, there are some folks in a very tight community, who owe me a favor."

~

Nellis curled up in the passenger foot-well of Bruce's baby-blue VW bug, under a long slender tasteless erotic painting and Katherine pretzelled herself into the narrow crevice behind the front seats covered with a paint-splattered tarp. Spratlin's son pulled down the winding drive and dropped the gearbox into second, whining up to the security gate, just outside the arch with the stately 'S' embossed on a burgundy crest suspended between regal golden lions, and rolled down the window.

The guard patted the roof, "I used to have one of these back in the day. My ol' man called 'em high speed thrills at low speeds."

"She's not fast but she sure is fun."

"Where ya' headed?"

"I've gotta to drop off this painting to a client and then I'm coming straight back for dinner with the family."

"Right," said the sentry, straightening up. "You know you're supposed to have a detail with you?"

Bruce turned on his haughty-bitch persona, "So, you don't see why I might have a problem showing up to sell radical pornographic art, that's supposed to give my very weird and kinky client a great big hard-on…with a Secret Service squad in tow. Are you out of your mind?"

The guard ducked to peek at the well hung naked man on the canvas as he backed away, "Just don't get yourself in any trouble between here and there and back, okay?"

Bruce rolled up the window with a sneer and gunned the little car down Maple Ridge, past lines of police and security vehicles wedged onto the grassy shoulders of the narrow road. "You guys okay? Stay put until I make the turn up here and we're out of sight."

Katherine's muffled voice erupted from under the seat, "That was quite a performance back there, you had that poor old man going."

Spratlin laughed, "As you know, Cameron's a very conservative community and most of the people I grew up with have never been exposed to gay people, or black or brown people, or many folk who aren't evangelically Christian, for that matter, and they really have no idea of how to react when confronted with someone who qualifies as one those 'others'. I fake it when I'm out and about because I don't want the hassle but I don't mind turning on the charm when some homophobic asshole dearly deserves it."

Nellis grunted and sat up under the canvas, "As they proved at the strike, most of 'em are ignorant country bumpkins who don't pay much attention to what's happening outside their little burg, unless something's trying to sully their way of life and then get the hell out of their way, 'cause they'll defend their turf until the last man gives up his last drop of blood."

The blue bug zipped around the corner and down a long winding back road through the forest to spit out on Fourth Street, two blocks from the Saint Francis Orphanage, where Sister Gwen awaited her newest, rather adult strays at the back gate to the alley behind the building.

Bruce circled the block, to make sure no one was following, and putted into the alleyway, just as the street lights sparked to life under the last orange rays from the setting sun tickling the treetops. The nun's white collar glowed in the twilight as Nellis and then Katherine untangled themselves from the tiny car.

They both hugged Bruce and Nellis said, "We owe you one, brother."

"It's not even close, you saved my sisters, then all the kids, and then our family."

"Tell your dad, I'm sorry I can't be there to help," said Katherine, with a kiss to his cheek, "and...that I think he'll make a fine president."

"Me too," added Nellis. "You give Sissy and Sammy a big hug for me and tell 'em I'll be seeing them real soon. Oh, and thank them for looking after my critters."

Sister Gwen opened the gate and welcomed them into a play yard behind the kitchens, as the blue bug motored down the alley. "Please come this way. I'm so pleased to have this opportunity to repay your many kindnesses. There are so many children and homeless souls, over at the shelter, who'd be out on the street if it wasn't for your generosity."

"I wish I could do more."

"We could all do more but you are certainly an answer to my prayers."

Nellis blushed, "I've arranged for another contribution to be delivered to you."

"Thank you," replied the nun with a curtsey. "From what you said on the phone, I think you'll be safe here, until we can make other arrangements."

"Thank you, Sister. We're humbled and frightened by our circumstance."

The woman took their arms, guiding them past a tidy little vegetable garden towards tantalizing scents wafting from the kitchen. "I've never had the pleasure of actually meeting either of you but I'm well aware of the work that you've been doing to salvage the lives of millions of desperate people in spite of the tragedies that you've faced. Whoever is after you is on the wrong side of humanity. Please come inside, we'll be serving dinner in a little while and I'm sure the children will be pleased to have guests who don't wear habits."

~

Nellis and Katherine huddled in front of a tiny television in Sister Gwen's office on the second floor of the orphanage, as the national networks opened a broadcast from the Great Plains Hotel, in downtown Cameron, Oklahoma, to present Stanton's first address to the American people, since the Democratic Party finally acknowledged his inherited rights as the nominee.

Grady Lewis, political anchor for Public News said, "Ladies and gentlemen, Representative Stanton Spratlin, Democratic Candidate for President of the United States."

Democratic Presidential nominee, Stanton Spratlin scowled into the television camera set up in the grand entry of stately Spratlin House, perched on a ridge overlooking the town. His speech was being broadcast by every news channel in the country. "My fellow Americans, I want to speak to you tonight about the assassination of our Presidential candidate, Tyrone Turner at the debate in Madison, Wisconsin, ten days ago by a paid assassin, who shattered history with a single shot.

I want to talk about the suicidal plane crash that killed or maimed hundreds of innocent people at the All People Matter rally in Chicago, the disgusting massacre of desperate demonstrators in Denver, the brutal white-nationalist riots in Atlanta, the deadly bombing in Houston and so many other attacks by the foot soldiers of a very exclusive group of tyrants who have every intention of deconstructing our government and dismantling our democracy."

Katherine noticed the tense creases at the corners of his steel blue eyes soften slightly, as he paused, staring straight into the camera.

"As all of you know, I am the most unlikely candidate in the history of presidential elections. I've been a loyal Republican for my entire life but…in hindsight, I've come to realize that through all those years I was too comfortable in my belief system to pay attention to the lies, the clever catch phrases excusing and promoting hate, bigotry and racism at the very core of the party platform. I contributed to the truckloads of dark money behind the elections of well-trained but completely unqualified candidates, who were elected to pass legislation in every state house and Congress to promote and protect the financial welfare of a small cadre of the wealthiest citizens in our land."

Stanton shook his head in disbelief, "I was absolutely astounded when Mayor Turner insisted that I become his running-mate. I hesitated for about two seconds because first, I believe in everything the man stood for and second, you don't say 'no' to Tyrone Turner, a six-six All-Star linebacker for the Atlanta Falcons and a Rhodes Scholar, with a doctorate in economics from Yale. He was bigger than life and he had a vision to unite all the citizens of this country to create a future for everyone together." His voice echoed in the empty hallway. "I will do everything in my power to carry his dream to fruition."

He paused, "I'm sure that most of you are familiar with the viscous attacks on the All People Matter movement and our campaign and I want to assure you that, no matter what the Republican propaganda machine splatters across the media, there's absolutely no doubt about who is responsible for the deaths of hundreds and injuries to thousands. We will be presenting proof in Congress, over the next few weeks, and we'll see whether the Justice Department is truly invested in justice.

In addition to all the murders, it appears that we've entered a new phase of their offensive which involves the disappearance of a number of our supporters who have been at the forefront of the All People Matter movement. So far, we know of thirty-eight people in six different cities who were visited and taken into custody by a clandestine governmental force known as the Alien Relocation Command and there are literally hundreds that we haven't been able to contact. None of the people who were arrested has been seen or heard from since they were seized and detained without warrants or judicial oversight. There is no record of any of them appearing in any court.

My staff has learned that this secret agency is funded through Homeland Security as a black operation for counter-terrorism but it appears to have been used to round up Latino immigrants who lacked proper documentation on their person and in many cases, dispatching them across the border without a hearing before a judge or an opportunity to say goodbye to their loved ones. Like our associates, tens of thousands seem to have just disappeared.

As you should know, the Republican Senate refused to confirm three different nominees nominated by our hamstrung President Gonzalez for that Secretarial seat and the second and third in command quit in protest of the blatant racism. So, now the Department is being run by Ozzie James, a radically conservative former Republican Representative from South Carolina, who resigned when four-thousand forged ballots turned up after his election. His office will not respond to our inquiries but I can assure you that he will be brought before the Oversight Committee to respond to these charges."

He paused again, "I honestly don't know whether my opponent is involved with this plot to hand the Federal Government over to the sponsors behind this enormous conspiracy but I do know that he is compromised by their financial support for his campaign.

Considering all that's happened over the past few months, combined with this paramilitary operation to silence and eliminate the opposition, I believe the coming elections should be postponed until Congress and a special prosecutor can guarantee truly free and fair balloting in every district in the country. We must have some assurance that this isn't just a sham produced by people who believe they deserve vast power and riches at your expense. At the very least, you should be able to trust that your votes will actually count.

Ladies and gentlemen, we've been working on our democracy for nearly two-hundred and fifty years. Hundreds of thousands of patriots have fought and died defending the very concepts that make our nation the envy of the entire world but in spite of how far we've come, we still have a long way to go before we finally become that shining city on a hillside.

I don't know about you but I'm not ready to hand all of this over to the richest few to raid and pillage, until our Constitution and the Bill of

Rights have no meaning, no value and no purpose. I don't believe we should return to the barbarity of feudalism or the cruelty of fascism and neither do you.

The only way to save our country is for every one of you to demand a full and honest investigation before one vote is cast. I call on my opponent to join me, if he's truly not in the pocket of the conspirators.

Every citizen needs to contact your senators and representatives, your governor and state legislators, your mayor and town council. I hope to see massive peaceful crowds shut down every city in the country until we learn the truth!

Let's stand together to defend the future of the nation and the promise of our democracy against this most vicious and virulent conspiracy festering inside our borders. Thank you and God bless the America we all believe in."

Sister Gwen bowed her head and crossed herself. "It's very easy to become focused on the welfare of our young charges and the future of this sanctuary and to lose track of what's happening out there in the real world."

Katherine took her hand, "More people should pay attention to the miracles you're performing here."

"Thank you, but I've always been fascinated by the patriots who smuggled Jews out of Germany during the Second World War and now I finally understand that their nightmare is being repeated in our own country and in God's grace, I will do whatever I can to keep you safe."

Nellis walked over and hugged her.

Stanley French led his guests through the massive salon of the cabin overlooking Jackson Lake and the snow-capped peaks beyond to his study, a masculine room bounded by thick logs and giant windows, with mounted trophies, gun cases displaying an arsenal of antique weapons, oversized leather furniture, and a massive slab of burl cottonwood for a desk.

He opened a portable safe with thick walls, "I'd appreciate it if you would contribute any phones, pagers, or other electronic devices while we're together. I can assure you that all of mine and the entire staffs' gadgets are in there too and the telephones and communications network in the house has been disabled."

"I appreciate your sense of security," said Blaho, pulling a slender laptop from his briefcase, "but this might qualify as extreme. We could have met in my SCIF or yours and avoided traveling through a blizzard to get here."

"We're miles from anything or anyone, so this might be the most secure location we could ask for." Ethan Tomlinson added a phone, before French closed and sealed the case. "Now, we can talk without worrying about surveillance, unless one of my satellites is monitoring us from orbit."

A waiter, in a starched white coat over faded blue jeans and polished cowboy boots, appeared with a tray bearing three champagne flutes and a very cold bottle of 1998 Boerl & Kroff Brut. He set the tray on a table, removed the foil wrap and popped the cork to fill the glasses, bowed and disappeared.

French handed a glass to each of his colleagues, "Gentlemen, I propose a toast to our imminent success."

The glasses clinked and each man sipped. "Ah, that is marvelous," said Tomlinson.

Conrad Blaho raised his glass, "And I would like to toast you, sir, for guiding us through the decades to this moment. Without your patience and foresight, we'd still be trying to win seats on school boards in rural counties."

"Thank you, but we all know that none of this would have been possible without our dedicated partners in The Forge, who put up the money for every battle in every district in every election over the years. We won some, we lost some, but everyone kept believing in the ultimate goal, which brought us to the brink of success."

"I received word this morning that the Relocation Command has taken more than eight-hundred activists into custody in the first week of the operation and they're on track to silence an additional two-thousand opposition leaders within the next few days."

"What are they doing with the prisoners?" asked Tomlinson.

"They're being transported on custom-designed, windowless high-speed trains to the half-dozen detention camps we've built out on abandoned military bases out in the boonies, where there is no escape, no legal remedies or ramifications, and no future for enemies of the state."

"We'll have Murphy tape a response to Spratlin's speech, suggesting that there is absolutely no proof behind his allegations and that he's just using the violence as an excuse, because he doesn't have the balls to fight it out."

"That should incite the faithful."

Tomlinson took another sip, "As soon as the Democratic Party puts their weight behind their candidate, we're going to launch a media blitz with all the grizzly details of how he screwed his employees out of their pension fund to save his company, how his wife is a bed-ridden drug addict as a direct result of his eight-year affair with Katherine Kennedy, the now missing voice of All People Matter movement, or his sons – one's a flagrantly gay artist and the other's a drug-addled vet with PTSD and a violent streak. By the time we get through with him, he'll be lucky to capture a majority of the votes in his home town."

"Are we sure we can control Murphy? He's a crazy son-of-a-bitch."

Blaho grinned, "We've got Milton Graves, Casper Wein, and Shephard Stone running his campaign and, from inside reports, Doc Billings is keeping him fired up when he's needed and sedated when he's not."

"Once he's elected, we'll put him out there to make some noise to keep the focus off Creighton Steil, who will take charge behind the smokescreen," said French, "and the real work of dismantling the government can begin in earnest."

"An action memo is already being prepared to guide the transition team to populate the administration with our people, vetted by our conservative wizards at America First, American Freedom, and Patriot's Heritage," said French. "They should be ready to roll out our agenda long before Murphy takes the oath in January."

Katherine turned to a gentle knock and Sister Gwen's soft voice, "May I come in?"

Nellis turned the latch and opened the door of their tiny room, secreted in the peak of the roof, to find their favorite nun in her black habit and white collar holding a trophy football that almost glistened in the dim light. "What do you have there, Sister?"

"I saw Hank Garrett a little while ago and he and a mysterious gentleman asked me to deliver this. He said that you would understand the significance. I have no idea of how the man made the connection or why this might be important."

Curious, Nellis took the ball and held it under a lamp to read, 'Most valuable player - Orange Bowl National Collegiate Championship – Oklahoma vs Wisconsin - 2003'.

Katherine's dark eyes opened wide, "Didn't I hear a crazy story about him dying tragically in Jessie's storm last year?"

Nellis turned to Sister Gwen, "Tell me about this guy."

"He's about six-two or three, two hundred pounds, solid build, athletic, maybe in his late thirties or early forties and starting to gray at the temples. She blushed, "He is very handsome and I almost feel as if I should know who he is."

"How could he possibly find us this fast?"

"The only person who knows we're here is Bruce and he wouldn't rat us out," said Nellis, turning to Sister Gwen, "Where is he?"

"He's over at the Soup Kitchen with Hank, sharing a cup of coffee."

Katherine took Gwen's hand, "Sister, you've dedicated your life to saving these wonderful children but I sense that your experience makes you a good judge of people. What did you feel about this man?"

The nun bit her lip for a moment, "He's a very masculine male, someone who hasn't lived by other people's rules, but I sense that he's on the right side of things. I didn't feel danger or aggression in him and he does have one of those genuine smiles, like he could be on the cover of a magazine."

Nellis looked at Katherine, "I'll go, you stay. One of us has to break free to tell the world what's happening, if this goes wrong."

"I know you're trying to protect me but I can't do this without you. We're going together or we're not going."

"Why do you always have to be stubborn when you know I'm right?"

"Because, I'm not letting you out of my sight, until we find a priest or a minister or someone who can marry us."

Nellis' mouth dropped open, staring into the fiery gleam in her dark eyes, feeling the tingling tension of her fight or flight fear intertwined with repressed rage fueling raw passion in the sincerity of her commitment. He dropped to a knee to kiss her hand, "I do."

Sister Gwen blushed again, as he stood up to kiss his fiancé.

They turned to the nun, "I'm sorry, Sister, I didn't mean to embarrass you."

"I think we could come up with a handy priest, if you really want one, and I certainly hope you'll let me attend your wedding."

"I'd be honored if you would be my maid of honor, so why don't you see if your priest is available in case we actually do come back?" replied Katherine with a kiss to each cheek. She looked up at Nellis, "If that's alright with you?"

"I'll say, 'I do' - tonight, tomorrow, or whenever it suits your fancy."

"Then, I guess, if we're going, we should get started."

They walked down three flights of stairs, through the darkened kitchen, scented with more than a lingering hint of garlic and onions from dinner's Marinara sauce, out past the vegetable garden, through the play-yard, and along the alley to Sixth Street. They strolled along an uneven sidewalk, fronting modest homes on the east side of the street away from the two street lights, arm-in-arm, like any couple walking home through reassuring stillness, save the dog barking behind a fence up ahead.

Katherine slowed, "How did he find us?"

"There's only two people who know about my relationship with these folks, besides you. Bruce and Ned and, if Ned's at the farm, he's probably smart enough to figure it out, but I honestly don't see how they could have connected."

"I sure hope you're right, because we could be walking right into a trap."

"You sure you don't want me to go in, while you wait outside in the shadows?"

"Where you go, I go."

They turned up another alley, past reeking dumpsters and a tabby cat darting through the shadows after a speedy mouse, to the back entrance of the soup kitchen. Nellis reached to try the door handle but Katherine grabbed his hand and kissed him passionately. "I just want to make sure that if this turns out to be a bad idea, you'll never forget our last kiss!"

"I love you."

"I love you, too."

Nellis reached for the handle and pulled the door open. They stepped into a dank storage room and pushed through a heavy steel door into a large kitchen where two men, loading dishwashers and scrubbing pots and pans, turned to look. Nellis smiled and waved, "Hank Garrett?"

The taller man pointed to the dining room, where the proprietor was sitting in the middle of a long table facing the kitchen, his bald head gleaming in the glare of a single bulb in a lamp dangling by wire from the ceiling, as he nodded in conversation with a husky man with dark hair streaked with gray. Garrett stopped talking and stood with a respectful nod, "I'm glad to see you're free."

"Glad to be free, for the moment," replied Nellis as the other man stood and turned.

Garrett said, "Nellis, believe it or else, this is Tate Sloan."

He handed the game ball to Sloan, "Never had the pleasure but your old lady and my friend, Jessie, sure have some tall tales to tell about you and not all of them were good."

"It's a long story," replied a graying Tate, "and we'll get to all that but first, you have to introduce me to this lovely lady, even though I already know your name and your reputation!"

Katherine extended a hand, "I'm happy to see you alive."

"Nice to be here."

"Before we go any farther," said Nellis, "we've got to know how you tracked us down so fast and who helped?"

"Well, actually, Mavis clued me in to what was happening in Dolphin's Bay and…"

"Wait," interrupted Katherine, "she knows that you're alive?"

"Well, only since Turner was gunned down but, as I said, it's a long story."

"Yeah, but that doesn't get you here," said Nellis.

"No, actually, I hired an old friend of yours, a while back. The guy's a wiz in accounting and also seems to have a mysterious talent of making things appear and disappear…me included. He's been helping me since not long after the hurricane but I made him swear to protect my secret, even from you."

"I always wondered why he walked away from his accounting career."

"Well, because he couldn't stand being cooped up in a cubical or even a stuffy office and he ended up taking me on as his only client…except you, of course, because I make it worth his effort."

"That lyin' son of a bitch, I'm never cooking for his sorry ass again."

Tate and Katherine cracked up and Sloan said, "I've heard rave reviews about your barbeque."

"So, the question becomes, why are you here now, considering the Federal bloodhounds are probably three doors down and I'm guessin' they wouldn't hesitate to indict anyone who happens to be in close proximity to us?"

"Because you two need to disappear and my old lady has decided that you're going to lead the revolution."

Nellis was bewildered, "Can't lead a revolution with us dead or in detention, so how do you plan to get us out of here, with the black shirts searching the whole damned town for us?"

Sloan grinned that cockeyed magazine grin, "Our personal magician, Ned, just pulled his newly painted classic uniform dry-cleaning van into the alley right behind you and there's a very fast plane fueled and ready at the airport to take us someplace far-far away."

"Why would you do this?" asked Katherine.

"Because, ever since Jessie tried to save my sorry ass, I've been helping other people escape their own weird situations and now, I'm signing on to rescue as many of your people as we can, so they can help organize a rebellion to stop the noble conspirators." His smile disappeared, "You can hide until the storm-troopers track you down or you can accept the challenge to save the world, it's up to you."

Katherine hugged Nellis and stared into his eyes, "There's something we need to attend to first."

He reached to shake Tate's hand, "If you guys would consider being witnesses for a very short ceremony, we'll be ready to go."

The Characters

Nellis Gray – cranky, craggy, lives with Katherine in an old farmhouse in a garden wonderland with five dogs and six cats, chickens, a few goats, plus raccoons, fox, bunnies, squirrels, possum, and flocks of birds.

Gracie – Nellis's shepherd/doberman mix

'Lucy' – Nellis' 1959 Goldtop Les Paul six-string electric guitar.

Nanny - his wife, who died of cancer and haunts the house, son (Nathan) took off when he was 17 and hasn't been heard from since, daughter (Ashley), a nurse, married to a college professor in Boston – no children, doesn't come home.

"Sissy" Shirley Ann Spratlin – 3rd grade, blond curls, pug nose with freckles, big green eyes - spritely, giggly, inquisitive, determined, and frightened.

"Sam" – Samantha Spratlin – 8th grade – slender, pale skin with dark eyes and auburn hair,

Brad Spratlin – oldest brother wounded in the war, post-traumatic stress, angry, violent, alcohol, drugs, flashbacks – hanging with bikers – hulking, burr cut, shrapnel scar on his right cheek, a dragon tattoo to chase away his demons on his right shoulder.

Bruce Spratlin – brother – gay artist / musician and activist, lives in a renovated loft in the barn, where he paints erotic art, and drives a baby-blue VW bug.

Stanton James Spratlin – father – distinguished, aristocratic, proper, hanging on to a time gone by, white hair – broad shouldered, always impeccably dressed, closet alcoholic, desperate to rebuild his family and fulfill his obligations as Temporary Congressional Representative.

Marjorie Murray Spratlin – mother – recovering from being a bedridden alcoholic hypochondriac, and reclaiming her place as matriarch of the family.

Mama Louise – cook – the good-humored backbone of the staff and the family, lives in renovated servants' quarters over the garages. Originally from southern Georgia.

Sibble Savage – nanny / housemaid – slender, aging waif, who looked after this generation and Stanton and his sister before them…more parent than their real parents and knows all the family secrets, which guarantees her place in Spratlin House until she joins her husband, who died in the Korean War.

Mr. Charles – houseman / chauffer – distinguished overseer - everything on the property must meet his approval, things are done as they have always been done and the honor and social graces of the family are to be protected.

Katherine Kennedy – Stanton's former secretary, mistress – long, lean, thick auburn hair, dark piercing eyes, high cheek bones, strong jaw, wide smile – intelligent, organized, and living with Nellis.

Ned Perkins - a beanpole with long straggly rusty blond hair and a full beard, accountant and transport driver for Nellis' marijuana crop

Jason (Jazz) Taggart – guitar player – Jazz Taggart and his Band of Merry Men

Maybelle Brown – deceased Representative Curtis Hall's former black mistress and mother to his four bastard children – Daniel, Hubie, Muriel, and Martin

Sister Gwen – the St. Francis Orphanage

Hank Garrett – runs the soup kitchen

Rev. Billy Joe Hardman – World-famous evangelical preacher who was arrested for conspiracy, fraud, failure to pay income taxes, and attempting to manipulate an election.

~

Tate Sloan – from Senders Creek, Oklahoma, as quarterback, he led the OU football team to a National Championship by defeating Wisconsin in the Rose Bowl. started TMS Oil Technologies, financed by his father-in-law, became notoriously rich and developed SunnyBreeze with his wife Mavis before disappearing during Hurricane Dot.

Mavis Simonson Sloan – Former OU cheerleader and sorority girl, who believed that there are only two classes of people, those special few who have and deserve enormous wealth and those who serve them, until she was confronted with the inevitable collapse of the American society and became the money behind the All People Matter movement.

SunnyBreeze – idyllic community on the south end of Breezy Key, created to bilk and brainwash wealthy tourists by Tate and Mavis Sloan, providing 'elite' vacation housing and every amenity in a safe, exclusive environment, until Hurricane Dot devoured it completely.

The New School at Dolphin Bay – Mavis' exclusive school in SunnyBreeze

Selby Simonson – Mavis' father - tycoon who made his first fortune using other people's money to punch holes in the Texas dirt, until he hit a massive field. Branched out to own pipelines, refineries, a fleet of ocean tankers, a giant real estate development and construction company, private jets, and the Rolls-Royce dealership in Dallas.

Chen Chen – very old Chinese assistant to Simonson, runs all his personal business, including the house, and is Selby's only confidant. Their relationship goes back to the war, when Chen saved Selby's life and took responsibility for his well-being. Helped raise Mavis.

James Robert Combs – 'Jimbo' – former NBA Allstar, turned semi-evangelical conman with an enormous congregation, transformed into the conscience of the All People Matter movement.

Jessie Cotton – former junior quarterback for the Wisconsin team that lost to Oklahoma, successful landscape painter in Dolphin Bay, leader of the All People Matter movement

Gracie – Jessie's Shepherd/Dobie mix – mirror image to Nellis's Gracie

Johnny Warmington, 9-year-old, who lives nearby with his single mother and younger sisters, loves to go fishing with best friend Jessie, and has an innate connection with animals and nature in the bay. Blue eyes, ginger hair

MissU – Johnny's boat that was destroyed in the hurricane

Bobbie Warmington – Johnny's mom

Cara and Stacy - younger sisters

Beatrice Rowlins – Bobbie Warmington's mother

Kate Crocket – Jessie's old college girlfriend and former lifestyle reporter for 'American Style' magazine in Atlanta, until she became the voice of the All People Matter movement. Tall, willowy, horsy, thick blond hair, piercing amber eyes, pretty without being glamorous

Marvin Standler – CEO of Brinksman Investments, cowboy hat and boots, a full head of silver hair, famous for leveraging buyouts to wring every last penny out of a company, until Mavis convinced him to lend his expertise to saving the middle class.

Ned Flint – hotel and shipping magnate, gay – snotty, arrogant – had an intimate relationship with Tate Sloan.

Bernie Baker – eighty-five, made his fortune in waste management in the Northeast. Last of his generation, opinionated, old-school, oblivious to real world

Police Chief – Trapper Johnson

Sammy Ball – tiny clerk in the Planning Commission's archives, bushy gray eyebrows, green eyes, leader of All People Matter movement

Benny Young – landscape maintenance for the city, face of the movement

Alva Thompson – Benny's sister

Derek Rangle – Tropical Paradise art gallery owner - a shock of white hair, dancing blue eyes behind thick horn-rimmed glasses, and the grin of an aging wizard

Eddie Glover – motorcycle shop,

Jimmy James – biker

Nomad – biker

Tabitha Hall – aging heiress who owns the newspaper, The Dolphin Times. The soul of the movement.

Hannibal Davis – Tabitha Hall's houseman

Gretchen Mowery – homeless woman who lived in a camp under the bridge at Pelican Turn with her three kids - Ted, William, and Betty until Eddie Glover offered them a small apartment above his shop

~

Stanley French – weapons production – the CEO of Dynamic Devices, the single largest contractor for advanced weapons systems in the country – running the conspiracy to own the president and the Congress- stout, goatee

John & Michael French – Stanley's sons

Conrad Blaho – steel and heavy industry - urban, pale, dark eyes, tennis knees, original partner with French in the conspiracy

Ethan Tomlinson – ultraconservative PR consultant, behind the scenes conspiracy campaign director – ImageSculptor

Will Terry – video producer

Casey Buck – owner of Global Oil, the largest private oil company in the world

~

Mayor Tyrone Turner – black Democratic Mayor of Atlanta - six-six former Rhodes Scholar, with a doctorate in economics from Yale, and all-star linebacker for the Atlanta Falcons

Phyllis Crane - the Mayor's personal secretary

Barry Clark - Head of the mayor's Security

Lincoln Todd - hardened biker, ex-con, and stanch white-supremacist, paid enforcer

Roger Stanislawski - Professional right-wing agitator

Henry Lorton – pilot - rental plane with "Free White America" banner

April Willow - doctor who shows up at Houston Links from West Memphis, Arkansas

Monica Hayes – Atlanta Chief of Police

Jasper Kline, the hard-right Republican governor of Georgia

President Phillipe Gonzalez – current democratic president

Brandon Beal - Eagle Security - slender, tailored, with a tidy moustache and blond hair, Military intelligence, Navy, top of his class,

Abe Sheldon – Career New York City cop - balding, dark owl-eyes, rumpled grey suit, spit-polished black tie-shoes with silent rubber soles

~

Martin McClintock Murphy – rogue radical right-wing radio show host, who becomes a candidate for president, beady dark blue eyes, pudgy face, thin lips

Jack Hannah – WBFK – engineer / station manager – Cincinnati

Milly Clark – secretary / fields calls during Murphy's broadcast.

Morgan Nance – 2nd term Congressman from Missouri

Katie's Chicken House
    Bernie – husband & bartender
    Sara – giddy daughter, receptionist and waitress

Shepherd Stone - political operative from Boston – campaign manager

Dr. Theodore Billings – greedy physician hired to keep Murphy upright

Haden Crawley – video director

Penny Baker - voluptuous makeup girl

Austin Crouch – Nashville producer and promoter – big stars, big shows

Milton Graves – Oil / mining – first mega-contributor to Murphy's campaign

Casper Wein - political organizer extraordinaire – convention coordinator

Senator Ted Sherman - Indiana

Clancy Hamilton – retiring Tennessee Senator and professional bigot

Democratic Candidates

Governor Jimmy Davidson from Massachusetts – Democratic candidate for president

Vincent Paul from California – CEO of Twyxys – a revolutionary software company - Democratic candidate for president

Joe Cassidy, the boring socialist Senator from the great state of Wisconsin – Democrat

Tippin Morton – aging Democratic Vice-President

Republican Candidates

Governor Jeffrey Grant, from North Carolina

Senator Saul Willis from Texas

Governor Billy Estes - South Carolina, who just barely got re-elected by his own people

Charles Garner – Florida Representative

Sam Trippet - up and coming loudmouth junior representative from New Mexico

Creighton Steil – handsome, charming, sleazy, homophobic, reportedly gay, extreme evangelical former governor of Indiana

~

Trevor Hobbs - renowned news anchor for International Public News, moderator

Melanie McQuade – co-anchor

Paige Phillips – Independent Broadcasting, Harvard degrees

Laura Poole – makeup girl in Madison

About the Author

Rick Stiller is a novelist, an award-winning commercial photographer, an accomplished musician, and a Master Gardener tending expansive gardens at the House of the Four Seasons.

Visit www.rickstiller.com to views his photographs, read first chapters, or listen to a sample of his music.

If you enjoyed this story, please post a five-star review on my Amazon page and like my 'Eric T Stiller – Author' page on Facebook.

Novels by Rick Stiller

Fiction

Dealer

The Redemption Series

Nellis Gray – Volume I
SunnyBreeze – Volume II

Young Adult

The Morgan's Knot Serial Fantasy

Morgan's Knot
Island of the Children
Ice Island
Islands of Concrete and Steel
Islands of the Mind
Islands in the Sky
Islands of Dark Miracles
Islands of Wisdom

Visit: www.rickstiller.com for more of his books,
photographs, and music and www.morgansknot.com for
the latest on the Morgan's Knot series.